The War Above the Trees

Operation Wayne Grey

Ron Carey

National Library of Canada Cataloguing in Publication Data

A cataloguing record for this book that includes the U.S. Library of Congress Classification number, the Library of Congress Call number and the Dewey Decimal cataloguing code is available from the National Library of Canada. The complete cataloguing record can be obtained from the National Library's online database at: www.nlc-bnc.ca/amicus/index-e.html

ISBN: 1-4120-3503-1

TRAFFORD

This book was published *on-demand* in cooperation with Trafford Publishing.
On-demand publishing is a unique process and service of making a book available for retail sale to the public taking advantage of on-demand manufacturing and Internet marketing. **On-demand publishing** includes promotions, retail sales, manufacturing, order fulfilment, accounting and collecting royalties on behalf of the author.

Suite 6E, 2333 Government St., Victoria, B.C. V8T 4P4, CANADA
Phone   250-383-6864   Toll-free 1-888-232-4444 (Canada & US)
Fax   250-383-6804   E-mail   sales@trafford.com
Web site www.trafford.com
TRAFFORD PUBLISHING IS A DIVISION OF TRAFFORD HOLDINGS LTD.
Trafford Catalogue #04-1331   www.trafford.com/robots/04-1331.html

10   9   8   7   6   5   4   3   2

THE WAR ABOVE THE TREES
Operation Wayne Grey

"The Unknown Battle in the Unknown Valley"

Written by Ron Carey

Dedication

This book is dedicated to the air crews of the 52nd Combat Aviation Battalion and all members of the 4th Infantry Division who paid the ultimate price in the Central Highlands of Vietnam.

In memory of Gator 297 and its crew, WO1 Martin Gehring Given (Aircraft Commander), WO1 Robert Lee Storey (Pilot), SP5 Billie Joe Ontis (Crew Chief), SP4 Eddy Gale Sumpter (Gunner) and passengers, SGT Charles Rein and SP4 Warren Haugen (of the 4th Infantry Division), all killed in action on Gator 297, November 21, 1968, in the Plei-Trap Valley.

i

Preface

I was a product of the baby boom. This term was yet to be widely used at the time. My parents had lived through the "Great Depression" and my father had fought in the Second World War. I was part of the first generation to grow up with television, integrated sports, and a thriving middle class in America. I was the oldest of six children in the typical American family of the fifties. My father worked and my mother stayed at home to raise the family.

As I grew up we enjoyed sports and playing soldiers with the many kids in my neighborhood. I had seen most of the war movies that had been made about the Second World War. From these I learned that it was my duty to serve if called. None of the horrors that were part of war were ever seen on the screen. Hollywood had made war a great adventure.

During high school, for me, the war in Vietnam was still a small conflict that few people were concerned with. A few major battles had been fought, but no one from my hometown had been killed or wounded. Having excelled more in sports than academics, I decided to skip college and enlist in the Army. I had wanted to learn to fly helicopters, but I missed the overall battery score by three points. If I couldn't fly them, then at least I would ride in them. I was signed up before graduation and left for Basic Training six days after I got out of high school.

Within six months I would be on my way to Vietnam. I arrived just in time for the Tet Celebration of 1968, which turned into the largest enemy offensive of the war. For the first time in my life I started to understand some of the things my father had said to me. War was not something you could describe in words, or show on a Hollywood screen. After spending my time in Maintenance learning the basics of the UH-1H helicopter, I asked for and was assigned to a flight platoon. I would spend the next ten months flying as a Huey crew chief in the Central Highlands. As my tour neared its end I felt a need to remain with my unit. I had seen combat but still felt I could make a difference. I volunteered for another six months.

At the end of February 1969 I was still two months away from my 20th birthday. Back in The World I was still considered a teenager who would not be old enough to vote, or even to drink beer. In Vietnam I was considered a combat veteran who had completed a year's tour of duty and was beginning a second. I was like many of the young soldiers who were now stationed in this country. Most were single and under the age of 22.

The Plei-Trap Valley is located between the borders of South Vietnam, Laos, and Cambodia. Unlike the A Shau Valley to the north and the Ia Drang Valley to the south, very few people have heard of this place. The A Shau would be made famous because of the US Marines' stand at Khe Sanh, and the Battle of Hamburger Hill, which was fought by the US Army's 101st Airborne Division. The Ia Drang is where the first major engagement between the forces of the 1st Cavalry Division and the North Vietnamese Army occurred in late 1965. Between 1965 and 1969, several battles would be fought in this area. In 1967 the Battle of Hill 875 by the 173rd Airborne Brigade would be well documented. The unknown unit that would fight and carry the burden of defending this part of the Central Highlands for almost five years would receive little or no press for its efforts. The 4th Infantry "Ivy" Division, which was comprised of mostly draftees, was not the type of unit the reporters flocked to. Their war was truly an unknown war.

Between March 1, 1969 and April 14, 1969, Operation Wayne Grey would become the last major engagement in the Plei-Trap Valley fought by the 4th

Infantry Division. Our country's role in the war would soon be handed over the Army of South Vietnam. By the middle of 1969, President Nixon would start to withdraw combat units from Southeast Asia. Other units would be relocated to different locations. The following year we would make one last sweep into Cambodia to destroy the enemy's havens of safety, before finally leaving Vietnam. In 1975, South Vietnam would fall as NVA tanks cut the country in two, moving through the Plei-Trap Valley and capturing Kontum City.

During 45 days, six years before, in 1969, I flew support to the troops who battled both the enemy and the jungle of the Plei-Trap Valley. If you were to ask any of the flight crews, they would have similar stories of what happened during this time. I have spent endless hours reviewing reports and working from my personal journal and personal memories. I have tried to tell what happened in the place we called "The Valley." We were not heroes or supermen. We were soldiers who were trying to do a job that none of us understood. Those whom we left behind are not forgotten. We shall carry each of them with us until the day we die.

The following poem was written by CPL James H. Mann, B Co. 1-327th, 1st Brigade, 101st Airborne Division. It was presented to a friend of mine who was a Huey pilot in Vietnam. Even after thirty years the one sound and image that still remains with most Vietnam veterans is the UH-1H (Huey) flying across the sky.

"On Thinnest Wings"

"On thinnest wings come those who dare to heed our
hollow lie, unspoken truth is fear of death and prayer for a
slick filled sky.

Eleven Bravo to UH-1…the LZ is clear we swear,
On thinnest wings and knowing truth comes to those who
really care.

From socked-in field in a far away place comfort for risk is
exchanged,and aircraft procedures and protocol are in
effigy soon to be hanged.

Over the noise of battle in progress, rotor blades can be
heard. And many times the enemy routed by, the grunt
protecting bird.

Thirty years later as Life-Flight goes by, the product of all
the above. The citizens for whom all this was done still
keep from soldiers love.

On thinnest wings of metal birds did many a grunt relay.
Oh how I wish I could thank them ALL before the day I
die."

Acknowledgements

Many people helped me as I tried to put this book together. An extra special thanks goes to my wife, Carla. She encouraged me during the many times when I was about to quit or give up. The many nights she listened to me as I relived the events I have tried to put down on paper. For the years she tried to understand the things I was unable to tell her. If not for her love and the support of my family I would not have been able to complete this book.

To all the members of my unit who contacted me during the past five years. Bob Kilpatrick and Al Mixer for their photos and the many notes that Bob sent me that helped me remember events that had faded from my memory.

To all the former members of the 4th Infantry Division who sent e-mails when I first started. Dave Fogg and George Heidt sent many reports that helped me stay on track. The eyewitness reports from Tom Lacombe, Dave Naranjo, Bob Ness, Chris Dressler, Albert Jacquez, and Greg Rollinger that added a personal meaning to those days. To Jack Leninger who wrote "Time Heals No Wounds" and got me started in the right direction as far as locating reports and other information. To the personnel of the National Archives who helped me locate many of the reports I needed.

Without all these people I could have not finished the story in these pages.

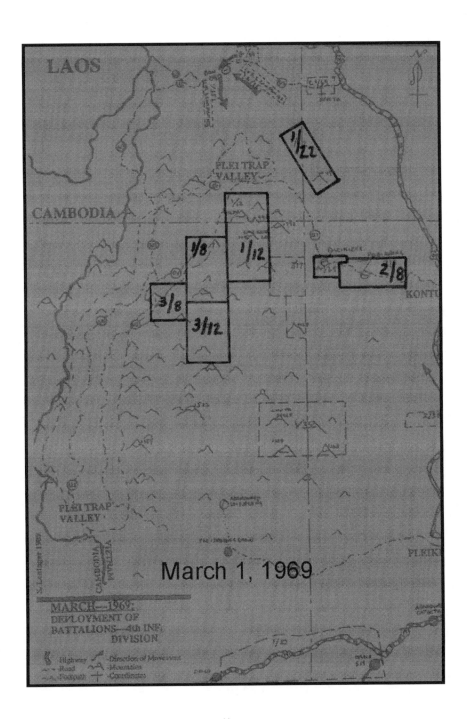

March 1, 1969

MARCH—1969:
DEPLOYMENT OF
BATTALIONS—4th INF.
DIVISION

TABLE OF CONTENTS

I	*March 1*	The Valley	1
II	*March 2*	What is that Smell?	19
III	*March 3*	Snoopy	34
IV	*March 4*	Short Night Long Day	52
V	*March 5*	The End of the Line	84
VI	*March 6*	My New Gunner	99
VII	*March 7*	LZ Brace	107
VIII	*March 8*	Task Force Swift	119
IX	*March 9*	Day Off	126
X	*March 10*	Gator 270	131
XI	*March 11*	Not Again	138
XII	*March 12*	The Assault	144
XIII	*March 15*	Phase II	189
XIV	*March 16*	Moving Day	195
XV	*March 17*	The Plei-Trap Road	199
XVI	*March 18*	The Beginning of Round Two	203
XVII	*March 19*	More Action to the North	208
XVIII	*March 20*	A Day with Gator 108	213
XIX	*March 21*	Just Another Day	220
XX	*March 22*	New Blood	227
XXI	*March 23*	Checkmate	233
XXII	*March 24*	March Madness	237
XXIII	*March 25*	Replacements and Build-Up	242
XXIV	*March 26*	The Beginning of the End	248
XXV	*March 27*	The Lift	253
XXVI	*March 28*	Fire Support Base 27	259
XXVII	*March 29*	Tactical Emergency	264
XXVIII	*March 30*	Task Force Alpha	272
XXIX	*March 31*	A Day of Rest	282
XXX	*April 1*	April Fool's Day	288
XXXI	*April 2*	Back to the War	291
XXXII	*April 3*	Nearing the End	294
XXXIII	*April 4*	One Last Push	297
XXXIV	*April 5*	The Last Bloody Nose	300
XXXV	*April 6-14*	The Final Act	302

Chapter I

"The Valley"

The end of February in Pleiku is like something out of a science fiction novel. The Dry Season is ending and the red dust of the area has covered everything. The landscape appears more to be the planet Mars than Earth. The new Company area is just awful. Having moved here in the beginning of January, the entire place is dirt. No concrete. No blacktop. No nothing. The only thing we have plenty of is red dust and more red dust. The barracks are long wooden buildings with concrete floors and screens at the top of the walls. There is nothing about this place that would come close to being comfortable or homey. The winds of nature and the rotor blade wash from the helicopters blow the red dust right through the screens. An engineering marvel only the Army could build.

This is the new home I arrived at three weeks ago. Now here I am for another tour of duty. September is beginning to seem a lifetime away. Besides discovering my new home, I was informed that the new helicopter that I crewed before my leave had been damaged in a "Hard Landing". Maintenance hasn't decided what to do with it, and until they do I have become the "Floating" crew chief. I have been on three different ships in so many weeks. The past two days I have been on "Gator 108". It's a good ship and I have my assigned gunner SP/4 Jeff Dana. The A/C (aircraft commander) is 1st Lt. Nicholas Burke. His call sign is Stoney. At least having the same crew I was with before my leave has made returning a little easier.

It's Friday night, February 28, 1969. Payday is a big thing in the Army. It means one more month toward the end of your enlistment. You have money for the things you really need like the big poker game that's going on in the Maintenance barracks. Most of the guys are there or

1

hanging out behind the mess hall drinking beer and swapping lies. I was sitting on my bunk writing home when the assistant platoon sergeant appeared at the mission board.

Tomorrow we start a new tour of rotation with the 4th Infantry. For the next sixty days we will be primary support to them. We will assign ten transports and four gunships during this time. As I follow the lines on the board I notice that all five ships from our platoon have the same mission status. Also we have a 0600hrs pre-flight inspection. With that I decide to walk down to the card game and let the guys know about the early pre-flight. As I pass the 2nd Flight's barracks I notice that their board reads the same as ours. I mention that to a couple of the guys standing by the board and they get the same puzzled look that I had. No sense in worrying about it tonight. We'll get the whole story in the morning.

The CQ runner throws the lights on at 5:00 A. M. (0500hrs). It's still pitch black outside. The air is heavy with moisture and a little chilly. I get dressed with one eye open. I'm not moving well at all. I gather up my gear and head for the mess hall. Not many people here this morning. The card game must not have broken up very early. I grab a big cup of coffee and throw some fruit into my flight bag and away I go. The walk down to the ship is not a long one. You just can't see anything; it's still dark.

As I open the cargo door and stow my gear under my seat I remind myself to write a note in the logbook that I need batteries for my flashlight. Dana shows up a little the worse for wear. He had spent most of the night behind the mess hall having some beers and telling some lies. He does have a case of C-rations and four canteens of water so at least we have lunch covered. As I pull the air intake filters off to start our pre-flight inspection, the pilots start to show up. With 1Lt. Burke is WO1 Jerry Miller. He will be our "Peter-Pilot" today. This is the title that new pilots

2

get. Mr. Miller has four months in-country and is a good pilot. It won't be long before he becomes an Aircraft Commander. Today should be a good one.

Aircrews are different from the rest of the Army. The pilots and crew are all about the same age and because of what we do, a person's rank doesn't get into the way of our being a team. As we go through the pre-flight we learn that we are doing a C.A. (combat assault) into the Plei-Trap Valley. We have a lift-off at 0700hrs. All ten ships will group along Highway 14 near the CIDG (Civilian Irregular Defense Group) camp of Plei-Mrong for a briefing. As we hover out of the revetment and start to stage as a single flight, our ship takes the position as flight leader. The tower clears us to take off and we head down the runway to the west, past the Maintenance hangar. I wave as we go by and then we bank to the right and start to head north toward Kontum. Another day has started for the 119th Assault Helicopter Company.

The flight is about thirty minutes. As we pass Artillery Hill and start to follow Highway 14 north, the crew settles in for the up-coming day. The pilots are going over radio channels that they were given this morning by Operations. Dana is sucking down a can of club soda that he has spiked with pre-sweetened Kool-Aid. How he can drink that is beyond me. I sit in the cool air with my head stuck into my flight jacket as I try to light a cigarette. The skies are clear and the sun is very bright this morning. As I finish my smoke we start our approach to the highway by Plei-Mrong.

We land on the highway that is nothing more than a dirt road and the grunts (infantrymen) lined up on both sides of the road give us the evil eye. I guess the menu of C-rations and coffee for breakfast was not supposed to have red dust mixed in. After we shut down and the pilots headed for their briefing, the enlisted crews started to gather at different ships. The first thing we do is try to get

3

a cup of coffee from the grunts. After a short chat we decide that they know about as much as us, that is nothing.

The rest of the crews are killing time the best they can. The crew of Gator 390 is lying in the cargo area of their ship. SP/5 John Schiffhauer ("Shifty") is trying to catch a nap. He played cards last night and was the big loser. PFC Leonard Thomas is talking endlessly to nobody because this is his first combat assault and his nerves are starting to show. We stop and talk to him for a couple minutes just to calm him down. We remind him to clear the ship and stay on his gun and he would be just fine. After almost an hour the pilots return. We are doing two combat assaults into the Plei-Trap Valley to establish new firebases. The first assault area is in the central part of the Valley that was an abandoned firebase. It would become Landing Zone (LZ) Swinger. This was at map location YA837965. Company A, 3rd Battalion, 12th Infantry Regiment (A/3/12) would be the lead element in the assault.

The reason for the long delay was the fact that infantry people don't understand helicopters. The brass had wanted us to carry six passengers in each ship. The pilots wanted only five. Their reason was that the Plei-Trap is not actually a valley. It's a grouping of mountains with ridges and deep gorges. There are several streams and rivers that run through the thick jungle that covers the floor of the valleys. The heat as the sun rises creates updrafts and downdrafts that cause control problems during a hover. Landing on a mountaintop that has an unknown landscape in the middle of an enemy-controlled area is not the easiest thing to do. Being two hundred pounds lighter might make the difference in landing or crashing. The brass was concerned about the turnaround time. The time between hitting the landing zone and returning to Plei-Mrong, getting a second load, and returning to Swinger would be about twenty minutes. This would also mean that instead of two trips into Swinger we would need three. The sooner the grunts were on the ground, the sooner the 155mm howitzers of the C/1/92 Arty (GS) could be in place. In the end the pilots would win out.

The assault would take place in the following manner. Artillery from LZ Bass had been employed in the early morning. A fire team (two AH-1G Cobra gunships) from the 4th Aviation Battalion's "Gambler Guns" would prep the landing zone for us. Our gunships (The Crocs) will provide cover as we make the assault. The slicks would set down one at a time to offload the troops. Operational control will be done on site by the First Brigade's Assistant Commander and their S-2. (Intelligence officer)

As our gun cover starts to take off I start to realize that I'm really back in the "NAM". The last three weeks I have only flown "milk runs" (easy, low risk missions). Nothing that would be hard or dangerous that might ruin my day. The platoon has really changed in the last two months. Most of the guys who were here in November are gone. I am one of just three crew chiefs who were here last year. We have lots of new faces, many of whom have not seen combat before.

"CLEAR," is the command that brings me to reality as Stoney starts the engine of the ship. "Clear left," is my response as the blades start to turn. "Clear right," echoes Dana as the blades start rotating faster. As we get our gear on and the engine has come to life the grunts start to move towards the ship. With the small cargo doors removed we start to load our human cargo. One is placed in the center of the cargo bay and two are facing each of the doors. We make sure that their weapons are clear and that they understand that they are not to exit the ship until I give them the command. Sometimes when we are entering a landing zone the grunts will stand on the skids and jump off as we hover above the ground. If the pilot is not ready for the change in weight on one side of the ship he might lose control of the ship. When Stoney says "GO," I give the command.

As we lift off we bank left to start to construct a "Daisy Chain" formation. Being the lead ship we circle until the rest of the ships are airborne and have gotten into their proper places. As we head west the formation is starting to take shape. A "Daisy Chain" has the first ship in the lead position lower that the rest of the flight. Each ship in turn is between thirty and forty seconds behind the ship in front of it and twenty to thirty feet higher. This way, as the first ship is touching down in the landing zone, the next is on its final approach to land as the first is leaving. The first set of gunships is heading for Polei-Kleng where they will refuel and monitor the radio while we make our first assault. They will remain there until we return for our second load. The two other gunships have gone ahead to the landing zone. Because of their slower speed, even with the head start we will catch up to them before we reach the landing zone.

The North Vietnamese Army (NVA) knew we are coming into the Valley. For the past two months LRRP (long range reconnaissance patrol) teams have worked the Valley. The "Sniffer" (a machine that gathers air samples that determines the presence of enemy forces) missions have also tipped our hand. The one place they are sure we will assault will be LZ Swinger. During the past two and half years that the 4th Infantry Division has been in the Central Highlands, the NVA have studied their tactics and their patterns. The need for a Fire Support Base (FSB) is one of the first objectives that our Army requires.

Unlike the American troops, NVA soldiers are here for the long haul. Their officers have fought their enemies for most of their adult lives. They fought the Japanese during World War II. After the war they then fought the French, who had returned to claim this land as one of their colonies. Now it is our turn. LZ Swinger was built in early 1967. It had been used for a short time before the units of the 1st Brigade had moved to Dak To. Located in the center of the Valley and large enough to accommodate the larger 155mm howitzers, it will provide fire support to the entire Valley.

Their plan is simple. They have concealed a 12.7mm anti-aircraft gun in one of the abandoned bunkers on the firebase. The old landing pad, which they thought is where we would land, was mined with command-detonated explosives. They will allow two or three ships to land before ambushing the next one on the pad. Once the pad is blocked with the downed ship and having fifteen to twenty men on the ground, we would be forced to either reinforce or pull the troops out. During this time they would be able to use the anti-aircraft gun to make this as costly as possible to us.

Entering the Valley, we make contact with our "C and C" ship. Command and Control will be done from a 4th Aviation Battalion helicopter. His call sign is "Blackjack 22". The man in charge is a Lieutenant Colonel with the call sign "Red 5". Our spotter is a LOH (OH-6A Light Observation Helicopter, pronounced "Loach") call sign "Hummingbird 3". The radios start talking as all the pieces of the puzzle start to go together. The Gambler Guns have completed their gun runs. "Hummingbird" will make the first pass over the landing zone and mark it with red smoke. This will help us determine the wind direction and the place where we are to land. The first gunship, "Croc 2," will follow the LOH to the landing zone. As they approach, the gunship fires two rockets into the base and opens up with his mini-guns. They will pass to the right of it and bank to the right. My ship will follow and as we enter the zone we will open fire to get any of the bad guys to lower their heads. Coming out, we will break left and return to Plei-Mrong to get the next sortie. As we leave, the second gunship will cover us and the next ship coming in.

I tap the passenger in the middle of the ship, who is a 1st Lieutenant, to let him know we are starting and that we will be going in "HOT". This means we will be firing our machine guns and that we are doing so as a plan and not actually receiving fire. The zone has been marked and we are setting up for our final approach. The rockets impact into the ground and the roar of the mini-guns can be heard over the sound of the rotor blades. The command "FIRE" blasts into my helmet. Our "sixties" (M-60 machine guns) start to rock at the same time. Clearing the outer perimeter with the tail rotor we start to land. "The tail is clear!" I inform Stoney as we start to hover. "Clear right!" Dana says as he still fires his gun. "Clear left!" I echo. About a foot off the ground the command "GO!" comes from Stoney. I yell "GO!" to the troops as we cease-fire. They exit the ship and my command is "We are clear!" and Stoney pulls pitch to leave the LZ. "We are coming out and negative fire," as we climb into the sky. No fire and no bad guys. This just might turn into a nice day.

"**Taking fire! Taking fire!**" comes over the radio. Our good day has just gone south. Gator 390 is the second ship in and all hell has broken loose. Out of the corner of my eye I see "Shifty's" ship taking fire from the left side of the landing zone. I open up to protect his side of the ship. Heavy fire is coming from the opposite side of where our gun cover is. "**My crew chief is down!**" is the only thing we hear as Gator 390 departs the LZ. "We are en route hospital, Pleiku." That would be the last transmission from Gator 390 that day. The landing zone disappears as Gator 603 hovers above the landing pad. The NVA have detonated the mines around the pad. Dirt and debris surround Gator 603 and it is impossible for us to see the helicopter. "**I'm coming out!**" is the only thing I heard as the helicopter slowly rose above the cloud of dust.

Mr. Hudkins (aircraft commander of Gator 603) informs the rest of the flight that he has wounded but the ship is flyable. He is also headed for the 71st Evac hospital in Pleiku.

"Taking fire! Taking fire!" again comes into my helmet. The fourth ship, Gator 606, is taking fire from the same spot. Again I open up but now "Croc 2" has broken his pattern and started to make a run towards the enemy fire. "My crew chief is down and I also have a wounded passenger," is Gator 606's response as they lift off. The Crocs are now raining hell down on the little people who started this fight. We call the two remaining gunships at Polei-Kleng. They have been monitoring the radio and are aware of what is going on. They are en route to our location. Meanwhile Gator 606 informs the flight that he is losing power and might not make it back to Polei-Kleng. We begin to follow Gator 606 in case he goes down. Departing the A/O (Area of Operations) it's becoming clear that things are going to get worse before this day is over. We pass our other gunships as we head for the airstrip. Gator 606 is leaking fuel and the engine is smoking badly. We have less than twenty people on the ground and we have lost three ships already. We have yet to return to Plei-Mrong for our second load. We stayed on station much longer than we should have and, having to follow Gator 606 to Polei-Kleng, we will have to refuel before returning to the LZ. The airstrip is in sight and Gator 606 will be able to make it.

Hovering into the refueling point (called "POL," for Petroleum, Oil, and Lubricants) to refuel, I watch as a Dust-Off helicopter lands near Gator 606. They load two people into it and then race into the sky headed for Pleiku. With a full tank of fuel we head back to Plei-Mrong. Arriving there at the same time as Gator 834 we load another sortie and head back into the Valley. Gator 834 had been the fifth ship into the LZ. They had received fire as they were leaving. Because the Crocs were working the left side of the LZ we would now have to bank right as we depart the area. Heading west, we pass the other ships that are returning for their next load.

Everything has gone to hell. Ships are running low on fuel and they will need to refuel before returning with their next sortie. Getting people on the ground is the main concern. The grunts are in contact and we need to get as many people as possible on the ground. The numbers game has already started. We had figured on getting the job done with ten ships but now we are down to seven and this day has only started. Once we get back on station things are not getting any better. The grunts are now fighting from one bunker to another. The fighting is more like the trench warfare of World War I, than the jungle fighting these troops are trained for. Hand grenades and .45 pistols are used to take each bunker. They are trying to expand their lines out from the landing zone. They estimate at least a platoon-sized force or greater. They have wounded but we can't pull them out until the area is secure. It would not do anybody any good to have one of our ships shot down in the landing zone. With the pad blocked we would not be able to reinforce or evacuate.

We drop into "Swinger" and offload without a problem. The grunts are making progress but things have slowed considerably. Blackjack is reminding us that we still have another assault on slate for this afternoon. Maybe if he talked to the NVA they would be so kind as to quit fighting so we could get back on schedule. It would take three hours before this battle would end. If not for the artillery strike prior to the assault, things might have been a lot worse.

The NVA had not planned on the gunships prepping the base before the assault. They had concealed their troops inside the base in and around what they

10

believed to be the landing zone. Two things they had not planned on. First were the gunships firing into the bunkers with rockets on their first pass. The second was that we did not land where they thought we would. Helicopters, as all aircraft, must land into the wind. We chose a landing zone away from their ambush point. The first assault troops moved out from this pad towards the enemy who were waiting to ambush the helicopters. This caused the enemy to fire on the second ship to hit the pad. Between the Gambler Guns and our gunships, the crew of the anti-aircraft gun had been killed. The troops of the first ship engaged the enemy immediately causing confusion and foiling the ambush.

After our third sortie is on the ground we are able to pull some of the wounded out. We race for LZ Mary Lou. One of the wounded is the lieutenant that was on our first sortie. He is pale but seems to be doing fine. I offer him a cigarette but he shakes his head. "I don't smoke," he yells over the sound of the rotor blades. By noon the bunkers have been cleared and most of the required equipment has been hauled into "Swinger".

The ships start to set down at Polei-Kleng for lunch. This is the first time we have had a chance to stop and catch our breath. A few of the guys walk over to see Gator 606. The crew chief SP4 Stephen Bowles got hit several times in both legs. The infantryman had been hit in the chest. The A/C, WO1 Jack Hawkins, (call-sign The Hawk) had done a great job of bringing the ship in. All of the damage was bullet holes. The engine and main rotor blades were the biggest problem. The guys from Maintenance would have to sling load it back to Camp Holloway under a big, twin-rotor Chinook in order to repair it. No word had gotten to us about "Shifty", or any of the crew that was on Gator 603. The crew of 606 was to be picked up by the ship that was bringing the Maintenance group in. They in turn would catch a ride back with one of the remaining ships at the end of the day.

Sitting in the cargo area of our ship, the crew breaks open the case of C-rations that Dana had gotten this morning. After picking through the twelve different meals the four of us have a little of everything we like. The canned fruit and pound cake are the first to go. Between this and the apples and bananas that I got this morning at the mess hall we have a pretty good lunch. Too bad we won't have enough time to enjoy it. We still have another assault plus we have to get the artillery people into Swinger. Within ten minutes we have eaten and refueled and are ready to go again. The troops from C/3/8 have been staged on the south side of the runway at Polei-Kleng most of the morning. We were to start moving them at 1000hrs. We are almost three hours late and missing three ships.

I am amazed at all the activity at Polei-Kleng. Back in November when I was last here this place was nothing but a runway and an old Special Forces camp. Not unlike many of the small hamlets in the Central Highlands, this little village has an asphalt runway that was built by either the French or American engineers. The French used these places as bases during their war with the Viet-Minh. After they left and the Americans showed up, the first CIDG forces were formed and based at these areas. The NVA has always used this area to stage troops and start operation against their enemies. The main idea is to cut South Vietnam in two. This was exactly how they would win the war in 1975. This was the reason why the 1st.Brigade of the 4th Infantry Division had been moving into the area. The Brigade is composed of the 1st Battalion, 8th Infantry; the 3rd Battalion, 8th Infantry, and the 3rd Battalion, 12th Infantry. Their primary fire support is the 6th Battalion, 29th Field Artillery. Their mission is to establish firebases and block and destroy enemy transportation routes in the Plei-Trap Valley. This is to be our new home for the next two months.

While the main rotor starts to crank Stoney briefs us on what is going on. We are to assault map location YA 816880. This will become LZ Pause. Unlike LZ Swinger this is nothing more than a mountaintop that has been shelled and bombed. There are no structures for the NVA to hide in and the artillery has pounded the area where we are to land very hard. Located southwest of Swinger, not only will this base be used for fire support; it will also used as a jumping off point to recon areas where suspected enemy bases might be located. All seven ships will be involved, plus the gunships. The Gamblers have hit the area and 'Blackjack' will again be on station.

As we start to pick up the first load of troops I again go through my little speech of what is going on. I explain that we will land and that they should just stay down until we leave. Back in July the ship that I was crewing was bringing new troops into Firebase 5 at Dak To. One of the "FNGs" (f_ _king new guys) who had less than two weeks in-country walked away from the ship, up a slight incline. The main rotor blade struck him in the head. He died before we could get him to the aid station. From that day on I made sure that nobody would walk into the blades. We also are told that there are no friendly people in the Valley. If we take fire or see anyone we are to throw smoke and return fire.

We head into the Valley for the second time looking for a fight. The smoke is still hanging over the landing zone. No need to mark, we can see it fine. I tell the grunts that we will be going 'Hot' and we head in. "FIRE!" comes over my intercom. Our guns are clearing the way. "The Tail is clear! We are clear right! We are clear left! GO! GO! We are clear!" The troops are on the ground and we bank left. I watch as Gator 834 enters the zone. If it's going to happen, it will happen now. The lump in my throat is the size of a baseball. They are coming out. Negative fire.

We head back to Polei-Kleng. We load the next group and head back. There are lots of smiles because the bad guys were not at home. With our third sortie we decide to change our pattern. Nobody has received fire so why press our luck.

Leaving the pad we bank right away from the LZ. **"I GOT PEOPLE!"** Dana exclaims as he throws a smoke grenade and opens fire. Stoney grabs some sky and heads out of range. Mr. Miller is on the radio calling for the Crocs. Dana explains that he saw three people near the stream that is west of Pause. They were carrying what he thought were buckets and they were armed. As we bank to the right so Dana can keep his eye on the spot where he had thrown the smoke, all I can see is blue sky. Soon the gunships are at our location. We will start our run into the target area so Dana can mark the spot with another smoke grenade. Starting our run, we open up with our guns and Dana throws smoke and all hell breaks loose. But not where we are.

"TAKING FIRE" comes over the radio. Gator 521 had just departed Pause and had banked left because we had spotted people. Now they are catching .50 cal. machine gun and light automatic weapons fire. The guns race toward Gator 521. They have spotted the gun emplacement and now they are bringing their wrath down upon the enemy gunners. The pilots of Gator 521 are grabbing as much sky as they can as they start back to Polei-Kleng. For the second time we are big brother for a wounded bird. Most of the rounds have hit the tail boom and maybe the main rotor. Nobody on board is hurt and the engine seems to be fine. "I'm going to go to Kontum rather that Polei-Kleng," is Gator 521's response when we ask how the ship is doing. The 57th Assault Helicopter Company is based there. Maybe they will be able to repair the ship. We continue with them to Kontum.

Hovering toward the hangar we are met by some of

the Maintenance personnel. The tail boom is shot and one of the main rotor blades will have to be replaced. The crew will have to hang loose until we are done and we can give them a ride back to Camp Holloway. While we are there, we find out that the 57th had lost a ship with its entire crew plus a LRRP Team just two weeks ago in the same area we are in now. It would have been nice if somebody had told us this before we started the assault today. After refueling we head back to the Valley. Over the radio we learn that every peasant with a flintlock has been taking pot shots at our ships. Actually it's more like .30 and .50 cal. machine gun fire. Also lots of small arms fire. We are running out of daylight and ships. The brass decides that we have enough people at Pause and that we need to start getting the artillery personnel and equipment into both firebases. We divide up the flight into separate groups. One starts moving the artillery unit into Swinger while the other works at Pause. We get elected to work Swinger.

The sky is fire red in the west as we leave Swinger for the last time today. Gator 608 is picking up the crew of Gator 521 at Kontum for their ride back to Holloway. We are informed that we will have to pick up a couple of passengers and some paperwork at the Brigade CQ and deliver them to LZ Mary Lou before we are released. It's been a long day. Lifting off the pad at Mary Lou the sun has disappeared.

Night in Vietnam is the darkest dark in the world. No highway lights. No traffic lights. Only the red glare from the instrument panel provides any relief from the darkness that surrounds us. In the distance we can see Pleiku. Crossing over downtown we contact "Holloway Tower." "Gator 108 you cleared to land at the Christmas tree and have a good evening". That's the best sound I've heard all day. Hovering toward our revetment I spot the platoon's 3/4 ton truck. Standing next to it are two familiar figures.

15

We haven't even shut the engine down as Sgt. Hall and his assistant Sgt. Tuminello approach the ship. Both are "Lifers" (career soldiers) and at times we don't see eye to eye. Sgt. Hall is an E-6 with about thirteen years in the Army. Most of that time was spent in Germany with what we sometimes called "The Real Army". He asked for Vietnam so he could get his next stripe. He has been here five months and will rotate to Battalion at the end of the month. During his time here, he has made it quite clear that he does not approve of the lack of discipline in our platoon. He believes that we should conduct ourselves in the manner which he was accustomed to in Germany. His only concerns are the flight status of our ships and that crews are available to fly. Any relationship between him and the members of the platoon could only be termed as strained.

Sgt. Tuminello came here as a gunner from the 101st ABN. Wearing "Buck Sergeant" stripes, he was actually a SP5, which is the same rank as me. Someone had heard that he was a cook before he came here. I had flown with him a few times when he first arrived in the Company. He is a hard worker, and a nice enough guy, but there was not any chance for a promotion if he remained a gunner. After a couple of months of flying he was moved to Assistant Platoon Sergeant. Sgt. Hall had found himself someone to handle us and deal with matters he found unpleasant. Tuminello has been in the Army six years and this is his big chance to make Staff Sergeant.

"What's the status of your ship Carey?" is the first sound out of Hall's mouth. **"Screw This Ship and the Whole Army!"** is the reply that greets him from both Dana and me. "How's Shifty doing?" is our next question. The look on his face tells us what we had feared. "I'm sorry," he starts out, "I didn't realize that you hadn't heard." "Heard what?" we asked. "Shifty didn't make it. He died before they got him to the hospital. Bowles is okay but his

16

legs are pretty bad." The grunt that was hit also died. Three grunts on Gator 603 were wounded as was PFC John Morrison, the gunner. John's flight helmet was destroyed but his wounds were minor. The crew chief, SP5 Bob Legasey, has what was termed a slight concussion. Later in life, Bob would lose most of his hearing because of this slight concussion.

Hall has stepped back so that it can sink in before anything else is said. The four of us just look at each other for a while. In the back of our minds we had all thought that he might have died but nobody had the guts to say it. After a long silence Stoney is the first to speak. "Do you need anything before we go?" "No Sir," we reply. The pilots load their gear into the truck and Tuminello drives them to Operations.

"My ship is just fine." I calmly say as Hall writes on his clipboard. "We do need ammo and smoke grenades." Dana adds. "I'll send Sgt. Bilbee by with his truck so you can get what you need. I have to stop by Maintenance before I go to Operations so it will be about a half hour." As Hall leaves, Dana gives him a dirty look. "I'm going to get the large mini-gun cans of ammo. After today I don't want to be running out of ammo in that place. I got to get something to eat. Want me to grab you something from the mess hall?" "No," I reply. Dana turns and starts to head for the Company area. In the dark I start my post-flight inspection. "Damn It." The flashlight batteries have gone dead. Walking toward the hangar I start to realize how tired I am.

On the taxiway in front of the hangar are sitting Gator 390 and Gator 603. Both have personnel working on them. The water truck is sitting between them. The blood is still on the floor of both ships. A few of the guys look up as I walk by. I continue into the hangar to get batteries from the platoon locker. The Maintenance personnel will have to work late tonight. With four ships going down

17

today we might not have enough to cover mission requirements tomorrow. I head back to the revetment to finish my post-flight.

Lights from the ammo truck appear as I climb down from the top of the ship. Dana has returned with the ammo and some cold beer. We load the large boxes into the ship. They each hold 1500 rounds and they weigh a ton. Drinking the beer and smoking a cigarette as we walk back to the Company area, we try to put some order to the day's events. Its 2200hrs and we have been on the go for seventeen hours. We are both dragging our butts and start to dread what might happen tomorrow. We can only hope that "Charlie" decides to give us a break tonight and not throw any mortars our way. I crash headfirst into my bunk without removing any of my clothes. I fall fast asleep. Saturday night back in The World would never be like this.

Our first day of "Operation Wayne Grey" was over. We had deployed troops of A/3/12 into the northern section of operational grid location 'YA'. The assault on Swinger had cost A/3/12 one killed and thirteen wounded. Our unit had one killed and three wounded. Four of our helicopter had been damaged. The move into the southern area with the troops from C/3/8 had been better. No casualties were taken. To the north of us, units of the 1/8 infantry, supported by ships from Troop A, 7/17th Cavalry had assaulted and secured bases near the Plei-Trap road. Very little action was reported during these operations.

CASUALTY REPORT
March 1, 1969

| SP5 John Schiffhauer | RA13858922 | 05/10/1947 | Age 21 |
| SP4 Doug J. Markovich | US51983710 | 08/31/1947 | Age 21 |

Chapter II

"WHAT IS THAT SMELL?"

I wake face down in my bunk. I can hear people moving but it's still dark in the barracks. I look at my watch and discover that it's 0430hrs. Sitting up, my entire body aches. I must have slept in the same position all night. Lighting a cigarette, I can make out the image of Dana sleeping in the bunk next to me. He still has his clothes on including his flight jacket. He has his cap pulled over his eyes as if to be blocking the sun. He must have lain down when the lights were still on. Thinking that I need a shower, I start to undress. My hair is full of dirt and the grit on my neck makes me feel awful. Pulling my clothes off while I move around to my footlocker I realize that every part of my body hurts. I am nineteen years old, not seventy. The air is cold and damp. That's another thing about this place. It's either too hot or too cold or too wet or too dry, too much dust and too many bugs. Not enough ships. Not enough hours in the day. I guess if they had a war where everything was perfect, they wouldn't need to have a war.

The shower is directly behind our barracks. At least we don't have to walk through the dirt to get to it. We share this with the Second Flight platoon. Wood skids have been laid on the ground to create a sidewalk to the shower. The walk branches off toward the revetments and is the main gateway to our beloved three holed out house. For going "number 1" a pipe has been dug into the ground and some stands have been placed around it to give the impression that you might actually have some privacy. Like nobody knows what you are doing. The shower is a ten by ten-foot building with six pipes and six valves for water. The water is supplied by a water bladder, which sits above the building on a twelve-foot tower. This is one time that gravity is our friend. The tower is also a place to hide if you aren't flying that day. On the days you don't fly the 1st Sgt. and the other sergeants would gather up people for work details. Heaven forbid that you could get a day of rest around here.

A couple other guys have the same idea as me. The water is cold but it does the job. The one light bulb makes it possible to shave. With yesterday's dirt off me I walk back to my bunk. The lights are now on and the platoon is starting to move about. Walking past "Shifty's" bunk I see that his gear has been collected and the mattress has been rolled up on his bunk. I didn't really know John that well. He had arrived in December while the platoon was on temporary assignment at Lane Army Airfield. I had left on leave at the end of the month and did not return until the beginning of February. He was the new guy and I really never talked to him. Maybe I should have made an effort but I didn't. I had lost a good friend in November. We had arrived in country at the same time. New guys sometimes become friends just because they are new together. I think that's why we had been friends. I try to put those things out of my mind.

Dana is up and sitting on the side of his bunk. With a cigarette and his morning can of club soda he is trying to pull his clothes off to grab a shower. "How's the water?" he asks. This was the question that would start our morning argument. "How do you think it is? It's cold. It's always cold". This was my comeback as I started to get dressed. "Yeah, well the headquarters platoon has gotten a heater for their shower. I was told that if I help them install it I will be able to enjoy their shower. Nice hot water would feel great about this time of the day." Jeff was now really trying to rub it in. "When was the last time they did anything for us to make life a little easier around here?" I shouted. "The only time we are able to get anything out of them is when they want something from us." Dana knew he had hit a nerve and now he was happy. "Well, I'm going to hit the shower and I'll see you at the ship." His smile told me he had completed his mission. Dana's Boston accent is a little heavy this morning. It gets like that if he had a couple extra beers the night before.

The mess hall is busy. Not many of the flight crews ate last night. I go for the chipped beef on toast (SOS, shit on the shingle) and coffee. Thank God for ketchup. I shovel my chow down and grab another cup to go and my normal handful of fruit. PFC Thomas is entering as I go out the door. Without saying anything I slap him on the shoulder and smile. He looks at me and he still has a tear in his eye. We pass without saying a word but I think we both needed each other's look.

The same crew as yesterday board Gator 108. Today, 1st Lt. Robert Nilius from the Second Flight platoon is flight leader. His call sign is "Penis." Like Stoney he is a great pilot. They each have their little personal things that make them different. Stoney thinks of himself as a rebel. Going his way and doing his thing. He is actually more straight-laced than he will admit. "Penis" on the other hand is a born entertainer. He always has a punch line to deliver and a laugh that only can belong to him. I can just picture him flying down to the gates of Hell. As he hovers there he would give Satan himself the "finger" and laugh that laugh of his as he flew away. Unlike the rest of the Army, pilots will rotate command so each one has a chance to get some experience. They treat the enlisted men with respect and we almost have a friendship. This is something the career soldiers (lifers) can't understand. As a matter of fact sometimes these guys go out of their way to mess with the sergeant's head because they can. I don't see many of these people becoming career soldiers.

The flight is a quiet one. Not much talking and the radios are very quiet. Everyone is tired and thinking about yesterday. Arriving at Polei Kleng, we pass over the east end of the runway. I can see a chaplain holding services out of the back of a 3/4-ton truck. I had forgotten it was Sunday. The only way I remember the date is because I have to enter it in my logbook. The only date that means anything is the day that you will be going home. D.E.R.O.S. [Date Estimated Rotation or Separation] is the one goal of every soldier in Vietnam.

We landed on the south side of the runway. Ten UH-1H transports (slicks) and four UH-1C gunships. The pilots head for their briefing and the rest of us start doing things on the ships that we didn't get done last night. The first thing was to figure out a way to mount the large ammo boxes that Dana had gotten last night to our gun mounts. Removing our guns and small ammo boxes from the mounts we try a couple different ideas. The best one we come up with is using the seat belts from the passenger seats to anchor the large boxes in place. We had pulled the seats out long ago and had stowed them in the side cargo compartment. They are only installed when we are flying some "milk run" and we are hauling passengers around. During combat assaults and resupply we pull everything possible out of the ship to make room and have the cargo bay as open as possible. The next thing we have to do is dump the ammo out of the boxes. The ammo is loaded backwards to the way it would feed into our machine guns. The reason is that when you load the trays of the gunships' mini-guns, the ammo is reversed. As you load the trays the ammo will now feed the proper way into the gun. So we dump the ammo on the floor of the ship before we mount the boxes in place. Once this is done, the next time we reload the boxes we can just load them in the usual manner. First time is always the hardest.

We were almost done getting the ammo in the boxes. Sitting on the ground for about forty-five minutes was time enough for the little people to get the first shot lined up at us. **BANG!** The sound of the first shot and the explosion near the middle of the ships came at about the same time. The NVA had moved a recoilless rifle into place during the night and now they had all these beautiful helicopters to use as targets. Running to the side of the runway we went down a slight slope away from the ships. Laying on the ground more shells came in. Being good soldiers we pressed ourselves into Mother Earth. Jeff Dana was digging in the dirt when "Doc" Kilpatrick asked the question. "What is that smell?" As we dug into the ground we start to realize that this was where the troops from yesterday were relieving themselves while waiting for us to move them to LZ Pause. By now Dana has unearthed toilet paper and worse. "At least it's a hole and cover," is Dana's only comment as he continued to dig. The gunships are starting to crank and the fire has shifted away from us. All the crews bolt for their ships at the same time.

Reaching the ship first, I jump into the pilot's seat and start cranking the engine. Dana unties the main rotor and starts getting his gear on. By the time Mr. Miller gets to the ship, I have it up to speed and ready to go. "Where's Stoney?" I holler as he gets dressed. "Don't know," was his reply. I am sitting in his seat because the main controls are on the right side of the ship. Miller gets into Stoney's seat so I can get out and get my stuff on. By this time several ships have taken off. I can see the Crocs banking toward the enemy fire.

What seems like hours pass before Stoney finally shows up. My helmet is not on and my gun is still lying on the floor of the ship. Mr. Miller is now pulling pitch and we are out of "Dodge" I have just had enough time to get into the ship as we barrel to the west in order to get airborne. Banking to the left I see the gunships laying waste to the enemy gunners. After I get my machine gun back on its mount I plug my helmet in just as the two

23

pilots start to argue. "Why are you in my seat?" asks Stoney as he buckles his shoulder harness. "Your seat?" answers Mr. Miller. "You're lucky we didn't leave your sorry ass back at Polei-Kleng. Skip (the nickname most of the pilots called me) was firing the ship up and I got in so he could get ready. If we had known it was going to take you so long to get here I would have had him hold the controls so I could get into my seat. What took you so long anyway?"

Stoney's face is now a little red as he starts to answer but Dana jumps into the conversation. "Yah, my grandmother is about that slow, but she is seventy and had polio as a child." Now Stoney turns his head and starts on Dana. "You guys get your gear on and start wearing your chicken plates (body armor) because we are doing another C.A. this morning." "Don't be worrying about us back here. You need to be taking care of business in the front," is Dana's comeback. So it goes for the next few minutes. We sound more like four brothers fighting over whatever it is that four brothers would fight about, which was anything.

Orbiting east of Polei-Kleng, we are briefed. Today we are to move elements of the 3d Battalion, 8th Infantry to the west of where we had gone yesterday. They are to establish a landing zone as a base of operations to the southwest of LZ Pause. This will be known as LZ Mary. Its map location is YA 784879 (map 1 location 1 page 32). The area has been prepped by artillery from LZ Mile High. This will be more of a hoverhole than a landing zone. Blackjack 22 will be on station as well as Hummingbird 3. The first Company in will be D/3/8. They have staged at the west end of the runway. All ships will bring two sorties apiece into the LZ. After we have gotten the first Company into Mary three ships will break away to resume moving the artillery unit (C/6/29) into LZ pause. Once we have the second Company on the ground two more ships

24

will start moving the other artillery unit (C/1/92) into LZ Swinger.

While we are doing the assault, CH-47 "Chinooks" will be sling loading the 155mm howitzers to Swinger. Both artillery moves were to be completed yesterday. We land and the troops are loaded. Flying to the west we head into the Valley. Meeting Blackjack at map reference YA784879 the smoke from the artillery is still hanging over what is soon to become LZ Mary. We are the third ship today. Lt. Nilius in Gator 409 is lead. Gator 834 is second. The area is not bad. Most of the trees have been knocked down and the ground seems level. One of the grunts pulls on my sleeve to ask what number ship we are. When I say three he looks somewhat relieved. I guess he didn't hear what happened yesterday to the third ship in. With everyone in place, Gator 409 drops into the landing zone. He unloads and leaves. Negative fire. Gator 834 sets down and leaves. Negative fire. Now it's our turn. I'm outside the ship watching the tail boom and main rotor. I have one hand on my gun the other operating the intercom button. I just know all Hell is about to break loose at any second. We hit the ground. The troops depart and away we go. Negative fire.

The turnaround time is only ten minutes. Stoney wants his seat back so, as we are flying back, he goes over his plan to switch seats. When we land he will get out of the right seat. I am to get in the right seat and hold the controls while Jerry (Mr. Miller) gets out of the ship, so Stoney can get into his seat. Once he is in the seat, he will hold the controls so I can get out and let Mr. Miller into his seat. Touching down, we execute the plan. It looks just like a "Chinese fire drill." One guy out. One guy in. One guy out. One guy in. And finally one guy out, one guy in. The grunts are watching this as if to say, "What the hell is going on?" Of course, Dana is laughing his fool head off.

Back in the air he suggests that maybe we should

start doing that every time we pick people up. Mr. Penny and the crew of Gator 608 also witnessed our little show. Mr. Miller informs them that the reason we are playing musical chairs is because Stoney has the top speed of a turtle. Stoney cuts off his mike and informs us that there will no more running jokes. All the while, the grunts are still trying to figure out what we are doing.

After our second sortie we refuel and then start hauling the artillery unit into Pause. The assault in LZ Mary has gone off without a problem. Two of our ships were damaged during the attack. Nothing serious and both are able to remain in service. While we continue our troop movements into Mary and Pause a company from the 2nd Battalion 8th infantry had completed their sweep north of Polei-Kleng. They confirmed that the Crocs had destroyed the recoilless rifle and killed its crew. Companies of the 1st Battalion 8th Infantry are also conducting assaults and sweeps this morning. They are directly north of us in operational grid YB. Their air support is Troop A, 7/17th Air Cavalry. They had started out of Polei-Kleng and Firebase 34 yesterday. Brigade had tried to cut down on having so many aircraft being in the same location. Now today, with three units of helicopters working the same general area, the sky is getting a little crowded. The larger CH-47s that are delivering artillery ammo and supplies by sling load into Swinger are causing us some problems. We have to keep our distance when they are around. One, because their propwash can really cause us problems if we are hovering near them. The second reason is that enemy gunners love to shoot at a nice big target. Every now and then one of the ships report they are taking fire but it's nothing that is concentrated in one spot and nothing but small arms.

By noon we have moved all personnel into Mary. We brought in food, water, and perimeter supplies. Our three ships shut down for lunch near the Resupply area.

The pilots head up to Brigade CQ for lunch and they have a briefing after. The enlisted crews of Gators 108, 834, and 376 gather for a little lunch and a bullshit session. Myself, Dana, SP5 Bob (Doc) Kilpatrick and PFC Gary (Eggy) Eggleston from Gator 834, and SP4 Jim (Ti Ti) Sempek and SP4 Bill Mutz from Gator 376. Dana and Mutz had been in the Engineers together. As a matter of fact, they had joined the Army together. They had gone to Basic and AIT (Advanced Individual Training). Then they came to "Nam" as engineers and were now here. Jim and I had been the crew of Gator 371. We had lost that ship to enemy fire back in November. After that, he decided to become a crew chief. If nothing else he could make E-5. Right now he is crewing SP5 Jim Fall's ship. Jim is close to going home and last night he had guard duty so rather than push it he took the day off. In October and November our Company had lost four ships to combat action. Three of those ships belonged to our platoon. In December I received a replacement ship but it was damaged in January. So we have been short ships for the past three months. Doc and Eggy are from New England as well as Dana. Sempek and I are from the Chicago land area. Six guys who that had never met before the Army sure have many things in common besides riding around Southeast Asia in helicopters. Dividing up the C-rations from our ships, we start lunch. Dana entertains everyone with the story of our Chinese fire drill and a couple of "slow jokes" about Stoney. We have a good laugh and for a moment the war is very far away.

After lunch the pilots return to let us know about what is happening. The remaining units of 3/12 have arrived at Polei-Kleng. These two companies had been trucked here from Plei-Mrong this morning. We are putting them in landing zones west of Swinger. Again we stage on the runway. Five ships will take B/3/12 to map location YA 734953. The other ships have C/3/12 going to

YA 743974. They will then begin a reconnaissance in force to the east. As we head west with our first load of troops we learn that units of the 1/8 had made contact and had discovered a truck convoy that was traveling east on the Plei-Trap road. Artillery and air strikes had been called in. This was the first contact for those units. Now we are looking for trucks and possible roads. What else is going to happen? We meet "Blackjack" and we are directed to the landing zones. Again they are just hoverholes that take a lot of effort to get into. As we orbit and hover into the jungle we watch for any movement or shape that doesn't look right. The Brigade was setting up to drive from the west to the east to cut off the NVA and keep him from retreating back across the border. We are so close to Cambodia I could throw a rock and hit it. Except for the contact that the 1/8 encountered things had been quiet in our area. The 2d Brigade which was to the north of us had received some incoming fire at LZ Mile High today. The attack at Polei-Kleng had done only minor damage.

As we flew back and forth to Polei-Kleng we learned that C/1/8 has discovered two Soviet one and a half ton trucks. They were abandoned south of LZ Susan in the area of the morning's air strikes. From documents they found it is believed that they are from the K25A and K25B Engineering Battalions of the NVA It is believed that they have constructed roads in and around the area. This is so they can prepare supply bases and bring artillery and anti-aircraft weapons to be used against US bases and aircraft. Also found in these trucks were a large amount of 105mm artillery rounds. As the units had moved out from their landing zones they discovered that some of the intelligence reports were right. Besides the Plei-Trap road many improved trails have been found. Company A/1/8 made contact with a small ambush. The enemy broke contact almost immediately. The first platoon encountered sniper fire en-route to their night location. The fourth platoon made contact with an enemy force in bunkers. They withdrew and called for mortars. They had one wounded and enemy casualties were unknown.

By 1500hrs we have completed the move. We now have to start resupplying the firebases with food and water. Arriving at Pause I am amazed at the amount of men and equipment that has been brought in. Sand bags, fence posts and barbed wire is stacked near the pad. The work is very hard. Some of the men are digging bunkers and filling sand bags. Others are cutting the downed trees into logs. The wire and posts start to outline the perimeter. All of this is done my hand. Picks and shovels and axes are the main tools. Looks like these boys are here to stay. Because of all the units working out of Polei-Kleng the one thing that the brass forgot about was fuel. We are now forced to go to Kontum to refuel. This just adds to the very long day. The last of the sorties are finally done. It's been a good day.

The hour is late and again we are told that we are to pick up passengers and paperwork for LZ Mary Lou. Hovering toward the CQ we see our last sortie of the day. As we set down the clerk tells us that he has to run back to get the mail poach that he forgot. "Glad it's not you running back for that thing. We wouldn't get out of here before midnight," is Dana's remark to Stoney. Our aircraft commander whips his head around and yells. **"GOD DAMN IT!" I CAN RUN JUST AS FAST AS ANY OF YOU BASTARDS. I WAS IN THE CAN WHEN THE ATTACK STARTED!!!"** The three of us lose all control and start laughing until tears start to form in our eyes. As the clerk returns Stoney starts to see the humor in the whole story and now he is laughing. Our passengers have no idea what is going on and the clerk has a look on his face as if to say we must be completely crazy. In the darkness as we fly toward Pleiku, each time Dana and I look at each other we start to giggle.

Landing in the revetment again we are greeted by Sgt. Hall and his shadow. Tonight Hall decides to wait before he says anything. None of us can still look at each other without laughing. It's not that it's that funny anymore than the fact we are tired and the long day has finally taken its toll on all of us. After we complete the logbook, the pilots and the NCOs leave. In the dark I finish my post-flight inspection. Dana helps because our guns don't need to be cleaned tonight. We realize that we had gone the entire day without firing a shot. By the time we head for the Company area the mess hall is closed. Looks like we'll have to hunt down something from an old care package or maybe some L.R.R.P. rations would be good. Maybe tonight I'll have enough time for a shower and I won't have to sleep in my clothes.

In March of 2003 I was contacted by David Naranjo. In March of 1969 he was a rifleman with Co. A, 2nd Battalion, 8th Infantry. The company was involved in the sweep after the attack on the morning of 2 March, 1969. The following are some of his memories of the day:

"The airfield ran east/west, and the Special Forces Camp was at the east end of the runway on the north side. LZ Bass was on the opposite side of the Special Forces Camp. The first day that we were there we made a sweep towards the west side of the base, more towards the mountain (Big Mama) maybe 200 meters from the edge of the runway. At the time we were in our tracks, ("APCs" or Armored Personnel Carriers.) While we sat looking west, a helicopter came from west to east over the jungle. It was probably on a routine mission, and as it passed this particular area, just 100 meters from where we were the NVA begin shooting at it with glee. I remembered we were all shocked at the fun the enemy was having shooting at this Huey.

"We estimated a company-sized unit from the amount of fire from the area. We got off our tracks and moved into the area. We ran into heavy fire from a heavily bunkered area. My squad shot up one bunker and a member of my squad reported hitting one NVA soldier in the head. They pulled us out so artillery could be used against the complex. We pulled back to the ridge where our tracks were located and we can't have been happier. We knew what was in the jungle area in front of us. A jet, I have no idea from where it came from, tried to drop a 750 pound bomb on the complex but missed it completely. By this time it was too late for us to recon the area, so we were pulled back to guard the perimeter at LZ Bass."

Two days later, David would be wounded during a rocket attack at LZ Bass. Also during this time he would be awarded the Bronze Star for Valor.

CASUALTY REPORT
March 2, 1969

| PFC Robert E. Diehl | US52817971 | 09/14/1948 | Age 20 |
| PFC James R. Taylor | RA11578241 | 03/07/1950 | Age 18 |

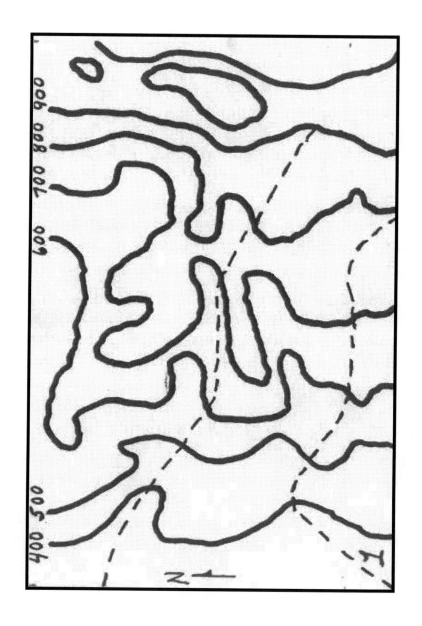

The Battle for LZ Brace

Solid Lines --- Ridge Lines
Dotted Lines --- Creeks or Rivers
Map not to scale

MAP 1
March 2, 1969

Location 1= LZ Mary   YA784879

Chapter III

"Snoopy"

For the third day in a row I find myself doing a pre-flight on Gator 108 at 0600hrs. After today she will be due for a one hundred-hour inspection in Maintenance. The Army is somewhat strict when it comes to the care of its helicopters. The main reason for this was because we have such a hard time replacing them. Tonight after we return I will have to pull all of my equipment off the ship. It has taken me too long to put together a complete tool kit and the things I need to do my job. That's the trouble with this place. We never have enough of anything around here.

Assault helicopter companies are set up to operate during combat to supply the needed number of aircraft while still being able to maintain the ships in an orderly manner. The guy who came up with that bit of garbage never visited sunny Vietnam. We have three flight platoons in the Company. The first and second are "lift" or transport platoons. The third is the "gun" platoon. Each flight platoon should have eleven ships. The third platoon has eight. The commanding officer also has a ship. Since I have been here we have never been to full strength. The most our platoon has ever had was ten. One of our ships is dedicated to the II Corps commander. Its only mission is to be used for the general or his staff. I had flown that mission a couple of times. It's a good deal if you had guard duty the night before and you needed to get some stuff from the coast. The pre-flights are always after 0800hrs. That would give you enough time to clean up and get anything on board that you would need to trade for the things that the platoon would need. It would also give SP4 Baker the day off. He had asked for the duty after he was shot down in November. He hates to fly but he also needs the money. He is one of the few guys who were drafted in

34

our platoon. He is married and has a baby.

His gunner, SP5 Mooney, is also married. Unlike the rest of us he is a career soldier. He had first come to Vietnam in 1965 with the 1st Cavalry Division. He rotated back to the states and was stationed in his home state of Alabama, and now he was back for another tour. He had nothing in common with any of us except Baker. So the match was made. They are both easy going and quiet. If you need help with something they are more than willing to help. They just don't want to go back into combat.

Because of the action the past two days, our ship count has dropped. Two ships were already in the hangar for maintenance. My assigned ship, Gator 488, was at the 608th Transportation Company because of the hard landing it had in January. Gator 390 had not been repaired yet. Then yesterday two of our ships had been damaged during the attack at Polei-Kleng. That had left us with three ships from our platoon for our primary mission. The second platoon was in the same mess as us. They also had two ships in the hangar. Gator 606 was still sitting next to Gator 390. Gator 521 remains at Kontum needing a rotor blade and a tail boom. The only ship to return to flight status has been Gator 603. With luck they would have six ships ready this morning. That would mean that the "Old Man's" ship would have to be pressed into duty. The gun platoon was the only one at full strength. They had all eight ships. One is in for maintenance, and two are pulling convoy cover. Four ships are assigned to us. This would leave one ship to be used where needed or to replace a ship lost during the day.

Once we are airborne, Stoney turns his head and smiles. Last night Dana and I had decided that we needed something to break the tension of the past couple of days. We each have two flight helmets. The helmets that we normally wear are the famous Army green. Olive drab is one color that nobody will ever wear once they get out of the Army. The helmets we have today are our own creations. A lot of time and effort have gone into the designing of these masterpieces. Dana has painted the main part of the helmet bright red. The visor is white with every color of the rainbow dotted or smeared on it. This is what Dana says an "acid trip" would look like. Across the back he has the printed in bold letters, "Bum Trip". My helmet is completely white. I have a picture of "Snoopy" the famous cartoon beagle by Charles Schulz. He is in his World War One flying suit ready to fight the "Red Baron". On the back I have painted a bulls eye. In every war that young men have flown, they have always been considered a little different or strange. To volunteer for something like this should be considered a statement that would question a person's sanity. It's just that some of us have a need to reinforce that statement. Every crewmember had something on their helmet.

"The CO is not going to like those helmets when he sees them. The last time you guys did that he threatened to give you an Article 15," (the Army's fine for minor infractions) is Stoney's comment. "What is he going to do? Send us to Vietnam and fly in helicopters?" responds Dana. "The problem with the Army is they have no sense of humor," I add. "If anybody asks, I warned you. Okay?" He just needed to cover his butt. Stoney was a little more straight-laced than he would like to let on.

This morning we are headed for LZ Mary Lou. Because of the attack yesterday morning, the pilots are getting their briefing here. The first order of business is moving D/3/12 into the area east of where we put companies Bravo and Charlie yesterday afternoon. Once we have them deployed, we will resupply the other two companies and the start the resupply to the firebases.

Picking the troops up at Polei-Kleng we head to map location YA747923. The landing zone is not bad. It is bigger than the hoverholes we had been using the past two days. The trees have been knocked down by artillery, so getting in and out proved to be quite easy. Once the troops are on the ground the ships divide up into four groups. Two ships will resupply Bravo and Charlie companies. Two ships will resupply the troops of the 3/8 by LZ Mary. That would leave three ships for Pause and three for Swinger. Yesterday as we brought troops into LZ Mary, they were to conduct reconnaissance in force in three directions. Delta was to RIF the center of the A/O. Alpha would go to the north and Bravo to the south. Alpha and Delta had not encountered anything. Bravo, which had gone south and southeast, had discovered a well-traveled trail and other signs of enemy movement. Alpha will now do a RIF to the east and northeast while Delta will move to the southeast. This will position the companies so Alpha and Bravo will drive the enemy towards each other and Delta can block any retreat to the west. From enemy documents and prisoners it is believed that some type of medical aid station or even a hospital unit is at or near map location YA830815.

We hovered toward the Resupply area. The CH-47s are now refueling at Kontum. The 7/17th are going to LZ Mary Lou for their fuel. This will help cut down on the traffic at Polei-Kleng. Hovering over to the Supply area I am greeted by a familiar face. His call sign is "Red Fox". He runs the Supply area for Brigade. We have worked with him many times at Dak To. The red hair and a large handlebar mustache are the reasons for his call sign. From his accent I think he must be from California. He has the "surfer" terms and the body language to match. That has become one of my hobbies since I joined the Army, trying to guess where people are from.

"What's happening?" is his greeting as we set down. He asks how much we are able carry. I let him know that I want to stay under twelve hundred pounds. Because of the area and the way we have to land, between our fuel and cargo we try to stay below three thousand pounds total. The brass was under the impression that we could carry four thousand pounds. In the states, where you fly and land on level ground, and you don't have to worry about cross winds hitting you as you hover into a bomb crater, or try to land on the top of a mountain, the total cargo limit would be acceptable. In Vietnam, the lighter the load the better the chance you would survive if you were to go down.

The first load will be C-rations and water. He hands me a red nylon bag. This is the most important part of our cargo. It's the mailbag for the grunts. I secure it to the bulkhead behind me with a "D-ring". The guys in the Resupply area quickly load us. Red has complete control of what is going on. He makes sure that the load is centered and nobody drops anything on the floor that might damage the control rods underneath that operate the flight controls. Once we're loaded, I tell Mr. Miller how much weight we are carrying and he writes it on the windshield with a grease pencil. We head to Swinger with our first sortie of the day.

Contacting Swinger, we inform them of what we have on board and ask which pad we should use. The larger fire bases have two pads. One is used mostly by the infantry company for passengers and resupply. The other is for the artillery unit. We will rotate pads so not to develop a pattern. That way, the bad guys wouldn't know which pad to zero their mortars on. As we set down, the guys unload the ship and we take three passengers and some empty water jugs back to Polei-Kleng. I've handed the red bag to the grunt in charge of the pad. He smiles and hands me back another bag. With care I secure it in the ship. They know I realize how important that bag is.

As we lift off I notice grunts moving through the wire and down the hill. I ask one of our passengers what is going on. He replies that they are checking the outer ring of the perimeter for caves or bunkers. Because of the deployments the past couple of days, and the task of setting up the firebase, the sweep of the outer perimeter had not been performed. Contacting Operations as we return to Polei-Kleng we are informed that we now have people operating outside the landing zones and we should not engage unless we receive fire. It would have been nice if we had been told that before we started the resupply. It would not be good to fire on our own people.

The morning passes with little happening. One ship received fire while en-route to Pause but no damage was reported. The gunships have been covering the large CH-47s when they take a load into one of the landing zones. We are under orders that we will not engage the enemy unless it is a large concentration of fire. Only after we receive permission to return fire would we be able to do so. Units from both the 3/12 and 3/8 are now operating outside their bases. Also the brigade commander, "Red 6," has issued orders that there is now a "No Hover Zone" near the Brigade CQ. We are to land on the opposite side of the taxiway when picking up dispatches or passengers.

The morning goes by quickly as our three ships move personnel and equipment into Swinger. It has been very uneventful. As we return with three passengers and more sandbags, the radio erupts. **"GATOR AIRCRAFT GATOR AIRCRAFT THIS IS 69. WE ARE UNDER ATTACK. WE HAVE INCOMING AND SMALL ARMS FIRE."** The gunships are refueling at Polei-Kleng. Stoney gets on the horn so we will have some gun cover. Clouds of smoke can be seen as the mortars and rockets impact at Swinger. We can see tracers coming in and going out of the perimeter. Our people are outside the wire and we have no idea where they are. The radios are now buzzing and are almost useless. The gunner on Gator 834 has spotted flashes at his four o'clock position. They will go in and place fire and smoke on the enemy location. We hang back to provide cover and Gator 525 will circle and try to locate any other enemy positions. On their first pass Gator 834 throws yellow smoke but they receive .50 cal. machine gun fire. We watch as they climb to get out of range but we don't see any smoke. The jungle is so thick, and the trees being one hundred to two hundred feet tall, it will take forever for the smoke to filter up to where we can see it. The gunships are coming on station but we have not been able to mark a target for them.

"I've got an idea," beams Dana over the intercom. Grabbing one of the first-aid kits he pulls a large bandage out and starts to tie it to a smoke grenade. "We can make our run and when I throw the grenade it will get hung up in the trees and mark the target," explains Jeff. "Hey, what do we have to lose?" says Stoney. With both Gators watching over us, we start our run. "I've got fire!" Dana shouts as he throws the smoke grenade. The tracers from the .50 cal. appear as big as basketballs. DAMN! Dana's idea worked. Banking right we can see the smoke hovering above the trees. The guns see it too. Upon starting their run the first of many rockets head toward the enemy gunners.

"Gator 108 this is 69, over." "Go 69, what's your situation?" "We have wounded. Can you evacuate?" "Get them ready. We are in-bound at this time." At this time Gator 834 contacts us. "Stoney, this is Bon-Bon."(1st Lt. Michael Bonthuis, Aircraft Commander, Gator 834.) "We are a little low on fuel. Let us get the first load. That way we can get them all out." "Okay Bon-Bon we will follow you." Swinger is still receiving small arms fire but we have to take the chance because we are all running low on fuel. Watching Gator 834 race toward the pad I brief our passengers on what is going on. I tell them to pitch the cargo out the door as soon as we hit the pad and then bail out as fast as possible so we can get the wounded aboard. Gator 834 hits the pad and just as they start loading

40

wounded a mortar round hits in the center of the fire support base. Five wounded are loaded before the next round impacts. Gator 525 has spotted another mortar tube. They head for the muzzle flash in order to mark it with smoke for the gunships. We land and as quickly as possible we unload them and load four wounded. We drop off the south side of the base and race for LZ Mary Lou. The second pair of gunships has come on station to lay waste to the target Gator 525 has just marked.

The wind has started to blow the blood around inside the ship. Dana has placed his flight jacket on one of the wounded, who is huddled on the floor of the ship. He has a back wound and is starting to go into shock. I have sat the one who has a head wound up against the bulkhead. I wrap another bandage around his wound. The other two seem to be all right. Setting down at Mary Lou, a medical team is waiting. Two are placed on stretchers while the other two are able to walk towards the aid-station. Dana has to run over and grab his flight jacket before the back wound is transported away. Taking off, we head for Polei-Kleng. We contact our other two ships. Gator 834 has gone to Kontum for fuel. He didn't have enough to return to Polei-Kleng. The gunships and Gator 525 are returning to Polei-Kleng to refuel and rearm. We tell them we will meet them at Polei-Kleng because we also need fuel.

Reaching Polei-Kleng, we hover to refuel. Sitting next to us is Gator 525. Their crew chief, SP4 Chuck Abrams starts pointing towards us as we set down. "Hey! Stoney! Take a look at your tail boom," is the transmission that comes over the radio as we start to refuel. Walking to the rear of the ship I discover three holes in the middle of the boom where "United States Army" is painted. I open up the side compartment and look into the tail boom. "We had better shut this thing down after we refuel so I can check the tail boom," I inform Stoney, as Dana continues to

41

refuel us. Once we are refueled, we hover to the taxiway by Resupply and shut down. The blades are still rotating as Stoney gets out of the ship. "Piss-Call," he announces.

It is now mid-afternoon and we have been going strong since 0800hrs. Dana has invaded my flight bag looking for my fruit and I have now gotten my flashlight and have started inspecting the damaged tail boom. The rounds have only done sheet metal damage. None of the control rods for the tail rotor were hit so we should be able to remain in service. The Red Fox has seen us land and has run over to us with four cold sodas. It's the best ginger ale that we have gotten all day. Having relieved ourselves and had a little something to eat we start the engine again. Hovering back into the Resupply area, we are loaded once again and head for Swinger. Back in the air, we learn that Gator 834 is unharmed. Gator 525 has taken fire as they had left Swinger. We are advised not to the bank to the north as we leave. Arriving at Swinger we use the south pad. As we unload a grunt comes up and hands me their red mailbag. With care I secure to the bulkhead and smile. He returns the smile and kneels down as we lift off. Over the radio we learn that one of Pause's companies is in contact west of the base.

The NVA would always establish their base camps in areas that were difficult reach by foot. They would use the high ground to defend against an attack. The area would have good cover and lots of fresh water nearby. The area between LZ Pause and LZ Mary had all of these.

Company A/3/8 had left their night location at 0930hrs. Moving to the east, they were to conduct a reconnaissance in force to map location YA812884. (Map 2, Location 2, Page 46) There they would establish a night location. As they had moved into this area they had found steps and trails leading up the hills and ridgelines they had to scale. They also saw signs that the enemy might be using elephants in order to move supplies. Arriving at

42

what they thought was their night location, they established a company perimeter. Shortly after 1600hrs, a SRP (short range patrol) from the third platoon encountered an NVA soldier. The enemy scouts were stationed at locations leading to their base camps. As the American forces would approach, these soldiers would break cover and run towards pre-planned locations where ambushes would be set up. The platoon leader in charge of the patrol informed the company commander. The forward observer assigned to the company recommended that artillery be called in. The CO elected to investigate without artillery support. The third platoon moved forward and at that time engaged the enemy. The ambush was designed to draw their enemy into a killing zone that covered three sides. Snipers were in the trees, along with booby traps and pre-sighted mortar locations, closed quickly on the platoon. The company moved to the rear of the third platoon and they started to receive fire. The enemy's ambush had by this time surrounded the third platoon, cutting them off from the rest of the company. The company radioed their position and called for help. They were actually at map location YA 804878. (Map 2, Location 3, Page 46) This was farther west than the planned night location. During this time most of the third platoon, the company commander, and the second platoon leader were killed. As the company continued to take casualties, the order to withdraw was given. They moved down the hill and established a makeshift perimeter as best they could. They were still under fire and greatly outnumbered.

Hovering into Resupply, our radio has gone crazy with everyone talking at once. "Blackjack 22" has taken off with "Red 5" on board. They and "Hummingbird 1" are headed to the contact area. We need to refuel and then head to B/3/8's location. They are cutting an extraction point so we can move them to the south of Alpha's position. Picking up the first sortie, we head north. The radios are now becoming our worst enemy. Between the number of people talking, and the enemy jamming different radio frequencies, we are having trouble determining what is going on.

Hummingbird 3 has spotted a location that we can use as a landing zone. It's at the base of a ridgeline in a creek bed. Our gunships prep the area and we head in. As we hover above the water, the first guy drops off the ship. The water is ankle deep so we will continue to bring the troops in here. This location is directly south of Alpha's scheduled night location. (Map 2, Location 4, Page 46) Before we can return for the next sortie, we are told to return to Polei-Kleng. We are to load ammo, claymore mines, and trip flares for the company in contact. Waving my arms as we enter the Resupply area, I'm yelling, **"AMMO! I NEED AMMO!"** The grunts have no idea what I'm yelling about. Red Fox has just learned what is going on. He runs over and starts to have his people load us with ammo. I can hear over the radio that the LOH is having trouble locating the company. I learn that we might have to drop the supplies to them. Hearing this, I grab Dana and we load several sand bags into the ship.

"What are you going to do with those?" Stoney asks. "You'll see," I answer as I cut the bags open and dump half the dirt out the door. "We can drop these out the door so we can find the guys on the ground. If we drop one of these boxes out and hit somebody we would kill them. This way we can find the guys and hopefully not hurt anybody." We divide the ammo between the two doors and each of us places three sandbags near our ammo boxes. Gator 409 from Second Flight is flying chase ship, and the Crocs are on station to provide cover. "Hummingbird 1" is hovering where the company is supposed to be. He has received fire but is still looking for the unit.

"BE ADVISED! WE HAVE SNIPER FIRE FROM ALL SIDES!" is all "ALPHA" can tell us. We circle and watch as the LOH hovers above the trees. Finally "Blackjack" tells them to pop smoke or we will never find them. After some protest they do pop smoke. **"SMOKE! I HAVE RED SMOKE,"** screams Dana. "WHERE?" asks Stoney. "FOUR O'CLOCK," is Dana's answer! Hovering at treetop level, Stoney tells everybody to stay off the radio so the guys on the ground can talk us to their location. As we hover looking for the company, we can hear firing below us. Tracers are coming up through the trees but they aren't coming towards us. I can't tell if they are firing at the ships above us or just shooting at the noise from our ship.

The wind is from the west. The trees are about two hundred feet tall. By the time the smoke has filtered up to where we can see it, the guys on the ground are nowhere to be found. The voice over the radio talks us to them. "I think you are to our Echo (east) Gator 108." Moving to the west, he continues to talk to us. The skids are touching the trees as we are informed that he thinks we are over him. I drop the first sandbag out. "That is too far to the November (north)." We move left and as Dana drops his bag we start receiving fire. **"RECEIVING FIRE, AT MY SEVEN O'CLOCK!"** I hear myself say as I open up with my gun. "We aren't leaving until those guys get this ammo!" Stoney states, as he holds the ship rock-solid. **"THAT'S IT! LET IT GO!"** is the response we were waiting for. (Map 2, Location 5, Page 46) As I am pushing the ammo out the door, my gun has not shut down once. Dana is now receiving fire on his side. As the last of the ammo boxes disappeared into the trees, I looked up at my field of fire. The wind from the rotor blades has parted the tree limbs and I can see the snipers taking aim at the ship.

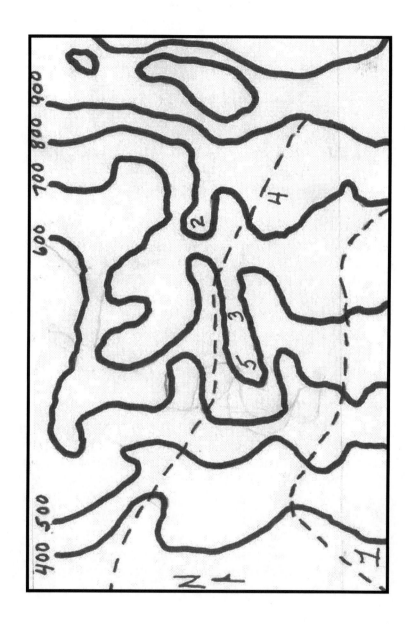

The Battle for LZ Brace

Solid Lines--- Ridgelines
Dotted Lines--- Creeks or Rivers
 Map not to scale

MAP 2
March 2, 1969

Location 1= LZ Mary   YA 784879
Location 2= Intended night location   YA 812884
Location 3= Made first contact   YA 804878
Location 4= LZ for B/3/8
Location 5= Area where A/3/8 had set up perimeter
                 after first contact

We both have spotted the snipers and their asses belong to us. We fire at our targets as the ship climbs out of range. For the better part of half an hour we have hovered looking for Alpha Company.

Circling the area waiting for the grunts to report I finally start to catch my breath. Its strange how short of breath you get after something like this happens. The guys on the ground report that three snipers have fallen from the trees. They also can see a few more bodies still hanging in the area that we were in. At this point Dana gives me a "High Five." Little bastards! That won't make us even for "Shifty" but it's a start. The rest of the flight has Bravo moved into the landing zone. The sun is setting and we can do no more to help the guys on the ground. Later that evening, the Company received a radio contact from one of their men who was wounded and still in the contact zone. A squad was formed and, under the cover of darkness, they were able to recover two badly wounded soldiers from the ambush site. The entire cargo area is covered with the spent brass from my gun. I must have fired eight hundred rounds. Half my ammo is gone. Returning to Polei-Kleng again, we are informed that we have passengers and dispatches for LZ Mary Lou.

Hovering toward the taxiway to pick up our final load of the day, the excitement of what had just happened to us is starting the wear off. The pilots are talking about what they are going to have at the Officer's Club. Dana is complaining that he has guard duty tonight. I am plotting on how I can get all of my gear out of the ship and back to the barracks before Maintenance takes the ship. The skids have no sooner touched down when, out of nowhere, this crazy man appears. He is overweight. He appears to be middle-aged, and slightly bald. Wearing only a towel and waving a .45 pistol, he runs up to the helicopter. "Who the hell is this?" I ask. "That's Red 6," is Stoney's response. The brigade commander had been in the shower when we had hovered up to the CQ. He was so outraged that his "No Hover" zone had been violated that he just snapped. As he continued his war dance the entire crew lost it. We are laughing to the point that tears are starting to form in our eyes, and this madman has now lost all touch with reality.

At this time he pointed his pistol at Stoney. Not wasting one second I pulled my machine gun to bear and yelled to this crazy fool, **"MOVE BACK AND LOWER THE WEAPON!"** I ordered. The look on everybody's faces had now changed. The passengers who were waiting to board our ship had watched this unfold, and now they actually believed that I might shoot this son-of-a-bitch. At this point is when I think he realized how stupid this whole thing looked. Or the fact that I might actually shoot him, and then how would the Army explain how he was shot in his bath towel inside a secure area? He raised his hands and smiled. Walking backwards away from the ship, he never took his eyes off me. The passengers were loaded and we had our important dispatches on board before anyone spoke. "Would you have shot that jerk?" asks Dana. "Not until he had plugged Stoney." I replied. "Thanks a lot!" is Stoney's response. We start to laugh again. Our passengers have not one idea what we are saying or why we are laughing. I can imagine the stories that would come out of this incident.

The flight back to Holloway was a quiet one. The war today had become very personal. During my first tour I had fired my weapon many times. I had been given credit for confirmed kills. I had never seen the horror of death as I saw it today. I saw the look in the enemy soldier's eyes as I fired at him. As the bullets tore into his flesh, his brain told his body that something was very wrong. He looked at me as if to ask, "Why?" I watched as his lifeless body disappeared towards the jungle floor, and he was gone. I felt neither remorse nor joy. I felt nothing, and that puzzled me more than anything that had ever happened to me. I only knew that, from that day on, I was a different person.

Returning to Camp Holloway, we are met by Sgt. Hall and some Maintenance personnel. They have us hover to the hangar and set down next to Gator 834. During its last trip into Swinger they took a round in the tail rotor. That ship will be ready for tomorrow. My ship will be there for at least two days. Between the maintenance that needs to be pulled, and the combat damage to the tail boom, the crews can't make any commitments as to when they will be done.

"Kilpatrick has guard duty tonight," states Sgt. Hall. "Would you crew 834 tomorrow?" I look at him as if I can't believe he asked that. "Lt. Bonthuis asked for you." Hearing that, I agree that would be fine. Sgt. Hall starts to help me carry my gear to Gator 834. This is not something that he would normally do. "I heard you and Dana got a couple of the little bastards today." "Yes, we did do that," I reply. I think he wanted me to continue but we had never talked to each other since he arrived. Any time we spoke was to ask or answer a question. I didn't even know what his first name was. We finished stowing my gear and we parted company. As he left he slapped me on the shoulder and said, "Good job today." It left me speechless because this was the most he had ever said to me.

Again it was 2200hrs before I got back to the barracks. I heated some water on Sempek's hotplate and made myself a LRRP ration. It wasn't the best chili, but it was hot and it filled my belly. Screw the shower. I would get one in the morning.

50

CASUALTY REPORT
March 3, 1969

SP5 Lynn D. Anderson	RA18960800	05/06/1949	Age 19
SP4 Melvin L. Applebury	US56346870	08/12/1948	Age 20
SP4 Philip L. Baker	RA26829658	12/03/1948	Age 20
PFC Paul J. Buczoloch	US54983432	12/30/1947	Age 21
SP4 Fred D. Burton	US52917389	09/22/1948	Age 20
SP4 Dennis J. Coll	US51983885	07/23/1948	Age 20
PFC Michael England	US53458364	02/20/1949	Age 20
SP4 Charlie Fields	US53704232	10/17/1945	Age 23
SP4 Rodger D. Force	US52968436	02/07/1948	Age 21
SP4 Rupert W Goebel Jr.	RA12810508	10/27/1949	Age 19
SP4 Jeffery K. Goss	US67040695	05/26/1948	Age 20
1LT Robert E. Griffith	05350686	09/02/1945	Age 23
SP4 Barry D. Horton	US5686669	12/01/1947	Age 21
SP4 Willie J. Hudson	US52941082	08/27/1947	Age 21
CPT. Dennis R.P. Isom	OF108670	04/05/1944	Age 24
SP4 Vernon E. Lail Jr.	US53530450	08/04/1948	Age 20
PFC William T Rector Jr.	US52917860	12/24/1947	Age 21
SGT George R. Robinson	US52759381	11/23/1947	Age 21
PFC Layne M. Santos	US56728606	10/17/1948	Age 20
SP4 William J. Schaaf	US51673516	10/07/1948	Age 20
SP4 Joseph Schmich Jr.	US56589866	11/23/1947	Age 21
PFC Harry B. Seedes III	US52817368	11/05/1948	Age 20
PFC David A. Seiber	US53911264	08/04/1948	Age 20
PFC Willard A. Wimmer	RA11580831	02/12/1949	Age 20

MISSING IN ACTION

PFC William M. Smith   US24425114   04/02/1949   Age 19
(Promoted to the rank of SGT E-5 and declared as "Died while captured" on 06/30/1970.)

Chapter IV

"Short Night Long Day"

My head is pounding as I'm shocked awake to the sound of incoming rocket fire. At 0200hrs the first of several rounds of 122mm rocket and 81mm mortar fire will land at Camp Holloway. Lying under my bunk, I pull my clothes on and wait for the rounds to stop. As the fire pauses I bolt from my hiding place and head for the bunker. Inside the bunker, our platoon stands in the darkness, listening for any more fire. **"THIS IS BULLSHIT!"** somebody says as the next mortar rounds impact in the distance.

Darting out of the bunker, I work myself between the barracks and the sandbags that line the outside walls. Moving toward the rear of the building, I can see our revetments. The flare ship has begun to drop its cargo, and the entire base is lit up. I watch for movement around our ships. Soon a couple of other members of the platoon move up to join me. The green star flare has not been fired so at least we don't have bad guys inside the camp. Nobody is moving for fear of drawing fire. The platoon has deployed itself around our barracks. We now wait until the platoon sergeant arrives to brief us. Thirty minutes passes before we get the word on what is going on. We are on 100% alert and we need to have all personnel report to the perimeter.

Sgt. Tuminello has arrived with the ¾ ton truck. The platoon starts to load up. I decide with a couple of others to walk. Grabbing my weapon and poncho liner we head for our perimeter bunker. As we walk, Jim Sempek, Sam Stella, and me, we talk about the last three days. Because of the long days and all that has happened none of us has been able to talk. Jim will be crew chief on Gator 390 tomorrow. It has been repaired and returned to duty. His gunner will be SP4 Clarence Vedder. He would have been with "Shifty" two days ago if not for being on guard duty the night before. Now he wants to take over as its crew chief. He has lots of reasons, but I think it is more guilt than anything. Sam thinks it's a good move because we are in need of crew chiefs who know what is going on. Besides losing "Shifty" we are about to lose SP5 Fall, SP4 Dana, and SP4 Mutz. They are all getting close to their DEROS.

Sam wants to know if we can get together some trading material. The II Corps bird will be going to the coast the day after tomorrow. He needs spray paint and a new operating rod for his machine gun. It is amazing what we have to do to get parts for our ships and guns. Jim got permission to convert the back part of the barracks into a bar. He has gotten plywood and other material to start the remodeling. The bad news is that we will have to move the bunks closer together. I spend so little time there anyway why would I care. The big news is that the headquarters platoon has gotten a water heater for their shower. They have made a deal with us that if we get the parts to install it and help get it running, we can use it. Somehow it seems like a deal with the devil. Arriving at the perimeter bunker, we survey the perimeter and find a place to rack out for a couple hours. Pre-flight is at 0600hrs.

Wrapped in my poncho liner, trying to get a couple hours sleep, I had no idea what was happening around us. Ben Het, which is located near Dak To, came under heavy attack. The enemy used fifteen PT-76 Russian tanks in support of their ground forces. This was the first time the NVA had used tanks in the war. Our tanks have engaged the enemy and they have retreated. Air strikes have also been employed. Polei-Kleng is under rocket and mortar attack. Later that night, a ground attack from the north and west would be repelled. LZ Swinger and LZ Pause were being probed. Their companies, who were located at different night locations, had not reported any movement. The remaining 68 men of A/3/8 sat out this long night as artillery and AC-47 (Spooky) gunships supported them. The claymore mines and trip flares that we had dropped had helped them establish a defendable perimeter. During the night a Dust-Off ship was able to extract some of their wounded. To the north, units of the 2nd Brigade were also receiving mortar fire and probes from the enemy. LZ Mile High was secured by C/1/12 and had units located in night locations north, south, and east, all of which remained at 100% alert during the night.

The platoon truck picked up the personnel who had pre-flights at 0500hrs. I was cold and having a hard time moving. The ride back to the barracks was short and very bumpy. A cold shower and clean clothes helped to start my day. A large plate of SOS with scrambled eggs and coffee got me to pre-flight. Instead of having the briefing at Polei-Kleng, we are to report to LZ Mary Lou again. The brass feels that the ships would be safer there because of all the action last night. Because Lt. Bonthuis is ranking officer, we are flight lead today. While the pilots are in the briefing, the crews talk. My gunner today is PFC Gary Eggleston. His accent is a cross between Dana's Boston colonial lingua and a New Jersey gangster. He has guard duty tonight. I have lucked out, because SP5 Jim Fall has decided to call it quits and stop flying. He has offered to pull guard for the rest of his tour. That would free up at least one crew chief a day. He starts tonight and he will be taking my place. Sempek and Vedder are going over Gator 390. If Jim had been the crew chief on 390 instead of "Shifty" nobody would have died. "Shifty" was hit in the right side of the neck. Jim is almost a foot shorter than "Shifty." The round would have gone over his head. They are number two today.

Today we are working a double-edged sword. First we need to get supplies into Pause and Swinger. Company A/3/8 has not been probed since early last night. The brass feels that they are to sit tight for right now so we can

54

get things arranged to reinforce their position. While we resupply the firebases, B/3/8 will prepare an extraction zone because they are too far to the east to link up with Alpha. The terrain is hampering their progress so we are going to move them to the north of A/3/8. Company D/3/8, southwest of Hill 947 (YA813864) is moving toward A/3/8. (Map 3, Location 7, Page 57) The Valley is starting to heat up in more ways than one. At 0930hrs everything turns to shit. D/3/8 has made contact as they moved from YA 800856(Map 3 Location 6, Page 57) to establish a blocking position to prevent the enemy from withdrawing to the south. The NVA knows that this Company is trying to link up with Alpha Company. They will now start to fight a delaying action until they can eliminate Alpha Company. The enemy had broken contact with A/3/8 during the night. This gave them the false security that they could move from their perimeter to recover their dead and missing from the previous day's contact. They moved out of their perimeter and again encountered a large enemy force and had come under attack. Three ships are scrambled to pick up B/3/8. Our ship is sent to Pause to pick up the reconnaissance unit of 3/8 for a combat assault to relieve Alpha.

The area we are to assault is northeast of where we had dropped the resupply the evening before. Map location YA828899. (Map 3, Location 8, Page 57) Artillery has flattened the trees, but we are still landing at the base of the ridgeline. During a flyover we determine that the best approach would be from the west. The trees would be less of a problem and we could depart without crossing the area where we had received fire the night before. "Red 6" has determined that it would be quicker to enter from the northwest because he says the landing area seemed larger, due to a finger that forms a valley. He also thinks that we might be able to get two ships in at one time. DUMB ASS! Like I said before, grunts don't understand helicopters.

The guns have set up to our left as we approach. We clear the trees and are about fifty feet above the ground when all hell breaks loose. **"FIRE! FIRE! I HAVE FIRE ON ALL SIDES!"** I point toward the tree line telling the grunts to open up. We are receiving heavy automatic weapons fire. There are people in the landing zone! **"BON-BON, THERE'S A GUNNER DIRECTLY UNDER YOU!"** is the warning we get from Gator 390. I look under the ship and there he is. He has a B-40 rocket launcher and I can't hit him with my gun. Sempek and Vedder are blasting at him but because they are higher than we are, they can't get the angle to hit him. I pull out my .45 and start shooting at him. Seeing me, he backs up to take aim at us. Bad move, buddy! Eggy has him in his sights and with the first burst he cuts him in two. The Crocs are throwing everything they have at them. "We're coming out!" radios Bon-Bon. The entire time our guns have fired into the ridgeline. Back in the air, we turn away from the landing zone. The gunships are out of ammo and the second set is on its way. Turning his head, Bon-Bon asks if anybody is hit and asks what we think. "I think we should have Blackjack go in there and get his ass shot up so the damn gooks will leave us alone," is Eggy's response. "Well this time we are going to do it my way," is how Bon-Bon informs Blackjack as we set up to the west. With the guns set up on our right we head in. Again we receive fire as the enemy counters our next move. Our machine guns are blasting the ridgeline. **"MY GUN IS JAMMED!"** I shout as it fails to fire. I grab my M-14 and start to fire into the tree line. We are being hit from all sides. **"GET OUT OF HERE!"** I yell as everyone in the ship fires into the tree line. We grab for the sky. The bastards are everywhere. The gunships have unloaded everything they have.

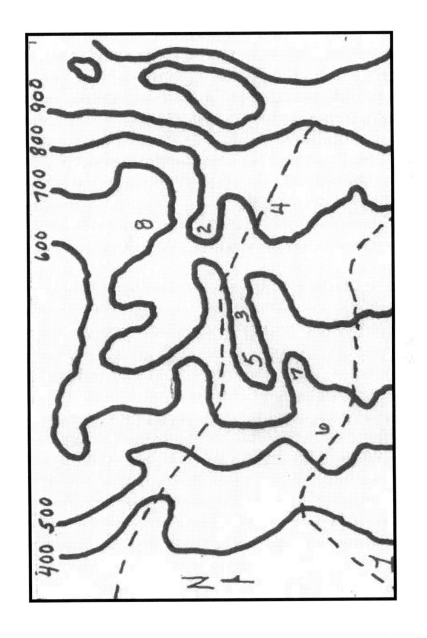

The Battle for LZ Brace

Solid Lines--- Ridgelines
Dotted Lines--- Creeks or Rivers
Map not to Scale

MAP 3
March 4, 1969

Location 1= LZ Mary   YA 784879
Location 2= Intended night location   YA 812884
Location 3= Made first contact   YA 804878
Location 4= LZ for B/3/8
Location 5= Area where A/3/8 had pulled back to
            and established a perimeter
Location 6= D/3/8 area of first contact   YA 800856
Location 7= Hill 947   YA 813864
Location 8= LZ for Recon/3/8 and B/3/8

Blackjack calls for an artillery strike. We are low on fuel and our gun support is gone. We are to return to Polei-Kleng. Once we refuel and rearm, we will try it again after the artillery strike.

Heading toward Polei-Kleng we radio to have ammo for both our guns and for the grunts waiting for us at POL. The grunts are talking and asking us what is going on. I explain we need fuel and ammo. This is the first time they have ever been in a firefight and not had a tree or something for cover. We land to fuel and the guys from Supply are waiting for us. I run to the opposite side of the ship and grab my extra barrel out of the side compartment. I had fired so many rounds that the barrel had actually drooped.

The grunts reloaded their magazines and we refilled our ammo boxes. One of the comments from our passengers was, "You guys must be nuts! How can you just sit there and return fire? I was scared shitless and I had a place to hide here behind the door post." The grunts are amazed at what just happened. I'm even more amazed that we did not take one round anywhere in the ship. Those guys are either the world's worst shots, or we are the luckiest bunch of bastards in the Valley. We head back toward Pause. During the time we were refueling, Swinger and Pause had been shelling the landing zone. They had also received incoming.

The smoke is rising as we enter the zone. Many more trees are down. It is difficult to determine how far above the ground we are. **"FIRE! I HAVE FIRE!"** is all that Eggy can say as we approach the landing zone again. The ridgeline has exploded with small arms fire. **"We're coming out!"** radios Bon-Bon. We break to the left and Bon-Bon yells, **"SCREW THIS!"** The next thing I realize is, he has kicked the pedals and made a hard left and we dropping back into the LZ. **"WE ARE CLEAR RIGHT! WE ARE CLEAR LEFT! WE ARE CLEAR ON THE TAIL**

59

ROTOR! WE ARE CLEAR RIGHT! WE ARE CLEAR LEFT! GO! GO!" The grunts are off the ship. "WE ARE CLEAR!" The gamble worked. Instead of leaving, Bon-Bon had pulled a U-turn and the "gooks" had dropped their guard. We were finally getting people on the ground. The enemy must now contend with the people on the ground. This helps to take the heat off us. As we moved the reconnaissance unit in, the rest of the flight has brought Bravo Company to LZ Pause. Once troops had finally gotten into this landing zone, the battle started to change almost immediately. The NVA who were engaged with A/3/8 broke contact to reinforce the area where we had assaulted. This gave A/3/8 a chance to retreat from the contact area and move towards an extraction point. Today nobody would be safe in the Plei-Trap. While we were doing our assault, Polei-Kleng had been hit with 122mm rockets. They had hit the 105mm ammunition that was for B/6/29. The Executive Officer of B/6/29 was critically wounded. He would later die from his wounds. The entire Valley had become a battleground.

Since 0615hrs a reconnaissance element of the 1st of the 12th that was set up at LZ Roberts had been probed and was under fire. They had requested gunships. The gunships are to be provided by the 170th Assault Helicopter Company. They are primary support for 2nd Brigade that is operating to the north of us. For the next twelve hours a running battle would take place. This would include two air strikes and several artillery strikes. Units of the 1/8 had again encountered trucks and enemy bunkers. They were in contact with an undetermined size force. One of the trucks they captured was brought to Polei-Kleng. The stories about ox carts and bicycles may show how determined they were to get supplies down from North Vietnam, but we had proof that some of those stories were bullshit. The four main fire support bases in the area would receive incoming fire. LZ Swinger and LZ

Susan would be hit by 105mm howitzer fire this afternoon.

By mid-afternoon Company A/3/8 had made their way out of the contact area. With the assistance of a LOH, they had followed a creek away from the enemy. Once the best possible extraction point was reached, a "Tactical Emergency" was called for us to remove the remainder of the Company. Several ships had been damaged. Some had taken rounds. Other had damaged their rotor blades as they were removing Bravo from their night location. Four ships had returned to base. Because of this, crews were scrambled from Holloway to help us extract what was left of A/3/8. Ships from the 7/17th would continue bringing B/3/8 into the assault area. The enemy and daylight were both against us at this time. Even with all the people who were on the ground, their ships would continue to receive fire. As Bravo and Recon expanded their lines out from the landing zone and started to assault the ridgeline, the pressure against D/3/8 was relieved. The enemy had already begun plans for tomorrow's action. They redeployed their assets in the area that A/3/8 departed. The next move was ours.

The Hummingbirds were waiting to guide us to the embattled company. It was not the best extraction point, but it would have to do. Dropping down into the creek bed, the clearing was a lot smaller than most landing zones. Unable to land because of the trees and the narrow creek bed, each of our ships would wait their turn. Once inside this small opening in the jungle, they would have to hover a couple of feet above the troops. Soldiers had carried their wounded a great distance and were exhausted. Many were without weapons and clothing. Crewmembers had to hang outside the ships as the men on the ground would use the last of their strength to lift the wounded up so that they could be pulled into the cargo area. As each of our ships departed with its sortie, the increased fear of an attack mounted. The troops were taken to Pause to expedite the extraction. As we unloaded the wounded of A/3/8, I looked at the fuel gauge. Being low on fuel would actually help us. Each time a ship returned, they would try to take an extra soldier on board. Finally at 1525hrs we had the last of the wounded and weary out. (Map 4, Location 9, Page 65) Once we had A/3/8 out of danger, the job of getting the wounded back to Mary Lou begun. Using both pads, the 7/17th continued to take troops back to the assault point. We loaded the wounded. The cruel facts of war took human form as we headed for Mary Lou. The first loads that we took are the ones who might make it. The medics would make the choices of who might live and those that were to die on this dirty little hill in a place most of these guys had never heard of. Passing out cigarettes, and helping to give water to the lucky ones who lay huddled on the floor of my ship, is the only aid that we are able to give. All have more than one wound. Many are almost naked. They have fought the fight of their lives.

At Mary Lou, several men help offload our damaged cargo. We refuel and head back to the Valley. The pace has taken its toll. Bon-Bon can hardly get out of his seat in order to relieve himself. The pilots have been in those seats for over eight hours. At least Eggy and I are able to move around and stand up to stretch once in a while. Returning to Pause we again load wounded. The soldiers that have died are wrapped in their ponchos and laid near the pad. We would take two more sorties to Mary Lou. The other Company of the battalion, D/3/8, which had been working its way towards Alpha, had set up a night location and had cut a small landing zone. They needed food, water, and ammo. They had fought their way to Hill 947(YA814869). Resupply would be accomplished by us dropping supplies to them. Some of their wounded would be extracted by Hummingbirds (LOHs) from the 7th of the 17th Cavalry, Rcn./3/8th and B/3/8 joined at YA

825890 where a night location was established. We would fly until the last light disappeared in the western sky. Departing Pause for the last time that day, we wished them luck. Many people had died or had been wounded in the past two days. The soldiers of the 3rd Battalion, 8th Infantry would have to endure another night in this place of terror. Company A/3/8 would not be considered an effective combat unit for almost a month. The Company started with one hundred and twenty-three men on 1 March 1969. During the last two days they sustained thirty-one killed. Another fifty-two were wounded. Four of these men would later die from their wounds. Four were missing

Flying in the dark toward Camp Holloway, we all sat lost in our thoughts. Smoking a cigarette and watching as the spent brass from my gun rolled around the floor, I was exhausted. My body ached from the effort of pulling the wounded into the ship. The events of the day seemed to pass in front of my eyes as if I watched a movie. The dried blood of the wounded had blended together on the gray floor to create a picture that was part of war. Operations informed us by radio that damaged ships were to park in front of Maintenance. They asked if any ship needed something special. I requested a water truck to wash the inside of the ship out. Hovering into our revetments, we are greeted by everyone in the unit. The Company commander and the first sergeant had ordered all personnel to help secure the ships tonight. The mess hall was open and hot chow was waiting for us. There were not many happy campers greeting us. They were pissed because they didn't understand why they needed to be there. Their attitudes changed as they saw inside the ships. Two started the post-flight. Another helped to remove our gear. Sgt. Hall informed me that I was on Gator 376 tomorrow. I carried my gear, with the help of a couple of guys from Maintenance, over to that ship. As I passed Gator 390 the crew and the personnel there were laughing and Sempek was red-faced and mad as hell. It seems that on our first attempt this morning he had tried to get the NVA who had run under our ship. Because of the angle he didn't get him. He had shot the front of the skid off. The one ship with combat damage that was self-inflicted.

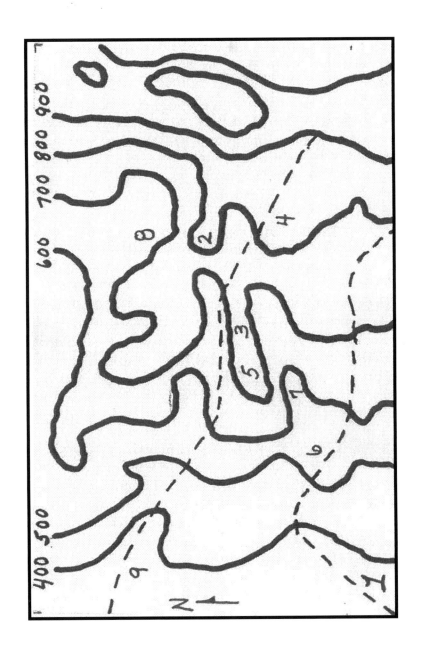

The Battle for LZ Brace

Solid Lines--- Ridgelines
Dotted Lines--- Creeks or Rivers
Map not to scale

MAP 4
March 4, 1969

Location 1= LZ Mary   YA 784879
Location 2= Intended night location   YA 812884
Location 3= Made first contact   YA 804878
Location 4= LZ for B/3/8
Location 5= Area where A/3/8 had pulled back to
                    and established a perimeter
Location 6= D/3/8 area of first contact   YA 800856
Location 7= Hill 947   YA 813864
Location 8= LZ for Recon/3/8 and B/3/8
Location 9= Creek bed where A/3/8 was extracted

James would not live this down anytime soon. I finished moving my gear and headed for the mess hall. They had chicken stew with mashed potatoes and gravy. The cold shower removed the dirt of the day and I finally got to shut my eyes.

In April of 2000, Albert Jaquez related his story to me on the events of those days. He was a member of A/3/8 and one of the few that was not wounded.

"When we arrived in the Plei-Trap we were told that there had been some enemy activity in the area. On March 3rd it seemed like we humped all day to reach the top of this hill. It was a hard climb and we found elephant dung and steps all the way up. It was getting late when we reached a flat area and spotted four NVA soldiers. They had come out of the woods and than ran back in. Our captain ordered third platoon to go and check it out. The other officers warned him not to do this. He sent them in anyway. Gunfire started and the platoon was wiped out. We rushed forward but were pushed back. We lost most of the chain of command. The commanding officer and the senior RTO were killed immediately. One of the platoon leaders and the acting first sergeant were also killed. We had walked into the 66th NVA Regiment base camp and didn't know it. We ran back to the flat area and dug in. We fought until dark. Then all went quiet. A chopper came in and dropped us ammo because we were very low. Snipers were in the trees all around us. The following morning it was quiet. We had a monkey swing by and scare the hell out of us.

"We only had one officer left. I believe his name was Williams. Anyway we went out to check out the damage from the night before. As we got to the area of the ambush I saw our bodies all stacked up. As we looked at them we were ambushed again. This time they followed us back to where we had dug in. We had artillery called in on top of us and then we bailed. We ran for our lives as the chopper kept them off of us. The only communications we had were with "Alpha Lima" on the chopper's radio frequency. All the other radio frequencies were jammed. We ran for about a mile and than the LOH helped us find a clearing so the choppers could pick us up. Once we got to the firebase this was the first time that the rest of the 3rd of the 8th realized that we weren't all dead. We stay there while the rest of the battalion went back to take the hill. It was almost impossible because they had bunkers on top of bunkers. We had bodies outside the wire for three days. They were so busy with the wounded and everything that when the dead came in we would just stack them by the pad. Finally they started removing them after things got quiet. I remained at the base for three weeks. During this time I watched B-52 "Arc Light" strikes during the day and at night "Puff the Magic Dragons" would be working out. The first of April they brought guys in from other units to make us a Company again. They sent us back into the very same place. It was a living hell. All the trees were burnt and split. No leaves anywhere and bodies were everywhere. You couldn't walk without tripping over the remains of the dead. That night we didn't dig in because of all the graves that we found. Lots of bad stuff. Without you guys in the air I would not be here today. Thank you my brother with all my heart."

During July and August of 2001 I exchanged e-mails with Bob Kilpatrick. Like me he had looked for some answers to what happened in that Valley over thirty years ago. One of his letters was about that day.

"I had guard duty the night before. My ship and crew were again in the Plei-Trap. I had been taking it easy and trying to catch up on my sleep. About two o'clock Tuminello and Hall came running into the Company area. They told Dana and me to get down to the revetments. They were putting together crews from all the available personnel. I spotted SP4 Mike Curran working on a nearby ship. Although he worked in Maintenance, he had flown with me several times. I drafted him as my gunner. There was a "Tactical Emergency" and we were going to fly with Second Flight. I don't remember the pilot but he was okay. As we headed to the Valley the pilot briefed us. I kept listening to the radio for Bon-Bon's voice. Once I heard him I knew that they were all right.

"Hovering into the creek bed I could see that these guys were beat to hell. It was horrifying. They were naked and had nothing as far as equipment or weapons were concerned. We had to pull them into the helicopter because we couldn't land. We got thirteen in the first time and headed for their firebase. I think that was a record. We unloaded and headed back for more. The second trip we just pulled guys in until no more would fit. I think that we made one more trip. After we had the company out, we started taking wounded to Mary Lou. Most of them were pretty bad. I don't know if any of them made it.

"We stayed with it until dark. Running back and forth to Mary Lou with wounded and then

69

taking resupply to the other landing zones. I sure did a lot of work on my day off. Getting back to Holloway that night we were met by the crew chief whose ship I was on. 'Where the Hell was he this afternoon? He can pull his own post-flight.' That night I had beers with Dave Silk and Mike. He told me that if he had known what I was getting him into, he would have never climbed into that gun well. I think that day is when he got the nickname of 'Shakey.'"

The following is a comparison of a typical infantry company in Vietnam and the actually strength of A/3/8 at the time they engaged the enemy on March 3-4, 1969. The source of this information is MTOE 176, and MTOE 178.

Organization of the standard U.S. infantry company [MTOE 7-177 Test used in Vietnam]: The rifle company headquarters consisted of two officers and ten enlisted men, with three rifle platoons (one officer, 41 enlisted each) and one mortar platoon (one officer, 25 enlisted). Each rifle platoon had a headquarters (one officer, two enlisted), three rifle squads, (ten enlisted with M79 and M16 weapons) and one weapons squad, and (nine enlisted with M16 rifles and two M60 machineguns and one 90mm recoilless rifle, the latter almost always was left at base camp). The mortar platoon contained a headquarters of one officer and seven enlisted and three mortar squads (six enlisted with one M79, 81mm mortar, and M16 rifles). Usually the 81mm mortars were also left at base camp and the squads used as rifle infantry. Totals: six officers and 158 enlisted.

From the research that I have done the total number in A/3/8 was six officers and 123 enlisted. I establish this figure from the Company roster, after action reports and casualty reports from those two days. Because of leaves, sick call and other personnel that were assigned to other duty post the Company had approximately 105 personnel at LZ Mary. Included in this number were two members from the artillery unit serving as a forward observation team and two combat engineers. Most of the companies who were involved during this operation were under strength. During one talk with a former member of A/1/8 he related that on the first day they assaulted LZ Turkey there were only 80 in his Company. From my own accounts I recall that the powers in charge were disappointed because our pilots would only carry five passengers. They had wanted us to carry six so that we could move a company with each ship doing two sorties. Ten ships, at two sorties apiece and five passengers would equal 100 men. I believe that the number of 105 for A/3/8 is very accurate.

The After Action Report that follows was filed by a battalion headquarters officer. It was written from eyewitness accounts and radio logs between the command and control ship, the company that was on the ground, and the battalion headquarters unit. Because of the stress of combat and the confusion of the battle there are conflicting reports between this account and other reported actions that day.

DEPARTMENT OF THE ARMY
HQ 4TH INFANTRY DIVISION
APO San Francisco 96262

AVDDH-CS
14 March 1969

SUBJECT: Combat Operations After Action Report.
RCS: MACV   J3-J2

THRU: Commanding General
IFFOORCEV
APO 96350

TO: Commander
United States Army Vietnam

ATTN: G3
US FORCES 96375

1.   NAME OR IDENTITY AND OR TYPE OF OPERATION: Reconnaissance In force, Company A, 3d Battalion, 8th Infantry.

2.   DATES OF OPERATION: 2 March1969, through 4 March 1969.

3.   LOCATION: PLEI-TRAP VALLEY, KONTUM Province [YA803879] Map 1:50,000 sheet 6537 IV series L7014

4.   CONTROL AND COMMAND HEADQUARTERS: 3d Battalion 8th Inf.

5.   REPORTING OFFICER: LTC. Pennel J. Hickey

6.   TASK ORGANIZATION: Company A 3d Battalion 8th Infantry.

7.   SUPPORTING FORCES:

a.   B and C Btry, 6/29 Arty   [105]   DS.
b.   C Btry, 1/92 Arty   [155]   GS.
c.   A Troop   7/17 Cav.
d.   52d Aviation Bn.
e.   7th Air Force.

8.   INTELLIGENCE:

a.   The 66th NVA Regiment was known to be in the general area of contact. Several intelligence reports and heavy 'Snoopy' reading were plotted approximately five kilometers to the south of the contact.
b.   After the battalion seized the ridgeline east of the contact, documents confirmed the presence of the K-25 Sapper and the K-8 Infantry Battalion of the 66th Reg.
c.   The terrain in the area of the contact [see sketch, Incl. # 1] was a north-south ridgeline extending east to west with fingers, and steep slopes on either side. The area is vegetated by triple-canopy jungle. Fields of Observation were limited to 25-30 meters. The weather was clear with afternoon temperatures in the 80's. At dusk a haze of smoke and dust impaired visibility for aircraft.

9.   MISSION: The 3d Battalion 8th Infantry had the mission of conducting combat assault into the southern portion of the 1st Brigade area of operations, and conduct a reconnaissance in force and ambush operations along the main enemy infiltration routes and in known or suspected base areas.

10.   CONCEPT OF OPERATION:

a. The 3d Battalion 8th Infantry was directed to conduct combat assaults with three companies to YA784879 and conduct reconnaissance in force operations in the respective areas of operation.

b. Company A was to combat assault to YA784879 following Company D, and conduct reconnaissance in force in the northern sector of the Battalion AO.

c. Company B was to combat assault to YA784879 following Company A and conduct reconnaissance in force in the southern sector of the Battalion AO.

d. Company C was to secure FB Pause and the Battalion CP.

e. Company D was to combat assault toYA784879 and conduct a reconnaissance in force in the center of the Battalion AO.

f. The Reconnaissance Platoon was to conduct a reconnaissance in force south of YA825895.

11.   EXECUTION:

a. On 2 March at 1049H Company A combat assaulted from Polei-Kleng to YA784879. The assault was made without incident and the Company began a reconnaissance in force sweep to the northeast. A night location was established at YA793879.

b. On 3 March Company A was scheduled to continue the reconnaissance in force to YA812884 where they were to establish a night location. At 1200H the Company laggard for the noon meal and then continued up the finger toward the crest of the north-south ridgeline. An eight men ambush force was left for rear cover. At approximately 1530H the Company reached what they believed to be their night location. Actually they were at YA804878. Captain Isom, the Company commander, who was new to Vietnam, assuming command on 12 February, established a company perimeter, assigning the 3d platoon the sector covering the portion of the trail leading up the finger of the ridgeline. Lieutenant Williams, platoon leader, dispatched a two-man team to reconnoiter the trail running up the ridgeline. The team surprised a NVA soldier who ran up the hill. The two soldiers returned to the perimeter and reported the information to Lieutenant Williams. Lieutenant Williams conveyed the information to Captain Isom. Lieutenant Flannigan, the forward observer with the company recommended that the area be prepped with artillery before the company investigated. Captain Isom elected to investigate immediately, and dispatched the 3d Platoon. Lieutenant Williams halted them in a clearing immediately behind a log across the trail. He had the squad set up a perimeter and moved up the trail with three other men. They found an NVA OP. with a cooking pot in it and continued a short distance up the trail. Suddenly, the point man saw a NVA soldier rise up from behind a brush. The point man engaged and killed the NVA. Lieutenant Williams observed three other NVA and fired at them. A machine gun positioned behind some logs opened up and was silenced with three hand grenades. The element withdrew back to the platoon location. Lieutenant Williams called Captain Isom and reported that he was in contact with a platoon or company of NVA. The enemy started to fire at the platoon from the front and gradually encroached on the sides. Some of the NVA were wearing fatigues and others wore shorts or black pajamas. The weapons squad located behind the logs returned fire, as did the rest of the platoon.

    c. Captain Isom, when he received word that the platoon was in contact, reported the contact to the 3d Battalion, 8th Infantry CP at 1621H. Electing to reinforce Lieutenant Williams, Captain Isom left one squad from each platoon at the night location and proceeded up the trail. The Company was in file with the Headquarters element leading, followed by the 2d, 4th, and 1st platoon. The last two platoons received sniper fire from the left, as they moved northeast up the finger. Captain Isom and the Headquarters element were able to join Lieutenant Williams behind the log, but the rest of the Company had to take shelter at the rear or behind the 3d platoon's position. Lieutenant Griffith, 2d-platoon leader, was killed shortly after reaching the 3d platoon's position. The NVA forces pinned down the Company with machine gun fire from the front. Meanwhile, NVA soldiers climbed trees to the flanks and started shooting down at the US soldiers. The Company commenced taking casualties, and at 1635H, Captain Isom reported to the 3d Battalion, 8th Infantry CP that he was in contact with a battalion size force and was receiving casualties. A short time later the RTO was wounded, Captain Isom, going to his aid, was killed. This left Lieutenant Williams and Lieutenant Flannigan, the FO, as the only surviving officers. The troops holding the left side of the perimeter were either dead or wounded, and the entire 3rd platoon weapons squad had been killed. Lieutenant Williams gave the order to withdraw. Specialist Gwin, a squad leader of the 3d platoon, pulled back to the rear of the clearing and turning to see if there was any remaining wounded. One man was crawling across the clearing to reach them. So Gwin and two others provided covering fire. Both of the men with Gwin were killed and when the wounded man crawling towards him was hit, Specialist Gwin withdrew. Later it was determined that the wounded man moving toward Specialist Gwin was Specialist Sowa.

   d. The Company reached their night location at approximately 1800H. They had suffered 17 KIA and 10 WIA or MIA. The force heard firing in the contact area, but they received only sporadic sniper fire at the night location. The Company dug in and prepared for an expected enemy attack. Lieutenant Flannigan called in gunships and artillery around the contact area but not upon it. A resupply helicopter was asked for because of a shortage of ammunition. The resupply helicopter arrived at approximately 1830H. Because of the triple-canopy the ship had a difficult time locating the Company. During this time the enemy fired toward the sound of the helicopter. After approximately 30 minutes the helicopter located the Company and pushed the supplies to the Company. As the helicopter left the door gunners opened fire and killed no less than five enemy snipers. These bodies fell from the trees. Others were seen hanging in the trees. Claymore mines and trip flares that were dropped by the helicopter were employed around the perimeter.

e. Later Specialist Sowa called the Company on the radio. He said he was lying wounded in the contact area and asked for help. An eight men patrol moved to the contact area and recovered Sowa and another wounded man and returned to the night location. A dust-off helicopter was requested, and, after receiving enemy fire twice, it managed to evacuate three wounded. This left 68 men in the perimeter. AC-47 (Spooky) and artillery fire supported the Company all night. The Company remained on 75% alert for an anticipated enemy attack that did not materialized.

f. Early the next morning, Lieutenant Williams directed the clearing of a landing zone to evacuate the wounded. Lieutenant Williams received the order to secure the bodies left in the previous contact area. He requested artillery preparation or gunship coverage, but his request was denied due to the possibility of friendly personnel remaining alive in the area of contact. Gunships were made available on call if needed. Sergeant Jones, the 4th platoon leader, organized a force of twenty-six men and moved out of the perimeter at 0940H. The force had just cleared the perimeter when a NVA soldier stepped out from behind a tree and engaged the point element. The first four soldiers took cover and returned fire. The rest of the men ran back to the perimeter. Sergeant Jones, employing fire and maneuver, pulled his remaining element back to the perimeter. The NVA initiated heavy fire all around the US position. Small arms, grenades, satchel charges, M-79, and M-60 fire from captured American weapons were employed. Lieutenant Flannigan called in artillery fire, but the enemy was to close to allow for effective fire. The claymore mines were triggered, but the ones on the north side of the perimeter had been disarmed. The reminder temporarily stopped the NVA attack. It quickly resumed as both sides exchanged heavy fire. Again enemy soldiers were observed in the trees firing small arms and throwing grenades. The contact continued for about thirty minutes, when some NVA soldiers on the north side of the perimeter yelled in English, "Hey Joe, don't shoot, it's Bravo." The enemy had evidently learned from the radios captured the previous afternoon that Company B was to reinforce Company A.

g. The reaction of the US soldiers was almost instantaneous as they jumped out of their foxholes and yelled to Company B. It was not until they saw a NVA platoon emerge from the area to the north that they realized the use of a ruse de guerre. They returned to their foxholes and continued firing. Their fighting spirit seemed to break under the pressure, and all they could think of was getting out of the area. One man bolted out of the perimeter, and was not seen again until two days later when he walked into a firebase. Lieutenant Williams passed the order around the perimeter to withdraw down the hill. Some of the personnel carried the wounded. A number of men were without weapons as a result of the enemy action, and most were short of ammunition. Sergeant Jones, who temporarily lost his hearing, observed the withdrawal and was the last to leave the position. He become separated from the Company during the withdrawal and evaded for ten days before he managed to reach a friendly firebase.

h. The Company withdrew off the ridgeline to a creek bed at the bottom of a draw. Where it regrouped and proceeded in a westerly direction in single file. The NVA continued to shoot at them from the top of the hill and sent squad size elements to pursue them. Lieutenant Williams attempted to contact the 3d Battalion 8th Infantry, but the batteries for the radio were too weak. NVA could be heard moving in the heavy undergrowth, so the Company moved to the top of a small hill. A small enemy force was observed coming up behind them in the streambed and was fired upon. The Company then moved to another streambed and commenced moving west. A LOH guided the Company to a landing zone where it was extracted at 1521H.

12.   RESULTS:

a. Company A sustained 29 infantry KIA, one artillery personnel KIA, and one engineer KIA. One infantryman remains missing. Fifty- two men were wounded, and three originally missing in action managed to evade to friendly positions. In addition, Company D, 3d Battalion, 8th Infantry recovered one man captured by the NVA on 6 March.

b. Enemy confirmed losses are 50 KIA by body count in the contact area. Further, the soldier captured by the NVA and subsequently recovered reported seeing a large number of NVA wounded along the top of the north-south ridgeline of the scene of action.

13.   ADMINISTRATIVE MATTERS:

a. Alligator 108 accomplished the initial resupply of ammunition, at 1835H on 3 March. The helicopter received ground fire as it approached the position and gunships were employed. Because of the thick trees and darkness the crew of the resupply helicopter had a difficult time locating the Company. Ground fire and the lack of a LZ dictated that the ammunition be "kicked out" at low level above the Company. The crew, who were exposed to the enemy fire, did everything to insure the resupply was delivered to the Company. Upon leaving they placed accurate fire and killed no less than five enemy snipers.

b. Company medics treated the wounded. Three of the most serious were evacuated by 'Dust-off' 32 by hoist at 2300H 3 March. AC-47 (Spooky-23) covered the evacuation.

c. The dense terrain and hill mass between Company A and the Battalion CP rendered constant communications difficult. During the initial contact, the battalion commander maintained radio contact by orbiting in a 06A-OH 'LOH.' At night, communications were maintained by relay through 'Spooky' aircraft and Head Hunter 0-1 aircraft. From 2230-0030H the Battalion Commander remained overhead in a C&C ship to maintain communications.

14.   COMMAND ANALYSIS:

a. Company A, 3d Battalion, 8th infantry was a well-trained, combat-hardened unit. It had participated in the actions of the DAK PAYOU Valley and was very familiar to the type of warfare employed in Vietnam. The Company commander was not a combat veteran and had only commanded the Company for a short time. He was, however, assisted by two quite capable platoon leaders, Lieutenants Griffith and Williams. The Company executive officer and two platoon leaders were in base camp on administrative matters. The 1st Sergeant was on R&R. Because of these reasons, the Company Commander, two platoon leaders, and one staff sergeant had been left to run the Company. The loss of the Company Commander and the most experienced platoon leader detracted from the strong chain of command and partially attributed to the loss of cohesiveness on the morning of 4 March.

b. Later intelligence has revealed that Company A probably encountered the K-8 Battalion, 66th Regiment. The statement of a US soldier captured by the NVA and recaptured by Company D, revealed that the 66th NVA Regimental Headquarters may have been in the area. The chain of events indicates that the NVA were surprised by the intrusion but quickly reacted. Their size and close proximity of their base area gave them a decided combat superiority.

c. Company A met a superior enemy force and aggressively engaged it. The numerically superior NVA force occupying the dominant terrain forced Company A to withdraw. US firepower was employed with unknown results during the night. The dense jungle aided the enemy by preventing either reinforcement or withdrawal. It also provided excellent cover and concealment, which was used by the enemy to surround the Company the morning of 4 March. Thus the NVA were able to employ devastating fire around the perimeter. The darkness, combat fatigue, casualties, and weakened chain of command, compounded by the enemy ruse, combined to reduce combat effectiveness. The Company consequently withdrew under difficult conditions.

d. Casualty reporting was complicated by the loss of the Company Headquarters element. No one else in the Company had knowledge of the unit strength or the whereabouts of the missing personnel. Consequently, Lieutenant Williams was unable to make an accurate account of his losses.

e. Smoke and haze conditions in the area presented a major obstacle to accomplishing resupply and medical evacuations. Poor visibility prevented pilots to pinpoint Company A's location. The 'Dust-off' helicopter, with the flare ship's assistance, spent one and one half-hours trying to locate the Company at night.

15.   LESSONS LEARNED:

a. Company A, 3d Battalion, 8th Infantry became involved in a contact with a larger enemy size force in dense double to triple-canopy jungle. Because of the vegetation, the Company could not be reinforced or withdrawn prior to the major enemy contact. Had a landing zone been available, results of the operation could have been very different.
RECOMMENDED: Landing zones be selected or a rapid means to cut a landing zone be supplied to small units and this be undertaken as soon as an area is occupied.

b. The loss or absence of the key company personnel adversely influenced the action. The casualty reporting, chain of command, and company structure were impaired by the shortage of key company personnel.
RECOMMENDED: Battalion reviews any shortage of critical personnel prior to any major operation and make adjustments accordingly.

c. If another company-size unit could have reinforced Company A within a reasonable period of time the tide might have been turned.
RECOMMENDED: When units move into an area where contact with a superior force is probable, company-sized elements should operate within reasonable supporting distance.

16.   SOURCES:

This report is based on the action report submitted by Battalion Commander (Incl#2) and additional research and interviews conducted by the 29th Military History Detachment. There are some differences between the two as a result of the additional research accomplished after the Battalion Commander's report was submitted.

FOR THE COMMANDER:

HERBERT J. McCRYSTAL, JR.
COLONEL, GS
Chief of Staff

This report contains the changes and updates from the final report dated 30 April 1969. After many hours of reviewing the reports of all the units involved in this action I believe this to be a very accurate account of what happened to A/3/8 on 3 March to 4 March 1969.

CASUALTY REPORT
March 4, 1969

SP4 Ben J. Rawlings	US67003707	06/29/1946	Age 22
SP4 Ronald P. Russell	RA18859818	12/19/1948	Age 20

Chapter V

"The End of the Line"

The history of the 119th Assault Helicopter Company had covered many years. Being one of the first units in Vietnam created many interesting stories that no other company would have. Between mid-to-late 1966 the unit would trade their old UH-1B model helicopters in for the newer model UH-1H and UH-1C ships. Because of this, they would become the only unit that had aircraft with consecutive tail numbers. The first group of ships that arrived had tail numbers 66-16371 to 66-16376. The second group of ships had the tail numbers of 66-16516 to 66-16526. The last group would contain numbers 66-16532 to 66-16536. The one odd ball of the group was 66-16540. This ship would become "Pa-Pa Gator." the commanding officer's ship. These ships were considered "sister ships" because of their numbers. This may have been another reason the 119th was such a close knit unit. During the next two years many holes would divide the numbering pattern. Now in March 1969 only one aircraft remained from the first group. "Gator 376" was the last of the sisters. Having flown over 1900hrs she was close to being retired. The Army would retire helicopters that reached 2200hrs. This was something not many ships did. The most amazing thing was the fact that she had never taken a round.

In April of 1968 SP4 Jim Fall had become her crew chief. During this time he flew the same mission as the rest of the platoon. Combat assaults, SOG missions, LRRP extractions and resupply. Not once had a round hit its mark. Jim was very proud to still have his "cherry." Now in March of 1969 Jim was close to getting out of the Army. He had decided to quit flying and spend the rest of his time on guard duty. This would give the rest of us a chance to get a break from the flying after a night of guard. The first one to benefit from this would be me. Instead of guard duty the night of March 4th I got to sleep in my bunk. I would be ready to fly the following day.

Another pre-flight inspection at 0600hrs found me getting up at 0445hrs. Standing in the shower trying to wake up, I realize that maybe I should start thinking about sick call. I'm not sick. Just dead tired. I sure could use a day off. I put that thought out of my mind. Only "strap hangers" (goof-offs) would pull a stunt like that. After the shower and breakfast I start to feel better. Maybe that's because I couldn't feel any worse.

This morning I have to pull the rest my gear off Gator 834 and transfer it to Gator 376. Being a floating crew chief really sucks. My temporary ship is still in Maintenance and Bob Kilpatrick will be back on his ship today. He gets to break in a new gunner because Eggy had guard duty last night. I have my favorite crew today. Lt. Burke and WO1 Miller are the pilots. Good old Jeff Dana will be hanging out on the right side today. I have a good feeling that today will be fine. We have "Snoopy" and "The Bum Trip" with us. Plus the good luck that 376 brings with it, what more could we ask for?

Because of the recent attacks at Polei-Kleng, we are staging at LZ Mary Lou again this morning. Of course, things around here are not as great as some people might think. Units of the 2/8 Infantry (Mech.) are starting to stage for their morning trip to Polei-Kleng. Convoys from Pleiku travel up Highway 14 to Mary Lou. From here part will go north to Kontum and Dak To and the rest head for Polei-Kleng. The main job for the 2/8 is to sweep and secure the road. At night, the bad guys have been placing mines along the road and setting up ambushes.

Sitting in the ship writing a letter home, I hear somebody swearing. Looking out the door, I see Kilpatrick storming down the line of ships. "You got anything worth trading?" he inquires. "I've got to get something really good for those grunts to deal with me." I start going through the stuff that I keep in the side compartment for emergencies. It seems that Bob's new gunner is being compared to "tits on a chicken." During the flight here the barrel on his machine gun fell off. Of course he didn't bring the spare barrel that he was issued. Now Bob is trying to find some goods that he can trade for a barrel. I have a large can of grapefruit juice. Also there are several cans from different C-ration meals. A few candy bars and a couple of packages of pre-sweetened "Kool-Aid." Bob takes the juice and the candy. "If they won't trade me for a barrel, maybe I can leave him here and one of those grunts will fly with me."

As I am putting my gear back in the side compartment, Dana asks what we have in there. We start to sort through the cans and other stuff. One pile we will keep. The other we will toss to the kids that are hanging around the staging area. Out of the corner of my eye I can see Bob still going from ship to ship, trying to find the right combination to finalize his deal. Dana is passing out the stuff we don't want and I start to put the other back in the compartment. As I finish Mr. Miller walks up to me. "Why do you carry that thing with you? I've never seen you wear it." I smile as I place my "chicken plate" in the compartment. "Each one of the crew should have one on board, sir. That's why they issue them." Mr. Miller just shakes his head. I was wounded the only time I had the damn thing on. So I figure that it must be bad luck. Besides, with all the moving that I have to do, it gets in the way. The Army's "one size fits all" shows how much common sense was put into that theory. I am 5' 6" and weigh 135lbs. My armor will fit one of the gunners in the gun platoon. He is 6' 1" and 200 lbs. Besides, between not wearing the body armor and my white helmet, it keeps the stories of me being a little crazy alive and well.

The pilots have returned from their briefing. We still have a little time before we start our engines. Because we are now using Mary Lou for our briefings, the gunships are landing over at Kontum rather than here. One of the "slicks" shuttles their pilots here and back each morning. Today it's Gator 409's turn to be the bus. During the wait, we watch as the tanks from units of the 1st Battalion, 69th Armor and the 1st Squadron, 10th Cavalry start moving into the area. They are here to serve as a blocking force in case the tanks that were spotted at Ben Het try to move toward Pleiku. Company B 1/69 remains at Ben Het. They had engaged the enemy tanks in the early morning of the 4th. One of their tanks had been damaged and two crewmembers were killed. The enemy unit had broken off the attack before the forces had completely engaged. Two enemy tanks had been knocked out, and were being evacuated so technical intelligence could inspect them.

Lt. Bonthuis has started giving us some insight about the tanks. His commission is armor tank warfare. As I listen, the tone of his voice has changed so that you can tell he would really like to get into one of those giants and go toe to toe with the bad guys. Somebody reminds him that the only difference between grunts and tankers is that grunts walk. Everybody laughs and we start to get ready for today's mission. Kilpatrick has returned with a barrel. He traded the crew of an APC (armored personnel carrier) for it. The price was more than he wanted to pay. He had to give up two cans of juice, my candy bars and a mixed carton of cigarettes. He was not happy, and swore that he would never fly with this guy again.

Heading to Polei-Kleng as we start our day is when we get the lowdown. Last night both Swinger and Pause received incoming. To the north LZ Mile High also received incoming and had been probed. D/3/8, on Hill 947, has received enemy probes by sapper units during the night. Unknown to us as we were flying west, D/3/8 is about to come under attack. Because of all the events of the past two days, we will divide the flight up into three groups. One group of four ships will move A/1/35 to LZ Pause. They had arrived from Ben Het this morning by CH-47. They are being transferred from 2nd Brigade and will be under operational control of the 1st Brigade. Once they are in place, we will combat assault with C/3/8 to map location YA828899. (Map 5, Location 8, Page 91) They will then coordinate with B/3/8 to assault on what would become LZ Brace. The second group of four ships would move companies B/3/12 and D/3/12 into LZ Mary. Those two units would combine as Task Force Swift. The remaining two ships would move C/3/12 to LZ Swinger. We would be moving A/1/35 to LZ Pause.

The staging area is at the western end of the runway. This is where Company A/1/35 was waiting for us. The remaining units of the 1/35th were still deployed near Ben Het. Because of what had happened they would be brought to Polei-Kleng by truck during the day. I told the first group to stay down when we got to LZ Pause because they had received incoming numerous times in the past two days. They told me not to worry. They had seen enemy tanks close up. They were glad to be out of Ben Het.

Moving an entire company with four ships would take four to five sorties apiece. The day is very bright and the sun is warm. Each time we travel into Pause we try to change the route and land at a different pad. The bad guys are enjoying themselves because they have been taking pot shots at everybody this morning. As the day goes on, they make things a little bit more interesting by throwing mortar rounds at the landing zones. With A/1/35 at Pause we regroup to assault with C/3/8.

Because of the short turnaround between Pause and the landing zone, we will only be using our four ships.

The rest of the flight will continue with the other moves. This was the same place that we had been shot out of twice yesterday. B/3/8 and Rcn/3/8 had moved south and were assaulting toward YA828880 (Brace). (Map 5, Location 10, Page 91) We got our first sortie and started towards the landing zone. I instructed Stoney on how we got in there yesterday. He agreed and we set up to enter from the west. "Blackjack" informed us that the area was clear. Again he pressed for us to enter from the northwest because it would hold two ships. DOUBLE DUMB ASS! This was exactly what the enemy wanted us to do. He controlled the high ground and had every square inch of the landing zone under his sights. The two units (Bravo/3/8 and Recon/3/8) which were on the ground could only provide limited cover fire for us. Most of their advance up the ridgeline had been accomplished by crawling from one downed tree to another. Any time a head got higher <u>than</u> six inches above the ground, snipers would open fire at them.

The NVA are very patient when it comes to baiting their enemies. They had probed and attacked D/3/8 that was located to the south of the assault area. Because the two units to their north had not moved against them, they realized that we would first reinforce before attacking. Yesterday we had first tried to enter from the northwest. Why? Because the area was larger and we could get two ships in there at one time. So they zeroed their mortars in to hit anything that tried to land in the larger area. They would now wait and as the first ship entered the trap they would engage the units to their north and also start shelling the landing zone.

Entering from the northwest, just as we had done the previous day, we are on short final. There are people up the ridge from us so we will not go in "Hot." Remember, the area is secure, and we will have no trouble getting these people on the ground. **"FIRE! FIRE!"** Both

Dana and I yell over the intercom as we enter the landing zone. The entire ridgeline has opened up. We return fire towards the top of the hill. The gunships have broken their formation and start firing into the ridgeline. **"INCOMING! WE HAVE IN COMING!"** The mortar rounds are hitting to our front and side. The dirt is thrown into the air, and for an instant we are blinded. **"THAT SON OF A BITCH!"** is all Stoney can say. He turns the ship and we haul ass out of there. Here we are at the same time, the same place and the same result. The only difference is that it is just one day later. As we had entered the zone, Company B/3/8 had also started receiving fire. Just the way the NVA had planned it. Using small arms and hand grenades, the NVA controlled the crest of the hill. We would return our cargo to LZ Pause while the artillery pounded the top of that ridgeline. D/3/8 had been now engaged for most of the morning. A pre-dawn mortar and rocket attack was followed by sappers and a frontal attack. Each time the attacks had been repelled with the help of gunships and artillery from LZ Swinger. The NVA were looking for an escape route, and going through their position would work but the soldiers of D/3/8 were not having any part of it. Two ships from the other flight had been pulled to stand by at Polei-Kleng. They would resupply them and pull out the wounded. One ship had been able to land and pull some of the wounded out. We dropped our troops off at Pause and picked up the wounded and headed for Mary Lou As we did that the NVA would toss a mortar or rocket at Pause every ten or fifteen minutes. This would be just enough to piss us off but not give us enough time so that we could locate his position.

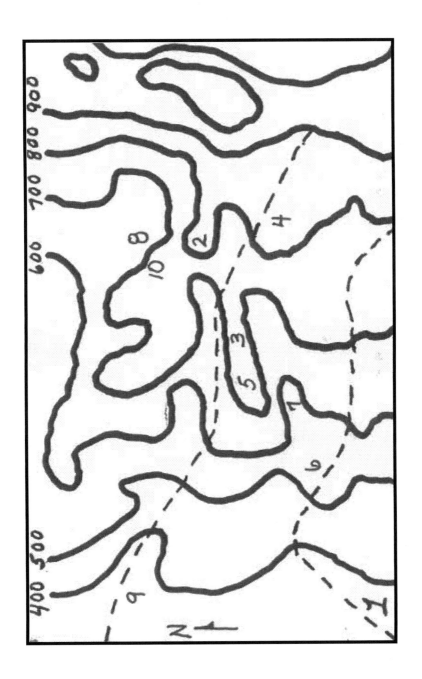

The Battle for LZ Brace

Solid Lines--- Ridgelines
Dotted Lines--- Creeks or Rivers
Map not to Scale

MAP 5
March 5, 1969

Location 1= LZ Mary   YA 784879
Location 2= Intended night location   YA 812884
Location 3= Made first contact   YA 804878
Location 4= LZ for B/3/8
Location 5= Area where A/3/8 established perimeter
Location 6= D/3/8 area of first contact   YA 800856
Location 7= Hill 947   YA 813864
Location 8= LZ for Recon and B/3/8   YA 828899
Location 9= Creek bed where A/3/8 was extracted
Location 10= LZ Brace   YA 828880

At Mary Lou we offload the wounded, and guess what I found? In the vertical fin is a hole. Just below the tail number and to the right of the drive shaft. I tell Stoney to shut her down so I can check it out. "Mr. Fall isn't going to like that," is Dana's comment. I inspect the entire ship. Just the one hole, but nobody could miss it. "Well it was bound to happen. The odds were always against her making it to retirement as a virgin," was Mr. Miller's remark. All I could think was, "It had to be me.'

After refueling at Polei-Kleng we again tried to assault the hill. Dodging mortar rounds as we loaded the troops, again we started. This time, we approach from the west. My guts felt like someone has kicked me. I know the bastards are still waiting for us. "The tail is clear." "You're clear on the right." "All clear on the left." "GO! GO!" "We are clear!" We pull pitch and head out of harm's way. DAMN! Thank God for small favors. We return to LZ Pause for another sortie. The artillery has done its job and we are able to get Charlie Company in without any more trouble. They will now move to the right and support Bravo as they advance to the crest of the ridge. The action continues in the rest of the Valley.

During one of the sorties to move B/3/12, SP5 Sam Stella's ship (Gator 498) has a main rotor strike as they hovered into the landing zone. A Second Flight ship (Gator 523) receives fire as they leave LZ Swinger. The main rotor had been hit, and also the tail boom. Both ships will have to return to Camp Holloway for repairs. Action in the YB area is still coming strong. Units have made contact throughout the day. The area around the Plei-Trap road is still a hotbed. The truck that C/1/8 captured has been lifted to Polei-Kleng. Troops from the 1/35th were placed under operational control of 1st Brigade. They started to arrive by late afternoon from Ben Het. They would spend the night at Polei-Kleng. We would not be able to deploy them today because of all the contact. In the 2nd Brigade area LZ Mile

High is still receiving incoming. The areas around LZ Roberts are being worked over by air strikes. To the north of Mile High, units of the 1/22 have made contact and are moving toward Hill 994.

With the troop movements completed, we start to resupply the different bases. Again we are short two ships. First we need to get supplies into D/3/8. They have been in contact most of the day. The companies at LZ Mary are next. Because of the incoming at both Swinger and Pause, we decide to only have one ship at a time at those locations. The NVA has broken contact with D/3/8 after almost four hours. Since then, the troops have been working frantically to enlarge the landing zone so we would be able to get in to them. We are ordered to Polei-Kleng. We would pick up some fresh people and supplies and head for Hill 947.

A battlefield has its own sights and sounds. It also has other characteristics that cannot be duplicated by a picture. The smell of battle lingers after the sounds have faded. Hovering down through the trees, I know that this place was a battlefield. The trees are split and most of the leaves are gone. Smoke from the burning wood fills the landing zone. There is equipment and junk everywhere. The gunpowder has also added the smell of sulfur to the air. It reminds me of the times when I would play with matches as a youth.

The guys are ringing wet from sweat, and many have bloody, bandaged limbs. We unload the supplies, and help the wounded into the ship. We try to take eight, but the ship won't lift that many men. I promised the one we have to put off that we would be back for him. We hover up and head for Mary Lou. The wounded had waited several hours for this ride. Their bandages had been applied with one thought in mind, stop the bleeding. The blood and dirt, along with their sweat, had now soaked through the dressings. We tried to make them comfortable. The metal floor of the ship added to their misery. They were cold and in pain. Muffled moans could be heard as they moved to ease their pain. We help with what we have; water and cigarettes, and a few lies that they would be all right.

We return to D/3/8 with more fresh people and supplies. This time the return load goes to Pause. It is their dead, wrapped in their ponchos. We can't take the time to get them back to Mary Lou. Right now we are interested in saving the living. Our brothers who no longer suffer must wait their turn. The remainder of the day is a blur. Each ship tries to carry a little extra in order to finish the resupply. We manage to finish with a little time to spare. The sun is low in the western sky. Maybe we will have enough time to read our mail tonight. An hour without the war would be nice.

Sitting at POL, refueling for the trip back to Holloway, we are ready to call it a day. Over the radio, Red Fox asks a favor. He wants to know if we can make one last run to Swinger. They need extra water because of the addition of C/3/12. He also has "SP" packages and their mail. The "SP" packages are large boxes that contain cigarettes, candy bars, chewing gum, writing paper, and hygiene products. They are the grand prize reward for the grunts in the field. You have to remember that these guys have been living on C-rations and warm water for five days. We agree and he rewards us with an "SP" for the effort.

We are loaded to the max. The large boxes are up to the roof of the cargo bay. The mailbag is hanging behind me and we are already fighting over who gets what out of the "SP". We land on the north pad and start to unload the prize sortie of the day. The grunts are overjoyed to get this shipment. I secure our bribe in the center of the bay in front of the transmission and we are headed home. We depart and bank left.

"OH SHIT!" The sound of gravel being thrown against a metal building can be heard. These are the bullets hitting the ship. The sky is full of red and green tracers as the enemy gunners zero in on our ship. I can feel the rounds hitting us and see some of them as they have come through the floor of the cargo bay. **"MAYDAY! MAYDAY! THIS IS GATOR 376! WE ARE HIT, JUST WEST OF SWINGER!"** Mr. Miller is on the radio calling for help. Lt. Burke is trying to gain altitude. The ship is shaking like crazy and the gauges have gone off the wall. "Can we make it?" Asks Jerry as he helps with the controls. "Don't know!" is Stoney's answer. The instrument panel looks like a pinball machine. Warning lights are flashing and audio alarms are blaring in our ears. I can see fuel and oil flowing out the bottom of the ship. **"GATOR 376 WHERE ARE YOU?"** blasts over the radio. It's the other ships, coming towards us in case we go down. **"WE'RE NORTHWEST OF POLEI-KLENG!"** Although the ship is shaking itself to death we still have power. "I think we can make it," Stoney radios to the other ships. Dana and I fasten our seat belts and start to brace ourselves as we near Polei Kleng. We can see the runway, but our luck has run out. We are out of fuel and we are heading in the wrong direction. Landing downwind will be the least of our problems. We clear the creek but we don't have enough altitude to make the runway. We hit hard in the dirt area between the runway and the creek. The tail hits the barbed wire, and we bounce into the air. Striking the ground for a second time the skids buckle and we nose into the dirt. The ship is full of dust. I can't see anything. I have undone my seat belt and have gotten to the rear of Stoney's seat. I pull the jettison tabs on the rear of Stoney's seat and, grabbing him by the collar, I pull him out of the ship. Dana has done the same for Jerry. We run away from the ship. People are starting to arrive at the end of the runway. Our ships have landed and the crews are running to help us. We are okay. Bumps and bruises, but nothing serious. The ship is a mess. The vertical fin has been torn off. The skids are bowed and the main rotor blades broken in two.

As the dust clears, we go over to the ship. It is now dark and we need to get out of here. I find my flashlight and we take our guns and gear and load them on Gator 834. The "SP" has several holes in it. Dana loads it as I take the logbook. The ride back to Holloway feels strange. I'm not used to being a passenger. Sitting on the floor we look at each other. Mr. Miller has had it. He is going to the Crocs. He has decided that it's time he should be able to shoot back. Dana has less than thirty days left. This was his last flight. Stoney just sits drinking out of a canteen. I'm trying to figure out what I can say to SP5 Fall. All that time, and let me crew the damn thing one time and look what happens.

In the revetment at Holloway we start to unload our gear. Sgt. Hall shows up and asks about the ship. I just hand him the logbook. Inside I have placed a "Red X" that tells a ship's crew that the ship is not flyable. Next to that I have written FUBAR. "What does this mean?" he asks. "F----ed Up, Beyond All Reconciliation," is my reply. I wait with Dana for the platoon truck. A couple of guys from Second Flight have given us beers. As I enter the barracks, I see the mission board. Carey and Matos, ship #108, pre-flight 0600hrs. At least I won't have to see Jim until tomorrow night. Maybe I can think of a good excuse by then. I drop my gear on the floor and fall asleep with my clothes on. I'm alive and that's all that matters for right now. The last of the sisters are gone. The old first flight nose emblem will no longer be seen on any of our ships. The pattern has been lost. With the way the war is viewed, it would be impossible to find a firm that would design another for us. Thank you, Gator 376, for bringing your crew home one last time.

CASUALTY REPORT
March 5, 1969

SP4 Juan Ayala-Mercado	US67192019	01/04/1948	Age 21
SP4 Wayne G. Bernoska	US5429813	07/27/1944	Age 24
1LT George A. Callan	05351543	07/13/1944	Age 24
SP4 Steven W. Dundas	US56722282	05/06/1947	Age 21
SSG Efrain Melendez	RA50162357	07/27/1942	Age 26
SP4 Antonio Garcia	US52814428	03/22/1948	Age 20
SGT Carlton J. Johnson	US53703553	12/29/1947	Age 21
SP4 Alfred Lallave	US67040592	06/15/1943	Age 25
PFC Larry G. Lacaeyse	US56464087	08/26/1948	Age 20
PFC Lavern M. Lamey	US68049226	11/07/1949	Age 19
PFC Johnny R. Lynn	US67115644	09/26/1948	Age 20
SP4 Kenneth Martin	US54979154	05/05/1948	Age 20
SGT Gary F. Rolfe	US55988781	12/19/1948	Age 20
1LT Ronald L. Warnett	05430643	05/30/1946	Age 22
PFC Joseph J. Strucel	US54985081	08/28/1948	Age 20

Chapter VI

"My New Gunner"

The ache in my head is no match for the one in my shoulder. As I try to move, I realize that the only part of my body that doesn't hurt is my flight jacket. As I sit on my bunk trying to move, a familiar voice is saying something. "Here. Take this. It will help." There stands Jeff handing me some "APCs" (all-purpose capsules) and his famous club soda. I don't know which tastes worse. I hope the aspirin starts working real soon. All I can do is sit and smoke a cigarette that Dana has lit for me. "What time is it," I ask. "About four thirty, I guess," replies Dana. I sit trying to get enough courage up to start getting undressed. "Are you going to get a shower?" asks Jeff. "Yeah. How's the water?" is my answer. "How do you think it is?" snaps Jeff. "Its cold! It's always cold! "

I struggle to get undressed. My arms hurt and so does my back. There's a large bruise on my upper arm. I must have gotten bounced pretty hard last night. I finally get into the shower. The water is cold but feels good. I stand for a long time before turning off the valve. Walking back to my bunk, not many of the guys want to make eye contact with me. I guess by the way I'm moving and the look in my eyes, they have decided that I am not ready to talk this morning. I finally get dressed and head for the mess hall. About all I can handle this morning would be coffee and some toast. I grab some fruit and head for the revetments.

Dana helps me get the gear and my machine gun down to the ship. Once we are there he starts helping with the pre-flight. With the ship just coming out of Maintenance, I need to check everything. It would not be good to have a rotor blade fall off, or the engine quit, because it ran out of oil. CWO Edward Thornton is the A/C today. He is a large man. He could have very well been a football lineman. His voice matches his body. "Thunder" is the only call sign that could match all of his qualities. Unlike most warrant officers, he is a career soldier. He has many hours of flight time under his belt and I have a lot of respect for him. He has always treated me fine, and given me the same respect. Our peter-pilot is Mr. Santos. He had started in the First Flight platoon but he just wasn't up to the task. They had first placed him in the supply room. Then they moved him to be in charge of the POL. He is a nice enough person, but not a pilot that you would want in a combat zone. Old Thunder will take good care of him today. He is one of those people that stay in complete control. My new gunner is SP5 Reynaldo Matos. He is from San Juan, Puerto Rico. His accent is very heavy and I have to listen really close to understand what he is saying. He has also extended for another six-month tour. He was in transportation prior to coming here. Today he has shown up with all of his gear, including his extra machine gun barrel. At least Kilpatrick did teach him one thing yesterday. My body is finally starting to work as the rotor blades start turning and we begin another day. As we hover out of the revetment, Dana waves and smiles.

Heading to LZ Mary Lou we learn that D/3/8 is under attack again. The gunships break for their location and we follow. Troop A/7/17th is on station when we arrive. They have silenced the mortar tubes, but our ships are to evacuate wounded and the Crocs will cover us. Hovering down into D/3/8's location again, the war is very real here. The enemy had begun the attack with mortars and CS gas (tear gas). They had probed the perimeter near the helicopter pad. The fierce firefight had ended, and the smell of gunpowder from small arms still hangs over the base. One bunker is damaged and I can see a couple of bodies trapped in the barbed wire. The medics continue to work as we land. The wounded line the pad, waiting to be evacuated. Our first sortie of the day is six wounded. These guys are

100

completely spent. Their spirit is gone. The looks on their faces reflect nothing but a blank stare, as they huddle together trying to stay warm. We arrive at LZ Mary Lou and help these poor souls onto the stretchers. Idling on the pad, our briefing today is short and sweet. Get people and supplies into the firebases. Water has become the most important item that we supply to the troops. The events of the past days have prevented us from supplying the units with the amount of water they need. It is also the hardest of the supplies to deliver. The five gallon cans are heavy and take up a lot of space on the ship. Plastic water bladders that hold two gallons of water are fragile and break quite easily if dropped. The temperatures on the Valley floor have reached the high eighties during the last two days. The quart canteens the soldiers carry will not replace the fluids that they will lose in just one hour, let alone the entire day. We are also given alternate radio frequencies because most of the channels are now being jammed by the NVA. We had experienced some problems for the past couple of days but now it was widespread. We are informed that we will be resupplying Pause today. We head for Polei-Kleng.

Arriving at Polei-Kleng I ask Mr. Thornton to hover to Gator 376. I need to check the ship so I can be sure everything is off of it. Landing on the west end of the runway, we are greeted by group of grunts from the 1/35th. They had been posted around the ship last night. "That thing is a mess," one of the guards informs us as we run by. "Yeah, I know," is my answer. Reaching the ship, I climb into the cargo bay. We had forgotten the first aid kits and the ammo boxes. As I go through the side compartments a few of the grunts start walking over. "Did anybody get hurt?" asks the sergeant in charge. "No, we did luck out on this one," I answer. "The brass wants to put this over next to that gunship that got hauled in here yesterday. Would it hurt anything if we did that?" "You can't hurt this old girl anymore. It's all yours." And with that I head back for the ship.

"How many holes are in the old girl?" asks Mr. Thornton as I plug in my helmet. "Anything over one is too many," I reply. We all laugh a little and head for Resupply. The Red Fox greets us as we sit down. I inform him that I expected another "SP" tonight before I leave. "No problem," was his answer and we are loaded with food, water, and ammo. As we flew to Pause I placed the intercom on private to talk to my new gunner. He said his nickname was "Mattie." I explained everything that he needed to do. He said that Kilpatrick had gone over all of that yesterday. I said okay, but we would go over it again because he was now with me and I wanted to go over everything regardless. I think he put up with my 'shit' just to humor me. Setting down at Pause, we unload the supplies then haul four passengers and the mail back to Polei-Kleng.

Returning to LZ Pause with our second sortie, the pains from yesterday are starting to disappear. The sun is warm and feels good. I had shut off the FM radio and was listening to our ships talk back and forth. The new face sitting in front of me has his eyes wide open. Judging from his fatigues he is brand new. I had checked both his and his buddy's weapons before we left. He was as scared as I was. I was just more tired right now. As we started our approach I did lower my weapon, but I also kept one hand on it. I let them know we are about to land and I tell them good luck. We clear the aircraft and we set down. They unload the cargo and the CQ runner hands me their mailbag. As I secure it behind me there is that sound. **"THUMP!"** Incoming! I didn't see the round hit but I felt the results. Dirt rained through the rotor blades. Thunder pulled pitch and we are gone. "Look for the tubes!" he instructs as we headed into the sky. We circled for ten minutes. The NVA knew we would be looking for them so they just stayed low and waited for us to leave.

Again the Valley was starting to heat up. Companies

B/3/8 and C/3/8 with Rec/3/8 had linked up last night. They would begin a coordinated assault on Brace this morning. On Hill 947 D/3/8 would continue to receive mortar and rocket fire. Task Force Swift was moving east from LZ Mary to block and destroy the enemy if they tried to withdraw from Brace to the west. LZ Swinger continues to receive 105mm fire from the YB grid locations. We will dodge mortars and rockets all day as we resupply LZ Pause and the surrounding landing zones. To the north the units of the 1/8th continue RIF and have scattered contact. In 2nd Brigade's area, LZ Mile High continues to receive incoming. They were probed last night but no contact was reported. As the morning ends I start working on Mr. Thornton about going to Kontum for lunch. We've had two close calls while sitting at Pause. Each time mortars had landed near the pad. I told him we needed to check out the ship and while we were there we should eat. I didn't have to twist his arm very hard. The 57th A.H.C. has an outstanding Officer's Club.

Shutting down at the Maintenance hangar, we walk past Gator 521. Because of her age they are declaring her a total loss. The boys have already started stripping the needed parts for other ships in the hangar. The menu today is beef stew, bread, and Kool-Aid. Let me tell you about the Army's beef stew. First of all, whatever meat was put in it may at one time have had four legs. It may have had a long tail. I will bet anything that it never did or could say, "Moo." Then we have the Kool-Aid. The Army has red Kool-Aid, orange Kool-Aid, and green Kool-Aid. It all tastes the same, just different colors. The good thing is that the food is hot and we can sit in chairs. Today it tasted very good.

The long days were beginning to show. While sitting at Pause unloading their sortie Bob Kilpatrick had noticed that the small cargo door was not latched. He had gotten out of the ship and as he was standing next to the door a mortar round landed. The pilot, not knowing this, pulled pitch and raced out of there. It wasn't until they were airborne that he checked and discovered that Bob was missing. Thinking that Bob had been hit and fallen out of the ship, he starts to radio Pause for assistance. That's when they radioed him back to inform him that his crew chief was there and was not very happy to be left behind. Returning to Pause, Bob climbed back into his gun well. Being the only person on the base wearing a flight helmet during the attack was not something that he would want to do again.

Some good news has arrived from D/3/8. They have recovered one of A/3/8 soldiers who were reported missing in action. He is in good shape and is being evacuated to Mary Lou. The assault by B/3/8 and C/3/8 has stalled. Enemy snipers and automatic weapons fire from the top of the ridgeline have kept both companies pinned down for most of the day. They have pulled back to their night locations, and are now waiting for artillery and air strikes. Their wounded are being moved back to the landing zone, but will not be able to be evacuated today. Enemy gunners still have that area zeroed in and one Scout ship from the 7/17th Cavalry has already been shot down trying to get in there. The crew is not hurt. A second Scout ship was able to land and evacuate the crew. We will spend the rest of the afternoon resupplying the units around Pause and Brace. Air strikes and artillery continue to pound the ridgeline. I think about Bravo and Charlie Companies sitting in their night locations. They have not been supplied in two days. We finish the day and I feel guilty as I collect my "SP" package from Red.

It's been a good day. I didn't fire my gun once. Again in the dark we head for Holloway. I have started to like my new gunner. We are so different but maybe things will work out. Thunder only yelled at Mr. Santos twice today. I have to laugh because Mr. Santos tries to be the big bad officer around enlisted men. You put him in that pilot's seat and he's at the mercy of the other pilots. I don't say anything because he was in Supply and sometimes I have to ask favors. A little game you learn to play in the Army. I pull my postflight and arrive in the barracks about 2030hrs. Jeff and Bill have joined Jim Fall as the permanent guards until they leave. I grab a shower and something to eat. Once again we have another 0600hrs pre-flight in the morning.

During March of 2003, I talked with two members of Recon/3/8. Bob Ness was the platoon sergeant and Chris Dressler was a squad leader. Even though Bob lives in Boston and Chris lives in Winston-Salem area of North Carolina they stay in contact via the internet and telephone. The following are some of their memories during this time:

Bob Ness: "I was the platoon sergeant for Recon/3/8 during that time. They put us in a landing zone north of where A/3/8 was under attack. The landing zone was "hot" and the enemy controlled the high ground. The only cover we had were the fallen trees that littered the landing zone and hillside. Our only movement was by crawling. Snipers would open fire at any head that was higher than six inches above the ground. The hillside was so steep even if we could stand up I don't think we would have been able to.

"We assault the hill for four or five days. We finally were able to take it. My platoon walked point or should I say crawled up that ridge during this time. I was slightly wounded on March 5th and my platoon leader was killed. We lost half of our 32 man platoon during those five days. I was evacuated and was out of the field for a week. When I returned I was put in charge of the Recon platoon and was given all new green replacements. I remained platoon leader until I left in May. Of the 32 men that were assigned to my platoon in the beginning of March only three were left by mid April."

Chris Dressler: "I was a member of the Recon platoon during March, 1969. The first two days on that ridgeline we barely were able to move. I remember either the second or third day a small helicopter tried to come in and pull some of our wounded out. He was shot down near the landing zone. Some of the pad guys were able to pull the pilot out. He was not hurt and another small helicopter was able to land and pull him out.

"After almost a week we finally reached the top of the ridgeline. Once the perimeter was established we started sending out patrols and ambushes. We discovered many trails and bunker complexes. I was assigned to walk point during one of those patrols. I was wounded and pinned down for several hours before the rest of the platoon was able to locate me. I was evacuated and did not return to the field."

Chris lay wounded on that trail for over twelve hours. During this time the remainder of his platoon remained in contact with the enemy until they were able to locate him. They took turns carrying him back to LZ Brace where he was finally evacuated the following day.

CASUALTY REPORT
March 6, 1969

1LT William D. Mc Allister	05351445	02/15/1946	Age 23
PFC Wilfred Perez	US52771487	09/28/1947	Age 21
SP5 James E. Ramsby	RA54953299	12/07/1944	Age 24
SP4 Paul P. Vavrosky	US54831255	06/29/1947	Age 21
PVT Clayton E. Fraley	US67004863	07/23/1948	Age 20
SP4 Frank D. Joynes Jr.	US67033380	07/31/1948	Age 20
CPL John W. Kobelin III	RA16919224	12/03/1944	Age 24
SGT Daniel M. Noeldner	US56565196	11/09/1945	Age 23

Chapter VII

"LZ Brace"

"CAREY! GET UP! LET'S GET GOING!" is all I hear as Sgt. Hall shakes my shoulder. "What the hell is going on?" I ask as I try to get out of my bunk. "You have to get into the air now," is all he can say. Pulling on my clothes, I realize that it's 0400hrs. What in the hell is going on? I get to the ship and my questions are somewhat answered.

During the early hours this morning, B/3/8 and C/3/8 with Rcn3/8 have taken map location YA828880. (LZ Brace, Map 6, Location 10, Page 117) During the night the enemy has retreated to the south. The enemy gunners who covered their withdrawal have been killed by artillery and by the assault platoons of the three companies. These NVA soldiers were chained to their weapons. We are moving troops and they want it done now. Mr. Thornton is our A/C again today. Mr. Thomas Trebby is the peter-pilot. We get the pre-flight done and we are in the air by 0515hrs. There's a briefing at Mary Lou, as soon as possible. The early morning air is cold and, worse yet, I haven't gotten my coffee this morning. I also learn that we are getting a few new ships in next week. Maybe I'll be done with this "floating" shit. We land at Mary Lou and, to our surprise, they have coffee waiting for us. While the pilots are briefed we get some breakfast. Pound cake and jelly could become the breakfast of champions; at least in 'Nam.

Sitting in Gator 834, we listen to the story of the forgotten crew chief. We all have a laugh except Bob. If it had been my ship I would have done the same thing. I just guess that with all that's happened and the lack of sleep, we aren't as sharp as we should be. Bob gives me the business about my new gunner and I remind him he still owes me a can of juice. Back at my ship I just about doze off when the pilots return. We have a serious game of musical chairs on tap for today.

We need to get people into Brace and Hill 947. (Map 6, Location 7, Page 117) The brass believes that the NVA may counterattack and they don't want to lose any more ground. Our flight will be transporting C/3/12 from LZ Swinger to Hill 947 to reinforce D/3/8. The other flight will move Task Force Swift from their night location at YA 788883 (Map 6, Location 11, Page 117) to LZ Brace to reinforce B/3/8 and C/3/8. Once they are in place, we will then airlift the 1/35th to LZ Mary so they can RIF towards Brace. The problem is we only have eight ships today. We will get help from the 170th AHC. We are moving the troops from Swinger to Hill 947.

Arriving at Swinger we load the first of many sorties for this day. Hovering into Hill 947 we can see that the landing zone has been enlarged. As the first troops get off, we take some of the less seriously wounded back with us to Swinger. I pass out some cigarettes and offer them water. These guys look bad. They have fought for that hill for three days. We drop them off and load another sortie. After ninety minutes we have the new company at Hill 947. Two of our ships are sent to join the rest of the flight to move the 1/35th to Mary. My ship and one other would stay to move the dead back to Pause.

The perimeter at LZ Brace was still being established when members of the assault force volunteered to sweep the area for A/3/8's missing and dead. In the early morning hours, they had made their way into the contact area and recovered most of the dead. The landing zone at Brace had not been completed, and the terrain was too difficult for the dead to be carried out. The order was given to enlarge the small hoverhole so that we could land.

The air in the landing zone was thick with smoke. Our rotor blades helped clear the air, as we slowly hovered towards the ground. The smell of death was everywhere. Each of the soldiers had been placed where we landed. They were wrapped in their ponchos. The white detonation cord from the claymore mines was used to secure the ponchos. The one thing we haven't brought in was body bags. The 4th Infantry thought that body bags were bad for morale. I guess, in some ways, I agreed with that. Food, water, and ammo were more important than those rubber caskets. Carefully, our ship is loaded so these soldiers could start their journey home. We land at Pause and soldiers wearing gas masks offload the dead. The Headquarters Company must first try to identify each one before we move them to graves registration. They are placed on the ground and the process starts. We return to the area and again we are loaded. This time they also place both American and NVA weapons on the ship. I grab one of the M-79 grenade launchers and also an AK-47. I will use them for trading material. We have to make three more trips before we need to refuel. Before we leave we stop at Swinger and pick up some wounded for Mary Lou. Two guys have the "million dollar" wound. One has a calf wound to his right leg and the other got hit in the left check of his butt. Both are happy to get out of the Valley, if only for a little while.

We are forced to fly large loops today around the Valley. There are many B-52 air strikes planned. The added time we will spend avoiding the Arc Light strikes will affect the amount of critical supplies we will have time to deliver today. To the south of Hill 947 is a main target area. The area to the northwest of Swinger is also going to be hit. They believe the howitzers that are shelling the landing zones are in that A/O. Before returning to Swinger we stop by Polei-Kleng for their normal resupply. Because of all the casualties, we are hauling more and more new guys into the bases.

As the morning slowly passed we could tell we would not see Holloway before dark. Having to stay away from the target areas of the B-52's, and the shortage of ships, was slowing everything down. Just before noon we were instructed to start transporting the killed in action to Mary Lou. Landing at Pause they placed six passengers on the floor. Our rotor wash blows the ponchos off the dead as we leave. I had been handed their identification cards, and was told to give them to the personnel at Mary Lou. Flying towards Mary Lou, the smell was unbearable. I had placed my face in my flight jacket to keep from getting sick. I looked at the cards. I did not know which card was for which body. Most of the cards had blood smeared on them. We arrived at Mary Lou and they placed each soldier on a stretcher. I gave the cards to one of the stretcher- bearers.

On the third trip to Mary Lou I was sick to my stomach. Between the smell and knowing that some of these guys had probably been on my ship when they went to LZ Mary five days ago, I was beside myself. I continued to light one cigarette after another so I wouldn't get sick from the smell. We landed and the first person to my ship started to pull the first poncho off the ship and it fell to the ground. The next thing I know, this crazy person is screaming at this guy. **"YOU NO GOOD ROTTEN SON OF A BITCH! HOW COULD YOU DO SOMETHING LIKE THAT? I SHOULD BLOW YOUR F---ING HEAD OFF RIGHT HERE!"** This maniac now has his pistol out and has this poor bastard by the throat and everybody knows he is about to shoot him.

The next thing I realize is that Thunder has his hand on my shoulder and he is calling my name. I release my grip and my prisoner escapes. I have totally lost it. Sitting on the floor of the ship, all I can do is sob. They have shut down the ship and a medic starts to talk to me. About fifteen minutes pass before I understand what had happened. Pulling myself together, we decide we should eat. Thunder radios the 57th AHC to see if they can meet us with their water truck. We set down in front of their hangar. Once the ship is washed out and I've had a chance to breathe some fresh air, I'm okay. Rather than going to the mess hall, I just sit with Mattie and pick through some C-rations. We talk a little, but mostly just relax. It is going to be a long afternoon.

We returned to Polei-Kleng for more supplies. We were loaded for Swinger. Maybe they decided that having us going to Pause was a bad idea. Later, I found out that I was not the only one that had been troubled over the past few days. Another crew chief had threatened to shoot two REMFs (rear echelon mother-f---ers) for taking pictures as their ship was unloaded. The word had come down from brigade that nobody was allowed near the pad when our dead were being brought in. The military police were now posted at the pad. We spent most of the afternoon resupplying Swinger.

The afternoon in the Valley had proven to be quiet. Our area of operations had many B-52 air strikes. The sound of thunder in the distance was "Arc Light;" bombs raining from the sky. The ground would shake and the echo of destruction was heard everywhere. Watching from the air, you could see the dirt and trees rise off the ground and be carried a thousand feet into the air. It was unbelievable to watch such power. The areas to our north were also being hit. One of the main goals was to hit the howitzers that had shelled our bases. LZ Mile High again was receiving their share of incoming. They were also encountering an increase of contact in the area of Hill 994.

Task Force Swift had assaulted the hill south of Brace. Map location YA 815872. (Map 6, Location 12, Page 117). No contact was made. They had now secured the three areas that had been the center of this battle. During the late afternoon we started to resupply the three landing zones that units from 3/8 and 3/12 had fought so hard for. Another soldier from A/3/8 had been recovered. He had walked into the latest landing zone, and was taken to Mary Lou. Still two soldiers from that unit remained missing.

The flight to Holloway was a quiet, almost restful, one as we flew in the darkness. I had offered the pilots some of the bounty from the "SP" package. They declined, saying that the crew of Gator 376 had earned it. I told them to let Stoney and Mr. Miller know I had one without holes in it. It was late as I got to the barracks. I found a couple of letters on my bunk. As I read them I realized how far away home was. Before I could finish the letters I fell asleep.

The battle for LZ Brace had cost the companies of 3/8 dearly. In addition to A/3/8's losses, Bravo, Charlie, Delta, and Recon endured 32 killed in action. A total of 125 were wounded and two were missing. An estimate of enemy losses was 241 NVA killed. During this time, artillery units B/6/29 and C/6/29 fired a total of 4478 rounds HE (high explosive) in support of operations.

This battle involved several chains of events for it to unfold as it did. On 2 March, Companies Alpha, Bravo, and Delta assaulted LZ Mary. Alpha sweeps to the north. Bravo sweeps to the south. Delta moves into the center. On 3 March, Alpha had gone east to what they thought was their night location. They in fact were farther to the west than they thought. They had walked into a battalion-sized base camp. They had failed to cut a landing zone and were unsure of their location. This made resupply difficult and reinforcement impossible. Bravo was moved to a location south of the planned night location. Because of the harsh terrain and the fact that they were too far to the east, prevented them from reinforcing Alpha. Delta had moved toward Alpha. They would also encounter a superior force. They were able to withdraw and prepare a landing zone, and they established a perimeter that they could defend. Although they were probed, mortared, and attacked, they were able to maintain their position. Artillery and air support proved to be the difference that enabled them to defend their position. Alpha had become separated and unable to locate their entire unit. Compounded by the fact that they were unable to receive artillery and air support, the enemy was able to surround this company.

The small extraction zone had hampered the

redeployment of Bravo. The lack of artillery support near Alpha prevented the use of a landing zone nearest them. The assault to a secondary landing zone found another heavily fortified area. The failure of command to recognize the need for additional forces in this area, and the fact that Bravo had an entire enemy battalion between them and Alpha, plus another hill, made it impossible for them to reinforce the embattled company. Alpha's only recourse was to break contact and withdraw.

On 5 March the assault of C/3/8 to reinforce came one day too late. The NVA had reduced Alpha's ability to be a factor in this battle. They continued pressure on Delta to keep them at bay so that they could direct their main efforts to the north, where Bravo was located. On 6 March, with three units assaulting the hill, the enemy was still able to deny them the high ground. It was not until artillery and air strikes pounded the hill that the objectives were realized.

After Delta was reinforced by C/3/12 on Hill 947, Task Force Swift was deployed to LZ Brace. From there they assaulted and secured map location YA815872. (Map 6, Location 12, Page 117) With units now deployed on LZ Brace, the hill secured by TF Swift and Hill 947 (Map 6 Locations 10, 12, and 7, Page 117) and units from the 1/35th located at LZ Mary and blocking their retreat to the west, the NVA withdrew to the south. At this time B-52 Bombers made several sorties to hit the fleeing enemy. The price 3/8 paid for the five days was 67 killed. The wounded would number 177 and two were missing. Of these numbers the soldiers who died of their wounds are not recorded in the after action reports. Once a soldier made it to the hospital and he was reassigned to that unit, he was no longer considered part of the 4th Infantry Division. This was one way to improve the kill ratio that the higher-ups looked at. Enemy losses were confirmed at 291 killed. Their losses from artillery and air strikes were believed to be over two hundred. LZ Brace would prove to be the most significant battle of Operation Wayne Grey.

The "Ivy Leaf," a bi-weekly newspaper printed by the 4th Infantry Division, contained the following article that described the events on Hill 947. Words cannot beginning to describe the horror of a battlefield. This was the reporter's story on March 30, 1969:

POLEI-KLENG – DRAGOONS SMASH NVA ON HILL 947

March 5-7th 1969. The men of Delta Company, 3rd Battalion, 8th Infantry set up their night position on Hill 947, 23 kilometers southwest of here; little did they realize that they would be pinned down at that location for a day and a half by NVA rocket, mortar, and sniper fire in a battle that would claim the lives of 139 NVA regulars.

The 4th Infantry Division's fighting men knew there was a good deal of enemy activity in the area. That day, they had met a six man NVA patrol on a heavily traveled foot path, killing four of the enemy and freeing a captured American soldier the patrol was escorting. Things were quiet as the Ivy men set up their night location on Hill 947. As darkness crept in on the camp, occasional movement could be heard along its perimeter. About 5 am the next morning, "Just as we were beginning to send out our OP's," related SP4 Donald Bosch of Bismarck, N.D. "We were hit with mortars, rockets and heavy sniper fire from all sides. We also found out that the earlier perimeter movement was caused by enemy soldiers setting up claymores facing us. These were also fired in the initial contact. After the outburst, enemy fire died off somewhat." "There were still snipers in and behind trees surrounding us," replied Sgt. Robert Edwards of Atlanta Ga. "Whenever we tried to moving from our holes, they would shoot and throw (fire) rounds at us."

During the entire day, the besieged 1st Brigade company was supported by artillery, gunships, and air strikes. The 6th Battalion, 29th Artillery's forward observer with the company; 1st Lt. Hank Castillion of Green River, Wyoming reportedly laid out in the open during the entire operation, calling in and adjusting artillery on the enemy positions whenever other methods of outside support were not being applied. That night, the NVA attempted to slip into Delta Company's position. They made frequent use of grenades in the short range probes.

Spooky 42 spent almost the entire night spraying lethal ordnance in support of the Ivy men. "Spooky began working out 400 meters from our location and worked his way in," explained 1st Sgt. Julius C. Smith of Harrisburg, Va. "He did a tremendous job for us, firing right into the edge of our perimeter." SP4 Arian Anderson of Battle, Neb., along with other members of the Company command post group, flashed lights on the trees nearest the entrenched Ivy men, showing Spooky how close he could fire. Spooky moved out the area about 7am the next morning.

Shortly afterwards, the enemy opened fire on the camp with mortars and gas. Light observation helicopters (LOH) from the 7th Squadron, 17th Cavalry came to the aid of Delta Company. "They sure did the job," commented SGT Edwards. "They came in at treetop level and cleaned out the enemy position. They found and knocked out the NVA mortar emplacements. It was located about 200 meters from our perimeter." Then the Ivy men heard something that had been absent for 36 hours, silence.

They cautiously moved from their holes that had provided cover during the attack. As they moved out to extend their perimeter, the men of Delta Company discovered 53 NVA bodies along with weapons and various ammunitions.

The next day, the Ivy men were joined by elements from the 3rd Battalion, 12th Infantry in a thorough sweep of the entire area. Additional bodies brought the total from the Battle of Hill 947 to 139 NVA dead.

CASUALTY REPORT
March 7, 1969

SGT Linnell Butler	US53610820	11/01/1947	Age 21
SP4 John A. Rivera	US52763633	12/20/1947	Age 21
SP4 Terrance L. Weant	US51837782	03/09/1947	Age 21
PFC John H. West	RA11766322	11/29/1948	Age 20
SGT Kenton E. Henninger	US51834525	09/19/1947	Age 21
SP4 Roger J. Mazal	RA11538847	07/23/1948	Age 20
SGT Robert J. Spence	US51980580	04/08/1945	Age 23

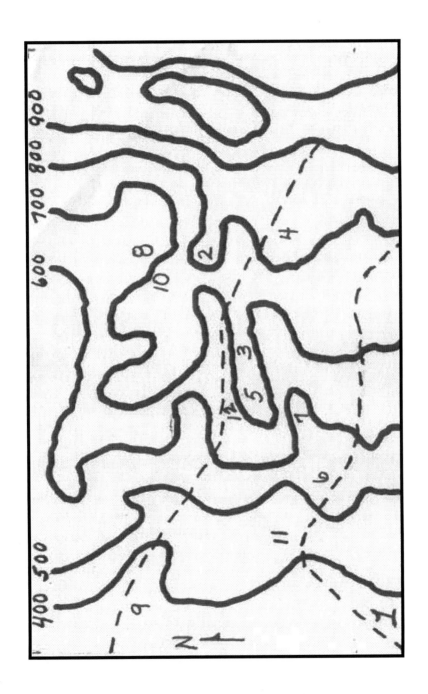

The Battle for LZ Brace

Solid Lines--- Ridgelines
Dotted Lines--- Creeks or Rivers
Map not to Scale

MAP 6
March 7, 1969

Location 1= LZ Mary   YA 784879
Location 2= Intended night location   YA 812884
Location 3= Made first contact   YA 804878
Location 4= LZ for B/3/8
Location 5= Area where A/3/8 established a perimeter
Location 6= D/3/8's first contact   YA 800856
Location 7= Hill 947   YA 813864
Location 8= LZ for Recon and B/3/8   YA 828899
Location 9= Creek bed where A/3/8 was extracted
Location 10= LZ Brace   YA 828880
Location 11= TF Swift's night location   YA 788883
Location 12= Hill assaulted by TF Swift YA 815872

Chapter VIII

"Task Force Swift"

The morning of 8 March 1969 started our second week in the Valley. Milling around my bunk in the dark, I gathered my things for a shower. Sempek asks if I have any shampoo. I do and I throw him the bottle. They have started to build the bar and finish the walls toward the back of the barracks. That's the one thing about the guys in this platoon. They can always manage to accomplish the impossible with nothing. Covering the walls with plywood and then using a blowtorch to burn the grain to highlight it. Once that is done they apply a coat of clear varnish. It really looks good. Jim has a line on a refrigerator and a black light. It's a done deal if we can get another AK-47 and two or three NVA pith helmets. The pith helmets are big with the clowns on the coast. Enemy weapons are confiscated immediately, but they are allowed to have the helmets. I tell him I'll see what I can do.

Standing in the shower, I learn that Kilpatrick is working on a deal for a .45 pistol. The .38 that he has is worn out. You have to rotate the cylinder by hand in order to fire it. He too had been busy gathering trading material yesterday. It is unbelievable what we go through in order obtain the things that we need. We are not a combat unit as far as the Army is concerned, we are a support unit. That means we do not receive priority when it deals with equipment or weapons. Most of the guys in this unit still have M-14 rifles. The reason for this is the ARVNs (South Vietnam Army) are equipped before we are. They have new M-16 rifles and all the equipment to match. The other problem is that we are at the end of the supply line. Everything that we receive starts at Qui Nhon where it is unloaded from the ships. It then goes through their Supply headquarters and is sent by convoy to An Khe. Once they have taken what they want it finally reaches us. So we are forced to deal with the black market and the REMF on the coast to obtain the things we need to stay alive. Great system, isn't it?

For some reason I have been taking a lot of time to get showered and dressed. Picking up my gear, I notice on the mission board a change that I missed last night. It has Gator 108 with the crew of Carey and Wyatt. I don't believe my eyes. Why would the First Sgt. be flying with us today? I had flown with him once before when he first arrived. But to have him going into the Valley just didn't make sense. What the hell could I do about it? He is a big boy and if he wants to go there, fine. I think 'Snoopy' will spend the day in my locker. I might be nuts, but not crazy.

After breakfast I arrive at the revetment. Mr. Thornton and Mr. Trebby are the pilots again. Sgt. Hall has driven the First Sgt. to the ship. The four of them talk as I start the pre-flight inspection. Mr. Trebby joins me on top of the ship to complete our inspection. With everything completed, we head for Mary Lou. Again we are not at full strength. Today we have nine ships.

The flight is a quiet one. The presence of Sgt. Wyatt has made things a little uncomfortable. This would be compared to having your girl friend's father sitting in the back seat at the drive-in. We set down at Mary Lou and they all leave for the briefing. Sempek and I are able to get some coffee and we have our own little briefing at "Doc's" ship. "Why is Top with you today," asks Eggy. "Damn if I know," is my answer. "Maybe he is here because of yesterday," adds Sempek. "Well, whatever the reason, we still have to get a few things so we can finish the bar." Almost an hour passes before the pilots return. Long briefings normally mean bad news for the flight crews.

Task Force Swift is to attack south and link up with the units on Hill 947. We are resupplying LZ Pause and LZ Brace today. Four of ships are assigned to the 1/8th. It seems that their support unit has been unable to provide enough ships. Brigade feels that we need to consolidate our resources. This translates into another long day for us. As we get ready, I explain the layouts at both landing zones. I stress the fact that we have been mortared while at Pause and we must get passengers and cargo off quickly. The area around Brace is a tight fit for us and need to watch the west side of the pad. The ground isn't level and we need to be in the center of the pad so we won't slide off the hill. Suddenly I realize that I'm talking to the first sergeant and not a new gunner. He agrees with all that I have told him and then he asks, "Where is Snoopy today?" I tell him he has the day off and is resting in my locker. His smile has broken the ice.

At Polei-Kleng we hit Resupply and start our day. Adding to the confusion, Flying Cranes (CH-54s) from the 355th Support Helicopter Company are now helping resupply the artillery units with shells. Carrying twice the payload of the CH-47's, this will ensure that plenty of ammo will be delivered to the bases. The 355th is the only unit in the II Corps Area with CH-54s. That means there are only six of these types of ships available. The 4th Infantry has been given one to resupply artillery rounds and nothing more. The "Crane" will be given two gunships as escorts into the firebases. Just what we need is a bigger target to get shot at. Our first sortie is going to LZ Brace. Food, water, ammo, and new people are loaded for the flight. The Red Fox is a little unnerved to see a first sergeant as my gunner. I let him know it's okay and I check to see that all weapons are safe. Hovering out from Resupply Sgt. Wyatt gets a good look at Gator 376. "She is a mess," he comments. The enemy still has snipers in the area so the approach to the pad at LZ Brace is, to say the least, unusual. We fly down the Valley at about 85 knots and then follow the ridgeline straight up and pop right onto the pad. The pad itself sits on a shelf that extends over the Valley. We have nicknamed it the "Perch". To depart, the pilot brings the ship to a hover and we just fall off the side of the pad. We gain airspeed as we follow the ridgeline down and this helps us into the air. Most of passengers do not like this roller coaster ride. To tell the truth, it scared the hell out me the first time we did it. We set down and unload, and pick up a couple of passengers and also a few weapons. I talk with the guys who are headed back to Polei-Kleng. Both are with Bravo Company. They have been through hell the past few days. They are going on R&R and not one minute too soon. The weapons are trash but one of the pith helmets is in good shape. That one finds its way under my seat. Now if I can get one more helmet or some type of enemy equipment, Stella will be able to make the deal.

Completing our resupply of Brace, we concentrate on Pause. So far things have been pretty easy. Just as we pull into our hover at Pause the first round lands. Directly in front of the pad the ground explodes. Just as Thunder swings the tail to the right to get out of here, another round lands at our seven o'clock. **Son of a Bitch**, they have the pad zeroed in and are blasting the hell out it. Somehow Mr. Thornton has us falling off the south side of the hill. We break hard left and then climb for the sky! "I got muzzle flashes at three o'clock," reports Sgt. Wyatt. We bank to the right and throw smoke at the tubes. We complete our run and have put the smoke in their lap. The guns have come on station and are now engaged with the crew that has tormented us for days. Continuing to circle while the gunships work, we watch for any other enemy movement. The Crocs have finished their runs and now a set of Cobras from the 7/17th have arrived to finish the gun crew.

Returning to Polei-Kleng, the news of the mortars arrived before us. We are given cold sodas as a reward. The first sergeant is very pleased with everything that has happened. I gave him a "High Five" and he returns it. Things loosen up and we start to chatter like a normal crew. The rest of the morning is spent resupplying Pause, without any problems from our old buddies. For lunch we shut down at Mary Lou. The crews of Gators 390 and 606 share our feast of C-rations and Kool-Aid.

Sitting in the shadow of the tail boom we eat and bullshit while watching the tanks and other vehicles of 2/8th move along Highway 14. The First Sergeant informs us that the last of the paper work has gone through and we are now an "Air Mobile Light" unit. That means that all of our support detachments are now reassigned to one "TO&E," Army-slang for "Table of Organization & Equipment." It also means that they can have us move anywhere in-country within 24 hours. We will be exchanging some of our older equipment for brand new items. He also asked if there was anything that we needed or felt that we could use. During this lunch the respect I had for this man increased 100%. It was the first time that a career soldier was in the thick of things with us and actually showed concern to know about what we needed.

After lunch we swapped missions and started resupplying units in the 1/8th area. We would get our first look at LZ Susan, LZ Turkey, and Firebase 20. The new area also brought new grid locations and call signs for me to remember. The inside wall of my gun well was covered with this information printed with a grease pencil. I have this need to know what is going on and where we are. I feel that with this information, in case we did go down, I could radio our last position to whoever may be looking for us. The radio is continually giving us artillery advisories and the coming of the next Arc Light strike.

The Plei-Trap road is again receiving attention, as more trucks have been spotted and artillery has been employed. The problem with the artillery being fired from so many locations is that we have to alter our routes between the firebases and Polei-Kleng. We are losing a lot of valuable time, and the possibility of not getting all the resupply delivered is very real. Because of the amount of support they are giving, the CH-47's have doubled their sorties to bring in more ammo. This limits us to times we are able to be at the bases, because it is very difficult to be there at the same time as the larger helicopters.

The word has reached us that in the 2nd Brigade area, one of its companies had found a large bunker complex. It is north and west of Mile High. This is near Hill 994. To compound the problem, Mile High is again receiving mortar and recoilless rifle fire. We continue to resupply, but our gunships are being called to support elements of the 1/12th, who have stepped into some deep shit. As the afternoon ends we are able to listen to the radio and hear that another battle has started in the Valley. Now Hill 994 will have its turn.

The resupply was completed just before dark. We are told to stand by in case we are needed. The flight sets down at Kontum and waits to see what is happening. While we wait, we have a chance to have dinner. We are spending more time at the 57th's mess hall than our own. It is almost 2100hrs before we are released. We have sat for two hours. Now we start our forty-five minute flight back to Holloway. The two hours spent were not wasted. We got a chance to write some letters and read the ones we hadn't had the chance to read. Some got to catch up on their sleep and others just sat with their thoughts and looked to the future.

Once the postflight was completed and the logbook filled out, I returned to the barracks. Not having Dana to talk to at night was starting to wear on me. With him being on guard every night and not flying during the day I have already started to miss him. The big news is that they almost have the water heater hooked up. With the stuff I got today they should be able to have it up and running by the day after tomorrow. I fall asleep knowing another day in the Valley awaits me tomorrow.

CASUALTY REPORT
March 8, 1969

SP4 William A. Beard	US52725014	06/10/1948	Age 20
CPL Jerry G. Ervin	RA12925684	02/21/1942	Age 27
SSG Dean H. Johnson	US51967504	01/15/1948	Age 21
SP4 Roy G. Zufelt	RA18864686	11/13/1946	Age 22

Chapter IX

"Day Off"

I had finished the pre-flight and was getting ready to leave when Sgt. Hall arrived at the revetment. A new ship was being delivered today, and it was assigned to me. I have to get it combat-ready for tomorrow. I pulled my gear off the ship and placed it beside the revetment wall. As Gator 108 departed I waved and started to realize how much work was ahead of me today. First thing was to get all this gear up to the Maintenance locker so I could stow it away. If I left it here it would grow legs and walk away. With Sgt. Hall's help we loaded my stuff into the truck and took it to the locker.

I arrived back at the barracks in time to catch Stella, who was going after the supplies we needed in the platoon. I told him I needed spray paint and masking tape. I then grabbed Dana to help me round up the equipment I needed for the new ship. Using the platoon truck we headed for the 608th. The first order of business was to get the gun mounts off of Gator 488. Once we had filled out the paper work we needed to remove the mounts, we had to return to the Orderly Room for the 1st Sgt. to sign them. Returning with the proper forms, we were able to remove the mounts. The paper work had taken almost two hours. To remove the mounts, twenty minutes.

Next we headed for the ammo dump. Things went a lot smoother there. Sgt. Greg Bilbee, who was in charge of it, had been a crew chief. There was no need for all the bullshit that might be involved. We loaded the three boxes of mini-gun ammo that we needed. The case of smoke grenades had the four colors we needed. The red and yellow grenades were for my side of the ship and green and purple were for the gunner's side. I had different colors so we would know who had thrown which smoke grenade. I also got two

"Willie Pete" grenades. The white phosphorus grenades were for destroying the ship in case it could not be recovered or secured.

It was almost noon before the ship was delivered. I had sorted through all the gear; and I had stored it in the locker. Most important was my toolbox. It had taken many months to collect all the needed tools. I had my personal gear that included my survival kit. I had also gotten a survival vest from the Air Force Base. It contained a hand held radio, which was the prize I wanted. If I went down I wanted to be able to talk to somebody. Also, I had collected many maps and radio frequencies that were used in the area. These I kept in a weatherproof bag. I had my M-79 and its ammo plus the ammo for my .45 and M-14 rifle. Everything was ready. All I needed now was a ship.

After lunch we accepted aircraft # 68-15270. She was brand new and had many improvements from earlier models. While the tech. inspectors checked the paperwork, I had a few items to correct. The first change to be made was moving the battery from the front nose compartment to the left side compartment. The factory installed the battery in the front prior to the Army mounting the armored pilot's seats. This would make the ship nose-heavy. Moving the eighty-pound battery would help the overall performance of the aircraft. Next, the gun mounts were installed, and then the safety equipment. Now that we had completed our work, the maintenance team would go over the entire ship. This would ensure that the aircraft was ready for flight.

The most important item that I needed to have done by morning was to paint a four-foot long section on the top of the main rotor blades white. This would enable the ships above us to see our ship against the trees. The rotating blades would appear as a round circle. I would have this done by 1700hrs. After dinner I would spend another three hours working on the ship. Many of the items that were to be done would take most of my free time over the next two weeks. The one thing that I was unable to decide was what I should name her. A good ship needs a good name. For the first time in ten days, I would be back in the barracks before 2200hrs. This would be my last day off for a while.

Although I spent a relatively safe day at base camp, our ships were still in harm's way. Three ships would be damaged this day. Two slicks would take ground fire while resupplying LZ Swinger. One of the Crocs would be damaged while providing support to units of the 1/8th. The Plei-Trap Road was again the scene of numerous enemy encounters. Several trucks had been spotted and also a large number of NVA troops were spotted in an open area near a suspected mortar position. Artillery and B-52s would again pound these areas.

Air strikes south of Hill 947 had continued. TF Swift had been given the mission to start bomb damage assessments in the area. They had spent their day being resupplied and preparing to move into these areas. The units of the 3/8 were being reinforced and reorganized. The battle for LZ Brace had taken its toll and they needed the time to prepare for their next mission.

The heaviest fighting during the day would be in the 2nd Brigade's Area of Operations. Although not considered part of Operation Wayne Grey, it still had a direct effect on us. The fighting at Hill 994 had increased. A large enemy force was encountered, and units of the 1/12th were taking casualties. Yesterday afternoon the 3rd platoon of B/1/12 had discovered a bunker complex at YB 898988. There were 150 bunkers that would hold three to four men apiece. They lined the northeast ridge of Hill 994. While pulling back from the area, the platoon was ambushed by a superior force. They were surrounded, but had set up a defensive perimeter. Company D/1/12 was also operating near Hill 994. That Company's third platoon was ordered to reinforce the embattled platoon. Before they were able to reach Bravo Company this platoon was also ambushed. Now two platoons prepared for a long night. The remainder of Bravo Company had departed Mile High this morning. By noon they had reached the area of the two platoons in contact. Working their way up the ridge, moving from tree to tree, bunker to bunker, they finally reached the platoons. Small firefights continued all afternoon as Bravo recovered their dead and wounded. Artillery and air support was employed several times as Bravo fought to secure a landing zone. Sniper fire proved to be deadly during this time. By evening the 3rd platoon had been accounted for. Eight were dead and thirteen were wounded.

LZ Mile High continued to be under attack by mortar and recoilless rifle. The thunder of the Arc Light strikes and the echo of the howitzers would continue all night. Fire Support Base 20 on this night would fire 167 rounds of 105mm howitzer ammo. Although we pounded the enemy, he showed no signs of withdrawing from the Valley. This became more apparent because of the discovery of bridges and roads that the 1/35th had found late this afternoon. These were well-constructed and would support the weight of trucks crossing over from Cambodia. A late afternoon resupply would be dropped to them so that these bridges could be destroyed.

The stress of the past days has starting to show. People would talk less and become angered over small, unimportant matters. This not only affected the aircrews, but everyone. The Maintenance personnel were working most of the night to keep our ships flying. The support groups were all taxed. The numbers game continued to hound us. We did not have enough ships or people.

Because of the amounts of supplies that were being used in the Valley each day, the convoys started to make twice the runs they would normally. The infantry units needed replacements and they were in short supply. If the press had labeled this an unpopular war back home, they really didn't need our views. We would continue to count

129

our days to DEROS and try not to question what we were doing in this Valley.

The heaviest actions of the day were in the northern part of the Valley. This is was the account of the Battle at Hill 994, one paragraph at the bottom of the front page of the 4th Division newspaper, the "Ivy Leaf."

Ivy Leaf
March 30, 1969

"The northern sector of the Plei-Trap Valley erupted again on March 9th as two platoons of Bravo Company, 1st Battalion, 12th Infantry were executing a reconnaissance in force 13 kilometers northwest of Polei-Kleng, exchanged a withering volume of small arms and automatic weapon's fire with an estimated NVA Company. When contact was broken by the enemy the two platoons swept, finding 36 enemy dead. U.S. casualties were light during the day long battle.

CASUALTY REPORT
March 9, 1969

SP4 Raymond L. Bethea	US67193281	11/29/1949	Age 19
SSG Raymond J. Bechard	RA51344935	11/03/1943	Age 25
SGT Clarence P. Burleson	US56829304	01/17/1948	Age 21
PFC Timothy M. Carroll	US67184389	08/14/1944	Age 24
SGT Buddy E. Channon	US52814184	04/29/1947	Age 21
SP4 Robert S. Gregg	US56592241	05/24/1948	Age 20
SP4 Timothy L. Hurley	US56428010	08/28/1947	Age 21
SSG Jerry C. Mc Donald	US54721266	10/29/1946	Age 22
SP4 Joseph H. Mears	RA11536954	06/06/1948	Age 20
SP4 Edward J. Millison III	RA11868169	01/11/1948	Age 21
SP4 Clarence Nofford	US67032903	02/04/1944	Age 25
SP4 Francis S. Oberson	RA11946986	11/18/1950	Age 18
SSG. Robert B. Protto Jr.	RA56834510	12/13/1945	Age 23
PFC Bobby J. Rollins	RA15932241	04/10/1949	Age 19
SGT Thomas G. Turner	US51670347	08/01/1945	Age 23

Chapter X

"Gator 270"

Another 0600hrs pre-flight inspection is how I would start this day. Having gotten my fruit and coffee from the mess hall, I arrive at the revetment. I have everything ready so, as the pilots show up, we can cover the improvements that this ship has. SP5 Matos is assigned as my gunner and he has gotten a new case of C-rations for the ship. He may work out after all. Once we have completed the inspection, we are ready for another day in the Valley. As we fly to LZ Mary Lou, Stoney makes a comment about the controls being a little stiff. I remind him that it's a new ship and they will feel that way. Each helicopter has their own little characteristics that make each of them unique. I now would have to learn what was special to this ship.

Arriving at Mary Lou, I make the pilots idle the ship while I check different things. This is for my own satisfaction that everything is working fine. These added precautions are just something that I need to do. This helicopter was built in Texas and flown to the coast. There, it was disassembled and placed in the hold of a cargo ship. Once it reached Vietnam it was reassembled and sent to us. With so many people working on this thing, I just won't feel right until I've had her for a week or so.

While the pilots are at the briefing I start to outline the pilot's doors for the unit's number. A small crowd has gathered to look at the new ship. It's like being at home when the guys would hang out at the gas station and check out each other's cars. Because that's what teenagers did back in The World and, in fact, that's what we were. Instead of street rods and hot rods, we had Bell Helicopters. Rumor was that we would be getting at least two more ships before the end of the month. We might get new ships but we were still short two crew chiefs. With all that has happened, not too many people have requested the flight platoons. At least with our short-timers pulling guard, we didn't have to contend with that. I have completed the outline on the first door when the pilots return. We have drawn Task Force Swift.

The Resupply area is busy this morning. Because of all the activity the firebases are in short supply of 105mm howitzer ammo. They are firing in support around the clock. They also need extra food and water. The area around Hill 947 has been plastered by the B-52s. TF Swift will be moving out of that location to RIF the areas south of them. Once we have them taken care of, we will then work on LZ Brace. Because we have personnel outside the bases, we are on restriction to any free-fire zones. If we receive fire we must first mark it and receive permission to return fire. We head for Hill 947 with the first sortie of the day.

To see the area south of Hill 947 is unbelievable. The trees flattened and the ground is still burning. It does not appear to be anything close to the triple-canopy jungle that had been there just three days before. The best description would compare it to a cornfield after the farmer has gone through with his combine. The ground is chewed up and the corn stalks are broken and destroyed. The landscape is now hills and valleys, not the level terrain that the treetops would lead you to believe. The power of the bombs would scar this area for years to come.

The landing zone is far different from the one I used four days ago. A perimeter has been built with barbed wire. Bunkers had been constructed, and the litter of war which had been thrown everywhere was now gone. As we unloaded, I could see some of the troops preparing to leave the safety of this place and start to move towards the area of the air strikes. For them the war was real twenty-four hours a day, and seven days a week. At least I was able to leave this hell at night. One of the guys handed me their red mailbag. I secured it behind me and we left for Polei-Kleng.

Some good news came from the units of 1/8th. They had located two enemy artillery pieces. Both had been destroyed by air strikes. They were in the process of securing the area and would try to extract the weapons so intelligence could inspect them. Hopefully this would take the pressure off our firebases that had been shelled the last week. Since the first of the month we had encountered enemy tanks, trucks, and artillery pieces. The theory of us fighting a bunch of peasants with flintlock rifles and pitchforks seemed to fade further away with each passing day.

Two of our ships had been assigned to the 2nd Brigade today. Due to the losses that all of the air support units have suffered, we were now being assigned to the units that were in need of us. The battle at Hill 994 had lasted two days. Those troops were in need of resupply and getting their wounded and dead out. The first reports would show seventeen killed and thirty wounded. Enemy dead were estimated at one hundred. The area around LZ Mile High continued with enemy activity. Besides the mortar and recoilless rifle fire, now the addition of sniper fire would plague those troops.

We continued to receive intermittent fire as we resupplied the firebases. It was as if the enemy knew he could get away with it. They would fire a burst with automatic weapons, and then melt into the jungle. LZ Swinger was still our biggest problem. Because of all the action to the north and south of this location, we had never really swept the area around this base. The snipers continued to fire into the perimeter and at us as we made our daily deliveries. The larger 155mm howitzers required the CH-54s to deliver their ammo. The larger helicopters would always draw fire. The good thing was the fact that we had nobody outside the wire at Swinger. If we received fire, we could return fire.

The units of the 1/35th were still operating out of LZ

Mary. They had been used as a blocking force during the battle for LZ Brace. They continued to find roads and bunker complexes. We also were supporting those people. LZ Mary had also become a major base of operations since the first days we were in the Valley. They had brought in engineers to enlarge the pad and reinforce the perimeter. On the trip to Mary we could really see the destruction of the bombing strikes. The passengers we carried would sit with their mouths open, not believing what they saw. By mid-afternoon the 1/35th has been given their marching orders. They would start to be withdrawn out of the Valley tomorrow and sent back to Dak To. As noon approached we started to contemplate where we would eat lunch. The past four hours, we had flown one sortie after another. It was time to get out of this ship and stretch our tired bodies. We would settle on Polei-Kleng.

The crews from Gators 834 and 390 would join us for lunch. A buffet was on the menu today. The crew of 834 had gotten bread and Spam from the mess hall. We would provide a large can of pork and beans while the crew of 390 appeared with two cans of tomato juice and apple juice. Breaking a claymore mine apart to use the C-4 as fuel for our makeshift stove, we proceeded to have a picnic lunch. It's amazing how good this stuff does taste if you are able to cook it. But then again, thank God for ketchup. Sitting in the cargo area of my ship we enjoyed our lunch and watched the war go by. The talk was the same as every day. What we would do when we got home, or what we needed to finish the bar back at Holloway. I was almost asleep when it was time to go back to work. I promised myself I would sleep for a month when I got out of here.

Sitting in Resupply, we receive the word that they are bringing the captured enemy howitzers to Polei-Kleng. Company D/1/8 had been airlifted from FSB 20 to map location YB 770026. They then traveled to YB 779028 where they encountered light enemy resistance and secured the weapons. These were two U.S. made 105mm howitzers. The manufacture dates were 1942 and 1945. From captured documents it is believed that they were assigned to the 40th Artillery regiment. They had also discovered several trucks and a large enemy complex. We were instructed to proceed to this area and help extract Delta back to Fire Support Base 20. We delivered one sortie to Swinger and then headed to the pickup zone.

Arriving on station we circled as the first two ships extracted Delta. The pickup zone was a hoverhole that they had cut so the CH-47s could extract the howitzers. Clouds of white smoke rise from near their location. They were destroying the trucks and supplies that they had discovered. When our turn came we had to stand outside the ship to clear it as we hovered down into the trees. They were approximately 50 feet tall. We loaded five passengers and several enemy weapons and other equipment. We hovered out of the hole and started forward. As we banked right that familiar sound rang out. **"FIRE! WE HAVE FIRE AT OUR FOUR O'CLOCK!"** Even with Mattie's heavy accent we knew what was happening. He had thrown smoke and the gunships were starting their run. **"Son of a Bitch!"** I just knew we had taken a hit in the tail boom. The damn ship wasn't one day old and it had lost her cherry. We would make one more trip before returning to Polei-Kleng. I did manage to get another AK-47 and two pit helmets. This would get the spray paint I needed to finish the ship.

Even before I could inspect the damage every ship in the Valley had learned that our new ship had lost its cherry. Setting down at POL I discovered three holes. One round had hit the cargo door and gone into the side compartment. That was just my type of luck, two holes with one round. The other was in the heel of the skid. The cap on the landing gear could be replaced without removing the whole assembly. We were still able to fly but the Maintenance crews would be busy tonight. We refueled and headed back to FSB 20. We were needed to haul the remaining enemy equipment back Polei-Kleng. Brigade wanted to go over the documents and personal effects that had been captured. After that, we returned to resupply of our firebases. The artillery batteries at FSB 20 would throw over 200 rounds of 105mm howitzer into the area where we had extracted D/1/8. U.S. casualties were one wounded. Results from artillery strike were unknown.

By late afternoon, TF Swift had arrived at their night location. Since the battle of Brace all units were instructed to cut landing zones to evacuate wounded or bring in reinforcements. The Brigade was not going to have another disaster like A/3/8. The reality that we were outnumbered and being in "Sir Charles" backyard had stacked the deck against us. As soon as the landing zone was cut we brought in claymore mines and trip flares. These steps would help the perimeter defenses. Artillery spotter rounds were fired to ensure that support was only one call away.

There was still daylight when we were released. We had passengers to drop off at LZ Mary Lou and some dispatches. The CQ runner met us at the taxiway. I guess they were still leery of having us hover near the brass. At Mary Lou, two artillery soldiers were looking for a ride back to Pleiku. They were going on R&R and had to get back to their base camp. The ride home passed quickly. Talking to our passengers and listening to what it was like being on one of those firebases made me glad that I was in aviation. We dropped them at Artillery Hill and they wished us well. We arrived at Holloway before the sun had gone down. That was a first since we started this mission. I finished my postflight and headed for the barracks.

I had just crossed the road in the rear of the Company area. It was twilight, and you could still see outlines of people moving about. All of the sudden there was this sound. It wasn't incoming and it wasn't an explosion. There was a bright flash and the sound of fire as if

136

gas had been thrown on it. The next thing I see is the shower behind the headquarters barracks erupt into flames. Guys are running and grabbing buckets and pouring water on this giant blaze. I now realize that the hot water heater that they have worked so hard on has exploded, and the shower and water tower are on fire. It's not funny, but I can't control myself. Standing at the rear of our barracks I have a front row seat. By now the fire department has arrived and they are getting the fire out. The First Sgt. is really going to be pissed off about this.

Seating on a sandbag, drinking a beer, I get the whole story. They had gotten the heater hooked up and filled it with fuel. Instead of using kerosene, they had put gasoline in it. Besides the higher flash point, they had also spilled some gas on the ground under the heater. When they put the match to it the laws of physics took over. The fire department saved the tower but the shower was not looking good. I may have not been able to enjoy a hot shower but I did have a good laugh. We sat there for a couple hours just talking, and drinking beer. The beer tasted like shit but the company I shared was the best in the world. By the time my head hit the bunk I was a little drunk. But I think I needed it on this night.

CASUALTY REPORT
March 10, 1969

SGT Jesse H. Archer	US53758176	08/06/1947	Age 21
SSG James L. Cameron	US54968491	09/14/1946	Age 22
SP4 Jeffery T. Cassidy	US52814184	01/11/1948	Age 21
SGT Leon Coit	RA11578829	09/16/1949	Age 19
SGT Art George-Pizarro	US51514750	04/28/1944	Age 24
CPL John E. Lortz III	US56725288	09/23/1948	Age 20
CPL Julius A. Mitchell	RA12894806	02/16/1950	Age 19
SP4 William J. Stedl	US56460783	07/06/1949	Age 19

Chapter XI

"Not Again"

The slightest movement of my head results in pain. This is the price I pay for drinking beer last night. I am not a drinker to begin with, and then to give me seven to ten beers, well, to say the least, I am not a pretty sight this morning. I finally get up and, after standing in the shower for twenty minutes, I am awake enough to actually function. As I walk to the mess hall I can barely make out the headquarters shower. Even in the dark it looks bad. The menu has pancakes this morning. I pass because I don't need a pound of that sitting in my stomach. The coffee and toast are enough.

Walking to the ship, I listen to Mattie ramble on about the fire last night. I guess he is starting to feel comfortable around me. He hasn't talked this much in three days. I have started to hear more of what he is saying and his accent isn't as heavy as it once was. The Maintenance crews have repaired the combat damage and the pre-flight is completed in twenty minutes. It's nice to have a new ship. If I could prevent the bad guys from putting holes in her, life would be perfect. We head for Polei-Kleng.

Brigade has decided that briefing will resume at Polei-Kleng. They feel this would have a positive effect on the morale of the men. All I know is this place scares the hell out of me. We have nowhere to go in case of attack and the thought of a 105mm howitzer round coming this way is not the picture I cared to paint. I work on the outline of the unit number on the other pilot's door. A maintenance crew from the 57th AHC has prepared Gator 376 for the trip back to Holloway. The slings are ready to go and they plan on transporting her tonight. Now that I've had a chance to look at her, the damage isn't that bad. There are only ten or so holes in the underside of the ship. The reason we went down wasn't because of an engine failure. Two of the rounds had hit the fuel cells; we ran out of gas. The vertical fin was torn off because the tail rotor had become entangled in the barbed wire and the torque had twisted it off. The skids buckled because we hit the ground so hard. Other than that, a little paint and some chrome and this bird would be as good as new. With luck she might make the coast before they scrapped her.

The pilots return and Stoney briefs us. We have Brace, Swift, and Hill 947. The first place we are headed is the night location of TF Swift. The enemy had launched a pre-dawn mortar attack against them. They had called in artillery and air for support. No casualties were taken and damage was termed "Light". They will be moving farther into the areas of the air strikes. They are south of Hill 947. At Resupply we load the usual cargo of water, food, and ammo. We head into the Valley. Arriving in the area of TF Swift we start to look for them. They pop smoke and we identify yellow smoke. They were on the side of a small hill just above a valley or saddle between two higher hills. The trees are still thick in this area. Although they have cut an extraction zone, it is very tight and we had difficulty getting into it. The breeze from the west isn't helping us because once we are below the ridgeline it creates a wind tunnel. On the ground Stoney tells an officer that they need to enlarge this area or we might not be able to get in here again. The officer tells us they are moving out. They were abandoning this zone, so there was no need to improve it.

Returning to Polei-Kleng we advise other ships to stay clear of that landing zone. We load up and head for Brace. Each day that we have Brace we continue to bring new troops to them. I have to go over my little speech and check their weapons. A couple of vets are also headed for Brace. Instead of checking their weapons, they are offered cigarettes. The one remembers my helmet. He was one of the guys from B/3/8 that we tried to get into Brace that first day. We talk as best we can over the sound of the rotor blades. At Brace we shake hands and depart. While we are sitting at Brace we can see the task force receiving mortar rounds. They are on the horn calling for artillery. We stand by waiting to see if we are needed. They have no casualties and are okay. We return to Polei-Kleng.

In the 1/8th's area they have located an anti-aircraft position. They had fired on Hummingbird 1 near location YB 827021. Artillery from FSB 20 was employed against this position. Air strikes continued in the area where the enemy howitzers were captured. Sweeps in the locations near the Plei-Trap road have been negative. A general sweep around FSB 20 and ambushes have been set to the south, southeast, and southwest. Something is in the works but we are not being told about it.

During the afternoon we start to move engineers into Brace. The increased amounts of sandbags and barbed wire suggest that they are going to reinforce this area for something. Just before noon, a short range patrol from C/3/12 southeast of Hill 947 discovered four dead NVA soldiers and fresh blood trails. They are at map location YA 817861. A platoon from that company is sent to sweep the area. Our peaceful day ends at 1420hrs. They have made contact with an unknown size force and are now receiving mortar fire at location YA 818858. The remainder of C/3/12 is being sent to reinforce the platoon. Company B/3/12 is dispatched to secure a withdrawal route. Company D/3/12 returns to their previous night location to secure a landing zone. Company C has walked into a large bunker complex. The NVA always have the advantage in these types of contacts. They have fortified positions and they are familiar with the area they are protecting. They stand and fight only to prevent their enemy from locating what they are protecting. Escape route and withdrawal plans are all determined prior to any contact. This is their backyard and

140

they know every inch of it. The Americans had traveled a great distance and are tired. The only supplies they have are on their backs. The enemy is hitting them with B-40 rockets, mortars, and automatic weapons fire. Outnumbered and unable to reinforce, they withdraw. They have wounded who need to be extracted now. Setting up a defensive perimeter near a bomb crater, they prepare a landing zone so we can extract the wounded and resupply them with ammo. They will then withdraw to the perimeter at the landing zone that they earlier decided not to enlarge because they were pulling out. We head into the Valley, fearing the worst.

Blackjack is on station as we arrive. The landing zone is a disaster waiting to happen. The bomb crater is surrounded by trees and the ground will not permit us to land. Stoney explains the problem to Blackjack. The winds have increased and hovering into this hole would be almost impossible. They would need to blow several of the trees so we could at least have a chance to get in there. The Company doesn't have any of the equipment needed to do this. We are ordered to go in and pickup the wounded. Stoney advises that at least someone should return and get extraction gear in case we crash in the landing zone. If we go down the zone will be blocked and then nobody would get in or out. Gator 390 heads for Polei-Kleng to get the extraction ladder and ropes.

Hovering above the hole we start our descent. I am standing on the skids outside the ship. Mattie is doing the same. "The tail is clear. You can move to your left if you need to. The right is clear. Hold It! Move forward. The trees are blowing toward the tail rotor. Okay. The tail is clear. You are clear left. You are clear right." We have jockeyed our way into this pit. I can see grunts along the outside of the crater and tell Stoney to have them move because our rotor blades are much to close to them The winds keep changing and we continue to flirt with disaster. Finally after what seemed like hours we touch down. The ground is uneven and we have one skid on the ground and the other about a foot above. Stoney fights to keep the ship level so we won't crash into the trees. They have eight wounded. We are low on fuel. It's a brand new ship. What the hell! Let's go for it. We load all eight on board. If we can get out nobody else will have to get in here. We start up. The wind has increased. Slowly we rise. Stoney follows every instruction to the letter. He is focused on our voices and nothing else. **"WE ARE CLEAR! LET'S GET OUT OF HERE!"** The nose of the ship eases down and we head for Mary Lou. Stoney has the peter pilot take over. He is dripping wet with sweat from the stress of what he had just done. All of the back seat crews agreed that our pilots were second to none because of their skills. The only way I could describe the way Stoney got into that landing zone is, he was able to fit a square peg into a round hole. Then his decision to take all eight of the wounded out so nobody else would have to enter this hoverhole showed the type of leader he was. We land at Mary Lou and the staff is amazed to see so many on the ship.

While we refuel, Gator 834 has dropped TF Swift chain saws and sandbags to improve the landing zone. Blackjack wants us to report to the taxiway near Brigade CQ. Setting on the taxiway Red 6 approaches the ship. It's the same person who just a week ago had charged our ship wearing only a towel and waving a pistol is again walking towards us. This time he is smiling from ear to ear. He enters the cargo bay and shakes everybody's hand. He gives me a long look before leaving. His aide takes our names and serial numbers and then leaves. We return to Resupply and load ammo and return to Swift's location. They are working to improve the landing zone as we return. We circle as they finish cutting down the trees that should have been cut down this morning. We land and unload ammo, then we load some of the wounded who were carried back to the perimeter. The enemy mortars are now starting to fall into this area. The task force needs supplies to reinforce their perimeter. We continue to resupply until dark before we are released.

The flight back to Holloway is quiet. The long hours that we have spent in the Valley have changed us. Anything outside of sleep is considered a waste of time. We no longer eat, or have the energy to shower, or read mail. The entire world is the Valley. We hate the place but feel lost without it. The question that nobody has yet to ask is why are we there? Being soldiers, we aren't allowed to ask that question. The red tip of my cigarette burns the same color as the lights from the instrument panel. This is the only time when I am at peace with the day. I know that for right now, it is over until morning. Tonight I will have a sandwich. I look at my mail, but won't read it. I fall asleep, but it brings no rest to my tired body. Tomorrow is another day.

CASUALTY REPORT
March 11, 1969

SGT William H. Barksdale	US53844419	01/06/1948	Age 21
SGT Wayne A. Bratz	US56460092	02/21/1949	Age 20
PFC Edward T. Cooper	US54931466	03/08/1950	Age 19
SFC Milfred H. Dingman	RA55020025	05/27/1927	Age 41
SP4 Vanderbilt Elliott	RA11931388	07/18/1947	Age 21
SP4 Terrell T. Ham	US53613661	09/11/1947	Age 21
PFC Samuel L. Holder	US5470436	09/26/1946	Age 22
SP4 Vincent G. Lew	US56837985	05/20/1948	Age 20
SGT Joseph A. Lewis	RA56836194	04/07/1946	Age 22
SGT Jean D. Martin	US54564582	09/10/1947	Age 21
PFC John F. Morris	US56840776	09/07/1947	Age 21
PFC Kenneth J. Robinson	US67179892	06/14/1950	Age 18
SP4 Carlos L. Tartt	RA12869763	10/11/1949	Age 19
PFC Howard G. Webster	US56730877	05/04/1949	Age 19
SP4 John R. Weir	US56721577	01/23/1948	Age 21

Chapter XII

"The Assault"

For the second time in less than a week, I am shaken awake by Sgt. Hall. "Carey! Get Up! They need you for pre-flight now." Sitting up, I light a cigarette and try to focus on what is going on. Several people are up, getting dressed, and starting to head for their ships. "Screw this!" They can wait five minutes so I can get a shower. I grab my towel and get into the shower. This "hurry up and wait" shit gets a little old after a while. I get my shower and then hit the mess hall for coffee and my fruit. I arrive at the revetment and there are no pilots anywhere. It figures. I start the pre-flight and Stoney and the peter-pilot show up. Mattie has gotten our rations and water. He also has two large cans of apple juice. We complete the pre-flight and head for Polei-Kleng.

During the night, Task Force Swift had been probed. They are in need of reinforcements and supplies. They are planning to go back into the area that they had been pushed out of yesterday. We are to resupply them at the earliest possible time. The area around FSB 20 has also seen action during the night. Brigade feels that something is about to happen. That's why we are being scrambled so early this morning. It's not bad enough that we have to fly home in the dark, but now we are leaving in the dark. I convince Stoney to slow down so we can close the doors. The air is cold and damp. We arrive just as the sun appears in the east. "Red 5" meets the ships on the runway. They have coffee for us and we are briefed as a whole rather than just the pilots. The landing zone has been improved and we should have no problems getting in there today. We finish our coffee and head for the Resupply area. We load four passengers and ammo. Arriving at TF Swift's location and we start our hover. They have enlarged the landing zone but it is still a bitch to get into. Finally we land and offload our cargo. We return to Polei-Kleng.

Our second load is ammo and food. By the time we arrive back at their location the first of the troops are moving out. The mood was tense because of what happened yesterday and everybody knew the beast was out there and he was hungry. On our way back to Polei-Kleng is when we hear the first news. The lead element had encountered bunkers and heavy resistance. The extent of the complex is unknown. It is very large and is built into the side of a ridgeline. The jungle is very thick on both sides, making it hard to flank and there is no approach to its rear. They were pulling back to regroup and hit the area again. The wounded were being brought back to the perimeter and we would evacuate them. The artillery from Pause was firing in support as we returned. Approaching the area we were starting to receive ground fire. With the first load of wounded we headed for Mary Lou.

"MAYDAY! MAYDAY! MAYDAY! THIS GATOR 408! WE ARE LOSING POWER AND TRYING TO MAKE PAUSE!" A Second Flight ship that had been waiting to pick up wounded had been hit several times as they circled to the west of the saddle. We unloaded the wounded at Mary Lou and started back to the Valley. Gator 408 had made Pause, but now it was a sitting target. The compression stage of engine had taken several rounds. The one pad they had was now blocked, and we had to get it out of there. As we circled I could see the crew chief and the pilots looking at the engine. They radioed us to say that the engine was damaged, and that we needed to contact Operations to get a crew out there to sling load her out of there. We gained altitude and contacted Operations. We explained what had happened and what was needed. They would have a crew ready and at this location within the hour. We picked up the crew from Pause and transported them to Polei-Kleng. We also needed to refuel.

The Task Force had again advanced toward the enemy. With the help of artillery and air support they had gotten a foothold at the enemy's perimeter. The enemy is determined, and uses B-40 rockets and automatic weapons fire against our assault. After thirty minutes, we again withdrew and call for artillery. Why is the enemy so determined not to give up this piece of real estate? They continue to pound our troops with B-40s and mortar fire as our artillery starts to fall. We again would have to evacuate the wounded and bring in fresh troops. The number of bunkers and the number of troops had surprised everyone. After days of B-52s pounding the area, it was unbelievable that anything was still in that area. We waited as the artillery hammered the bunker complex.

While we were engaged, the northern part of the Valley was heating up. Company A/1/8 had made contact with an NVA unit, which was dug in at YB 852003. Company C/1/8, which had moved along a parallel line as Alpha also encountered an enemy force. Alpha Company had moved from their night location to recon to a new location. A large bunker complex and hospital were discovered. The complex was heavily defended, and a fierce firefight erupted. Following the initial contact, the Company fell back to reorganize and prepare an assault plan. The Company assaulted the area and again met heavy resistance. Suffering casualties from the large volume of fire, they again fell back. Two additional assaults would yield the same results. The NVA defenders employed automatic weapons and B-40 rockets to drive the Company back on each occasion. Greatly outnumbered, and with several of their officers and senior NCOs wounded, the Company withdrew. A young squad leader who led the Company during the final assault and organized the withdrawal would be nominated for the Medal of Honor for his actions this day. For heroism and valor that day, Sgt. Jerry Loucks

146

would be awarded the Distinguished Service Cross. Many of the members of his Company were disappointed that the medal had been downgraded. During this time Charlie Company had also encountered a large enemy force. The NVA were positioned between Charlie Company and Alpha to prevent the two companies from linking up during the action. They were also forced to withdraw because of superior enemy numbers. These contacts would continue until late afternoon. During the day and into the night, batteries of A/6/29th artillery would fire 405 rounds of 105mm howitzer to support these units. Things were quiet in the 2nd Brigade's area. Companies A and C 1/14th had spotted NVA soldiers two kilometers north of Mile High. They were following them towards the river, but lost the trail after they had crossed the river. The units of the1/12th at Mile High had been flown in hot chow that morning. By mid-afternoon over forty men were sick. The chicken that was flown in must have been tainted. Anyone who had eaten it was now suffering with food poisoning.

For a third time, Task Force Swift attacked the bunkers. Again the enemy refused to give in. The Air Force was called and now napalm is employed from the silver wings of F-100s. While the fires burn in the bunker complex, a crew from Holloway works to prepare Gator 408 for its ride home. By late afternoon the CH-47 hovers in to lift the disabled bird into the sky and back to Pleiku. The Task Force finally obtains its goal. The bunker complex has been taken. Even as they secured the objective they started to receive mortar and small arms fire. Again we have to evacuate the wounded. The number of enemy casualties from the air strikes and artillery were unknown. The final assault resulted in five NVA killed. For these two days U.S. casualties were ten killed and 56 wounded. This was not a fair price to be paid at YA 818956. With the southern A/Os secured, the second phase of the operation would soon begin.

Once the wounded were evacuated and the dead taken out, we would resupply until dark. We were now working with the 170th AHC and sharing responsibilities. Both units were having trouble supplying enough ships to cover mission requirements. The losses to Troop A/7/17th were even worse. Their sister Company, C/7/17th would replace them on March 20th. Driving the enemy out of the Plei-Trap Valley had become a very costly operation. Units of 1/8 would report four killed, thirteen wounded and two missing for this day.

During the next two days March 13th and 14th, units would regroup and reorganize for the second phase of "Wayne Grey." The first move would be A/3/12 going to LZ Mary. This was to prepare for an assault at YA 829799. This would become LZ Cider. The assault was made the following day without enemy contact. This would be followed by C/3/12, Hq/3/12 and Battery B/6/29 being moved from Polei-Kleng. B/3/12 and D/3/12 would move over land to YA 808856. From there they would continue to YA 821853 to establish LZ D-Handle. This would be a firebase for 4.2-inch mortars.

The Cu Don is a mountain on an extension of the ridge south of Brace. It was a known enemy base area and suspected to be on the withdrawal route of the 66th NVA Regiment. The 3/12th received the mission of establishing blocking positions and interdicting enemy movement throughout the area.

The final move was to airlift the remaining units from the1/35th from LZ Mary to Plei-Mrong. During their operations in this area, they had discovered bridges and one of the largest weapons caches in the central highlands to date. They would establish blocking positions in the south and west to prevent the NVA from escaping and moving toward Pleiku. Once they were in place, those units were returned to the operational control under 2nd Brigade.

During these two days we would fly from sunup to

sunset. During these two days, no U.S. casualties were reported in our area. The best news being that the last missing soldier from A/3/8 had managed to walk into LZ Mary. He had become separated during the withdrawal along the river. He had evaded the enemy and survived the bombardments for ten days. This would close the chapter on A/3/8.

CASUALTY REPORT
March 12, 1969

SP4 Fred J. Bridges Jr.	US67132664	01/09/1948	Age 21
SMAJ James C. Gilbert	RA44041639	06/01/1926	Age 42
SP4 Fred A. Moody	US53527444	08/10/1947	Age 21
SP5 David G. Rankin	US55943931	04/14/1947	Age 21
SP4 Charles J. Revis	RA12809948	02/14/1949	Age 20
SP4 Franklin J/ Runge	RA16609874	07/14/1940	Age 28
CPL Robert E. Shaffer	US55948833	02/18/1950	Age 19
SP4 Sigmond M Sikorski	US52767329	12/04/1946	Age 22
SP4 James A. Franklin	RA12940521	01/27/1947	Age 22

MISSING IN ACTION

SGT Floyd H. Robinson	509466564	01/28/1949	Age 20

Promoted to the rank of SSG E-6 and declared "Died while missing" on 07/05/1975.

CASUALTY REPORT
March 13, 1969

SP4 James P. Fullerton	US56717148	11/06/1949	Age 19
PFC Thomas L. Vendelin	US56834414	07/30/1947	Age 21

CASUALTY REPORT
March 14, 1969

None reported

When I first started my research I was contacted by Tom Lacombe. Tom was a rifleman with B/3/12 during this operation. Tom has looked for many years to find answers about Operation Wayne Grey. Last year, Tom's book, "Light Ruck" (available from Loft Press) was published. The following is his memories of March 11, 1969:

The morning of March 11th was warm and bright. We were preparing for an assault on the next hill over from our position. For right now, we were to sit tight while the B-52s worked the area. I spent this time reading some letters from home.

Charlie Company had sent out an eleven man patrol early that morning. They had encountered an NVA soldier. They followed the fleeing soldier and soon were ambushed. They were pinned down with four dead and several wounded. Our first platoon was sent to reinforce them. A friend of mine walked point on this mission. Within an hour, I heard he had been killed.

My platoon was alerted. We were told to take only ammo and water. We were to secure a landing zone for the dead and wounded. Shortly after we started down the trail we heard shots. First were the sounds of a Russian AK-47. That was answered by an American M-16. We took cover and waited. A few minutes later there was movement coming towards us. Two members of my platoon were carrying our point man. He had been killed in the brief firefight.

We continued towards the ambush site. We arrived within a hundred yards of where our troops were busy cutting a landing zone. My platoon provided security and acted as the rear guard to the landing zone. I could hear the choppers coming in, but I was unable to see them because of the jungle.

150

Enemy fire could be heard in the distance.

As light was fading, we were told that the wounded had been evacuated and we were to move out. Some of the dead had to be carried out. I sat and watched as the other platoons passed. Most looked very tired. We were the last to move up the trail. We had only moved a few hundred yards when a B-40 struck a tree in front of us. I was knocked to the ground with another member of my squad. Several moments passed before I was able to stand. Our squad again moved up the trail when explosions and screams were heard from the rear of the column. Our medic, who had become separated from the column, had two wounded men with him. One could walk if helped. The other had to be carried. We took turns carrying our wounded comrade. By this time we had become separated from the rest of our unit. It was pitch dark and we could hear movement to our flanks.

We slowly moved up the trail. We hoped we were heading in the right direction but not sure of anything. We continued to trade off carrying the wounded soldier. After what seemed like hours we joined up with another platoon that was also moving towards our base location. We finally reached our perimeter.

Tom's full detailed account of this day is part of his book, "Light Ruck." Tom's war was the war of a grunt. His book tells the story of his tour in Vietnam. It will give you the story I am not able to tell.

Greg Rollinger and Jerry Horton were both former members of Company A/1/8. They, along with several other members of that Company, have put together a great web site dedicated to their Company. Jerry is also working on a book about this operation. Being a member of a rifle company, he will be able to tell a much better story than I of what it was like being on the ground. Before the operation in the Plei-Tray Valley was completed, Jerry would be wounded and evacuated out of the field. Thirty years after he was evacuated he was able to locate the pilot who pulled him out. His book should prove to be very interesting.

On March 12, 1968, Greg Rollinger, manning an M-60 machine gun, was with the 2nd squad of the 3rd platoon. The following are some of his memories of that day along the Plei-Tray Road:

> We were on a BDA (bomb damage assessment) on this day. Intelligence reports believed an enemy hospital complex was located in this area. The 4th platoon, which Jerry Horton was part of, was on point. My platoon was second in line. The NVA sprung a three sided ambush on the point element. This was designed to trap them and cut them off from the rest of the Company. We ran forward to support them. This separated us from the rest of the Company. The 4th platoon was pinned down by heavy automatic weapon's fire and B-40 rockets. My squad and one other remained to provide support. The remainder of the platoon rejoined the Company to organize an assault on the bunker complex. The first assault was made but we were unable to reach the 4thplatoon. A second assault was tried and again we were driven back. By this time all of the officers and ranking NCOs were either killed or wounded. Jerry Loucks was in the 3rd squad of the 3rd platoon. He basically saved all of our asses that day. He organized what was left of the Company and moved them forward to relieve the pressure on the 4th platoon so they were able to withdraw. He then over saw the evacuation of our wounded. I can still picture him walking around as if he were bullet

proof telling us where to move and helping with the wounded. Every soldier in our Company owed his life to Jerry that day. Why he didn't receive the Medal of Honor is beyond me.

The following is a story that ran in the Ivy Leaf newspaper on March 30, 1969. It details the ordeal of Sgt. John R. Jones of A/3/8. John was the squad leader who became separated from his unit during the withdrawal on March 4, 1969. He survived ten days alone in the jungle without a weapon.

Ordeal Has a Happy Ending
By Cpt. David R. Fabian

Camp Enari
For ten days and nights, Sergeant John R. Jones, a squad leader with Alpha Company, 3rd Battalion, 8th Infantry, was a man alone.

Separated from his unit, the twenty-year old infantryman from Pike Road, Alabama, mustered all of his cunning and courage to evade a main-body enemy force. Wounded and without a weapon, he successfully out-witted the enemy and overcame the ominous, hostile jungle environment. Without a moment's respite he faced-up to the extraordinary demands that the ironic circumstances of war had imposed upon him.

Harrowing Ordeal
The harrowing ordeal began on March 4 when Sergeant Jones was called upon to lead a twenty-six man patrol toward a hill-top facing opposite the ridgeline where his Company had spent the night.

The afternoon before, his unit exchanged

heavy fire with an enemy force dug in near the crest of the hill. Contact broke by evening and throughout the night lethal US artillery sliced through the thick jungle canopy and onto the enemy positions. Now his patrol was moving stealthily along the vine-entangled jungle floor to assess the situation. "We thought that after the artillery prep fires, the hill-top might be cleared of NVA," Sergeant Jones recounted.

Taken Under Fire

"We had moved about seventy-five meters up the hill when we were taken under heavy fire. Five of us covered the withdrawal of the others. "As the enemy fire increased, I rolled behind a nearby tree. It was during this time that my weapon was destroyed by enemy fire. The NVA blasted it to pieces as they raked the trail with automatic weapons fire," said Sergeant Jones.

Sergeant Jones shouted for the four other members of his patrol to employ fire and maneuver so the five might leap-frog their way back to the perimeter. "It took time, but the maneuver was successful," Sergeant Jones continued. "All five of us got back safely. Along the way I picked up a machine gun and fired up all the available ammo into the enemy positions before I was forced to throw the gun down and catch up with the others."

Enemy Threw Grenades

As the Company began to pull back and call in artillery fires, the enemy soldiers who had been in pursuit of Sergeant Jones and the four others began lobbing grenades inside the perimeter. Dazed temporarily by a wound in his head, Sergeant Jones fell behind the Company. "They must have been about 100 meters ahead of me when I rolled down the side of the hill. I knew I had become separated from my unit, but my only thought was to get away

154

from the NVA, so I just headed over toward another ridgeline that ran parallel to our night location. I had one grenade with me. The NVA were still firing, so when I got over the ridge I hid in the hollow of an old rotten tree."

For the remainder of the day, Jones observed the ridgeline opposite him. He suspected that another American unit might be inserted to reinforce the contact, so he wanted to be ready to attract their attention. At dusk the sergeant inventoried his resources- one grenade, one pocket knife, one Red Cross metal mirror and a plastic battery bag that he later decided to use as a canteen.

Didn't Give Up

US Forces did not return that day or the next, but Sergeant Jones did not abandon hope. During the first five days he roved the ridgeline, never allowing himself to get further than a kilometer away from the point of contact. At night he would ease down the stream at the base of the ridge and fill the battery bag with fresh water. "I practically lived on water alone for the first five days," said the sergeant. "Later I tried eating leaves, but my better judgment warned that I might become sick so I decided I had better quit. The jungle animals were a temptation too. I saw many squirrel-like animals but couldn't catch them. I thought that when I really became desperate I could use my boot laces for a bow string. The arrows would be easy to make."

The patience of the young sergeant paid off during the third day. Overhead, he heard the drone of American gunships. He decided to chance a dash into a nearby clearing to signal the pilot with his mirror. Once in the clearing he jumped down beside a log, lying on his back, and flashing his distress signal skyward toward the sound of the chopper.

Watchful Sniper

"A sniper must have spotted the signal," said Sergeant Jones, "because within a minute I was being fired at. I took off into the heavy wood line." Each night, Sergeant Jones carefully prepared his hideaway. He would always select a different location. Since US artillery was pounding the enemy hilltop, he invariably sought resting places near heavy rocks and boulders that would afford him ample protection from shrapnel. He brushed aside leaves on the ground lest he roll over at night and gave away his position.

"One night- I think it was the fourth- I woke to very loud voices that seemed to be closing in on my position. I prepared to evade. Then I discovered it was a Chieu Hoi broadcast plane flying overhead. I was quite relieved." On the fifth day Sergeant Jones heard voices from the opposite ridge. Shouts of "fire in the hole" carried over to his hideaway, so he knew US Forces were back to blow a landing zone (LZ) and probably make a sweep in search of his body. By the time he has traversed top the parallel ridge, the soldiers had gone. Artillery again rained over the area.

Decided To Move

It was the morning of the sixth day that Sergeant Jones decided to move toward the sound of the nearest US heavy gun that continued to shell the enemy hilltop. "I traveled from first light to dusk. One night I tried to travel by moonlight but it was far too risky. There were too many steep drop-offs and the terrain was too irregular." By the seventh day Sergeant Jones had diagnosed his head wound was light. He was certain it was healing. His confidence grew, and he began navigating by terrain. Still, he knew caution would be the key to his successful return, so he moved slowly but deliberately.

All went well until dawn of the eighth day when an episode with a tiger nearly forced him to give away his position. He awoke in the uneasy presence of the huge cat that stood stone-like approximately 15 meters from his location. "Once I had an experience with one of these cats when I was leading a short range patrol, so this time I reached for my grenade, but I figured the explosion might give away my position. I jumped up, and surprisingly enough, the big cat turned tail and ran. I immediately used my pocket knife to implement a five-foot spear to defend myself against any other wild animals."

The terrain near Landing Zone Mary, 25 kilometers due west of Polei-Kleng began to flatten out and the boom of the gun resounded louder and louder. Exhausted and dirty, Sergeant Jones came upon a stream bank and heard American voices. Peering carefully through the overgrowth he noticed several Americans on the opposite bank providing security while their fellow soldiers were bathing in the water. "I had been through too much to be shot now, so the first word out of my mouth was 'friendly.' They directed me to a shallow spot and I crossed over with their help. When I told them how long I had been in the jungle humping without a weapon they didn't believe me."

Sergeant Jones was then escorted to the landing zone, where a First Sergeant with a Company from the 1st Battalion, 35th Infantry, immediately notified Sergeant Jones' unit that he was alive. The sergeant was given a thorough check-up by the medic. "Aside from losing twenty-five pounds, I was told that I was in good condition. I was fed and given new clothing, but I didn't dress right then. I wanted to swim in the stream.

"A dust-off took me to the 71st Evac for another physical. Later I was able to contact my parents by phone. They couldn't believe I had made my way back. In fact, near the end of our conversation my dad decided to put me to a final test. He asked, "What color is our barn, Son? Charcoal brown, Dad, charcoal brown. Thank God, Son."

Today, Sergeant John R. Jones of the Famous Fighting Fourth Division is back to tell his story. Truly, it is a manifestation of an infantryman's confidence in himself and his will to survive. There is no doubt in Sergeant Jones' mind that he will see that charcoal brown colored barn again.

I talked to John vie e-mail during the time when I was doing my research. He still lives in Pike Road, Alabama. He seems to be doing quite well. He was on the radio the evening that my ship dropped supplies into their location. He told me that some of the supplies fell outside the perimeter that day. I did not know that until he told me. I told him I was sorry we didn't get all of them closer. He said it was okay and he thanked me for being there that day.

Plei Trap 1969

Gator 834 sits on the pad at LZ Swinger during Operation Wayne Grey. The following photographs are from the collections of Bob Kilpatrick, Al Mixer, and the author. Many of these were taken in and around the Kontum and Dak To areas of the Central Highlands of Vietnam.

The left gun well of a UH-1H helicopter. The passenger
seats would be removed during assaults and resupply.
The smaller ammo box would be replaced with a larger
one during Operation Wayne Grey.

The triple-canopy jungle in the Plei-Trap Valley sometimes made it impossible to locate the soldiers on the ground during resupply. Marking enemy positions was also very difficult. Trees would average in heights between one hundred and three hundred feet tall. In the center and to the right of this photo is the red smoke we were looking for that marked the friendly position.

A landing zone created by a "Daisy Cutter". The ten-thousand pound bomb would clear the jungle but would make the ground so hot that the boots of the soldiers would melt if we assaulted the area too soon. At the top of the crater one of our ships is about to land. Many of the landing zones in the Plei-Trap were made by these bombs or heavy artillery bombardment.

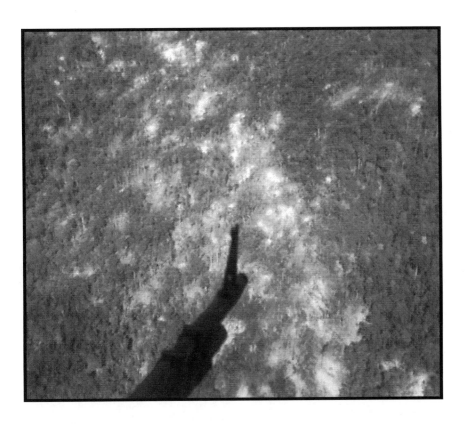

A B-52 strike commonly called an "Arc Light" would destroy miles of the jungle at one time. This is only one strike near a suspected enemy gun emplacement. The area south of LZ Brace received so many strikes that most of that area looked more like the surface of the moon than the jungle.

The infantrymen of the 4th Infantry Division. Called "Grunts" because of the sounds they would make as they moved with their heavy packs on their backs. Regardless if it was a "Hot" landing zone or a firebase, they carried everything they owned plus ammo, food, and water on their backs. These were the men who fought and died during Operation Wayne Grey. The scrub trees in the background are nothing compared to the triple-canopy jungle they would have to "hump" through in the Plei-Trap Valley.

The red mailbag was always secured in the safest place of the ship. It was considered just as important as ammo, food, and water. It was the grunt's only contact with the outside world. Many nights after I returned to Camp Holloway my pockets would be full of letters I had been handed at different firebases during the day. I made sure that each one was put in the mail slot before I turned in.

The command was, "GO, GO, GO!" These grunts un-ass our ship as we hit the landing zone. They will move to protect the landing zone and secure the area. The terrain played a big part in the assault. Tall trees and bomb craters made it difficult to land. Flat areas with elephant grass were sometimes a greater danger. The enemy would booby trap these landing zones with land mines and anti-personnel mines.

The OH-6A was the main Scout ship of the 7/17th
Cavalry units. These small ships that had a two-man
crew would hover above the trees trying to locate enemy
positions. Their big brothers, the Cobras, would circle
above waiting for them to draw fire. Many times these
small ships would land in tight landing zones to evacuate
wounded. Scout duty on a LOH was considered the most
dangerous of all flight duty assignments.

The CH-47 Chinooks, or "Sh--hooks" as we called them were the workhorse for the artillery units. They could move the 155-mm and 105-mm howitzers into the firebases along with ammo to support the infantry. They were also the favorite targets for enemy gunners.

A wounded soldier is helped aboard one of our ships.
Our primary mission was assault and resupply. Many
times we were called upon to evacuate wounded.
Passing out cigarettes or water and a few words of
comfort were all we could do for them.

PFC Gary (Eggy) Eggleston. Assigned as the gunner on Gator 834, Gary flew many hours with Bob Kilpatrick. For his actions on March 4, 1969 during the assault to reinforce A/3/8 he was awarded the Air Medal for Valor.

SP5 Bob Kilpatrick, crew chief of Gator 834. He flew
many hours during Operation Wayne Grey. We spent a
lot of time drinking coffee while the pilots had their
morning briefings. He was a good crew chief and friend.

SP4 Jim Sempek. His nickname was "Ti-Ti" which in Vietnamese means small or tiny. Although he was just over five feet tall, he had the heart of a lion. We were a crew from August 1968 until November. During the assault on the ridgeline at LZ Brace, Jim stood outside his ship trying to shoot the gunner who had run under my ship. If not for his actions that day I might not be here today.

SP4 Jeff Dana wearing "The Bum Trip." Jeff was more
than my gunner. He was a good friend and almost a
brother. We argued about everything and then laughed.
For his actions on March 3, 1969 he would be awarded
the Air Medal for Valor.

Looking to the west from the Resupply area at Polei-Kleng you can see the mountains of the Plei-Trap rising towards the sky. The low clouds meant the Monsoon season was not far away. The daytime temperatures in the eighties and the dust our helicopters created made life miserable for the guys working the Supply area. Enemy gunners shelled Polei-Kleng several times during March 1969.

As the loadmaster watches, another Gator aircraft
approaches the Resupply pad. Food, ammo, and water
were the primary cargo. Passengers would be limited to
three because we would always take supplies into the
firebases with each sortie. The average load weighed
1200 pounds. That would depend on the temperature,
the winds, and the power the engine was producing that
day.

Sitting between two high ridgelines, the Plei-Trap Valley
was actually a series of mountains and valleys that ran
from Polei-Kleng in the east to the Cambodian Border in
the west. The triple-canopy jungle along with its many
rivers and streams made it an excellent place for the
NVA to stage and attack the center of the country.

The typical firebase in the Plei-Trap Valley was established atop some mountain or ridgeline. This is FSB 29 that was located west of Dak To on the northern edge of the Plei-Trap, a place we called the back door. Looking southwest from here you could see Cambodia and looking northwest is Laos. During May and November of 1968 this base's perimeter was attacked and breached. Each time the enemy was repelled, but at a cost of several American lives.

The airstrip at Dak To where the 1st Brigade of the 4th Infantry was stationed during 1967-1968. Many enemy engagements were fought in the ridgelines during this time. The mountains in the background are the northern border of the Plei-Trap Valley. Most of my first tour was spent resupplying and working from this base. This picture was taken as we entered the POL (refueling) area of the base.

Two "fast movers" make a low level pass over the runway at Dak To. Support from the Air Force by F-100s and the Navy's F-4s were common in the Tri-Border area. Almost every type of aircraft saw action in the Central Highlands. B-52s from Thailand and Guam rained bombs in what was called an "Arc-Light."

This Spooky gunship (C-47) was shot down in April 1968 over Laos while supporting Special Forces. The pilot was able to land at Ben Het. The same type of aircraft worked the Plei-Trap during Operation Wayne Grey. An enemy 37mm anti-aircraft weapon was used to down this aircraft. That same type of weapon was used against our helicopters in the Plei-Trap.

The beginning of each day would find us shut down while the pilots were given their morning briefing. Most of the crews would gather at different ships to talk and share a cup of coffee. The friendships and bonds that have lasted a lifetime were started here. This picture was taken at the airstrip at Old Dak To. We were flying support for the Special Forces across the border during this time. The water jug in the picture was something we borrowed from the mess hall. First Sgt. Wyatt had a sense of humor when the Mess Sgt. found out we had it. He let it slide but never forgot about it.

Once the briefing had ended our day would start. Regardless if it was an assault or resupply, each crew was prepared for the up-coming day. This scene would repeat itself every day we flew in the Plei-Trap.

A flight headed into "Harm's Way". Unless it was a
combat assault, most ships worked alone or in pairs. This
reduced the possibility of enemy ground fire. Having
another ship with you while working the Valley gave the
false sense of security that if you went down, at least
there was somebody close by who could pull you out.

This is one of our ships that became a victim to enemy gunners during Operation Wayne Grey. Although heavily damaged, the crew walked away from it. The skills of our pilots and the durability of the aircraft saved many crew members lives. If recovered, many of these aircraft would be sent back to the States and be rebuilt to fly another day.

A pair of Cobra gunships from the 7th of the 17th Cavalry. These fire teams would work with the smaller OH-6A Scout ships to locate and engage enemy positions. Even with so much firepower, they could not match the close support that our Charlie model gunships provided us.

The UH-1C "Charlie model" gunship. Armed with 14
ten-pound rockets and 6,000 rounds of mini-gun ammo
these ships would escort us into the landing zones. Our
brothers in the 3rd platoon were always there to cover our
butts when we got in trouble. Most of their pilots were
once "slick drivers" with the 1st and 2nd platoon.

The day didn't end when the rotor blades stopped turning. The aircraft needed to have its postflight inspection and be made ready for the following day. Many nights would be filled with either guard duty or flare stand-by. The white helmet I wore would sometimes get me in trouble.

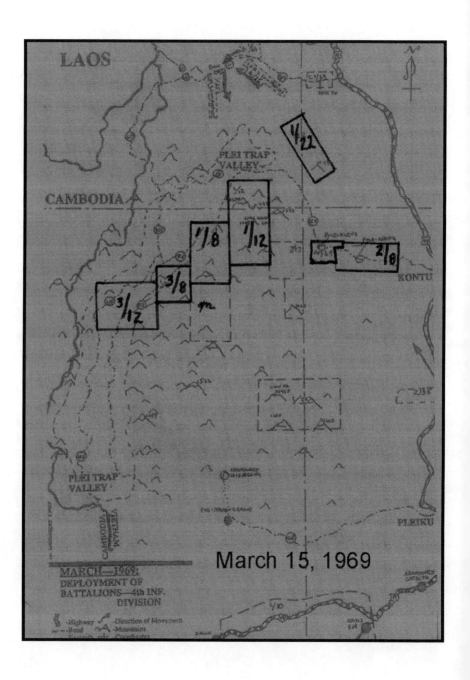

March 15, 1969

Chapter XIII

"PHASE II"

March 15, 1969 would begin the second phase of Operation Wayne Grey. As if a game of chess were being played on this giant squared board, the units of the 1st Brigade were positioned against a worthy opponent. The problem we faced was that many of our pawns had been taken out of the game. The areas of responsibilities would now overlap and we would find ourselves pushed to the limits. On this day we would complete the final stages of deployment before engaging the enemy again.

The Cu Don Mountain south of LZ Brace had been pounded for the past week by B-52s and artillery. It is a known enemy base camp area and possible escape route for the 66th NVA Regiment. During the past two days we have brought troops from the 3rd of the 12th into this area. They were to establish firebases, set up blocking positions, and interdict enemy movement in the area. As we continue the action against the enemy, we are moving farther from our lines of supply and closer to the Cambodian border, where the enemy had stockpiles of weapons and men. They were the only troops left to work this part of the Valley. The remaining units from the 1/35th had been recalled to Dak To and had been airlifted out of Plei-Mrong.

For the first time in several days we are at full strength. After briefing we are split into two flights. The first flight will move engineers and equipment into Brace to finish the construction of that firebase. The other will resupply Swinger and D-Handle. We also have to finish moving Battery B/6/29 into LZ Cider. This will be accomplished between the sorties that the CH-47s are running in order to transport the 105mm howitzers from Polei-Kleng to Cider. We are given D-Handle and their outposts.

The first sorties of the day are mainly base plates and tubes for the "Four-Deuce" 4.2-inch mortars that will be used at D-Handle. The parts are heavy and the first plate that they load on my ship is dropped by the FNGs who are loading the ship. **"HEY! DON'T DROP THAT SON OF A BITCH ON THE FLOOR!"** The grunts jump as I scream at them. I make them pull the damn thing off so I can inspect the floor. Red Fox comes over and starts chewing their asses. These guys don't understand there are control rods under the floor. Break the rods or prevent them from moving properly and the ship is down. Everything is okay but that's the last time any of these guys will drop something on my floor. I calm down and we finish loading and head for D-Handle.

D-Handle is another hill on a ridgeline southwest of LZ Cider. Air strikes and artillery have flattened the trees. The engineers had been working to construct a pad and mortar pits. Everybody is busy with some task. Bunkers are being built and barbed wire is being placed. The look on these grunts' faces tells me that they were expecting food and water not mortar tubes. We unload and take two passengers back to Polei-Kleng. We will take two more sorties of mortar supplies before we load food and water.

The first sortie to the outpost was supplies to reinforce their perimeter. This was manned by B/3/12. Since the move here they had split up TF Swift. Bravo Company was here and Delta was at D-Handle. From here Bravo would send out SRPs (short-range patrols) and RIF the areas around D-Handle. They had cleared a nice, large area for us. After what had happened at the saddle I guess they had learned their lesson. The ride back to Polei-Kleng proved to be interesting.

"FIRE! FIRE! WE HAVE FIRE AT TEN O'CLOCK!" A quad fifty has started blasting at us between D-Handle and Cider. I have thrown smoke and returned fire but Stoney is grabbing sky. We move to the north and circle while we wait for the gunships to arrive. "Keep your eyes on that spot," Stoney advises me. "Don't worry. I have them." The Crocs have arrived. We advise them of where the fire is. As we circle I take my M-79 grenade launcher and pop two rounds toward the enemy. I guess I was close because they returned fire. Now the guns have their position and they start their run. While they are doing their thing, a Cider aircraft from the Air Force arrives. After the Crocs are done the Air Force joins us for some napalm and high explosives.

We refuel and load another sortie. While we are doing this we learn that other ships are taking fire all over the Valley. The area around LZ Cider has become very active. The presence of the CH-47s was the main reason for that. We complete this sortie and are then pulled. The 7/17th needed a chase ship and we are the closest one.

Operating in the area of YB 862997 they have spotted a possible U.S. MIA in a bomb crater. One of their slicks would attempt a rescue but needed back up. The guns had set up and the slick entered the bomb crater. **"FIRE! I HAVE FIRE!"** The NVA had tried to ambush the rescue ship. The guns pounded the area. We pulled back as artillery was called in. While we waited another slick from the 170th AHC relieved us. We returned Polei-Kleng to continue resupply. The MIA who was later reclassified as KIA was part of Tracer 5. Tracer elements were members of Company E/1/8. These small units were assigned to different companies in the brigade as scouts and recon forces. They were highly trained and considered the "Pathfinders" of the 1/8 brigade. On March 12th, Tracer 5 was cut off from A/1/8 during that Company's engagement. Two members of the unit had evaded the enemy and were able to rejoin Company A that evening. Today, two more members would walk into Company A's position unharmed. This would leave one member still MIA. (See page 149, Missing in Action)

The morning passes and we finally shut down for lunch. Since my return from leave, any extra weight I had gained in The World is gone. My clothes are so baggy that two of me would fit inside. After only a few bits of food, most of us obey the soldier's rules: 1. Never stand when you can sit down. 2. Never sit down when you can lie down. 3. Never stay awake when you can sleep. For years after the service I could still take a twenty-minute catnap and feel great. It was our only escape from the reality we faced while we were awake.

Having taken care of D-Handle and the patrol base we were assigned to start moving everything out of Pause and into Brace. This was something that would never make sense to me. We would constantly play musical chairs with these firebases. We would fight like hell to get control of them only to leave two weeks later. Of course, "Sir Charles" would not let us do this without making things interesting.

While we are sitting on the pad, loading the first sortie, the familiar sound of a mortar round exploding gets our attention. "Son of a Bitch!" is Stoney's only response as he pulls pitch and we grab as much sky as we can. We circle looking for the tubes. It's like looking for the famous needle in the haystack. We head for Brace. The same thing happens to the next ship in. Again the tubes are nowhere to be found. Now Blackjack and Cider come on station. They have a plan. They will circle while we land and hopefully they can spot the tubes as they fire. What a great plan this is. I have a better one. How about if we circle and have Blackjack land and draw fire. Of course we won't do that because I guess Blackjack has better eyes than we do.

We land and load another sortie. The bad guys know what is going on. We leave with negative fire. The next ship does the same. We don't find the tubes but at least we aren't receiving fire. The amount we can move is limited because we don't have enough daylight to get the large artillery piece out. This will be completed tomorrow. Again we are pulled to help in the1/8th area.

Because of the depleted numbers in their ranks, a new task force is being created. Company's Alpha and Charlie of the1/8th have been operating in the vicinity of the Plei-Trap road since the beginning of this operation. Delta is moving to FSB 20 and these two units have moved to Hill 467. Map location YB 803034. There they will combine into Task Force Alpha. They will need perimeter supplies and the basics of food, water, and ammo. Starting this in the middle of the afternoon is crazy.

Back at Polei-Kleng, we find out the real reason we are there. Red Fox has some special supplies that need to be delivered and he knows we can do the job. The cargo includes pop, beer, several cans of fruit juices, bananas, apples, and fresh bread. Because Stoney is an infantry officer they all know he has a soft spot for the grunts. They also know that "Snoopy" will get the job done. We load the unauthorized supplies and head for Hill 467.

The area has been cleared and a pad constructed for us to land. Two of Alpha's grunts have accompanied the supplies from Polei-Kleng. Most of this stuff was bought with the grunt's own money or traded for with enemy equipment that the REMFs were interested in. The look on those guys' faces reminds me of Christmas. They are all dirty and dripping wet from sweat. They all look tired as hell but the arrival of this sortie brings them all to life. The added surprise of getting their mail proved too much for some. I saw a few tears of joy as I handed the red mailbags to the CQ runner. They were heavy so I can only guess that they had not received their mail in a long time. Every now and then this job can make you feel good.

The next sortie would contain clean clothes and SP packages. The brass must have felt that those guys needed something to raise their morale. The final sortie of the day was large containers of hot chow. Beef stew with mashed potatoes. If only for one day, these guys would actually feel human again.

The trip back to Holloway found us pretty pleased with ourselves. The day had ended on a happy note, and that's all we could ask for. That night we also received a reward. The mess hall was open and we had hot chow waiting for us.

The units in the southern areas in the Valley were almost ready to start daily patrols and recons. The firebases were manned and ready with LZ Swinger in the middle to provide heavy support. LZ Brace now secured and Hill 947 acting as a patrol base. LZ Cider would now have the 105mm howitzers that could protect all of the areas south and west. LZ D-Handle had their mortars in place, and now patrols would be working the area.

CASUALTY REPORT
March 15, 1969

PFC Bruno Baran	US54833724	03/11/1946	Age 23
CPL Tommy J. Dixon	US53814199	08/10/1947	Age 21

Chapter XIV

"Moving Day"

The routine of the 0600hrs pre-flights has become old hat. As I become accustomed to Mattie as my gunner, I have started to trust him more. That is a big factor when determining a crew. You must trust the people with you with your life. Once you have done that, you can concentrate on your own job. He now takes care of the things that he needs to without me saying a thing. We have a busy day scheduled today.

The first order is to complete the move from Pause to Brace. We will alternate sorties so that the CH-47s can also move the large guns during this time. An uneasy feeling hangs over this place. We know the enemy is still out there and he can hit us at any time. The first sortie is loaded and we head for Brace. While at Brace it started. **"In-Coming! In-Coming!"** The CH-47s had no sooner arrived than the first mortar rounds fell at Pause. We race back to try and spot the tubes. The gunships have come on station and we are all looking for the damn mortars. The perimeter guards at Pause believe that the rounds came from the northwest. We look for possible gun placements. Using my M-79 I fire at likely locations. I'm either not close to them or they know what we are trying to do. Nobody returns our fire.

While two more of our ships move in and out of Pause, we circle with the gunships. The CH-47 returns and bingo, we have them. "I have smoke at nine o'clock," reports Mattie. He has thrown smoke and I have moved to the opposite side of the ship. I get three rounds into the trees before the Crocs start their run. While the Crocs work out, we continue to circle. **"BANG!"** They just got a secondary explosion. That has to be where the tube was. We get another explosion. The next thing we know, the whole jungle has exploded. It must have been an ammo dump. Blackjack is now on station and calling Swinger to get their 155mm howitzers into the picture. We return to Polei-Kleng while the artillery does their thing.

Scout teams from the 7/17th have also been busy this morning. They had sighted two 2 ½-ton trucks and several bunkers near the Plei-Trap road. They have destroyed the trucks and what they believe to be an anti-aircraft gun. The Air Force is now pounding the target. They continue the draw small arms and automatic weapons fire around and near FSB 20 and Hill 467.

After refueling we are back to the move at Pause. As we continue, the rest of the flight works the Valley. D-Handle and the patrol base have activity but nothing that creates any trouble. It seems that the NVA is happy just to spar with us. They will throw a couple of punches; a mortar round here or a rocket there, and enough small arms fire to keep us on our toes, but nothing like the first days. The attacks at Polei-Kleng have ended completely. Nobody has let their down guard. We know that this could change at any time.

Shutting down for lunch, we share large can of chili we have liberated from the mess hall. SP5 Sam Stella is from Hollywood, Florida. His gunner, SP4 Clinton Murphy, is from Atlanta. If you didn't know better you think they were brothers. They talk alike and even look somewhat alike. If you need something for your ship or anything else, Sam is the man to see. He has connections on the coast. Many times he has been the crew chief on the II Corps bird. His latest venture is to complete the transactions needed for our bar. Breaking a claymore mine apart for our fuel to cook, and using an ammo can as our pot, we prepare lunch. We have more than enough to share with Red Fox and his crew. Over lunch Sam and Red start to deal about getting beer for SP packages. The beer we get is shit. It's either Black Label or some garbage from

Korea. Sam has a line on some Coke and Budweiser. As they wheel and deal I shut my eyes and with the help of a full belly I quickly fall asleep.

After lunch we are pulled to extract the reconnaissance platoon from Task Force Alpha's location back to FSB 20. They are in need of reorganization and reinforcing. We head for Hill 467. The first sortie we are greeted as if we were gods. They remember the goods we brought them last night. The first sortie is loaded and we head for FSB 20. A couple of these guys are going on R&R. They ask if we can get them back to Polei-Kleng. I tell them sure, once we get everybody moved to have their radioman call us and we would take them back when we returned to Polei-Kleng. Completing the move, we pick up our passengers and return to Resupply.

The afternoon finds us resupplying the different bases and becoming a taxi service for many of the grunts out in the field. The NVA is not the only enemy in the Valley. The heat and living conditions are also taking their toll. The biggest problems are open wounds or cuts. They become infected very quickly and spread very fast. Getting a shower and a clean dressing normally would do the trick. On the firebases, showers and staying clean are impossible. The brass has decided to take this time to get some of the soldiers with the worst wounds into base so these things could be cared for. Most of the wounds appear to be on their legs and arms. Trying to walk through the jungle is like wrestling with knife blades.

The late afternoon found us hauling mermite cans into the firebases. These contained hot chow. Most of these guys had been eating cold C-rations for the past two weeks. Along with the food we also took clean clothes and SP packages. We were greeted with the same looks of joy that we had seen last night. We finished as the red sky in the west told us another day was done. We headed home tired, but a little pleased with ourselves. Again we had picked up a couple of men from the artillery unit hitching a ride back to Pleiku. Stoney started to get on my butt about flying so many hours. I told him I would take a day off when the ship went into Maintenance. Besides he had flown just as many hours as I had. We argued for a couple of minutes and then made the deal that the next day he took off, I would take off. I knew that would never happen. We were not short of pilots. We were short of crew chiefs.

After postflight, I returned to the barracks to find a black light and cold pop and beer in our new bar. Sempek had his tape recorder playing the "Guess Who" and other songs. I sat in one of the folding chairs that was probably stolen from somewhere and enjoyed a soda. I sat and talked for about an hour. Finally I got up to shower and found something to eat. One day closer to DEROS.

CASUALTY REPORT
March 16, 1969

CPL Albert A Beauchamp	US68023026	09/07/1944	Age 24
MSG Robert G. Daniel	RA14454709	03/21/1935	Age 33
1LT Francis E. Sievers Jr.	05349833	04/20/1942	Age 26
PFC Marlon W. Troxel	US6507939	09/03/1948	Age 20

Chapter XV

"The Plei-Trap Road"

Because our losses had affected the whole Battalion's performance, we start today sharing mission responsibilities with the 170th AHC and the 7/17th Cavalry. Within the next couple of days Troop "A" will be replaced by Troop "C". Our numbers have grown only because replacement aircraft have started to come into the unit. We are now supplying twelve ships for today's mission. Our good luck the past few days has encouraged many of us.

The main focus today is supplying units of the 1/8th with large quantities of explosives so that they can crater and destroy the road network south, north, and east of FSB 20. Task Force Alpha has moved to YB 804034 and established a patrol base. Company A/1/8 has two platoons in the vicinity of YB 794022. They are our first stop.

Contacting them on the radio, we ask for smoke to identify their location. We spot red smoke and they confirm it. Hovering above the trees, we drop sandbags to locate their position. Once we have found them we drop the supplies through the trees. We are the real, live sitting duck as we hover above the trees. We bring two more sorties before they are ready to detonate the explosives. They accomplish their mission and start to move to the next location. While they are moving we start to resupply the patrol base.

The turnaround time between Polei-Kleng and FSB 20 is about fifteen minutes. Now that we are becoming familiar with the area and the different units' locations we are delivering sorties quite easily. Food, water, ammo, and mortar rounds are the majority of our sorties. A few of the passengers are heading for sick call or other assignments. We complete several trips before Alpha calls for another sortie of explosives. They have moved south and are again popping smoke. This time they confirm yellow smoke. Hovering, we drop the sandbags and then the explosives. Two more sorties are delivered before they are ready. Once this is completed they will move east and call us for another load.

Company C/1/8 encountered three NVA to our north. They have engaged but with negative results. They will continue northeast to map location YB 815022. They will set up a company-sized ambush in that area. Bravo and Delta companies have platoon-size ambushes designed to monitor the roads east, south and southwest of FSB 20. Because of all the personnel moving in our area, we are restricted from returning fire. This is one of the little games that the NVA are good at. They would position themselves between an aircraft and a ground unit. They would then fire at the aircraft so the aircraft would return fire towards the friendly ground forces. They are very patient and very good at the waiting game. It has taken us many years to learn his tricks.

The rest of the Valley has been quiet. Some small arms fire near LZ Cider and some possible movement near D-Handle are all that has been reported. Most of the ship-to-ship talk is about the show that is scheduled at the Officer's Club tonight. The morning has gone by very quickly, and most of the ships are headed for Kontum or LZ Mary Lou for lunch. The break away from Polei-Kleng and the chance for hot food and a place to sit down for lunch has helped morale considerably. We hit Mary Lou and get chicken stew and potatoes. The guys at Kontum didn't fare as well. The main course there was liver and onions.

The road between Mary Lou and Polei-Kleng is still a big question mark. The units of the 2/8th continue to patrol and guard convoys going to Polei-Kleng. Their APCs (armored personnel carriers, or "tracks") are constantly on the move. The NVA continue to place mines and try to disrupt the convoys. A pair of our gunships is still pulling convoy cover between Pleiku and Mary Lou. This is the lifeline of this operation. Besides the basics, we are also bringing in large quantities of barbed wire, sandbags and fence posts. These are all the needed items for setting up the perimeters. The increased need for replacements has also increased the volume of traffic to this area. We continue to check any replacements' weapons prior to their getting on the ship. We also continue to ferry troops back and forth so they can get cleaned up and receive medical attention for the increased amount of jungle rot that they have suffered.

After lunch we return to TF Alpha's location with another load of explosives. They again pop red smoke and we locate their position. It's hard to believe there is actually a road below us. As we hover, I search in vain to see anything except trees and the jungle. Once they have accomplished this mission they will be setting up their night location. We will need to resupply them with food and water. We return to Polei-Kleng and resume supplying FSB 20 and the other units in the area.

Again in the late afternoon we start to haul hot chow out to the bases. The brass must figure this is the best way to improve morale and, with rotating men back to base for showers and clean clothes, this will improve the health and will to fight. I don't know about the latter but to see those cans on our ship when we land at the bases, I realize that hot chow is the next best thing to receiving mail. We finish our day as we have done so many times in the past two weeks; we refuel in the twilight and return to Holloway in the dark.

Returning to the barracks, we discover a large pot of soup heating on the hotplate. The guys have liberated bread and cheese from the mess hall and, along with some Spam and peanut butter and jelly, we have sandwiches for tonight's dinner. We sit around and talk about our day. We now have two lists posted behind the bar. One is a wish list for things that we need. The other is things that are needed for trading material. Believe it or not, the first item at the top of the list needed for trading is cases of C-rations. The one thing we have tons of. The next is enemy equipment and weapons. Being an E-5, I was allowed to purchase a bottle of "Jack Daniel's" every month. This was the one thing that I never would give up. At the Air Force Base I could get a C-130 transport with it. This was where I would get the special things that my crew would need. As hard as they tried, my bottle of booze was never thrown into the mix to be traded.

I was able to write a couple of letters. They were just a few lines to let everyone know I was alive and well. I got a shower and finally went to bed about 2300hrs. My body ached and the few hours of sleep never provided the rest I needed. At least it was a bed and a roof over my head. My brothers in the Valley would have given anything for this.

CASUALTY REPORT
March 17, 1969

SSG Benedict M. Davan   RA11426391   02/10/1946   Age 23

Chapter XVI

"The Beginning of Round Two"

For the third time since we started this operation, we are scrambled at 0430hrs. The firebases are receiving 105mm howitzer fire again. Units in both the YA and YB map locations are being ordered out of their night locations to find these guns. We are to resupply them "on the run" as they move through the jungle. By 0530hrs we have completed our pre-flights and other duties and we are headed to the Valley before first light. The early morning air is cold, so we keep the doors closed as we fly north.

The briefing is short and sweet. We are going to D-Handle and the patrol base. Elements of the D/3/12 are already doing a RIF south of D-Handle. We are under restriction to return fire only at positive enemy targets. There are many of our people outside their perimeters and we don't need to get careless. The enemy is good at causing us problems. Nobody will get trigger-happy today.

At Resupply we are loaded with mortar rounds and ammo for the firebase. Things are a little tense at Polei-Kleng this morning. If the bases in the Valley can be shelled by the enemy's howitzers, so can this area. The problem is, where the hell are they? You just can't throw one of these large guns over your shoulder and carry it somewhere. It has to be towed by a truck and driven to wherever it can be fired. There must be another road that we have not found yet. The other question is, how many guns do they have out there?

We arrive at D-Handle and unload the first sortie. We are given the radio frequencies of the units in the field and a general idea of where they are. Three more sorties will be taken to D-Handle before we start to supply the field units. D/3/12 has divided into platoons and is RIF in three directions from D-Handle. One is southwest of the firebase. Another is directly south, and the third is southeast. The area is again triple-canopy jungle and very hilly. Finding them is a chore and, judging from the distance they have covered since this morning, it must be very slow going. Once the smoke is spotted we again hover and drop sandbags to locate their exact position. We are carrying as many as two dozen bags now. This has been the most reliable way to locate the people on the ground.

Task Force Alpha continues to crater the Plei-Trap road. They are also deploying platoon size ambushes and LPs (listening posts) in order to find the enemy howitzers. Because so many units have split up into smaller forces we are forced to resupply twice the number we had been doing prior to today. The aircraft are spread very thin between all these units and of course, something was bound to happen.

A large bunker complex is discovered by C/1/8. It covers an area between YB 779035 to YB 779032. There are approximately 75 bunkers with commo wire running between them. These two-man bunkers are well-camouflaged, but show no sign of recent use. Not to take any chances, three of our ships will help bring troops from FSB 20 to reinforce Charlie Company. As we are about to be pulled, our unit has just stepped into some deep shit.

The third platoon of D/3/12 has become heavily engaged at YA817839. They are working the area southwest of D-Handle. We stand by while the second platoon is told to reinforce them. Because of the terrain we are used as a relay between the unit and the firebase. They have also discovered a bunker complex. This one is occupied and the defenders are willing to fight for it. As the second platoon moves to reinforce the third, they now have made contact with an enemy force. This force has positioned itself between the two US units. During this time we are relieved by Blackjack and are told to refuel and return to this location. At this time artillery and gunships are supporting the people on the ground. We return and now the two platoons have linked and are withdrawing back to D-Handle. They have wounded that need to be evacuated.

As the first of the wounded arrive, we transport them back to Mary Lou. At Mary Lou we unload the wounded and head back to D-Handle. Two more ships have joined us to evacuate the wounded. We must wait as the platoons arrive back with the wounded. Rather than cutting a landing zone they have elected return to D-Handle. The most serious was the first load we took to Mary Lou. The majority of the remaining wounded are not critically injured. Most will be treated and released, but we still evacuate them as a precaution. The last sortie loaded for Mary Lou is the dead. After this load we need to get replacements into D-Handle. This action has caused four US killed, nineteen wounded, and three missing. The enemy losses are confirmed at seven killed.

There is no time for lunch today. We continue as the day goes on to bring replacements and supplies into the firebases. LZ Cider is again receiving small arms fire and many of our ships have taken rounds during the day. We still have to get supplies to all the units that are positioned throughout the Valley. This is taking a lot of extra time because we need to locate them while hovering above the trees. Plus, because the artillery units are pounding the hell out of the areas where the bunkers were located, we must detour to avoid the artillery being sent to "Sir Charles."

During the middle of the afternoon we are pulled to move the recon platoon from FSB 20 back to Task Force Alpha. They have been reorganized and are now ready to rejoin the task force. We will use one of the craters that they have blown in the road as our landing zone. Hovering into the crater I get my first real look at the Plei-Trap road. I'm amazed at the size of this thing. It is almost two lanes wide. The ground is well-packed and it is also slightly raised so rain will drain off to the sides. Being from a rural area, it reminds me of the country roads back home. From the air you would never think this was here. We make two more sorties to complete the move.

We finish up the day going to Cider. As we are leaving, **"THUMP!"** In-Coming! Two mortar rounds land inside the perimeter. Out of the corner of my eye I have spotted the tubes. I have Stoney circle and I send a couple of rounds from my M-79 toward the enemy. **"BANG!"** We get a secondary explosion. We call for the gunships and throw smoke at the target. While we wait, we circle and take turns firing our machine guns and putting grenades on the target. The guns show up and take over. Once the guns finish, the firebases start putting 105mm and 4.2 mortars on the target.

Brigade has four passengers that need to get back to Pleiku tonight. Two are Red Cross girls, better known as Donut Dollies, and their escorts. They were to fly out on a 4th Aviation Battalion ship but they were pulled for some reason. Hovering near the CQ we pick up our passengers. Spent brass is rolling around on the floor and we have bloodstains from the earlier evacuation at D-Handle. We sweep the brass out and offer to put in the seats. The girls say it's all right, so we share our seats in the gun wells and their escorts sit on the floor. We talk as we fly toward Pleiku. It's hard to hear over the sound of the rotor blades but we manage. The basic small talk of what's your name, where you are from, and how much longer before you rotate home. One wants a picture of my helmet, so when we land at the Air Force base I pose near my gun for the picture.

I catch a lot of grief from the guys about my "date."

At least she smelled a lot better than most of the guys I had to haul around today. I have the water truck meet us at our revetment. Besides the postflight inspection, the inside of the ship needs to be washed out. The ship is real close to having its 100-hour inspection. I check with Maintenance and they are going to extend it until tomorrow night. That gives me something to look forward to. The day after tomorrow, I get a day off.

When that night comes, I will line up help to get my gear off the ship. Tonight, Dana has the night off from guard duty so we bullshit for a good two hours before I finally get to sleep. I miss flying with him. I don't blame him, though. If I had less than three weeks before I got out of the Army I wouldn't be flying either. Because of the short night last night and the beers tonight I had no trouble falling asleep.

CASUALTY REPORT
March 18, 1969

PFC Robert L. Barrett Jr.	US56715927	07/25/1947	Age 21
SP4 Dan M. Britt	US53948166	04/18/1948	Age 20
SGT Mark F. Daniels	US54967769	09/29/1946	Age 22
SP4 Larry K. Davis	US56837976	06/05/1948	Age 20
PFC Joe B. Eastern	US67156916	08/23/1948	Age 20
PFC William L. Johnson	US67074705	12/03/1947	Age 21
SP4 Jimmy L. Larsen	US56649610	03/18/1944	Age 25
SP4 Danny R. Mack	RA56838514	03/25/1948	Age 20

Chapter XVII

"More Action to the North"

I have an easier time getting up this morning. Just knowing that I have a day off tomorrow seems to make things better. I get my shower and even eat breakfast this morning. Pre-flight is a snap, and Stoney is already planning his day off. I have the truck lined up for tonight so I can get my gear up to the locker and I won't be stuck half the night. Mattie has gotten the smoke grenades and ammo we need, so we are ready to go.

We arrive at Polei-Kleng and are given to the 1/8th. We are supplying FSB 20. The first sorties will be food and water. We need to hurry because they also need 105mm ammo. The CH-47s will be delivering that, so we have to get our first sorties in or we will have to wait until they are done. We are in and out before they even show up.

We now head back to Resupply for explosives to be delivered to the companies along the Plei-Trap road. First sortie is close to where we dropped off the recon platoon last night. They pop us red smoke and we confirm. Hovering over the trees we drop our sandbags and locate the unit. Before we can deliver another sortie we are held at Polei-Kleng while an "Arc-light" is employed in our area.

Shutting down at Resupply we get a cup of coffee and a short break. Talking to Red Fox we learn that we have about eight artillery sensors that they are going to plant this afternoon. These things look like 105mm artillery rounds that have a plate welded on the flat end and an antenna sticking out the top. The operator drops them out of the ship and they are supposed to stick into the ground and, on impact, the signal device should activate. After watching my sandbags drop and hit branches and spin and flip before they hit the ground I have little faith in these things. The operator has been listening as I express my doubts. He asks that we be used to drop these things, and then I can see close up how they work. After lunch, we have a date.

The air strike started at 0915hrs. We are given the all clear at 1000hrs. Another sortie is loaded for FSB 20, and we are on our way. While we were standing down, one of A/1/8's platoons has become engaged at YB 805053. They have one killed and one wounded. The NVA have used automatic weapons and B-40 rockets. A second platoon is moving to link up with the platoon in contact. We drop our sortie and then remain on stand-by. The two platoons link up at YB 801043. The enemy breaks contact and melts back into the jungle. The two platoons establish a defensive position in order to evacuate the wounded soldier. The dead point man remains in the contact area. A "Dust-Off" is on station to remove the wounded soldier. The gunships have arrived on station, so we return to Polei-Kleng.

While we refuel, we listen to Alpha Company. They are going back to retrieve the KIA. The wounded man was extracted by basket, so we return to Resupply. Heading back to FSB 20 we continue to listen to Alpha. Both platoons are now in contact. They are receiving intense ground fire. The enemy has regrouped near the initial contact and they were employed in a horseshoe-shaped ambush. Alpha pulls back without the KIA. The enemy is determined not to give up this piece of real estate. Our people call for mortars from Task Force Alpha's location. Again we must make a wide swing to avoid the mortars.

No sooner do we arrive than we get the call. A mortar round has exploded in the tube at Task Force Alpha's location. They have twelve wounded. Wasting no time, we head to the landing zone. We arrive before the "Dust-Off." We load six and head for Mary Lou. Most are minor, but we have one with a head wound. A head wound will bleed like crazy and I'm always afraid they will go into shock before we get them to help. I get him to sit up against the bulkhead and have him smoke a cigarette. This slows the bleeding and keeps him awake. We reach Mary Lou and offload the wounded. Another ship has pick up the remaining wounded, so we break for lunch.

As we eat lunch, several people swarm our ship from battalion and brigade to inspect these sensors. Listening as to the theory and development of these devices, I continue to have my doubts. First, we have to drop these things out of the ship and they are supposed to hit the ground point first and drive themselves into the ground. Then, on impact, a signaling device is triggered so they can be monitored at the firebase.

After dropping sandbags out of our ship for almost three weeks, I know what will happen. They will hit a dozen branches as they fall. The trees are 150 to 200 feet tall. How many times will this thing be defected? The ground is not level. Hovering above the trees you can't even see the ground. The area is so varied in features that many times we have to serve as a relay for ground troops to radio the firebases. What makes them think they will even be able to locate the signal if everything does go well?

Four of the sensors are loaded on our ship. I have to dig through my gear to find a splitter so both the dropper and I can be plugged into the intercom. The others are loaded on a 7/17th ship. We have Blackjack and another ship going on this mission. The Cobras from the 7/17th will be our gun support. This entire circus is now complete except for a couple of elephants; the clowns are already flying above us. We circle to the west of FSB 20. The people and their equipment have been delivered to the CP. A Hummingbird leads us to the first drop zone. Hovering above the trees, I search for the ground. I see nothing but darkness.

The order is given, and the first sensor is dropped. I can see and hear this thing crashing through the trees. If it even made it to the ground, it would surprise me. We gain altitude and wait while they try to find the signal. Nothing can be found. After ten minutes we are told to drop the second one. Again we hover, and I watch as the sensor falls to earth. I now estimate they have thrown out the cost of the new Mustang that I want to buy when I get home. Again we circle as the people at the firebase search for the signal. Same results as before.

The second ship now deploys two of its sensors. While this is going on we sit and bite our tongues because of the passenger we are carrying. He is an officer in the Signal Corps, and he is very upset that these devices are not working. After two hours, we have deployed all of the sensors. None of them seem to be working. We drop our passenger off at the Brigade CQ and we continue our resupply.

The area of the bunker complex that D/3/12 had encountered yesterday has been pounded by air strikes all day. A few aircraft have taken fire but no damage has been reported. None of the firebases or patrol bases has received mortar or sniper fire. The lack of action may be related to the heat. Today is very hot with very little wind. The pilots are soaking wet from sweat, and when we are loading a sortie it doesn't take long before the sweat starts dripping from inside my helmet. The NVA are more than likely taking it easy and waiting for night to arrive. Because of the mortar accident at Task Force Alpha's location, A/1/8 was unable to return into the contact area. They established a night perimeter and registered artillery around their position.

We finish the day and are finally released. No passengers are looking for a ride, so we might get back at a decent hour. On the way back I get the logbook filled out and have Stoney radio Operations to let them we are

211

headed in. We are informed to land in front of the hangar. That's great! I can carry my gear right inside the hangar to the platoon locker. I won't need a truck or anything. After shutting down, we unload the ship. The pilots catch a ride back to their barracks, and we carry the gear into the hangar.

I am just about finished when Sgt. Hall arrives. It seems that the second platoon got a replacement ship today. They had been using Gator 108 because they had been short two ships. Now we are getting her back. Abrams is going on R&R in the morning. We are still one crew chief short. They need the ship for tomorrow, so who will be flying tomorrow? TAG! I'm it. I didn't need a day off anyway.

CASUALTY REPORT
March 19, 1969

SSG Harvey C. Avery   RA18577854   2/15/1942   Age 27

Chapter XVIII

"A Day with Gator 108"

I have the CQ runner get me up at 0430hrs. I need to go over 108 before pre-flight. Sometimes a float ship is not taken care of the way it should be. By the time the pilots show up, I have all the compartment doors and half the inspection panels open. Mr. Thornton is the pilot today. Looking through the logbook, he finds a half-dozen things I have written up on the ship. None of these are major, but I feel that a Tech Inspector should look at these defects before we leave. He radios Operations to have Maintenance send a TI to our ship. While we wait, I grease the main rotor and tail rotor and start to close the unneeded inspection panels.

The inspector arrives and we go over what I have found. Two problems were broken safety wires that I replaced. The one thing that concerned me is the amount of play in one of the eyelets of the main rotor control rod. He agrees that it should be replaced. While he completes his inspection, I head for the hangar to get another eyelet.

I talk to the crew leader who will do the inspection on my ship. I am told that the ship will be ready tonight. He will take care of anything that was my responsibility, because I am flying today. By now the rest of the flight had begun leaving and I watched as they moved down the runway. Once back at the ship I replace the broken part. Mr. Thornton starts the engine and we check all the flight controls. He is satisfied with the way it feels so the inspector signs off in the logbook and we are ready. We are forty-five minutes late, but I feel a lot better knowing everything is in proper order.

We have a new peter-pilot today. He has already figured out that he is the fifth wheel in this operation. He has forgotten his grease pencils, so he is unable to write the radio frequencies on the windshield. Mr. Thornton is all over him. I bail him out by loaning him the two spares I have in my flight bag. He is told that they will be returned tonight. He is again told that call signs are black and radio frequencies are red. It will be a long day for Mr. Mathews.

At Polei-Kleng we are given to the 1/8th. The first sortie is headed for Task Force Alpha's patrol base. We have food, water, and a large amount of explosives. I ask Mr. Thornton how much weight he felt comfortable with. Each pilot and each ship are different when it comes to the amount of cargo we haul. He decides that 1200 pounds is a good number, so that's where we would start today. This might change as the day goes on depending on things like the wind, temperature, and where we are going. This would be our starting point and Red Fox would be able to determine the number of sorties that would be needed today.

Thunder has allowed Mr. Mathews to fly the first sortie. Because of his years of experience, Mr. Thornton is the Company's instruction pilot. He is considered the old master. He asks for my help in finding Alpha's position. I show him the way and describe the pad location and condition. At Alpha's location we ask to have them pop smoke to check wind direction. They are not happy with this request because this would give enemy gunners a fix on their location. Mr. Thornton agrees, so he takes the controls and we land at Alpha's location. I tell the guys on the pad we have a new pilot with us and I ask them to place a flag near the pad so we can check wind direction. I explain about the FNG and they laugh. We load empty water cans and three passengers and return to Polei-Kleng. During the return flight, the pilots discuss "what if" situations and get familiar with the area. I hate days like this. It's like being in a classroom and having somebody who keeps asking questions, so the teacher can't finish the lesson. Today we are not a crew. We are four guys who happen to be flying in the same helicopter.

Back at Polei-Kleng we load another sortie. We will return to Alpha's location with this load before we start to resupply the units along the Plei-Trap road. I tell Red that I will need some sandbags and he already has them filled and waiting for us. Mr. Mathews is able to return to Alpha's location and land without a problem. We get a general idea of where the companies are operating today, and on the way back we fly near their locations.

During this time D/3/12 has again attacked the bunker complex on Hill 800, Map location YA 817839. Artillery and the Air Force have been pounding that hill for two days. Some of our ships are on standby as the attack begins. We are to continue resupply but are to monitor the radios in case we are needed.

Near the Plei-Trap road we locate A/1/8. We hover above the trees and drop their supplies to them. They are making a sweep in the area of yesterday's action. They will be cutting a landing zone at this location prior to the operation. They have already started to cut trees in the area. I am able to see the ground and the troops below. Mr. Mathews is a little unnerved at how close the skids are to the tops of the trees. What will he do when we hover down into the landing zone?

After refueling we are now headed for D/1/8. They are doing a RIF to the east of FSB 20. They are to move overland and link up with two platoons from B/1/8. We are now in a restricted fire zone. The winds have picked up, and we can see storm clouds to the west. Hovering near Delta's location, we have a very hard time locating them. The trees are very thick and the smoke they have thrown is being blown everywhere. I have dropped almost all of my sandbags before we locate them. By the time we drop our supplies the storm has arrived. The sky is black and the rain is pouring down. We head back to

Polei-Kleng. My gunner, PFC Thomas, and I move into the cargo area of the ship to keep from being drowned.

We set down on the taxiway near Resupply to wait out the storm. Our ship appears to be bleeding because the rain is washing the red dust from its compartments. It's a fast-moving storm that only lasts thirty minutes. It has turned the entire area into a large mud puddle. We have time for one sortie before lunch. This is an easy one. Food and water are the main supplies for FSB 20, along with their mail. We return with three passengers for Polei-Kleng.

The nice thing about flying with Mr. Thornton is we always get a hot lunch. He loves the food at the Officer's Club at Kontum. While the pilots are there we can grab lunch from the mess hall. The chow at the 57th is the best. The rest of the base has a lot to be desired, but they do excel with their food. We probably eat more meals here than in our own mess hall. Two other crews have joined us. From them we learn that D/3/12 did not take the bunker complex. They did recover two missing in action from March 19th, however. They would pull back to D-Handle and again, artillery and air strikes would be used against Hill 800.

After lunch we return to Resupply. During a run to FSB 20 we learn that A/1/8 is in contact. They have recovered one killed in action from yesterday, but they have wounded and they are pulling back to the landing zone they cut this morning. Again the enemy has used machine guns and B-40 rockets against Alpha Company. We hurry into FSB 20 and drop our load and head for the Plei-Trap road. Reaching the landing zone, we wait for instructions.

The first of the wounded have arrived and we are asked to transport them out. We hover into the zone. The wind is causing us problems because it keeps blowing the trees towards our rotor blades. We work our way down.

Slowly we hover, stopping and turning every now and then so the tail boom can clear the trees. Finally we touch down. We load six passengers and start our way out. I inform the guys that they need to drop a couple of the trees behind the ship to make it easier to get in. It takes us just as long to get out as it did to get in. Clearing the trees I now can start to tend to the wounded. Placing added dressings and passing out cigarettes is about all we can do. We watch for shock and reassure them that all will be okay. Some of these guys don't look good. We arrive at Mary Lou and return to the Valley.

Company C/1/8 has sent two platoons to A/1/8 to help with the wounded. We circle and listen to the radio. The two companies have linked up and the rest of the wounded are being brought to Task Force Alpha's location. We are low on fuel, so we drop into the landing zone and load the two dead soldiers from A/1/8 before we return to Mary Lou. Mr. Mathews is getting a crash course in the Vietnam War today. We have done just about everything possible in one day. Today's action has caused one US killed and eleven wounded. There are four confirmed NVA dead.

As the late afternoon sun moved lower in the western sky we continued to resupply our units. On our last sortie to FSB 20 we heard the call. **"MAYDAY! MAYDAY! MAYDAY! THIS IS GATOR 606! WE ARE HIT AND GOING DOWN!"** Dropping everything, we head towards Gator 606. They had been working the units near LZ Cider. Coming on station, we discover Gator 606 sitting on the pad at LZ Cider. They had just lifted off and received heavy automatic weapon's fire. Mr. Hudkins, as cool as could be, just kicked the pedals and rotated the bird 180 degrees and dropped right back on the pad. The engine was smoking, but everyone was fine.

Unlike the other firebases, Cider only had one pad. We would have to get a ladder from Kontum in order to evacuate the crew. Our ship and Gator 409 are sent to the 57th to get the ladders and a crew to secure the ship. This way it can be picked out of there the first thing in the morning. We race to Kontum because darkness is now our enemy. Installing the ladder and picking up a maintenance crew, we head back to the Valley.

Hovering on the far side of the base, we drop the ladder and the crew climbs down to the firebase. Once on the ground, four passengers who were on Gator 606 climb up the ladder. They need a ride to Polei-Kleng. With them on board, we head for Polei-Kleng while 409 gets the crew from 606 on board. Returning to Cider it is almost dark. We need to circle while they finish rigging the ship. Two other ships and a pair of Crocs keep us company while we wait. Finally, they complete the task and we pick them up.

We arrive at the 57th hangar and remove the ladder and drop off the rigging crew. Gators 409 and 390 have stayed with us. We will make up a flight of three to return to Holloway. On the way home I break out a large can of apple juice. Mr. Mathews admits he needs something stronger. I tell him it's the best I can do. The flight back is quiet. It is almost 2030hrs when we finally arrive. I need to get the postflight done and check on my ship.

By the time I have moved my gear back to my ship and completed the duties for today it is 2300hrs. A sandwich and some fruit will be my dinner tonight. I am too tired to get anything else. To my surprise, I learn we have gotten a new crew chief from Maintenance. He will be taking over 108. That will put us at still one crew chief under strength. The next time my ship is down maybe I will get that day off.

The rest of the spray paint I needed has arrived. Sam must have gotten the last items of his order. I carefully place it in the bottom of my footlocker. I don't know when I'll get a chance to use it, but at least I now have all the colors I need. The rest of the platoon seems to be zombies just like me. Our energy is gone and we are lucky to find our bunks at night to fall asleep. This is the worst I have ever seen it. Hopefully things will get better.

CASUALTY REPORT
March 20, 1969

| PFC Harold B. Johnson | US56839273 | 11/05/1948 | Age 20 |
| SP4 Karl J. Taschek Jr. | US56463034 | 01/22/1950 | Age 19 |

Chapter XIX

"Just Another Day"

Taking my time, I shower and then head for the mess hall. I know everything is fine with the ship, so I've decided to drag my feet a little today. Besides the coffee and fruit, I also have gotten two large cans of fruit cocktail from the mess hall. These are for Red Fox. He has made sure we have gotten cold pop and water so this is just payback. Even though I tried to be late for pre-flight inspection, I'm here five minutes early.

On the way to Polei-Kleng I have to listen to Stoney give me hell about not taking the day off yesterday. As if I had my choice as to which days I would be able to take off. Besides, if I didn't fly, I would end up on some work detail. Doing this is better than burning grass out of the perimeter, or decorating the Company area with rocks. I guess my ideas about what the Army would be, and what it actually was, ended up as two completely different things.

We are again working with the 1/8th. Once we have FSB 20 and Task Force Alpha resupplied, we are rotating troops between those two locations. The main problem today is getting Gator 606 out of LZ Cider. Last night they received mortar and recoilless rifle fire. There was little damage, but the reason for the attack was the ship sitting there. Besides, they need to clear their pad in order to receive resupply this morning.

Red Fox is a little surprised with the fruit cocktail. This will ensure cold pop for this afternoon's break. Besides the normal supplies, we have several passengers headed for our two firebases. Most are replacements, and there are a couple who have returned from R&R. I split the load with three passengers and 600 pounds of cargo. First stop is FSB 20. The ground haze is very thick this morning.

The rain yesterday has added to the humidity on the Valley floor and this is the end result. We had no sooner crossed the first set of hills when we started to receive fire. The NVA are good at games. They know it would be useless for us to throw smoke; all they want to do is screw with us. They can't see us but they sure can hear us. So they load their magazines with all tracer rounds to make sure we can see they are shooting at us. I popped an M-79 round back at them. That's just to let them know we saw them. The new guys are about ready to shit as they watch me playing tag with bad guys below us. I told them it was no big thing, just enjoy the ride. This adds to the myth about door gunners being crazy.

At FSB 20 the CQ hands me their mailbag and we load empty water cans. On the return flight, we again draw fire. This will keep up until the fog lifts. The rest of the ships are reporting the same as us. We see the CH-47 with Gator 606 swinging below it as we return. The grunts will be happy now that the big target has been removed from their base. Three more sorties are flown before the haze starts to lift.

The better part of the morning passes before we are ready to move troops. Company A is being brought back to FSB 20. They will assume security guard duty and get some rest. Company B will be taken to Task Force Alpha's location and then deploy into the areas that Company A was in. We will start at the landing zone near the Plei-Trap road and extract Alpha to FSB 20. Arriving at their location, we discover they have enlarged the zone to twice its original size. We are in and out with no trouble. The turnaround time is only ten minutes. With three ships we complete the move in less than one hour.

The day has actually become somewhat boring as we pick up troops and complete the turnaround between Hill 467 and FSB 20. All of this comes to an end as we complete the last of our sorties. **"MAYDAY, MAYDAY,**

MAYDAY! This is Blackhawk Zero-Niner. We are taking fire and are ejecting at this time!" Blackhawk 09 is a photo-recon bird from the 225th Aviation Company. The OV-1 Mohawk is a two-seat fixed-wing aircraft that was equipped with the Martin-Barker Ejection seat. Their mission this morning was to photograph the areas near the border where suspected enemy gun emplacements might be located. They found a 37mm anti-aircraft position and had paid the price. Cider aircraft had spotted their parachutes and were directing aircraft to their position. At a time like this, every aircraft in the Valley responds to the Mayday. Cobra gunships along with our Crocs provided cover as Dust-Off helicopters and our ships came to assist.

The first to ship to arrive near the downed aircraft is Gator 573. In the early hours of this morning this aircraft had been released from Maintenance. It was still not mission-ready at 0600hrs. As the rest of us had left Holloway, the crew had continued its work on the ship. Because they were late leaving base camp, they had been assigned to the Dak To area to support elements of the 1/35th. The crew was being given a break from the Valley today. This chain of events would alter the fate of the ship and its crew.

They were en-route to FSB 29 with supplies when they heard the Mohawk's Mayday. Realizing they were the closest aircraft, they landed at FSB 29 and pushed the supplies out of the ship and headed to the disabled aircraft. As they neared the area of the Mayday, they spotted the parachute of SP5 Leonard McCauley, the flight observer. He had been wounded and was now landing in a field of tall bamboo. At this time, they were joined by Gator 390, commanded by CWO Thornton. Knowing that their gun support was still fifteen to twenty minutes away, the crew of Gator 573 decided to evacuate the downed crew member while Gator 390 provided cover. Because of the height of the bamboo, Gator 573 was unable to land.

The bamboo would have punctured the bottom of the aircraft just as easily as enemy bullets. As SP5 Paul Schmitz hung outside the aircraft, his gunner SP4 Richard Fosmo held his ankles to form a human chain. Gator 573 hovered down just close enough that SP5 McCauley, the wounded observer, was able to grab hold of the aircraft's skid. He was then pulled into Gator 573 by SP5 Schmitz. Thinking that he was now safe, McCauley had only a few minutes to relax before he would be shot down for the second time in less than thirty minutes.

"MAYDAY, MAYDAY, MAYDAY!! This is Gator 573, we are taking heavy fire and losing power!" These words sickened me. Another one of our ships was in trouble and we needed to get to them now. Racing to the north, we listened to the radio. As Gator 573 had started to gain altitude, an enemy gun emplacement armed with a .50 caliber machine gun had zeroed in on them. The Aircraft Commander, WO1 "Judge" Pruitt, struggled to gain altitude as Gator 573 continued to lose power. The crew chief, SP5 Paul Schmitz was wounded. Gator 390 was flying chase for the disabled bird as they headed towards Ben Het. By this time most of our ships had arrived on station. Gator 573 is unable to reach Ben Het but is able to land in a dry creek bed. Gator 390 evacuates the crew and is now headed for Dak To. SP5 Schmitz has received several wounds in both legs. He will first be taken to the 71st Evacuation Hospital in Pleiku and then later sent back to the States. He will recover from his wounds. For now our crew is safe, but another man still remains on the ground.

Orbiting as the Dust-Off helicopter hovered over the downed pilot, we searched the ground for any movement. The last thing we need right now is Sir Charles bothering the rescue attempt. Captain David B. Peterson, the pilot of the Mohawk, had remained with his ship until SP5 McCauley had ejected. He knew that McCauley was wounded, and he wanted to ensure that his observer's parachute had opened before he himself ejected. These few moments would prove fatal to the young pilot. As he circled, his aircraft was again hit by enemy ground fire. Although seriously wounded, he was still able to eject from the aircraft. The Dust-Off had found him and gotten a hoist cable to the pilot. As he was being pulled up, he fell from the line. The medic now rides the cable down to assist the wounded pilot. After what seemed like hours, which in reality was twenty minutes, the pilot of the downed bird is safe and on his way to Pleiku. We return to the Valley.

This day has become very hot and humid. During the short time we are in Resupply and Refueling the heat has gotten very uncomfortable. The pilots are baking when the ship is not moving. The sun is getting even with us for the rain showers we had yesterday. We will be hauling twice the amount of water this afternoon than normal. Next to ammo, water is the most valuable cargo we haul. By the morning's end the pilots decide that Kontum is the place for lunch. No complaint from the rear of the ship because we know the mess hall will be cooler than the shade of the tail boom.

After lunch we return to Resupply. Red Fox explains to us that a soldier in B/1/8, which we just moved to Task Force Alpha's location, needs to be picked up. A chaplain and an officer are waiting to go with us. His father has died and he is going on emergency leave. We hover into the zone and the two passengers talk to him before they get on the ship. He has not been told until now what has happened. After a few minutes they are able to get him on the ship. We hover out of the zone and start for Polei-Kleng. At this time we are told to return them to Hensel Field at the 4th Infantry Base Camp.

It's a forty-minute flight from Polei-Kleng to Hensel Airfield. I try not to listen as the two officers talk to the soldier. To be in this hell, and then to have this happen, would be too much to endure. We try not to talk as we head toward Pleiku. This is the first time in a long time that we have seen the road on the return trip. At Hensel a jeep is waiting for our three passengers. We then return to Polei-Kleng.

The flight back is like playing hooky. I enjoy the ride and the warm breeze feels good. I almost doze off, I'm so relaxed, but I jerk myself awake and drink some warm Kool-Aid from my canteen. I have changed the radio to AFVN and enjoy some music. Normally I listen to ship to ship chatter, or the grunt radio stations, or a combination of the two. My hour-and-a-half vacation from reality ends as we enter the Resupply area. It is time for us to go back to work.

First sortie is back to the Plei-Trap road with explosives and water. While we are there one of C/1/8's platoons has made contact. We stand by until we learn if we are needed. They have killed two and have no casualties of their own. We continue with resupply. As the afternoon grew later, several reports of fire were received around Task Force Alpha's location. Most had been just small arms but this was the first time in many days that the enemy has fired at us near one of our bases.

The convoys coming into Polei-Kleng that are the life-line to the units in the Valley are starting to catch hell from our determined enemy. Today's convoy received enemy small arms and B-40 rocket fire along the entire route from Mary Lou to Polei-Kleng. Several trucks were damaged and two US soldiers were wounded.

The Valley is starting to show signs of life as the day ends. The bases are not bothered, but the aircraft are starting to draw more fire than usual. The NVA are up to something; nothing they do is done at random. We finish our resupply and are released at 1800hrs. The few extra hours I will enjoy tonight may be enough time to write home and just relax. I need a day off. Our day ends on the down side as we learn that the pilot of the downed Mohawk died before reaching the hospital.

CASUALTY REPORT
March 21, 1969

SP4 Robert S. Davis	RA18846956	08/09/1949	Age 19
CPL Mickey W. Hill	US53532363	12/15/1948	Age 20
CPT. David B. Peterson	OF114638	03/30/1946	Age 22
SP4 Stephen L. Weigt	RA18912735	10/14/1947	Age 21
SGT John J. Valero	RA56834206	07/23/1947	Age 21

Chapter XX

"New Blood"

With the arrival of Troop C 7/17th we are being reassigned to the northern area of the Valley. We are primary support for the 1st of the 8th. Because of the past few days, I am very familiar with the area and the change will do us good. We will also continue to resupply LZ Swinger as one of our duties. The turnaround times between these places and Polei-Kleng are far shorter than what we are used to. Today, the new pilot from two days ago has joined Stoney and Mattie in our crew. Mr. Mathews is learning fast, which is good. The last thing we need is a "Dead Head" flying right seat.

Our first sortie is for FSB 20. Company A has patrols and ambushes to the north and east of the base. Company B continues to work the Plei-Trap road, building roadblocks and cratering the road. Company C is working the areas north of Task Force Alpha and Company D is east of that location. Because of the number of people outside our bases, we are restricted to return fire at only confirmed targets. This game of "Hide and Seek" that we have been playing for the past three weeks is really starting to get old.

Food, water, and ammo are again the main items we haul this morning. The number of new guys waiting around the Supply area is very noticeable. Most will have to wait until their units have cut landing zones so we can get them in. That won't happen until this afternoon, when they reach their night locations. Their first day, and we drop them in about two hours before dark. That would be a big kick in the ass. The number of places that need to be resupplied has grown to the point where it is almost impossible for us to accomplish our mission. Lack of sleep and the many hours spent in the air has taken its toll on all of the crews. But as we enter our fourth week, we continue to do our jobs.

Before we even start to load our first sortie of the day we are placed on hold because D/3/12 has attacked Hill 800. Heavy air and artillery strikes have pounded the hill for two days. We stand by our ships, waiting for some word about what is going on. Two ships from the 170th Assault Helicopter Company are to help us in the northern A/O but at this point anything can happen. After two hours we are released to start resupplying our units. D/3/12 has seized the hill without opposition. The last MIA from March 18th has been recovered and they have no casualties. We start the day two hours behind schedule.

We are partnered with Gator 834. Because of the rains and high humidity we are only carrying one thousand pounds of cargo. Being two hundred pounds lighter will help the pilots handle the ship better while hovering above the trees, but the lost weight on each sortie will add up by the end of the day to where we might not be able to deliver all the supplies that are needed. Our first stop is Bravo's location. They are still patrolling the Plei-Trap road and continue to crater and destroy the road. The winds from the west have picked up and, combined with the heat rising through the trees, we have a very hard time hovering while we try to locate Bravo.

Stoney's patience is running thin as the guys on the ground direct us towards their location. The ship is like a bucking bronco. The winds keep pushing us from side to side. The heat from the jungle floor creates updrafts that push us toward the sky. We drop three sandbags before we are able to find our target. By the time we depart, all of us are a little the worse for wear. We need a better way to locate the people on the ground. The jungle is so thick that it is impossible to shoot a signal flare. They just bounce off tree limbs before they can clear the top of the trees. The smoke grenades are somewhat useless because the smoke drifts so far by the time it filters through trees, it does more harm than good.

As we return to Polei-Kleng we are informed that Scout ships from A/7/17th and C/7/17th would help us locate the units on the ground. The brass has decided that all of the supplies needed to be delivered before dark. The Hummingbirds would locate the units while we returned to their location. Hovering above the units would speed up the resupply but expose these smaller ships to enemy gunners. Of course their big brothers the Cobra gunships were just a phone call away. Orbiting high above, they were ready to blast any hostile fire below.

Returning to Bravo's location, we deliver our second sorties. Gator 834 had been supplying Delta's location with a Hummingbird's help. During this time Charlie Company is moving toward YB 812022 and has made contact with an unknown size enemy force. A brief firefight ends with one NVA killed and one US wounded. They deploy an ambush at YB 796026 and move the wounded GI back to Task Force Alpha's location. Because we were returning with Charlie's supplies, we are asked to drop the supplies at TF Alpha and pick up their wounded soldier. We offload the cargo and pick up the wounded and head for LZ Mary Lou without incident.

"RECEIVING FIRE! RECEIVING FIRE!" Gator 834 was heading into Task Force Alpha when all hell decided to break loose. Just as they came to a hover they were hit from all sides by heavy automatic weapons fire and anti-aircraft fire. Pulling pitch to grab as much sky as they could, the crew pushed as much of the cargo out as they could so the ship would climb faster. Once they were out of this deadly crossfire they called for help as they headed for Polei-Kleng. They still have power and the gauges are all in the green. The ship is vibrating but seems to be flying quite well. We monitor the radio as we race for Mary Lou. Chase ships follow Gator 834 to Polei-Kleng and we breathe a little easier when we hear they have landed safely. After we drop off our wounded soldier we return to Polei-Kleng.

Landing near Gator 834 we walk over to talk to the crew. Bon-Bon is sitting inside the cargo area smoking a cigarette. The peter pilot, Mr. Trebby, is on top of the ship with the crew chief and gunner. Bob Kilpatrick and Gary Eggleston were inspecting the main rotor blades. Each blade had three or four holes in them. There was some sheet metal damage to the tail boom but none of the flight controls had been damaged. The decision was made to fly her back to Holloway for repairs. We helped the crew close up the inspection panels that we had opened and they departed for home.

Cobra gunships from C/7/17th and our own Croc gunships had been working the area around Task Force Alpha since Gator 834 caught hell. They also received heavy fire. At this point Cider aircraft called for air strikes. We were advised to load supplies and stand by until the air strikes were completed and the gunships had rearmed and refueled. They will escort us into Alpha's location. While we waited, Mattie and I checked our guns and test fired them to ensure they were working properly. If we needed them, we wanted to be sure that they worked. Sitting at Resupply we learn that a convoy is being ambushed near Plei-Mrong. Cobra gunships and our own Croc ships are flying support for the unit in contact. We are told to stand by in case we are needed. We sit and listen to the radio as the battle continues near that single lane dirt road where we had started this operation twenty-two days ago.

A convoy of fifteen trucks, escorted by four APCs (armored personnel carriers) from Company B/2/8th, had left LZ Mary Lou late this morning. Their final destination was LZ Bobbie located northwest of Plei-Mrong. Arriving shortly after 1400hrs at Plei-Mrong, the convoy continued northwest to LZ Bobbie. Approximately two kilometers northwest of Plei-Mrong, the convoy is ambushed from the west side of the road with heavy automatic weapons fire and B-40 rockets. Two of the armored personnel carriers are hit by B-40 rockets and are burning. Artillery and gunships are called. The enemy strength is estimated to be at least company-sized or better. At least two are wounded and one of the supply trucks has been hit. The gunships arrive on station and artillery is starting to deploy on the enemy.

After a forty minute wait we are released to complete the remaining resupply for our units. Flying as low and as close to the trees as possible, we race towards the patrol base with their much-needed supplies. Dropping like a rock onto the pad, we pushed the supplies out of the door, pulled empty water jugs and three passengers aboard, and departed just as fast. By the time the enemy gunners realized we were there, we were gone. We made three more trips into Alpha's location in the same manner. Each time we received fire as we climbed out of range. With those sorties completed we helped deliver artillery rounds to Swinger. One of the 170th ships that were helping us developed engine problems caused by the amount of dirt that had been sucked into the intake filters. He was having trouble maintaining power in a hover, so he also returned to Holloway. We continued to deliver supplies until the last light of the sun disappeared in the west.

During the flight home we learn that two aircraft were lost while trying to evacuate wounded from the ambushed convoy. Blackjack 400 from the 4th Aviation Battalion, and Bikini 69 from the 170th Assault Helicopter Company, were destroyed. Eight air crew members were wounded. One would die from his wounds the following day. The units involved with the convoy suffered ten killed and eighteen wounded. We have to make a detour around this area because artillery continues to pound suspected enemy targets.

Working by the light of my flashlight, I completed another postflight in the dark. Walking back to the barracks in the dark had become second nature to me. My feet could find their way home without any help from my head. My eyes just stared at the red tip of my cigarette as I tried to erase another day in the Valley. Eating and reading mail no longer mattered. Just let me shut my eyes so I could sleep. Maybe when I woke up I would find this only to be a bad dream.

CASUALTY REPORT
March 22, 1969

SP4 Richard W. Anderson	US56934363	07/12/1947	Age 21
SP4 Roscoe W. Ball Jr.	US67009526	11/29/1949	Age 19
SFC Armin J. Blake	RA17379020	09/19/1934	Age 34
SP4 John R. Brandborg	US56505726	09/27/1945	Age 23
SP4 Harvey G. Enz	US56504753	03/12/1948	Age 21
SP4 Michael E. Hermsen	US56459275	12/12/1946	Age 22
SP4 James A. McKechnie	US51600439	04/16/1947	Age 21
PFC Lauvi P. P. Peters	RA18865629	04/07/1949	Age 19
SP4 Angel Reyes	US67052618	02/25/1945	Age 24
SP4 Clyde S. Sweatt	US67087872	04/22/1946	Age 22

Chapter XXI

"Checkmate"

This day begins with some good news for a change. I learn that Sgt. Hall is being transferred to battalion at the end of the month. Sgt. Tuminello will take over the platoon for the time being. I am the ranking E-5 in the platoon, so most of the guys already have me become Assistant Platoon Sergeant. But I don't think I could work with Tuminello, and becoming a "Buck Sergeant" really doesn't impress me that much. Besides, my job is flying, not sitting around base camp waiting for the ships to return. Stoney gives me a little speech on why I should think about it during pre-flight. He is also getting "short" and may only fly a few more weeks, so losing me as his crew chief would give him a reason to pull some of the safer duties before he has to leave. I start to think about different things as we hover towards the runway. It might be safer but I still love to fly, and I'm not ready to give that up.

Gator 834 is still down after yesterday's contact. Our Company has eight ships mission-ready and we have two from the 170th AHC on loan. We are divided into two flights. We will again be supplying the units in the YB area. Charlie Company is still at TF Alpha's location. Bravo is working the Plei-Trap road west of that location, and Delta is to the east. Last night, artillery was employed against possible truck movement near Bravo's night perimeter. Results from the air strikes around TF Alpha yesterday have proved to be negative at this time. Things have been quiet, but we also have not given the enemy any targets to fire at. The Hummingbirds will again help us locate the ground units. Their big brothers will be there close by if we need them. Our first sortie is for FSB 20.

The supply area is very busy today. Several

replacements have arrived for deployment to different companies in the Valley. We will fit them in between the food and ammo cases we are delivering. Today is a little cooler, so we start the day with eleven-hundred pounds of cargo. If the bad guys leave us alone, we might increase it to twelve-hundred by the end of the day. First load is food, water, and the mail. We head for FSB 20. Passing to the east of Alpha's location, we can see where the air strikes had hit yesterday. The entire Valley becomes more scarred with each passing day.

At FSB 20 we are informed that they have received two rounds of incoming mortar fire already this morning. We plan to land quickly and unload as fast as possible. No reason to give those gunners any targets if we don't have to. Hitting the pad, we push the cargo out the door and I hand the mail bag to the NCOIC on the pad. His crew throws empty water cans on board, two passengers climb in, and we are out of there. Banking right, we hear and see a large explosion near the firebase's north perimeter. A White Phosphorus shell, "Willie Peter," from a 105mm howitzer has landed there. We grab for the sky as we search for the gun. That damn thing could be as far as five miles away. No sooner has the gunships moved towards our location, then the supply ship at TF Alpha's location start receiving fire. Sir Charles is very good at this game. He dumps a couple of small rounds as spotters into FSB 20 and then waits for the first ships to start landing. Then he throws a big shell in to pull the gun cover away from a weaker base, so he can start blasting away at the supply helicopters. This will make for a long day.

Back at Polei-Kleng we load up for the next sortie into FSB 20. Everything is placed next to the doors. The replacements are put in the middle of the ship. They are told that when we hit the ground, they are to push the stuff out the doors, follow it out, and then stay low so we can get out as fast as possible. While we were gone they had received one round of high explosive. This round also fell outside the perimeter. The bad guys still didn't have the range, but they were getting close. Racing in at treetop level so not to give the enemy a target, we drop onto the pad, dump our load, and beat feet out of there. The remainder of the morning we would play this cat-and-mouse game, while Cider and Headhunter aircraft would look for the enemy artillery pieces. Because artillery support from Ben Het was being employed we had to make detours to the south and west to avoid their fire. This increased the turnaround time, so again we started to fall behind. By noon we had a pretty good idea of what was going on. The NVA would fire a couple of rounds towards FSB 20 and then move the gun to another position. This would keep the gunships busy so the people around Task Force Alpha could zero in on the supply ships trying to work that location. It was working because none of the units outside of Alpha's perimeter had received supplies today. That would be our job later this afternoon.

After lunch we directed our efforts towards LZ Swinger. They have received sniper fire today, but nothing big. Listening to the radios we learn that one of Bravo's platoons has made contact approximately 350 meters west of Task Force Alpha. Mortars from Alpha's location are employed in support and later a Spooky gunship is also used. As this is happening, Delta has encountered another enemy force as they moved to their night location. These fights last about a half hour. Delta has killed one enemy soldier and they have no casualties. Bravo isn't as lucky. They have killed four but they have suffered one killed and eight wounded. The wounded and dead are being brought back to Alpha's location. Two of our ships are dispatched to pick up these men.

To the south, in the area around LZ D-Handle, light contact has been made by all companies of the 3/12th. Most of the ships that are working that area have received fire at one time or another today. FSB 20 would receive seven rounds of white phosphorus and twenty rounds of high explosive today. Artillery and air strikes worked the suspected areas most of the day with unknown results. B-52 bombers would hit the areas southwest of Task Force Alpha during the night. Our day would end in the darkness as so many days before had.

I return to the barracks to find everyone milling around the bar talking and drinking beer. The first thing I hear is that we are getting a new platoon sergeant, and Tuminello would stay an assistant. Next I'm told that Tuminello is the platoon sergeant, and one of the crew chiefs from Second Flight would be his assistant. The one thing that the Army is good for is rumor upon rumor. At this point I don't even care. Making my way to my bunk, I find two letters. I pull out a tin of crackers from my locker before I open the first letter. Halfway through the letter, I fall asleep.

CASUALTY REPORT
March 23, 1969

| SP4 Larry J. Conklin | US52969184 | 11/11/1947 | Age 21 |
| SP4 Alley O. Stephens | RA54823116 | 10/29/1945 | Age 23 |

Chapter XXII

"March Madness"

This morning's surprise was not one I was ready for. It seems that Stoney has been grounded for the next two days. He is reaching the maximum number of hours that a pilot can fly in one month, so he will be sitting out the next couple of days. It's not a bad trade because for the next two days Mr. Hudkins will be our A/C.

Mr. James Hudkins was a career soldier prior to becoming a pilot. By career soldier, I don't mean a "Lifer". He is the real deal. His first tour of duty in Vietnam was with the Special Forces. After that he re-enlisted to become a helicopter pilot because he believed that this is where he could do the most good. He is a great pilot and afraid of nothing. He respects the enlisted crew members and treats us good. The only problem is that he will go into some really bad places that might not be any good for our health. I would fly with him into the barrel of a cannon. His call-sign is "Hud".

After yesterday, we will treat every sortie as if it were the last one we will be able to deliver today. We make sure the most important items will go in first. These include food, water, and ammo. We are not hauling any passengers in or out unless they are wounded. FSB 20 seems to be the biggest problem. Enemy gunners have the base zeroed in and are throwing shells in at will. The brass seems to think there is more than one artillery piece in that area. Good call, stupid! We have not been able to locate these guns, and the fact that they are probably moving them from one place to another is the reason we haven't destroyed them. The boys who sit in the rear have truly underestimated the enemy's strength and his ability to move in this Valley. Plus, if you add in the fact that most of the companies that started this operation were understrength, and our ability to resupply them as they moved through the jungles was very limited, no wonder things are working out the way they are.

Bravo Company is moving toward the southwest of Task Force Alpha today. An Arc Light strike was employed 3000 meters southwest of Alpha's location last night. They will continue to destroy the Plei-Trap road and do RIF in that area. This will be one of our first stops today. Because of what has been going on we were unable to resupply this unit yesterday. The Hummingbirds will again help us find the ground units. While they are doing this, their gunships will be doing bomb damage assessment recons in the area of last night's Arc light. Leaving Polei-Kleng with the first of today's sorties, we contact our Hummingbird.

We spot the Hummingbird at Bravo's location. He talks us in towards the unit and we drop sandbags to confirm exactly where they are. Dropping the first load, we head back to Polei-Kleng. Listening to the radio we learn that both FSB 20 and Hill 467 are again taking incoming. Alpha's location has received small arms fire and a few mortar rounds. Picking up the second sortie for Bravo, we again head for the Valley. **"FIRE! I HAVE FIRE!"** shouts Mattie as we hover near Bravo's location. The bad guys can't see us but they do hear us. Tracers rise out of the jungle in our general direction. We drop this sortie and then barrel out of there in the opposite direction from which we came. The Hummingbird has spotted the location of the fire and starts calling for the gunships to lend a hand.

Bravo has also started to move towards the sound of the gun fire. For now, the mission of destroying the road will have to wait. This contact might lead them to the 105mm howitzers that have been shelling FSB 20. This has become to primary mission of all units on recon. The last of their supplies will have to wait because they are now on the move. We start to bring Delta's supplies to their location. We must find them on our own because the Hummingbirds are scouting for Bravo. They are east of Alpha and following a small stream that runs from the northeast to the southwest. This is one of the main reasons why the NVA are here. They can hide in the heavy jungle and there is lots of good water running through here. The stream is hard to find from the air. The trees grow over everything, and in the case of the stream, it is hidden from above. Only the wider rivers can be seen from the air. The enemy stays away from these, so they won't be spotted. These small streams are where units of NVA will be stationed. We spend almost twenty minutes before we find Delta. While we were delivering this sortie Task Force Alpha comes under attack. Mortars and rockets, along with small arms fire, hit the base.

We circle to the east as the attack ends. They have casualties and are requesting a "Dust-Off" to their location. Dust-Off Three-three is in en-route and we are to act as chase ship in case something happens. They receive heavy fire as they approach Alpha's location and they abort their landing. Mr. Hudkins gets on the radio and informs Alpha to get ready as we are on our way in. Racing at treetop level we drop onto their pad and load four badly-wounded men. We inform Dust-Off that we are headed for Mary Lou and to have assistance waiting for us. I wrap my flight jacket around one of the wounded who has a large back wound. He has no shirt on and the cold air is blowing right on him. I think he might be going into shock, so I sit him up and give him a cigarette. At LZ Mary Lou we have eight people waiting for us. Two of the wounded are rushed into the field hospital at the base. Two medics work immediately to stabilize my guy with the back wound. I grab my jacket as they take him away. We need to refuel before returning to the Valley. Landing at Kontum, we refuel and the pilots take turns getting out of the ship to stretch.

I can't say anything bad about the Dust-Off crews, but sometimes I doubt their pilot's skills at getting into some of our landing zones. I just don't think they had the ability to race into these places and drop on the pads the way our pilots did. Our job was to assault and resupply the guys on the ground. We also made it a point to pull out the wounded if the need arose. The only problem was we only had small first-aid kits, and no real training to deal with the wounded. All we could do was hope to keep them alive until we got them to a place that could help them. This day we would make it a habit of getting the wounded out of places like this.

Task Force Alpha would be attacked several times during the afternoon. Ships from our unit would pull wounded out on three different times today. One ship, "Gator 409", would receive heavy fire and return to Camp Holloway for repairs. The skies in our A/O were very crowded this day. Air strikes were being called in on suspected enemy positions. The 7/17th spotted an NVA near Bravo's location as they were encountering light contact. One US soldier was slightly wounded from friendly fire. He was moved to Alpha's location and evacuated by our ships. Delta Company killed one NVA as they patrolled along the stream to the east.

The NVA were again planning some type of move along the Plei-Trap road. These attacks were designed to keep our troops in one place, so the NVA could move or hide their equipment. The afternoon was spent resupplying all the bases as best we could. Flying in at low level, dropping our cargo while trying to dodge enemy mortar and rocket fire, was really taking its toll on all of us. By day's end, four of our ships would be damaged by enemy gunners. The last sorties of the day would be getting the new replacements into their Company's locations. The number of wounded had depleted all of the brigade's units. Most were operating with less than one hundred men. Platoons were one-half their normal strength and they needed to be reinforced. The artillery units were also in need of replacements. Company C/1-92 Arty (GS) at LZ Swinger was in need of six replacements for their 155mm howitzer crews. Swinger had received enemy fire the entire time since it was established on the first day. This would be our last sortie of the day. Dropping off these passengers and grabbing the base's mail bag for the return trip, our day was over.

I listened to the radio as we headed for home. The music from AFVN out of Saigon made me that much more homesick. Most of my friends would be hearing these same songs as they were cruising around in their cars and going on dates. Here I was stuck in this God-awful place, and for what? At this point I started to doubt the reasons we were here. Maybe I was just so worn out that none of this made any sense. Tomorrow would be better. It sure couldn't get any worse.

CASUALTY REPORT
March 24, 1969

SGT Raymond F. Eade	RA56833834	08/15/1947	Age 21
SP4 Phillip H. Fleming	RA12980046	09/09/1949	Age 19
SGT Arthur J. McIntyre	US51728510	01/26/1947	Age 22
SGT Minor W. Pattillo	US53366323	05/28/1939	Age 29
CPL Benjamin R. Turiano	US52762123	11/10/1943	Age 25
SGT Michael Valunas	RA11862743	06/02/1948	Age 20
SP4 Gary L. Weekley	US51839410	08/15/1948	Age 20

Chapter XXIII

"Replacements and Build-Up"

Our day hasn't even started and our gunships are already being called upon for support at Task Force Alpha. Between 0630 and 0700hrs a LP on the west side of their perimeter spotted three NVA soldiers. They called for mortars in that area. A recon squad was then sent into the area and came under fire. The point man was wounded. The squad tried several times to reach the wounded man, but was unable to recover him. They withdrew back to the perimeter, and a reaction force was formed to recover the WIA. Twenty-five meters outside the perimeter, this unit came under fire. The reaction unit had to withdraw because of wounded and heavy enemy fire. They were able to reach the perimeter with their wounded. Another unit was formed and headed into the contact area. This time they were able to recover the wounded soldier and returned to Alpha's location.

The gunships waited on station until all of our troops were clear of the contact area. The NVA have learned to keep as close to the American units as possible while in contact. This renders our air and artillery support useless. The fear of inflecting casualties on our own troops limits the use of this deadly power. Now they are free to work the area. While they keep the enemy busy, our ships were going in for the wounded. Thirteen have been wounded and one killed. Small arms fire is intense around the area. The gunships have received fire from all directions during their runs. Once they have completed their mission and returned to Polei-Kleng the Air Force is brought in. For the next hour, propeller-driven A-1E "Skyraiders" and F-100 and F-4 jets would pound the areas around Task Force Alpha.

Having evacuated the wounded, we start our day

resupply of our units. We are assigned to take replacements into all of the unit's locations. The brass is planning another move but, before we are able to do this, the understrength units need replacements. Our first stop will be FSB 20. Company A/1/8, which has been providing security at that location, is to move out to YB 855074. They are to set up platoon-sized ambushes and establish an outpost for FSB 27. Some of the new guys will start their tour as guards at a firebase that has been receiving enemy artillery fire for the past ten days. The others will be thrown right into the enemy's backyard. I explain everything we will do to get them into the base. This does nothing to prepare them for what actually happens as we race into FSB 20. We complete four sorties to their location. Twenty new souls are delivered to this place called the Valley.

Our next sorties are slated for Company D/1/8. They are moving from their night location towards Task Force Alpha. We will deliver the replacements there and they will also get refitted and supplied before moving out in the morning. The area around Alpha is still hot. They continue to receive small arms and mortar fire. We again race into that location as we had done the day before. Banking to the north as we depart, I can see the smoke still rising from the air strikes employed this morning. Between the 500-lb bombs and the napalm, that part of the jungle will remain a clearing for the next thirty years. The morning passes without incident. Most of the replacements have been delivered to their units. We completed our last sortie just in time for Bravo to "step in it."

Bravo had left their night location at YB 797023 to continue to crater the Plei-Trap road. Shortly after noon, they made contact with a squad size element of NVA soldiers. After thirty minutes contact was broken and they called for artillery support. We had started bringing supplies into Alpha's location, but remained on the radio in case we were needed. Most of our aircraft were reporting they were receiving small arms fire at all locations. The areas west, south, and east of Alpha's perimeter have become "free-fire" zones now that Delta has arrived at their location. If we take fire we can return fire without getting permission. We have no troops in these areas.

Approximately 90 minutes after contact was broken Bravo again engaged the enemy. This larger force is willing to stand and fight. The threat of artillery and air support being called in doesn't deter them. Another half-hour passes before the enemy pulls out. Bravo has wounded and they need a Dust-Off as soon as possible. Two Cobras from the 7/17th will fly cover while we provide the chase ship. We orbit as the medevac hovers above the trees and Bravo talks them into their location. They lower their basket and are able to get the first of the wounded out. During the second try everything goes to hell.

"FIRE! FIRE! This is Dust-Off 52; we are taking fire." The tracers fill the air. The gunships have the enemy locations and start returning fire. The Dust-Off hangs tough and retrieves their basket with the second wounded before "getting out of Dodge". Our gunships come on station as the Cobras depart the area. Bravo still has two wounded that need to be evacuated. We don't have a hoist or anything to pull wounded out with. We wait until Dust-Off 33 arrives on station to pull the last of the wounded out. Bravo still has seven slightly injured men along with one killed. At the present time they also are missing six men. They are ordered to return to their night location from the previous night, and we would resupply them there. The NVA have something to protect at this location. They only stand and fight for a good reason.

At Polei-Kleng we load supplies for Bravo. Gator

390 will help us get the supplies delivered. They are in need of all the things required to set up a night perimeter. Trip flares and claymore mines are loaded on our ship first. This load has to get in so they are able to defend themselves during the night. The other ship has food, water, and ammo. We wait around for twenty minutes to give Bravo a chance to get where they are going. No sense flying around the Valley and giving the NVA something to shoot at.

The Cobras are back on station, along with a Hummingbird to help us locate Bravo. Hovering above the trees, we drop our sandbags. We finally locate the troops on the ground. We carefully drop each box so they won't have to move far from their location to retrieve these supplies. They are understrength and also have wounded. We move out and Gator 390 moves in to deliver their cargo. Just as the last box goes out the door they receive fire. "This is Gator 390. We have taken fire and are returning to Polei-Kleng." Mr. Thornton's voice was just as calm as if he were talking on the phone. The gunships have spotted the gunners and are blasting the hell out of them. We follow Gator 390 back to Polei-Kleng.

The damage to Gator 390 is only sheet metal damage to the tail boom and the side cargo door. Jim Sempek got a close-up view as three tracer rounds hit that door only eighteen inches away from him. He is a little pale, but ready to go back to work. We still have several sorties left to deliver and we are running out of daylight. Because of our little side trips today, most of the basic needs are still sitting at Resupply. Food, water, and ammo need to go to FSB 20 and Alpha's location. There also are personnel who didn't get to their units today. They will be put on hold until tomorrow because we just won't have enough time to get them and these supplies all in before dark.

We have to detour to the northeast because artillery

from FSB 20 and LZ Swinger are registering their guns for Bravo and Task Force Alpha's locations. Short range patrols have moved out of Alpha's perimeter towards this morning's contact area. This is now a restricted fire zone. Assessments of the bombing this morning have determined that two gun emplacements were destroyed and two NVA soldiers killed. Totals from the other actions today include ten NVA killed. Our units included three KIA, 24 WIA, and six MIA. Two helicopters were damaged. Gator 390 and Dust-Off 52 both had taken rounds but were able to continue their missions.

I am greeted at the revetment by Jeff as we set down for the night. He is all smiles. His orders have come down for his separation from the Army. Billy and Jeff have about fifteen days left before they leave. Jim Fall is also on his way. I am happy for him, but also mad to think I still have so long before I can get out of this place. He has brought me a beer and wants to figure out when my ship will go into Maintenance, so we can party one last time before he leaves. Judging from the log book and the normal amount of hours we have flown in the past week, I guess about three days.

He helps me complete the post-flight. He has not shut up once since we landed. I guess if I were him I would be the same way. He fills me in on all the news I have missed over the past couple of days. They started to rebuild the headquarters' platoon shower. Sgt. Hall is leaving in two days and Tuminello will be in charge until the new guy shows up. The rest is rumors and bullshit. I spend another hour listening to Dana. The beer and my long day finally catch up with me and I fall asleep before a shower or getting undressed.

CASUALTY REPORT
March 25, 1969

PVT Walter E. Brown Jr.	US67110494	09/03/1948	Age 20
SP4 Jewell R. Green	US53456820	05/12/1948	Age 20
PFC Miles B. Hedglin	US67059361	08/04/1949	Age 19
PFC Phillip E. Lynch	US55947331	03/15/1948	Age 21
PFC David G. Smith	RA12850478	05/06/1949	Age 19

MISSING IN ACTION

PFC Fred D. Herrera   585320923   08/07/1949   Age 19
Promoted to the rank of SFC E-6 and declared "Died while missing" on 07/24/1978

PFC Prentice W. Hicks   416623614   10/11/1947   Age 21
Promoted to the rank of SFC E-6 and declared "Died while missing" on 07/17/1978

PFC Richard D. Roberts   381466230   04/30/1948   Age 20
Promoted to the rank of SFC E-6 and declared "Died while missing" on 07/31/1978

CHAPTER XXIV

"The Beginning of the End"

Stoney returns after a two-day rest. He is a little hung over but seems to be in good spirits. I tell him that Dana has received his orders. He wants us to come over to his hooch tonight for a drink. I tell him that he has guard duty tonight, and he says not to worry about that. He will have the night off for sure. While Mr. Trebby and I complete the pre-flight, Stoney hunts down Sgt. Tuminello so Dana will have the night off. Once that is done we are ready for another day.

For the first time in several days, we are told to come to LZ Mary Lou for a briefing. Something must be up. A few of us gather at my ship. The talk is everything from what's happening in the Valley, to having a party for Jeff, Billy, and Jim. I still am getting shit about becoming the assistant platoon sergeant. Stella seems to think that things would be a lot easier for all of us. I just can't see this happening. He also thought with my bottle of Jack Daniels and a few pieces of enemy equipment we could get a heater for our shower. After what happened the first time, the 1st Sgt would skin us alive. Besides, no way do I give up my bottle of booze for a community project.

The pilots return, and we learn about the big briefing. The brass is sending one platoon from Company A/1/8 from their night location to secure the area around FSB 27. Once they are in place we will airlift D/1/8 from Task Force Alpha to that location. This will be done this afternoon. Delta Company will first leave Alpha's location and link up with Bravo and return them to that location. Bravo is in need of reinforcements. If they make contact with the enemy again, they would be in trouble.

Today we are again playing taxi for the new replacements. The first couple of sorties take us into the

YA A/O. These people are going to LZ Cider and LZ D-Handle. We have not been into these locations for almost two weeks. LZ Cider is easy to find. It sits atop a twin peak ridge. They have constructed a second pad that we are able to use. Sitting down we offload our passengers and pick up some empty water jugs and two other passengers. The guy in charge of the pad recognizes me because of my helmet. He had been one of the soldiers on my ship when they first established the base. We talk for a couple minutes and then Stoney asks me to find out where LZ D-Handle is. All of these bases are starting to look alike. I am told it is directly west on the second ridgeline from here.

Flying to D-Handle with our first sortie, I realize how close this is to the Cambodian border. We are less than one kilometer from the border. D-Handle is a clearing on top of a small ridgeline. It is not as big as Cider, and does not have the reinforced bunkers. It falls more into the class of a patrol base. I would compare it to Task Force Alpha. They have patrols working the areas north, south, and east. They have encountered enemy contact, but nothing compared to what the units of the 1/8th have dealt with the past couple of days. The morning is spent working these two areas. I am almost uneasy with the lack of action in this place. Sometimes, the waiting for something to happen is worse than the actual event.

The seven wounded soldiers from B/1/8 were evacuated this morning by a Dust-Off. Once they link up with D/1/8 they will return to TF Alpha's location. We will then move D/1/8 to FSB 27. This plan goes to hell at 1100hrs. Gator 110 had been resupplying Task Force Alpha this morning. As they sat on the pad, they came under small arms and mortar fire. They were hit several times as they departed but were able to return to Polei-Kleng. It was determined that they must return to Camp Holloway for repairs. During the next seven hours both Task Force Alpha and FSB 20 would come under attack.

We are sent back into the YB area to help resupply LZ Swinger and FSB 20. Because they are taking 105mm howitzer fire, the brass doesn't want the CH-47s delivering artillery rounds into these bases. Guess who got elected for this duty? Sure enough, our ships are now loading up these large shells for delivery. We are given one soldier to help unload the crates when we touch down at the bases. Of course, he is one of the new replacements who had no idea of what is going on.

Flying into FSB 20 I explain what needs to be done. We have stacked as much as we could in the doorways and all he has to be is push the stuff onto the ground. Don't get off the ship and, if they have wounded, just pull them aboard because we aren't sitting on that pad longer than two minutes. We arrive at FSB 20 and they are still under attack. Orbiting to the east I can see shells impacting inside their perimeter. These aren't mortars. These are big shells. We search the ground trying to spot where the enemy guns are firing from. A 105mm howitzer can fire from a distance of five miles. They could be sitting across the border for all we know. Twenty minutes pass before the shelling stops. We wait five minute before we start in. They have wounded. We back off until Dust-Off arrives. The gunships escort him in, and we will become chase ship if needed. Dust-Off loads two wounded and departs without taking fire.

Landing on the pad, we push the ammo out the doors. Three guys hand our loader the corner of a poncho that contains another wounded soldier. We are out of there in less than two minutes. Climbing into the cargo area I start to help the wounded soldier. He is not wounded. He is dead. Plugging my helmet back into the intercom system I inform the pilots he is dead. After crossing his hands I wrap the poncho over him. I tell the new guy there is nothing we can do, but this doesn't help his state of mind. I return to my gun well and light a cigarette. We take our brother to Mary Lou. Before returning to Polei-Kleng, we stop to refuel at Kontum. The remainder of the afternoon is spent dashing into the firebases with ammo.

Task Force Alpha had received fire most of the afternoon. They had wounded who needed to be evacuated. Dust-Off 52 had tried to land but received heavy fire. On their second attempt they were escorted in by gunships, and again they had to abort. Sitting at Resupply, we decided to give it a try. Mr. Hudkins in Gator 606 was game. Lt. Nilius in Gator 409 would be our chase ship, and the Crocs would supply cover. Stoney explained to our loader what was going on, and told him that he didn't have to go with us. He would have none of that. He had stuck with us all afternoon and he wasn't about to be left behind now.

The gunships had set up to the east of Alpha's location. We would make our approach from the southeast. C/1/8 had patrols in that area and reported that things were quiet. Racing in, we flared the ship as we broke on top of the pad. Stoney dropped it in and scared the hell out of all the guys around the pad. We loaded three guys as quickly as possible and pulled pitch. No sooner had we cleared the pad than two rounds impacted inside the perimeter. Listening to the radio as Gator 606 followed our lead, we headed for Mary Lou. They were able to pull the other two wounded out. Shutting down the ship at Mary Lou, I checked for damage. We had been lucky. Our loader wanted to know how he could become a gunner and be in our unit. We told him just to ask when he got to his unit. We were always looking for crew members. The sun was starting to set low in the sky as we returned to Polei-Kleng. We dropped off the guys who had helped us so much this afternoon and we wished each other luck. The brass had decided to release us because the bases were still receiving fire. It was Sir Charles' way of telling us that he was out there and he wasn't going away.

At Holloway that evening we were met by Jeff, Billy, and Jim, who were there to help me with my post-flight. In less than twenty minutes we were squared away and riding over to Stoney's hooch. Not only had he gotten Jeff out of guard duty, but he also got Tuminello to drive us over to his hooch. That evening we ate crackers and cheese with different lunch meat sandwiches, and drank ice cold beer. Not the garbage beer that we normally had, good beer. We enjoyed Budweiser and some of Stoney's scotch whiskey. For a few hours, we were just friends who enjoyed each other's company. We talked about the funny things that had happened to us. By midnight we were all a little drunk. We said our good-byes, and the three who were leaving promised that we would all get together back in The World. We all knew that might never come true.

I fell asleep that night somewhat happy for the first time in almost a month. It was the beer, not my day. The enemy had shelled both FSB 20 and Task Force Alpha with over one hundred mortar rounds. FSB 20 received twenty-five rounds of 105mm howitzer and TF Alpha, forty-four. They had suffered four killed and fourteen wounded. Tomorrow would bring more of the same. The good news for the day is that, during their return to Task Force Alpha's location, B/1/8 found four of their missing in action. They were in good shape. The fate of the other two was still unknown.

CASUALTY REPORT
March 26, 1969

PFC Daniel K. Hinkel	US51840410	07/05/1945	Age 23
SP4 David Stone	US53456024	01/31/1948	Age 21
PFC Donnis G. Willis	US54828135	04/07/1949	Age 19

CHAPTER XXV

"The Lift"

The hangover I had was a small price to pay for the fun I had last night. I felt good about myself and was able to let go for a short time. Breakfast would be just coffee and toast. I was amazed that my headache was gone by the time we completed our pre-flight inspection. Stoney was a veteran of several of those types of nights, so he was in pretty good spirits this morning. The flight to Mary Lou passed quietly.

The briefing was nothing compared to what was going on along the road. Fourteen helicopters lined the road, eight from the 119th. Three were from the 170th AHC. Two were from the 57th AHC and one was from the 4th Aviation Battalion. Nobody seemed to know what was going on. The three crews from the 170th had talked to other members of their unit who had been in the Valley helping us, but the others were in the dark. We let them know what we had been doing, but we had no idea why they were all here. We learned the whole story when the pilots returned.

The brass had decided that, because of the artillery that had been used against Task Force Alpha, we needed to get D/1/8 out of that location as quickly as possible. A second platoon from A/1/8 had also moved to FSB 27. That area was considered secure. Delta Company has 105 personnel to be moved. The plan was for each ship to drop into that location at staggered intervals and load five-to-six passengers at a time. This way, each ship would only have to make one trip and there would be no turnaround time involved. We would have two sets of gunships on station at all times. Once this was accomplished, four of the ships would be released, and we would do our normal resupply.

The flight of fourteen ships took off to start the lift.

Gator 409 would be the first ship in. The rest of us would orbit to the northeast and hope that the enemy artillery spotter was unable to see us. **"FIRE! RECEIVING FIRE!"** As Gator 409 lifted off, the perimeter was hit from all sides by sniper fire. They are able to escape, and the fire ceases. We make a long count of one hundred and then head in. Each ship would use their own count and try to stay off the radios, so as not to give the enemy any help as to what we are doing. Grabbing six passengers, we race out. There aren't any of our guys outside the wire, so once we clear the perimeter our guns go hot. We don't receive any fire as we leave. The next ship would have a mortar round greet them as they came in. One set of gunships had already expended their ammo, so another pair was on its way in. We arrived at FSB 27 and dropped off our sortie, then waited and listened as each ship went into Alpha's location. Within ninety minutes we had completed the lift. Three ships were damaged but we had suffered no casualties. Two of our ships were damaged but would remain in service, and the other was from the 57th AHC. Two ships from the 170th AHC would stay and help us while the others were released.

The attacks on FSB 20 have continued. They received 105mm howitzer fire for almost an hour this morning. Twelve rounds landed inside their perimeter. They had two wounded. The remainder of the morning is spent resupplying the firebases. No contact is reported by the ground troops and none of our aircraft have received fire. We decide to break for lunch at Kontum. The mess hall is crowded today. Everyone had the same idea as us. We enjoy a hot meal and some laughs before we start the afternoon. Our lunch is cut short as we are scrambled back to our ships.

Company C/1/8 had moved from Task Force Alpha towards the area where Bravo Company had made contact the day before. They had made contact and were withdrawing to call in artillery, when they came under attack from a 105mm battery. This forced them to return to Alpha's perimeter. The enemy continues to defend this area of the road. During this engagement, a Cider aircraft had spotted the big gun's location. Artillery from FSB 20 and Ben Het were now being employed against this location. While the gun crews resupply their gun locations, the Air Force continues to pound this area. We were again being used to bring artillery rounds into the fire bases. Although our sorties are not as large as the CH-47's, we make up for it with speed. At about the same time, a platoon from A/3/12 in the area around LZ Cider has engaged a small enemy force. Two of our ships are sent to that location in case they are needed.

While we resupply the firebases, we are informed that we will have gun support from the 7/17th but their slicks have been pulled to support the 3rd Brigade. The Valley has taken its toll on all the air units. We have taken ships from 2nd Brigade to cover our losses and, in turn, 2nd Brigade has pulled ships from the 4th Aviation Battalion to cover their losses. And so on and so forth. The madness continues into the afternoon.

Hummingbird 5 reports that he confirms one enemy gun has been destroyed by our artillery. He and a team of gunships will continue doing damage assessments in that area. These reports put them near the Cambodian border. I am willing to bet they are on the other side of the fence. Maybe this will bring some relief to the guys on the fire bases.

Once again Charlie Company tries to move out of Alpha's perimeter. Again they receive mortar and small arms fire. They fall back to the perimeter and allow the gunships to work the area. The gunships come under heavy fire. A second team arrives and also expends on the target area. Now artillery and mortars are called in. During this time they don't receive any enemy mortar or rocket fire. It is believed that this area might be where an enemy forward observer was stationed. We are unable to supply Alpha for the remainder of the day because of all the enemy activity in this area.

The action to the south has increased. The unit from A/3/12 had moved back into the contact area after the artillery strike, and again they engage an unknown size force. This time they encounter automatic weapons fire and B-40 rockets. Gunships were brought in as support, and the platoon withdrew to LZ Cider. They have eight missing from this contact. The terrain that our troops are fighting has taken its toll. Once outside the firebases, the thick jungle, and endless hills and ridgelines, make it almost impossible for our troops to operate. The fear of leaving a wounded soldier behind wears on everyone.

We finish the day getting supplies into FSB 27. The troops have been working like crazy to build up their night positions and make this deserted fire base defendable. This is just another move on this giant chess board. The how and why is no longer the question that any of us asks. The sooner we get out of this place, the better I'll like it.

I complete my postflight inspection and realize that, by tomorrow night, my ship will be due another 100-hour inspection. I need to stop by Maintenance and let them know, and make arrangements to get my stuff off the ship. The best thing is, I just might get the day after tomorrow off. This sounds pretty good to me. Most of the guys are having a beer by the time I arrive at the barracks. Beer is the last thing I want. I drank my fill last night, and I still have the taste in my mouth. I settle for some lemon-lime soda and a can of beans and franks for supper. Dana has got most of his gear packed up and ready to ship home. He has cleaned out his locker and thrown some stuff on my bunk. I can use the two pairs of socks and the sweater he will no longer need. Under my bunk, I find his cleaning kit and spare parts for his machine gun. This is worth its weigh to gold. I put this in my foot locker for safekeeping. I will sure miss him, but am glad he is going home. I wish I were going with him.

CASUALTY REPORT
March 27, 1969

PFC Robert S. Hardison	RA12968434	11/29/1948	Age 20
SP4 James R. Long	US52859984	10/21/1948	Age 20
CPL Willie D. Martinez	RA15784869	05/13/1950	Age 18
1LT Anthony J. Urrutia	O5348250	10/02/1944	Age 24
SP4 Rodney A. Vore	US54976014	01/10/1948	Age 21
SGT David O. Wilson	US56591520	04/02/1948	Age 20

MISSING IN ACTION

SGT Ray G. Czerwiec   325367898   02/21/1944   Age 25
Promoted to the rank of SSG E-6 and declared "Died while missing" on 04/28/1976

PFC Gail M. Kerns

On March 27, 1969, Raymond Czerwiec and Gail Kerns were riflemen with A Company, 3rd Battalion, 12th Infantry on a reconnaissance mission in Kontum Province, South Vietnam when their platoon came under hostile weapons fire and were forced to withdraw with a number of people missing. An attempt to reenter the area that afternoon was unsuccessful. Another attempt was made on the 28th but it was also unsuccessful. Air strikes and artillery fire were placed into the enemy area for two days. On March 30th Company A attacked the enemy again and was again forced to withdraw leaving people behind, including SP4 Clarence A. Latimer, who was a rifleman with the Company and had been severely wounded during the attempt. Two Long Range Reconnaissance Patrols (LRRP) were sent back into the area a week later to recover the bodies of the missing. Sweeps were made in the area for two days, but no remains were found. On March 3, 1973, Gail Kerns was released by the North Vietnamese. He had been held in South Vietnam, and moved to Hanoi prior to his release. No word had ever gotten out to the U.S. that Gail had been captured. Kerns was not conscious when he was captured, and did not know the fate of Ray Czerwiec, nor did he have any information regarding Clarence Latimer. He was promoted to the rank of SGT E-5 and classified as "Released Prisoner of War".

CHAPTER XXVI

"Fire Support Base 27"

The day hasn't even started and I already receive some bad news. My ship will brought into Maintenance tonight and a crew will work all night so she is ready in the morning. We have so few ships that are mission–ready, they are scraping the bottom of the barrel. We are to the point where three damaged ships are being stripped to make one flyable ship. Two ships from our platoon are in need of tail booms. The guys from the sheet metal shop are patching patches, and now the airframes are starting to show signs of wear because the outer strength is gone. These ships are now missing their main rotor blades so two other ships can be made flyable. Because of the hard work of our maintenance crews, we are able to get nine ships out of seventeen ready for today.

Task Force Alpha has spent a very uneasy night. They have seen movement all night. Artillery from both FSB 20 and Swinger had been deployed around their perimeter. Between constant enemy contact and being shelled, plus the fact that most of these guys have not slept in two days, they have the makings of a bad situation. Our first sorties for today will be hot food and fresh replacements. Low morale and despair are as deadly to an Army as enemy bullets. These guys are at rock bottom.

The Resupply area is very busy this morning. The CH-47s are again delivering artillery shells to the fire bases. The amount of ammo that has been used over the past three days is unbelievable. The amount the Chinooks are able to haul in one slingload is equal to four of our sorties. The gunships will be providing cover as they make their deliveries. We load up jugs of coffee and containers of scrambled eggs with all the trimmings. This will be their first hot meal in two weeks.

259

The area around Alpha seems to be quiet as we land on the pad. Their breakfast is unloaded and we load several empty water cans and other things that have been sitting around the pad for the last several days. This is the first time we have picked up anything in a week. The place is a mess. Garbage from empty C-ration cases, along with damaged or destroyed equipment, is everywhere. Several of the bunkers are in need of repair. The smell of burning jungle and death hover over this place. I realize how easy I have it. At least I get to leave this place at night. These guys are stuck here every minute of every day.

On the way back to Polei-Kleng, I read a leaflet from a handful that one of the guys on the pad had given me. A shell containing these had exploded near the perimeter last night. It said that we should stop fighting and come over to their side. It also contained statements from POWs on how they were treated well. A runner was waiting for us as we landed at Resupply. I handed over the entire stack of leaflets that had been given to me. He made sure that I didn't keep any of them. I must have looked as if I might be ready to surrender or something.

Our morning passed without any trouble. The only thing wrong was that there was nothing wrong. By mid-morning, elements from both B/1/8 and C/1/8 had moved outside of Alpha's perimeter and were sweeping the area and assessing artillery damage. We were supplying FSB 27 when the shit would again hit the fan. Bravo had encountered a small patrol and had engaged it when the first 105mm shells started to fall again. During the next ten hours, a total of 120 rounds impacted in and around Alpha's location. The attacks were designed more at keeping the units inside Alpha's perimeter than to inflict casualties.

The afternoon began as A/3/12 again moved back to YA 826811 to recover their missing. They received small arms and rocket fire from a large enemy force. Gunships were employed to cover their withdrawal, and then artillery was called in on the position. They were unable to recover their missing, but at least they did not suffer any casualties from this contact.

Our afternoon was spent resupplying most of the bases in the Valley, but with a twist. Because none of the Cider or Headhunter aircraft had been able to locate the enemy gun positions, we were now flying large circles while delivering supplies. Staying at two to three thousand feet above the jungle, we would slowly loop around the Valley trying to spot these gun emplacements or draw fire. We were now being downgraded to targets in this cat-and-mouse game. Artillery was still pounding the area where the first gun had been sighted. This made for a long afternoon. None of our ships reported fire or spotted enemy gun emplacements.

Company D/1/8 reported movement to their north. A possible enemy convoy was moving in that area. As they adjusted artillery on that target, they came under small arms fire. Gunships were sent in, but no damage assessments could be determined. Late in the afternoon we were sent to FSB 27 to pick up four passengers. These guys weren't straight line grunts. This was a LRRP team. Judging from the way they looked, I guessed they had been out in the bush for a while. I offered them candy, gum, and cigarettes out of my flight bag. They passed on the candy but helped themselves to the gum and cigarettes. I asked them how long they had been out and was told six days. We took them directly to Brigade Headquarters and that was that.

During the entire time that our Company worked in the Valley we never once put any LRRP teams in. How did they get there? Who put them in? This mystery would not be answered for several months. Prior to the beginning of this operation, intelligence knew there were several large units massing in the Plei-Trap area. Since the end of

January, the 57th AHC had been putting teams into the Valley. In February they had lost a ship with its entire crew and the team. The brass wanted this intelligence, but they believed it would be compromised if known outside this small circle. So they decided to operate in the following manner. Teams were put in and pulled out just before dark or dawn. We had received reports of aircraft in the Valley during the night from fire bases and the guys on the ground, but we never thought anything about it. These ships would arrive just as we were departing, or starting the day, and they used us as their decoy. The enemy would assume they were part of our flights that were resupplying or whatever. These teams would hide in the jungle for days and spy on enemy movement. During the night, they would count the number of flashlights they saw. Write down the number of trucks that moved along the Plei-Trap road. After we would pull out of the Valley, they would again go in and search for our missing in action, and assess enemy casualties. The only reason we were allowed to pull this team out was because our involvement in the northern section of the Valley was almost over, and we didn't even know it.

Tonight we landed in front of the Maintenance hangar. There is no need to remove any of my gear, because the ship should be ready in the morning. At least tonight I won't have to pull a postflight. The mess hall is open, but not many people are interested in liver and onions for supper. With a little luck I'll get to write a short letter home before I fall asleep. I find a can of corned-beef hash and some crackers I was saving for times like this, and proceed to heat my meal on Sempek's hotplate. Most of the lights are out except around my bunk and the bar. Being alone in a crowd of people is something that I will never be comfortable with. This is the part of the Army that those who have not "been there" never understand. I eat, and actually finish writing a letter home, before falling to sleep. One day closer to go home.

CASUALTY REPORT
March 28, 1969

PFC Julius P. Pignataro   US527700898   08/11/1949   Age 19

CHAPTER XXVII

"Tactical Emergency"

The lights are thrown on and loud voices jolt me awake. Sgt. Hall and Tuminello are rushing from bunk-to-bunk waking people up. Sitting up to clear the sleep from my head, I try to focus on what is being said. We need to get to our ship now. They need help in the Valley. My brain still doesn't understand what is going on. I start to pull on my clothes but I just can't make my body work. Slowly things start to work and I realize what is going on. We jump into the platoon truck and head for our ships. Its 0400hrs and we need to get to Mary Lou now. Maintenance is not quite done with my ship. I start to check things out as three more guys help install the remaining inspection panels. We complete the pre-flight inspection and are airborne by 0430hrs.

Task Force Alpha has been probed all night. They have fired at movement outside their perimeter and artillery from LZ Swinger, FSB 20, and Ben Het has adjusted most of the night. Intelligence believes there is a large force massing to attack. Spooky gunships are standing by, and Cider aircraft are ready to bring in "Tac-air," fast-movers, if needed. We are to land at Mary Lou, where troops from the 2/8th are waiting in case we need to reinforce Alpha. Our gunships will stand by at Polei-Kleng to either support Alpha or provide cover for our assault.

When we arrive at Mary Lou, we are told to shut down and stand by. The troops gather around each ship so we can leave on a minute's notice. Most have no idea what is going on. We tell them what we know, and then we wait. The air is cold and I am dying for a cup of coffee. It is pitch black, and the idea of heating water is out of the question. A sniper would see that a mile away. I settle for a can of apple juice that I had in the side cargo compartment.

After an hour the sun is starting to rise. Nothing is going on. Suddenly, we are scrambled to head for Polei-Kleng.

There has been another attack at Alpha's location. They have wounded and also need ammo. Our ship and Gator 409 will resupply Alpha. The rest of the ships will remain at Mary Lou and stand by because LZ D-Handle is under attack and they may need to be reinforced or supplied. We load as much ammo as we can and stack it in the doorways. Artillery is being lifted so we can get in. Our approach will from the northeast. This is where the least amount of movement was seen last night. The best guess is that Alpha is surrounded so there is no good way in or out. The smoke from the artillery is hanging over the Alpha's location and we first need to circle to get our bearings. We head in while the gunships cover our approach. Hitting the pad, we drop the ammo and pull three wounded aboard. Because we didn't receive any fire on the way in, Stoney decides that we are going out the same way. He picks us up to a hover and rotates the tail 180 degrees and we barrel out of there. Negative fire. We wait long enough for Gator 409 to make his delivery and depart before we head for Mary Lou. The wounded are in good shape and are not emergencies.

LZ D-Handle was also busy last night. One of their short range patrols encountered a small enemy patrol just before midnight. Also one of the ambush squads was fired upon during the night. This morning at dawn the base was attacked by rocket and mortar fire. During this attack, sappers and ground troops tried to breach the wire. Artillery support was called in and, after an hour, the attack was repelled. They have wounded, and they need reinforcements and resupply.

Three of our ships are sent to pull the wounded out of D-Handle. The other three are sent to LZ Cider to pick up a platoon from A/3/12 to reinforce D-Handle. Our ship and Gator 409 will pick up ammo and other supplies.

Companies B and D/3/12, that were located at D-Handle, had received over fifty rounds of 82mm mortar fire. Two bunkers were destroyed by sappers and B-40 rockets. Two were killed and twenty-eight wounded. Twenty-seven NVA soldiers were found in the wire and several drag marks were found leaving the perimeter.

Once the wounded were evacuated and the platoon from A/3/12 was on the ground, we headed in with the resupply. The air was again heavy with the smell of smoke from artillery. Soldiers were already rebuilding the two bunkers that had been destroyed during the attack. Several soldiers were pulling the dead NVA out of the wire and searching the bodies. Once the ammo had been unloaded, the two dead soldiers were placed aboard the ship. Several enemy weapons and other equipment were also loaded. We headed to Mary Lou.

I looked at the ID cards that were handed to me at the fire base. Two more mothers would learn what I already knew. Their sons were dead. They had died on a little dirt hill in the middle of nowhere. What was the point to all of this? I stared into space as we flew back to Mary Lou. Out of the corner of my eye I saw Mattie looking at me. A tear moved down his cheek and I knew our thoughts were the same. I offered him a cigarette and he took it. We sat for the longest time before we finally arrived at our destination.

The pad at Mary Lou is deserted when we arrived. They were busy with the wounded and our two passengers would have to wait. Several minutes passed before another stretcher team arrived to take our fallen brothers away. We helped place each of them on a stretcher, and then dumped the captured weapons and gear on the ground before we lifted off. At that moment, I could care less about that pile of junk. We refueled before leaving Mary Lou, and were finally able to get that first cup of coffee before starting back to Polei-Kleng.

We formed up with Gator 409 and Gator 390 at Polei-Kleng to airlift the Weapons platoon from D/1/8 from FSB 20 to FSB 27. Yesterday morning, two platoons from A/1/8, the ones who had secured the firebase for our lift of D/1/8 to that location, were ordered to return to FSB 20 overland and to RIF to that location. Because of the enemy buildup around Task Force Alpha last night, the need to reinforce Delta is important. FSB 20 has not received any enemy fire this morning, but we aren't going to take any chances. We will come in at treetop level at different intervals. The artillery that has been firing in support of Task Force Alpha most of the night will have to stop so we can accomplish this mission. This will give those boys a break, and make our job a lot easier.

Our gunships provide cover as we start the move. Gator 390 makes the first pickup without incident. We drop in second, and Gator 409 after us. The turnaround time from FSB 20 to FSB 27 is less than five minutes. The terrain is so bad that it will take the two platoons from A/1/8 a day-and-a-half to cover this distance. Within an hour, the move is complete. We will now return to our resupply mission of the different bases. We are advised that enemy movement around Task Force Alpha has increased. The sounds of things being moved through the jungle can be heard and we have no troops out at this time. If we see anything we are to place fire upon it and report our location.

Things are quiet around LZ D-Handle. B/3/12 is outside the perimeter and sweeping the area. That area is now a restricted fire zone. Patrols around LZ Cider have been recalled to provide security until replacements can be brought in. The numbers game continues on the ground, just as it does in the air. Less than half of our unit's aircraft are flyable. Each day we continue to borrow ships from other units, which in turn shortchanges somebody else. When will this madness end?

We grab an early lunch before starting to resupply the Valley. We have already put in a full day, and it's not even noon yet. Today we try LZ Mary Lou for lunch. This has become our main meal of the day. By the time we return to Holloway most of us are too tired to eat. Besides, the mess hall is normally closed by the time we return. The Army's canned beefsteak burger is always a favorite at Mary Lou. It's a combination of beef, pork, fat, and grease. A far cry from a "Big Mac" but still great when compared to liver or some of the other things that the Army would try to pass off as food. Stick this between two slices of one-inch thick bread, and drown it with mustard and ketchup, it would feed a family of four Vietnamese or one hungry US soldier. Army chow was not meant to taste good. Its only purpose was to keep you alive and fill your stomach.

Things started to heat up as the afternoon began. FSB 20 had received two rounds of 105mm. Sniper fire on the east, south, and west side of the perimeter at Task Force Alpha was limiting movement into the base. This area included the chopper pad, so any deliveries would have to be dump and run. Bravo Company was operating outside of the perimeter and we are now being restricted to return fire at their location. The CH-47s were not being allowed into these places, so we were again pressed into service to deliver artillery rounds plus our normal cargo. Light contact around LZ D-Handle resulted in two NVA killed by elements of B/3/12 as they continued to sweep the area south and west of their location.

Our afternoon was spent hauling cases of 105mm shells into FSB 20. During the entire day they continued to support Alpha and also fire on suspected enemy gun emplacements. We were lucky to not to be at the wrong place at the wrong time. A total of sixteen shells hit around FSB 20 this afternoon. Twelve of these would impact inside their perimeter. There were no casualties. Each trip provided a different show to watch. The Air Force was working the areas to the west. Five-hundred-pound bombs and napalm could be seen impacting the ridgelines along the border. The gun crews from Ben Het were throwing their giant 175mm shells into the area plus some help from LZ Swinger's 155mm guns added to the fun.

An NVA soldier was spotted near Alpha's perimeter, waving a white flag. One of our ships scared him away as they were landing at that location. Because of the propaganda leaflets that the enemy had employed yesterday, the brass decided to send a psychological team into their area to broadcast our own brand of propaganda. The enemy's willingness to surrender must have been overestimated: the LOH no sooner arrived and starting broadcasting when the enemy opened fire on them. They escaped with light damage. Two of our ships would take hits during the afternoon, but all would remain in service. Three more wounded were evacuated from Alpha's location before the end of this day.

Fifteen hours would pass before our day would finally end. We had survived another day. We were greeted by every available man in the unit as we returned tonight. The word had come down that as many ships as possible would be mission ready in the morning. We were taken to the mess hall to be fed and then get some sleep. Unknown to us, the plans were already in motion to pull the 1st Brigade out of the Valley in the morning. FSB 20 had fired over 800 rounds of 105mm and 200 rounds of 4.2-inch mortar fire in support of Task Force Alpha in the last 24 hours. All of the units were understrength and in need of regrouping. Most of the enemy movement in the area around the Plei-Trap road had slowed or stopped completely. The damage to the road itself would make it unusable for a long while.

Stoney had reached the maximum number of hours that he could fly in this month. Tomorrow I would have a different aircraft commander. This was the last day I would fly with Stoney. The events of the next few days would change the remainder of my tour. Tonight I would sleep as if death itself had taken over me. I would not remember eating or lying down on my bunk.

CASUALTY REPORT
March 29, 1969

SSG Stephen D. Board	US51713821	09/23/1947	Age 21
PFC Danny F. Perkins	US53532434	10/21/1946	Age 22
CPL Kenneth H. Visintin	US56960335	09/06/1947	Age 21

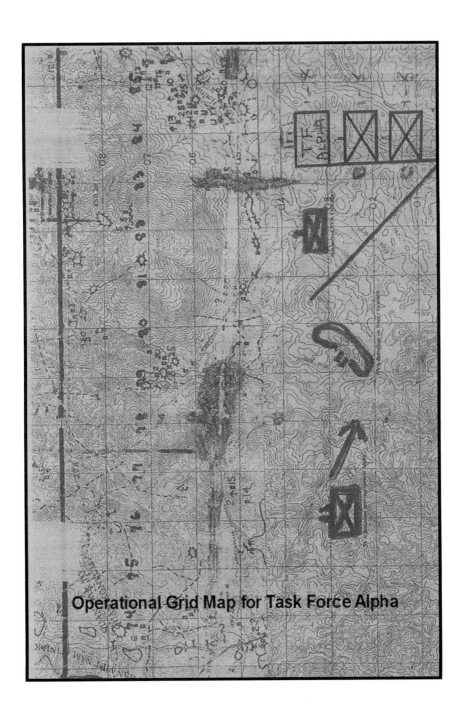

Operational Grid Map for Task Force Alpha

271

CHAPTER XXVIII

"Task Force Alpha"

I could hardly move this morning. I must have stayed in the same position the entire night. Standing in the shower, as the cold water fell on my head the life started to return to my body. I ate breakfast this morning just to have something in my belly. I wasn't hungry, but I ate because I had the chance. Mr. Klimaszewski, from the Second Flight platoon, will be the A/C today. WO1 Eugene Klimaszewski is a small man with a baby face. He looks more like a sixteen-year-old who should be studying for his driver's license than an aircraft commander. During the past six months, he has tried to grow a mustache three times. He thought it would make him appear older. Each time, he was forced to cut it off because of all the grief the other pilots had given him. Because of his name, the only fitting call-sign for him is "Ski". Mr. Elson is the peter-pilot. I had never flown with either of them, but I knew they were both good pilots. Several of the ships had mixed crews today. Maintenance had been able to get ten ships ready for today.

The briefing at Polei-Kleng was quite long this morning. This is where we first learned about the withdrawal from the YB A/O. All short range patrols were pulling back to their bases this morning. We would have Cider and Headhunter aircraft ready to call in air support. Artillery from Swinger and Ben Het were registered around the units we were extracting. The first unit would be Task Force Alpha. We were to bring them to Polei-Kleng. The turnaround time would be twenty minutes. We would use the grab-and-run approach to extract the troops. They had caused Sir Charles a lot of grief, so we felt that they weren't going to let them leave without a sendoff. Once this was completed FSB 27 would be next.

As we were extracting FSB 27, CH-47s would start removing the large guns from FSB 20. Our last mission would be to pull the remaining troops out of FSB 20. The entire lift would take most of the day. Our gunships would provide cover. Two flights of guns would remain on station with us, and one pair would stand by at Polei-Kleng. We would start at 0900hrs.

The sky was clear and there was no ground fog as we started our orbit to the east of Task Force Alpha. We just had to make it in and out of the meat grinder two or three more times, and we could forget about this part of the war. All of their patrols were inside the perimeter, so it was now a free fire zone around the complete base. Gator 409 would be the first to go in. We were slated as number four.

The first sorties out would be the mortar platoon and their equipment. Base plates, tubes, and ammo would slow the extraction, but we could not leave this behind. Because of the enemy artillery and sniper fire, it was not wise to destroy any of the bunker or the perimeter until all the forces were extracted. After we had completed our job, artillery from LZ Swinger and air strikes would destroy anything that had been built on Hill 467. We had never tried to extract an entire firebase while under fire.

The gunships started their routes as 409 headed in. Racing above the trees, the first ship dropped onto the pad. Base plates, tubes, and other equipment were the first items thrown into the ship. Two of Task Force Alpha's mortar men were the first to leave this place in hell. "This is Gator 409 on the pad and negative fire." This would be the radio transmission we all hoped to give, once we were on the ground. A minute later we received the transmission of, "Gator 409 coming out. Negative fire." One sortie completed but we still have a bunch to go. **"RECEIVING FIRE! RECEIVING FIRE!"** The next ship in was Gator 606 and all hell had broken lose. Tracers from

273

small arms and machine guns can be seen. A rocket impacts near the perimeter. The gunships open up but Gator 606 continues into the base. With complete disregard for the fire and the warnings from the ground, Gator 606 drops on the pad. Mr. Hudkins, with this one act of determination, would inspire every other crew this day. If he could get in, we could all do it. The fire continues as they lift off with more equipment and men on board. We wait as Gator 108 heads into the pad. Again they receive fire, and the gunships place covering fire. He is coming out, and now it's our turn.

Starting our run we open up with our sixties. No sense in reporting fire because we are catching it from all sides. I have thrown smoke just to give the gunships an idea of where the greatest amount of fire is coming from. We flare as we come over the base. "CLEAR LEFT! CLEAR RIGHT! THE TAIL IS CLEAR!" Mr. Klimaszewski has dropped us right in the center of the pad. Grabbing arms and pulling people into the ship as fast as possible we have six passengers on board and we are out of here! Everything is moving in slow motion. Being on the ground for only a minute is a lifetime. The tracers are flying over the ship. I can see the terror in each of the soldier's eyes as they climb into the ship. Banking to the left as we leave, I continue firing my machine gun until we climb out of range. The stress and fear of the past month disappears from our passengers faces. They are ready to party. There are big smiles and they are patting each other on the back as if to say, "WE MADE IT!" I tell them that once we hit the ground at Polei-Kleng, get out of the ship and just kneel down so we can get back into the air. We have several more souls to save today. The radio tells the story as each ship races into Alpha's location. No matter which way we come in, there is enemy fire. The base has started to receive heavier in-coming mortar and rocket fire, but none of it has landed inside the perimeter.

We don't even squat down on our skids and the grunts are off the ship and we are rolling into the air. The perimeter continues to shrink as each sortie departs the landing zone. Our biggest fear is the enemy attacking and over-running the base before we can get all of the defenders out.

Our second set of gunships is now on station along with a pair of Cobras from the 7/17th. A1E Skyraiders have dropped CS (tear gas) and smoke in order to screen the extraction. Gator 110 had taken several rounds in their main rotor blades. Once they dropped their sortie off, they would have to return to Holloway. We wait our turn and plan how we are going in there this time. Mr. Klimaszewski was happy with the way we got in the first time. That approach gives him a little lead time before he has to flare the ship and drop onto the pad. That's the way we'll go in. The area east of Hill 467 is more open than the other approaches. Scrub trees and high elephant grass dominate the area. There are still plenty of places for enemy gunners to hide. I know they are waiting for us.

We drop from our orbit and head into Alpha for the second time. We receive fire as we break over the trees and we return fire. The next thing that I see is a bright flash and I hear a loud explosion. **"MAYDAY! MAYDAY! MAYDAY! THIS IS GATOR 270! WE HAVE TAKEN AN AIR BURST AND ARE RETURNING POLEI-KLENG! ARE YOU ALL RIGHT BACK THERE?"** I can hear Mr. Klimaszewski but for some reason I can't answer him. **"MATOS! CHECK CAREY!"** Again I can hear this, but I can't respond. Mattie is now helping me into the cargo area and starting to shake me. I open my eyes, but I'm having a hard time focusing. Mattie raises my visor and now I can see the inside of the ship. "I'm okay," is my response as I wave at Mr. Elson. "No you're not," is Mr. Klimaszewski's answer. He radios for a Dust Off to meet us at Polei-Kleng. By now I'm awake and realize that my leg hurts and I have pain in my hands. Looking down, I

275

can see the blood running down my leg. Rolling up my pant leg, we discover a gash in my shin. A piece of metal is sticking out of my leg. I am able to pull the object out and Mattie presses a bandage over the wound. By the time we reach Polei-Kleng, I am smoking a cigarette and I don't need a medic.

We shut down the ship and the medic from the Dust Off comes over to the ship. While I show him the wound, the rest of the crew inspects the ship. The entire area around my gun well has been peppered with shrapnel. The roof, cargo door, and my gun mount have small holes or dents. There is a larger hole in my ammo box that goes completely through. The medic has found a few nicks in my hands and several marks on my helmet. My head is ringing but I am fine. Our best guess would be that, as I returned fire, one of my rounds struck a B-40 rocket that had been fired at the ship. This round detonated the rocket directly in front of my gun well. The hole in my ammo box was either a larger piece of the rocket or a bullet from a rifle. By the time it had traveled through my ammo box the impact to my leg was like being hit with a rock. The medic tells me that I need a few stitches and a tetanus shot. I also might have a slight concussion. I tell him to wrap up my leg so we can get back to Alpha's location. Another ship had been damaged while we were here inspecting ours. The ship is flyable, and I'm fine. The loss of two ships would slow the extraction and create a greater danger to the remaining crews. We refuel and head back to Alpha's location.

Everyone is surprised to hear that we are on our way back. While we were gone, Croc 242 had taken several rounds and was headed back to Polei-Kleng. A large caliber round had gone through the bottom of the ship and stuck the peter pilot's seat, then went through his door. WO-1 Jack Cloud would tell us that he just knew his ass had been shot off. The impact of the round caused his legs to fly up in the air. His butt felt like one hundred bees had just stung him. Nothing but his pride was hurt.

Again we raced into Alpha. I was scared to death. I started to realize how close we had come the last time in here. The fire was still intense, but we made it in. We pull six more passengers on, and we are out of there. I explain to the grunts what they need to do when we arrive at Polei-Kleng, and ask them how many are left. The one guesses about fifty or so and another says twenty. No matter what the number, we will have to go in one more time. We have pulled twenty-some sorties, and we have two slicks and one gunship out of service. That would leave us with eight slicks to complete the rest of the lift. Landing at Polei-Kleng is starting to feel like a football game. As we sit down the guys around the runway cheer and wave as we head back to the Valley. Hugs, hand shakes, and tears greet the latest soldiers to be pulled out. For the past thirty days they have lived in the shadow of death. Many of their friends were either killed or wounded. This is the first time they have something to be happy about.

There are twenty guys left on the ground. We have three ships en-route at this time. It's decided that the next two ships would try to take seven passengers and the last would get six. Because my ship was the newest and has a strong engine we get to go in first. The gunships really pour the lead into the enemy as we race for the pad. We drop on to the pad and pull seven aboard. Mr. Klimaszewski pulls the ship to a hover and sets it right back down. "I CAN TAKE ONE MORE!" he yells as he waves to the grunts huddled around the pad. The perimeter is now the small area around the pad. I pull one more abroad, and again he pulls us into a hover. Clearing the tree, we climb into the sky. Knowing the two other ships were older, and because we were low on fuel, Mr. Klimaszewski had decided that if he could pick the ship up easily with seven then he could get eight on board. We wait until all of the sorties are complete. The last two sorties joined us as we flew towards Polei-Kleng. Setting down on the runway, the last of B/1/8 departs from our ships. As they are greeted by their friends, I get the feeling that we have finally done something good. We hover over to refuel. Mr. Klimaszewski asks how my leg is, and tells me we are going to Mary Lou so I can get it taken care of. It's almost noon, so I figure, "What the hell." I was looking forward to a hot meal. Besides, this was a good reason to celebrate. We had gotten Task Force Alpha out of that living hell and, with a little luck, we would never have to go back to Hill 467.

While Mr. Klimaszewski walked with me over to the dispensary, Mattie and Mr. Elson headed for the mess hall. Once all the forms were filled out and questions answered I was taken to an examining room. My leg was swollen and had a large bruise, but the bleeding had stopped. I was told there was no need for it to be stitched but I would have to get a tetanus shot. I think the shot hurt worse than being wounded. I was given some pills for the pain and was told to rest for a couple of days. Once outside, I told Mr. Klimaszewski that I could rest tomorrow because we had already lost three ships to combat damage and I felt that I should stay. Besides, the other ships had already left for Holloway, so there was nobody to replace me.

FSB 20 was still receiving enemy artillery fire. None of the attacks would be considered heavy, but they were more than enough to hinder their withdrawal to Polei-Kleng. Their artillery pieces were being moved by CH-47s to Polei-Kleng, while their mortars would be used to cover our extraction of FSB 27. Besides being short three ships, as we started the move of FSB 27, action around LZ D-Handle forced us to release one of our ships to that location. They were again in contact near the area of March 27th

278

engagement.

Company A/3/12 had moved into the area to recover the missing from three days ago. Although artillery and air had pounded this area, the enemy was still here. Unable to recover the missing, they withdrew to their night location. Because of increased small arms and mortar fire, C/3/12 was sent to secure the night location. Light contact would continue for most of the afternoon.

The first few sorties into FSB 27 were tense ones. We all believed the same type treatment would be waiting for us that we received at Hill 467. None of the ships received any fire during the first lift. The trip to Polei-Kleng was made longer by the detour that was caused by our artillery from LZ Swinger. They were shelling the area around Hill 467. They were making sure that anything that had been left by Task Force Alpha would not of any use to the NVA. The extraction would take most of the afternoon. We would use the same grab-and-run tactics that had worked earlier today. As each ship completed a sortie, the force on the ground feared an enemy attack at any minute. We completed this lift, and not one round had been fired at us.

All of the large 105mm howitzers had been removed by the time we started extracting people out of FSB 20. The first to go were the last of the artillery personnel. One CH-47 had come in and taken a sortie of them before we arrived. This would help us greatly. One of their sorties equaled about fifteen of ours. We took these people to the eastern end of the runway. The pace had slowed considerably since this morning. We have several sorties to be pulled, but our sense of urgency was not as great as it was morning. Once this was done, the next group to be pulled out was the mortar platoons. The heavy base plates and tubes slowed the loading of our ships, but we still were able to make pretty good time, considering everything that was going on. These guys were taken to the Resupply area. From there they were would rejoin their individual companies. Some were headed for Mary Lou, while others would stay at Polei-Kleng tonight. The last to leave would be A/1/8. It had been a long month for most of these guys. Among the last to leave was Red Fox. He had been in charge of getting the ships loaded and getting everybody out. If anybody deserved a medal it was him. He kept these guys supplied for the entire month. Between jockeying loads and destinations, and making sure that replacements made it to their units, the whole operation would have been garbage without him.

Having pulled the last sortie out of FSB 20, we waited on the runway at Polei-Kleng. Company C/3/12 had moved to help A/3/12 secure their night location. Company A/3/12 had broken contact, and we were standing by if needed. My leg was bothering me, but I was afraid to take the pain pills. Trying to find a night location is bad enough without having a buzz working my head from some drugs. It was dark before we were released. It had been a very long day.

We were told to set our ship down at Maintenance. The crews would repair the sheet metal damage around my gun well. All ten of the slicks had received some type of damage today. Three of the four gunships were also damaged. We learned that all ships were on stand-down tomorrow. We had only three ships flyable. These would be used for stand-by if needed. I guess the higher ups decided we weren't much good to anyone, so we got the day off. I enjoyed a few beers and the pain killers that night. I didn't have to worry about tomorrow, so tonight I relaxed and thanked God I was still alive.

CASUALTY REPORT
March 30, 1969

SFC. Art M. Bradberry	RA24503966	08/07/1931	Age 37
PFC James C. Fox	US56732555	05/27/1947	Age 21
SP4 Johnny A. Gibson	US54762951	04/18/1948	Age 20
SGT Charles M. Lamby	US51776631	06/04/1945	Age 23
SGT Fred D. Smith	RA16967834	05/31/1949	Age 19

MISSING IN ACTION

SP4 Clarence A. Latimer   298677077   08/27/1947   Age 21
Promoted to the rank of SFC E-6 and declared "Died while missing" on 07/31/1978

CHAPTER XXIX

"A Day of Rest"

The barracks was very bright and hot as I tried to open my eyes. I found myself lying on my bunk, still in my clothes from last night. Sitting up and looking around my area, I had no concept of what time it was or anything. I could smell coffee and hear people talking at the end of the barracks. After taking off my shirt and lighting a smoke I started towards the bar. My leg was sore and I was having a hard time walking, but I was able to locate the coffee that was brewing behind the bar.

"How's the leg?" Was the greeting I received from a few of the guys who were sitting around the bar. "It's still there," was my best come back. After I had made my morning visit to the piss tube I enjoyed some of Sempek's fresh-brewed coffee. We shot the bull about yesterday, and started to make some plans for the day. It was payday so, if nothing else, we had to get dressed so we could get paid.

I took a long shower. The dirt from the past month was embedded in my skin. I looked like a prune by the time I walked back to my bunk. Jeff helped me change the bandage and I got dressed. It was the middle of the morning before we got to the Orderly Room to get paid. Of course, the First Sgt. has to tell me that I need a haircut, but he also asks about my leg and then tells Dana that if I need to go to the dispensary, to come and get his jeep. We sure couldn't pass this one up.

We no sooner get back to the barracks than Dana has a plan. He'll go and get Top's jeep, and then we can motor on over to the Air Force Base for lunch at the NCO club. We can do this. Besides, I could go to the 71st Evacuation Hospital and have them look at my leg, just to be legal.

The Air Force has no idea there is a war when it

comes to their bases. All of their buildings are concrete block, with windows, and most have air conditioning. The NCO club has great hamburgers and French fries. The beer and sodas are cold, and not the garbage we have at Holloway. I'm talking Budweiser and Coke. Because we are the Army, we can't just walk into the place. They actually have a dress code. Your uniform has to be clean, and there must be a reason for you to be on the base. With that, and maybe a bribe, we might rate an invitation. We will bring a case of C-Rations, just in case we need the bribe option.

The first stop is the hospital. I explain to the clerk at the front desk what happened, and I give him the orders the doctor at Mary Lou had given me yesterday. I'm taken into an examination room where a nurse checks my leg and places a new bandage. They give me a set of crutches and tell me to stay off it for two days. These crutches will become the feature prop in our little story. No need to use the rations when we can use the old pity story. Dana tells the airman at the door how I was wounded yesterday and he is my gunner. He asks if it would be all right if we grabbed a bite to eat before returning to Holloway, because the hospital was busy and by the time we return, the mess hall will be closed. You would have thought we were General Abrams' personal body guards. We were seated at a table near the bathroom. By the way, did I mention that this base had indoor plumbing? They bring us our food, and then Dana drinks about twelve free beers bought for me, that I couldn't drink because of the pain killers. After spending the better part of the afternoon in this air conditioned paradise, I now have to load Dana into the jeep, because there is no way he can drive back to Holloway. The trick will be getting him back and returning Top's jeep without being seen.

Sneaking in the back way from the hangar, we arrive at the barracks. A couple of the guys help get Jeff

283

into the barracks and Sempek drives the jeep over to the Orderly Room. I stop in and thank the First Sgt. for the use of his jeep. "Where's Dana?" he asks, as I'm about to escape with our lie intact. "He had to get ready for guard," is my reply. Again he asks about my leg and tells me that if I need anything, just ask. Jeff has racked out for a nap with the help of the beer he enjoyed.

The rumor machine was going at full speed by the time I got back to the barracks. It seems that the 1st Brigade of the 4th Infantry will be moving to An Khe. We are to be assigned as their primary support, and we will also be making the move. Now we know why our TO&E (Table of Organization & Equipment) had been changed, and we were now considered an Airmobile Light Unit. This plan had been in the works for a while. During the next few days, part of each platoon will RON (remain over night) at An Khe while plans are completed for the rest of the Company to move.

My ship will remain at Holloway, because now that Stoney is getting ready to go home, he will no longer be flying as platoon leader. Lt. Bonthuis has become the platoon leader, and my ship and its crew have become a float ship. We will remain at Holloway, assigned to whatever unit might need a helicopter that day. This is not what I wanted at all. We also have a new platoon sergeant. SFC Young has been in the Army for over twenty years. This is his second tour in Vietnam. I have not yet met him but it will be just a matter of time before that happens.

Entering the mess hall for supper, I was greeted by a posting that brought a smile to my face. Sgt. Wyatt had gotten the special services to show a movie tonight in the Company area. Being at the far end of the camp, most of us never ventured over to where the movies were shown. We were going to be treated to "The Green Berets" starring John Wayne, the "true story" of the Vietnam War. Growing up in the "Fifties" I had seen this great American hero win the Second World War. He flew "Flying Tigers" to defend Burma. He had stormed the beaches of Iwo Jima with the marines. No matter what branch of the service or what enemy he faced, without him the war would have been lost.

As darkness started to fall we gathered to pick out our spots for the show. The mess hall, which was not big enough for all of us to watch the show, was not used. Instead, the area between our barracks and the mess hall became our theater. The screen was set up at the far end near the shower. We gathered as the stars appeared in the evening sky. Sitting on the sand bags that protected our barracks, we ate cheese and crackers and drank Black Label beer as the movie started.

Watching as John Wayne did all the things that I had loved as a youngster, I started to remember the comments of my father who had watched his movies with me. "BULLSHIT!" My father had spent the war fighting in the Pacific. Having enlisting during the Depression at the age of sixteen, he was already in the service when Pearl Harbor was attacked. During the movies, he would speak his disapproval under his breath so I wouldn't hear. War was not the great adventure that Hollywood made it out to be.

The catcalls and comments flew as the movie continued. The scene where the helicopter is hit three times in the front radio compartment, and does the Hollywood auto-rotation before it crashes and burns, was given a standing ovation. About three-quarters through the movie, the projector jammed because of the dirt that had blown into it. More beer was consumed before the final scene. As John stood with his arm on the small boy's shoulder, telling him that he was there to fight the war for him, the sun was setting on the South China Sea. As great as John Wayne was, I just couldn't believe that he could get the sun to set in the east. The movie ended and, if nothing else, we'd had a good laugh.

After the movie, Sgt. Tuminello showed up to post tomorrow's missions. He asks if I can fly and I tell him yes. We have a 0630 pre-flight and Mr. Thornton is the A/C. I decide to walk over to the hangar and see what kind of shape my ship is in. Mattie joins me. We bullshit as we walk towards the Maintenance hangar. The card games are beginning as we start our walk to the hangar. I think he is still not comfortable around the rest of the guys, because of his accent. While I check over my ship, he meets two of the maintenance personnel who are from California. They speak Spanish and he seems at ease with them. After checking the ship I start back to the barracks. Mattie stays to talk with his new friends. I have made this same walk many times since my return. This past month has been the worst of my entire tour. I pray that things will be better starting tomorrow.

CASUALTY REPORT
March 31, 1969

SP4 Daren L. Drinski   US54825238   10/26/1947   Age 21

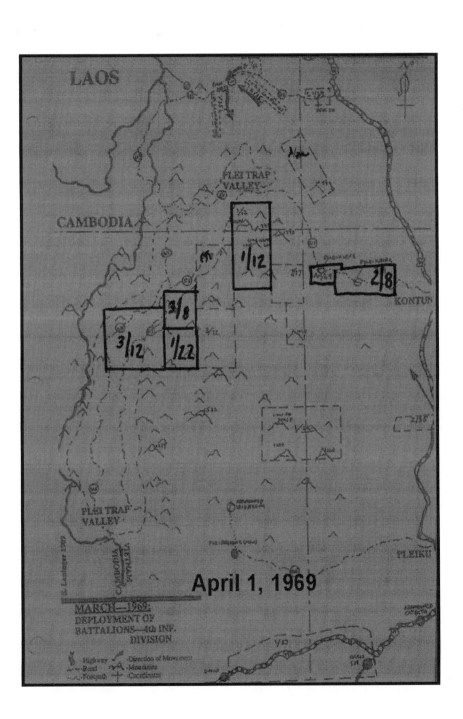

April 1, 1969

MARCH—1969:
DEPLOYMENT OF
BATTALIONS—4th INF.
DIVISION

CHAPTER XXX

"April Fool's Day"

The pre-flight inspection at 0630hrs is like sleeping in before starting work. I have plenty of time to shower and eat breakfast before walking to the ship. Mr. Mathews is the peter-pilot today so I have several questions to answer before pre-flight is done. From the small talk we share as we fly towards Kontum, I learn that Mr. Thornton is transferring to the 361st. They are the Cobra unit that came to Holloway last September. He has decided he is tired of being shot at and it's time he got the chance to shoot back. This starts me thinking about my future in this unit.

There are three ships from our unit that report to LZ Mary Lou this morning. The two other ships are from the Second Flight platoon. It looks as though they have been condemned to the same fate as my ship. Two of our ships will help the 170th AHC move troops from the LZ Mile High to Polei-Kleng. The other will be stuck as C&C bird for the convoys moving out of this area. Mr. Thornton has his choice so we are moving troops out of Mile High.

The action around LZ D-Handle has slowed. In the early morning hours of March 31st Companies A and C/3/12 had received mortar fire at their night location. They suffered no casualties, then moved back to LZ Cider during the day. For the next forty-eight hours B-52 strikes would be carried out in the areas south and west of LZ Brace The troops that we were bringing into Polei-Kleng were being supplied and refitted to assault into this area in the morning.

LZ Mile High has been under the command of the 2nd Brigade since November. It is the main firebase south of Dak To and sits on the northern-most ridgeline of the Plei-Trap Valley. The twin peaks of this mountain were referred to as "Big Mama". The base is well-built and they have a good helicopter pad. Mr. Mathews will get plenty of practice landing and taking off from this mountain top today. We fly high over the Valley and I can see most of the places we visited yesterday. The area around Hill 467 is still smoking from all the artillery rounds that were used to destroy the base. We can hear and feel the Arc Light strikes as they pound the southern end of the Valley.

The troops we move from LZ Mile High are members of Charlie Company, 1/22nd Infantry. The rest of the 1/22nd will be brought to Polei-Kleng during the day. They are being placed under the operational control of the 1st Brigade. Although viewed as replacements for the 1/8th that has departed the Plei-Trap, they will be working the southern part of the Valley. They will spend the day preparing for tomorrow's assault.

The morning passes very slowly today. We drop the troops off at Resupply and we are loaded with the basics for our return flight. Food, water, and ammo are the main items. The pace is nothing compared to a week ago. This was one time that "boring" was a good thing. Sitting in my gun well, I enjoy the warm sun and listen to the radio as we fly back and forth. By noon I'm ready for a short nap and a little time out of the ship.

I spend my time during lunch talking to the newest arrivals to Polei-Kleng. Most ask questions about some of the rumors they have heard. I tell them what I can but I have few of the answers they are looking for. I enjoyed a few minutes of sleep before the pilots return.

The afternoon proves to be more of the same. I find myself dozing off as we fly between Polei-Kleng and Mile High. By 1700hrs we have completed the move and we are released. This might not be as bad as we thought. Being a taxi and going into a relatively secure area and then being released before dark is something I could learn to like. No enemy contact had been reported all day. Maybe the bad guys needed a day off too. For the first time in a month, I am able to do my postflight without a flashlight. To my surprise, half the platoon is gone by the time I reach the barracks. As their ships were made flyable they were sent to An Khe. Sgt Tuminello will stay here while Sgt Young will be with the rest of the platoon in An Khe. We have just started to get the place fixed up, and look what happens. Sempek and a few others have already decided that we are taking the bar with us. At this point I could care less. I spent the rest of the night catching up on my mail and relaxing.

CASUALTY REPORT
April 1, 1969

PFC James J. Curry   RA11625710   03/06/1948   Age 21

CHAPTER XXXI

"Back to the War"

We are back to the 0600hrs pre-flights. A total of four ships are again assigned to the 4th Infantry. The morning is cool, and some low clouds can be seen to the north. The beginning of April is the start of the monsoon season in the central highlands. The rains will start towards the end of the month, but we will now start to have the cloud cover and cooler temperatures in the mornings. By the middle of May we would start having trouble getting into the fire bases early in the morning because of the clouds. Before the end of that month we would be flying only two or three hours a day because of the rains and poor visibility. This would be the last month until October that we would be able to fly every day. Hopefully, we will be out of the Plei-Trap before then.

Today, all units of the 1/22 will be under the control of the 1st Brigade. We will be part of an airlift this morning. The 189th AHC has become primary support for the units in the Valley. We are assigned to help with the lift. Sitting along the runway while the pilots receive their briefing reminds me of what happened a month ago. I have Mattie untie the main rotor and I get the controls set in case we have the same thing happen. A few of the crews from the 189th have gathered by our ships. Because of the damage that is still visible and some of our stories, they are getting the idea that this is not a nice place to be.

We have a two-part operation today. First we will lift Companies A and C/1/22 into LZ Cider. Once they are in place, they will RIF towards the areas that the B-52s have been pounding for the past two days. Once that is completed we will combat assault Companies B, D, and Recon/1/22 into YA806827. This is the area southwest of Hill 947 where some of the heaviest fighting at the beginning of the month had taken place. The knot in my stomach is as big as a beach ball. The past month has taken most of my courage, and I am now left with this overwhelming fear. After two sorties into Cider I breathe a little easier. No problems or bad guys that would cause us any grief. Everything is moving along pretty smooth. By late morning the lift is completed and we break long enough to grab something to eat, and stretch, before we start the second half of the mission.

Blackjack is waiting as we form up on the runway. We are the last ships in the formation because the 189th is in charge of the lift. This is fine by me. I have no problem letting somebody else be the first into a place where you could get shot to hell and back. Most of the guys on my ship appear to be fairly new. I explain that we are near the end of the formation and we would only start firing if we received fire. Over the location of the assault we can see the landing zone. It's a large bomb crater in the middle of the strike area. Most of the trees have been knocked down and the ground is still smoking from the attack. The gunships escort the first ship in and they open fire as the slick lands. The first ship departs with negative fire. As each ship lands we learn more about the landing zone. The crater is the best place to land because the ground is very unstable due to all the trees that were uprooted. It is large enough for the entire ship, but we have to make sure that the grunts stay put until we leave. We don't want any of them walking into a rotor blade. I explain everything to them in detail so they understand what to do. I guess my voice sounded a lot calmer than I felt, because a few of the guys smiled at me as if to say thanks for caring.

We started our approach into the landing zone. I had seen this place many times during the first few days of the operation. This was the route that we had taken into LZ Mary. I could not believe this was the same place. The jungle was gone. Large craters marked the ground. The smell of war entered the ship as we neared the ground. The burning wood and ground was the first to hit you. Then the smell of gun powder and the gas fumes from the napalm were next. Finally the smell of death surrounded us. People had died here. Touching down, I gave the command of **"GO"** and the troops dropped off the ship. We headed back to Polei-Kleng for our next sortie.

The entire afternoon would pass before all units were deployed into the landing zone. A few ships reported fire as they flew between Polei-Kleng and the landing zone, but none were damaged. We had gotten a foothold on the Cu Don Mountain without suffering one casualty. The hope that the new month would also bring good luck was on everybody's mind.

Our day would not end until after dark. Once again I finished my postflight by the light of my flashlight. Entering the barracks, I discover that only three crews are still at Holloway. We would remain here until we were rotated to An Khe to replace one of those ships when they required maintenance. I've just about had it with this garbage when I hear that there might be an opening in the gun platoon. I walked over to their barracks and after talking to a few of the guys I find out the rumor is true. In the morning I will ask for a transfer. I have nothing to keep me here. Jeff and Stoney are going home and maybe it is time that I get to shoot back with something more than a machine gun.

CHAPTER XXXII

"Nearing the End"

For the third day in a row, we are again assigned to help the 189th in the Valley. The good news was that there were no casualties yesterday. This is the first day in a month that no one died during this operation. Being the odd members we are elected to resupply LZ Swinger and LZ D-Handle. Most of the other ships will be supporting the 1/22. They are working the area southwest of LZ Cider. The traffic around the Supply area has dropped to nothing, now the 1/8 has moved out of the northern section of the Valley. The Red Fox is still there to greet us as we land.

As the ship is loaded, we talk about everything that is going on. I tell him Stoney and Jeff are about to leave and our platoon is being sent to An Khe. He is also getting short, and was hoping to be out of this place by the end of the month. We have about 1100 lbs of ammo and water ready for LZ Swinger before we head out.

The perimeter around Swinger is starting to get pretty full of garbage. Cardboard boxes from the C-Rations and cans are piled near the landing pad. The large brass casings from the artillery rounds are stacked nearby. These will be placed in a sling and hauled out by the CH-47s. By now, most of the bunkers are actually comfortable. This is either the second or third time that this base has been used. I wonder how much longer before we abandon it again. We return with a couple of passengers and their empty water containers.

While we resupply, C/1/22 has moved from their night location at YA 821795 and they are advancing towards the area southwest of LZ Cider. This area has been pounded with five B-52 strikes in the past week. The enemy continues to remain and fight for this area.

Once we have completed the resupply of Swinger, we start moving supplies into D-Handle. The area in this part of the Valley looks more like the surface of the moon than the jungle we were flying over a month ago. The bomb craters are everywhere and most of the trees are twisted, smoldering match sticks. The ground is black, and small fires still burn where some of the trees remain. This is the area where the 1/22 is now operating. The good thing is that we would not have any trouble landing, because the trees are nowhere to be seen.

As noon approaches, we receive word that one of the platoons from C/1/22 has made contact with an unknown-sized force. We are told to stand by and to refuel in case we are needed. The main body of their Company has moved to reinforce the platoon. We sit for almost an hour before we are given the word. C/1/22 has broken contact and is withdrawing. They have wounded, and we are to evacuate them. Blackjack is on station and will guide us to the company.

We have no trouble locating the company once we are over the Valley. Hovering into the bomb crater, we load six wounded. The ground is very hot. The heat can be seen rising as we sit on the ground. The dirt and ash is stirred into the air as our rotor blades turn. It is becoming hard to see. We finally leave this living hell with our wounded cargo. At Mary Lou the routine has become very old. We help unload the wounded and head back into the Valley. By the time we return, the wounded are all out of the landing zone. While we return to Polei-Kleng to continue resupply, another company makes contact. B/1/22 has made contact east of where C/1/22 had engaged the enemy. We continue to Polei-Kleng for ammo and water in case it is needed by this company.

We return to learn that the enemy has broken contact and B/1/22 has pulled back to their night location. They have one of their Kit Carson Scout slightly wounded, but he should be able to remain with the company. We are to first drop this load of supplies at C/1/22's location and then return to resupplying the rest of the companies.

We spent the rest of the afternoon running supplies into the firebases and night locations. Even though there are ships from the 189th working the area, it is like we are alone. There is none of the normal talk between ships that I have been accustomed to for the past month. Being an orphan is not how I would like to spent the war. I can only hope that I will be transferred to the gun platoon.

The empty barracks does nothing to improve my mood. I feel completely deserted and alone. Why did I decide to return to this awful place? I don't think I will last until September.

CASUALTY REPORT
April 3, 1969

SP4 John T. Montgomery	US51838583	05/08/1949	Age 19
PFC Edward F. Morrill	US51731323	01/03/1948	Age 21
SGT Gene L. White	US54820771	09/13/1946	Age 22
SGT Ronald V. Hacker	US51835645	04/08/1948	Age 20

CHAPTER XXXIII

"One Last Push"

I received the news that I would be going to the gun platoon by the end of the month. This makes things a little better as we complete the pre-flight. I am flying with the "Hawk" today. At least I have the comfort of a good pilot flying my ship. We head for Polei-Kleng with one other ship from the company.

Shutting down on the runway near Brigade Headquarters, we wait as the pilots are briefed. Sempek is bound and determined to figure a way to get the bar to An Khe. At this point I could care less. Just get me out of this Valley and this platoon. I can see several trucks unloading troops in the Resupply area. Most appear to be brand new. I wander towards the mess hall to get a cup of coffee and bullshit with some of the guys who are stuck on KP. The word is that the brigade will be pulling out of the Valley in the next few days. If the brigade is doing that, why are there so many new guys hanging around the Supply area? New guys mean reinforcements. Reinforcements mean only one thing. We are staying for a while longer.

The pilots finally return, and we find out what is going on. We are moving new people to LZ Brace and there A/3/8 and C/3/8 will rotate personnel to make two companies. The few survivors of A/3/8 have been at Brace since March 4th. They have been used mostly as security guards for the base. Once they are reorganized, both units will move into the same area as the 1/22. The brass wants to make one last sweep in that area before pulling out of the Valley.

Hovering into Supply, I get my first look at the replacements. All have brand-new equipment and that look of complete hopelessness. Seeing them actually makes me feel better. I know what is going on, and I will be going home in September. These guys still have an entire year before they can even think about going home. As far as not knowing what is going on, they might be better off that way. I check weapons and explain to them what is going on today. Don't jump off the helicopter and to stay low as they move away from it.

We spent the morning moving people to LZ Brace and hauling empty water containers back to be refilled at Supply. The morning passes pretty quickly, and nothing of any interest happens as we ferry the new troops in. The crew talks about the possible move to An Khe. Mr. Hawkins would like fly in different areas other than Kontum and Dak To. Mattie doesn't care one way or the other. He just arrived here and he wouldn't know the difference of one from the other.

After lunch we start to resupply the firebases. The 189th are now moving A/3/8 and C/3/8 into the areas southwest of LZ Brace. They will set up night locations and in the morning start to sweep the area with the 1/22nd. LZ D-Handle is now considered Ft. Apache. They are in the middle of "Indian" country, and we are their only way in or out. The area to their east is completely destroyed. There is only a narrow strip of jungle between the bombed out area and their base. To their west is Cambodia. Everybody knows the bad guys are only a stone's throw away. Most of these guys were part of TF Swift. They have been here the entire month.

Mail, food, and water are a welcome sight. We take two guys back with us because they are going on R&R. The looks on their faces tell me that they never want to see this place again. Things have been very quiet the past few days. Two small firefights in the past five days are nothing compared to a week ago. We all hope it will continue.

Our day ends as most had during the past month. We fly home in the late evening and I pull my postflight with my flash light. I drop by the gun platoon barracks before I head for mine. I have a beer with some of the guys. I catch a lot of grief about being one of the only crews still flying the Valley. I tell them I'm thinking of asking for the II Corps bird. They all laugh knowing Baker would kill me before giving up that job.

I find several letters on my bunk when I get to the barracks. Most ask the same question. Why haven't I written home in so long? I don't know what to say about this place. I sure can't tell them the truth. I guess I will just stay with my standard lines. Hi. I'm fine. How are you? That way they would at least know I'm still alive.

CASUALTY REPORT
APRIL 4, 1969

None Reported

CHAPTER XXXIV

"The Last Bloody Nose"

Unlike the past week, this morning is cloudy and there is haze that covers the ground. The signs of the monsoon season are starting to appear. The hot, dry days will soon be replaced with day-long rains and temperatures that will actually seem cold. Our days in the Valley are numbered. By the end of the month, we might have trouble getting out of Holloway in the morning because of cloud cover.

We have supplies to deliver to several bases today. LZ Cider and D-Handle will be our main customers and, if time permits, some of the outposts. The mood at Cider is tense. Several units are working the Valley today, and it's just a matter of time before something happens. For the second day since the start of the operation, we had no casualties yesterday. If the brass were smart they would throw in the towel and start pulling these units out of here. If something bad did happen, we no longer have the means to reinforce as we did two weeks ago. Most of the 1/8th has left the area for An Khe. The 3/8 is still way under strength. The 1/35th is still involved at Dak To and there aren't any units left without pulling out of LZ Mile High. We are now between the famous rock and a hard place.

Company C/3/8 has left their night location at YA 826906 and will sweep towards Hill 871. They are moving towards units of the 1/22nd that are now working as a blocking force near YA 806825. Just before noon a platoon from D/1/22 spots soldiers in a bunker complex. They withdraw and call for air and artillery strikes. We monitor the radios as we fly our supplies into the bases. After the attacks are completed the platoon moved back into the area. The platoon is ambushed from a second bunker complex as they enter the area. Another platoon from D/1/22 is sent in to help. They encountered a flanking force and also become engaged. Gunships and Cider aircraft support the troops as they try to regroup and fall back. A running battle continues until 1620hrs when contact is finally broken.

We start to pull the wounded out once the units have secured a landing zone for us. They have one dead, five missing (killed) and seventeen wounded. We are the second bird in and we pull six souls aboard. After dropping them off at LZ Mary Lou, we stop at Supply for ammo before returning to D/1/22's location. At their location we learn that we are pulling the company out. We pick up the first load for LZ Cider. The brass has decided to pound the area with artillery and air strikes. It is dark before we finally get the last soldier to LZ Cider. The rest of the units have been instructed to pull back and starting tomorrow, we would start to pull all of them out of the Valley.

CASUALTY REPORT
April 5, 1969

CPL James A. Brock	RA14937588	07/30/1948	Age 20
CPL Louis Brown	US67107099	06/07/1947	Age 21
SGT Donald L. Cline	US67111158	02/25/1950	Age 19
SGT Steven J. Hubert	US 6565282	05/15/1947	Age 21
SGT George J. Hyatt	US56961045	10/06/1946	Age 22
CPL Burley D. Kiracofe	US54981697	11/18/1947	Age 21
CPL Steven Michalski	US56460529	08/30/1947	Age 21
CPL Michael L. Wertman	US52860317	09/28/1948	Age 20

CHAPTER XXXV

"The Final Act"

For the next three days, we dodged artillery and air strikes as we supplied the firebases in the southern section of the Valley. The enemy had either pulled back into Cambodia, or had just dug in and waited for us to leave. There were no attacks, and few bullets were fired during this time. At the end of the third day, LRRP teams were sent in to recon the area for enemy forces and to recover our missing.

On April 10th and 11th units from 1/22nd and 3/12th recovered a total of sixteen missing who were now known to be dead. Following these last sweeps of the area, all units closed on the nearest firebase for extraction.

April 12th and 13th were the days that all of the units from the 1/22nd were extracted from the area around the Cu Don Mountain to Polei-Kleng. Companies A, C, and Rcn/3/8 Infantry were also extracted.

The final extractions came on the 14th of April. The last units out were the first to have been put in. The 3/12th closed LZ D-Handle and moved to LZ Mary Lou, where they would board trucks and prepare to deploy with the rest of the 1st Brigade to An Khe. Troops from the 3/8th would fall under 2nd Brigade's control until units from Dak To could join them at Polei-Kleng. The last casualties of this operation would come on April 6th and 14th. SP4 Robert A. Wojtyna, US 52858703, 02/08/1948, Age 21, on April 6th; and SGT Bobby L. Denton, US 54512456, 12/07/1947, Age 22, on April 14th.

Operation Wayne Grey had begun on 1 March 1969 and ended 14 April 1969. During this time US casualties totaled 179 killed (I have included some members of the 2nd Brigade in the casualty reports because I feel that they were also caused by this action. Kontum Province was a very unstable place during these two months and several events contributed to the battle that took place.), 1,015 wounded, and eight missing. Enemy losses were 575 killed and four POWs. An accurate number of wounded could not be established but unconfirmed reports puts the number over 1,500. Because of the amount of enemy equipment captured, it is believed that this number is valid. The main mission was to interrupt enemy supply routes and hinder his ability to wage war in the central highlands. This, for the time being, was accomplished. As for the 119th Assault Helicopter Company, we would suffer one killed and five wounded. Of the nineteen transports (UH-1H) that would start this mission three ships were destroyed and fourteen received combat damage. Of the eight gunships (UH-1C), all but one would be damaged during this time. For their efforts during this time 54 decorations for heroism and valor would be awarded to the air crews of the 119th. The untold stories of the people who kept us flying should have rated another two hundred medals. For every soldier who entered the Valley, there should be a medal. I know that, when our time comes, each of us who were there will enter the gates of heaven because we have served our time in hell.

The following reports are part of a web site that was put together by two soldiers who were on the ground during this operation. The make-up of the first report came from the daily journals and after action reports of the companies of the 1/8th Infantry. Two of the authors of this web site are Mike Trebbe and Jerry Horton. They deal with all of the action that took place in the northern section of the Valley. This is often referred to as the YB area of operation, or A/O. As a member of Company A/1/8, Jerry Horton was wounded during the later stages of the operation. He is also writing a book about his time in the Valley. The second report is the brigade "After Action

Report" that was filed with the Department of the Army in May 1969. As you read these reports, remember that these are taken from after action reports and daily journals that were written as the events unfolded. The stress of combat, and the confusion that occurs during a battle, contribute to some of the conflicting reports of certain events. I did add information to the first report that I discovered from reports other than ones from the 4th Infantry Division. Some of this information did help clarify some of the conflicting information that I discovered while doing my research. In writing this book I have tried to give the reader a feel for what it was like to be above the war. Only the soldiers who fought on the Valley floor can understand the true horrors of war. They lived, ate, and slept in the hell that I only visited during the day. They are the true heroes of the place we called "The Valley".

SUBJECT: After Action Report for Operation Wayne
Grey (1st Bn, 8th Infantry Reports Follow)

I.   Operation conducted by 1st Brigade, 4th Infantry
Division from 1 March 1969 to 29 March 1969.

On 27 February, the 1st Battalion 8th Infantry's tactical
order from 1st Brigade while located at LZ/FSB Patt where
they were located with Company C 1st Battalion, 8th
Infantry. At the time the operations warning order was
received, Companies A and D were under the operational
control of the 2nd Battalion, 8th Infantry, on operations
north of Kontum City. B Company was under the
operational control of the 2nd Brigade and they were
located at Fire Support Base 34 near Ben Het Special Forces
Camp.operation center received a warning

First Brigade operations gave 1st Battalion, 8th Infantry the
mission as shown in attached overlay (see Appendix A).
On 28 February, Companies A and D moved to LZ Mary
Lou under the operational control of 2nd Battalion, 8th
Infantry, where they were passed to the operational
control of 3rd Battalion, 8th Infantry. From Mary Lou the 2
companies were moved by convoy to LZ Bass at Polei
Kleng Special Forces Camp. Company C minus,
Headquarters minus, with the reconnaissance and mortar
platoons moved by convoy from LZ Patt to LZ Bass at
Polei Kleng. The remainder of Company C was moved
from LZ Bobbie by airlift to LZ Bass. The 1st Battalion, 8th
Infantry minus was at this time prepared to combat assault
into sub AO 1. Bravo Company located at Fire Support
Base 34 was prepared to combat assault into Fire Support
Base 20.

1 March, 1969: 1st Battalion, 8th Infantry on 1 March began
its first CA by moving Company B from Fire Support Base

34 to Fire Support Base 20. Headquarters minus and A Battery, 6th of the 29th Artillery (Direct Support Battery) were moved from LZ Bass at Polei Kleng to Fire Support Base 20. The battalion mortar section minus was moved from LZ Bass to Fire Support Base 20 along with Headquarters minus. Companies C, D and A along with Headquarters minus remained at LZ Bass in preparation for Companies C and D's move to LZ Susan and Company A's Combat Assault to LZ Turkey. The reconnaissance platoon remained at LZ Bass to work in liaison with Company A. Artillery at Fire Support Base 20 employed 45 rounds of 175 mm support fires from Ben Het.

2 March, 1969: 1st Battalion, 8th Infantry on 1 March continued combat assault operations from LZ Bass to LZ Susan with Companies C and D. Company A made a Combat Assault to vicinity YB 822031. Company D proceeded along the northern axis of advance and established NL at 740047.

After Combat Assault, Company A walked to LZ Turkey. At LZ Turkey Company A was to establish a blocking force for Company C sweeping on the southern axis and Company D sweeping on the north. These axes are centered on trails vicinity YB 762032 and 765055 running from east to west respectively. Company A reported light contact with an ambush by the 81 platoon and some sniper fire while en -route to the Night Location. The 4th platoon reported contact with an enemy force in bunkers, vicinity YB 820025. They pulled back employing 81mm mortars. Enemy casualties were unknown. One U.S. wounded in action.

Company B secured A Battery, 6th of the 29th Artillery (Direct Support Battery) at Firebase 20 with local security, patrols and Short Range Patrols. The reconnaissance platoon was employed in liaison with Company A. The mortar platoon (-) supported Company A's activities at LZ Turkey, and the remainder supported battalion operations from Fire Support Base 20.

Company C proceeded in the vicinity of an air strike on an enemy truck convoy. They found vicinity YB 765030, an abandoned but intact enemy truck. One platoon secured the truck while the main element moved to a night location at 755034. Company C discovered in the air strike area, on the back of the truck 52 rounds of 105mm howitzer ammunition (Chicom). The discovered truck was a 1-½ ton 4-wheel drive with assorted motor pool equipment. Company C's 81 platoon, vicinity 860033, observed 2 individuals, one with a flashlight at 2100 hours. Claymores were employed, individual with flashlight was seen falling and the flashlight continued to burn. At 2155 hours, 4 additional individuals were sighted in the same place, one saying "Lai Day". Claymores were again employed and the platoon moved back to the company's main element.

Air Support: Troop A, 7th of the 17th Cavalry encountered heavy fire from vicinity YB 765030. This fire encountered was on the combat assault into LZ Susan. The Cavalry also reported two 2-½ ton trucks destroyed by air strike vicinity YB 760033. Three NVA soldiers were confirmed killed (Airforce). Air strike employed 765034 on an enemy vehicle in the open.

Artillery: LZ Susan had 200 HE 105mm howitzer rounds fired from Fire Support Base 20. LZ Susan had 25 HE rounds of 155mm fired in their support from LZ Swinger. LZ Turkey had 125 HE 105-mm rounds fired from Fire Support Base 20. LZ Turkey had 25 rounds HE 155mm fired from LZ Swinger. Company A's 84C upon contact fired 105mm from Fire Support Base 20 at grid 8002.

3 March, 1969: 1st Battalion, 8th Infantry on 3 March

continued reconnaissance in force operations with Companies C and D sweeping from west to east and Company A blocking at vicinity LZ Turkey. Company B continued to secure Fire Support Base 20 with local security, patrols and two platoon sized ambushes. Company B ambushes were located at vicinity 808068 and 824066. Company A reported contact vicinity 819029 with enemy in bunkers. Mortars and artillery were employed with unknown results. Elements were drawn back to night location so air strike could be employed. One U.S. WIA in initial contact and 2 NVA were found in a sweep after the air strike and artillery were employed. At vicinity 815023 Company A's 1st and 4th platoons found one NVA who had been killed in action and 2 AK-47s. Company C reported contact in the same vicinity of the vehicle captured vicinity 760033. Contact resulted as the point element moved past the vehicle. Results were one U.S KIA, 3 NVA KIA (BC). The truck captured on the 2nd was later extracted and taken to LZ Bass. Company D continued from their previous night location to 754049 along the trail without incident. They established local security and ambushed the trail. Reconnaissance platoon Trace 5 operation in liaison with Company A sighted 4 or 5 NVA near their night location at 846024. The mortar platoon (-) supported battalion operations from Fire Support Base 20. The 81 section supported Company A's operations at LZ Turkey.

Air Support: Troop A, 7th of the 17th Cavalry supported Company C when they heard vehicle movement near their captured truck. They drew ground fire vicinity YB 761034. Gunships employed rockets and Cavalry reported 2 NVA killed. Gunships were employed at 819029 in support of Company A. Gunships also sighted and engaged bunkers at grid 815023 and 814026. Cider 10 emplaced air strikes on 819029 in support of Company A.

Artillery: Grid 762033. Company C's 4th platoon employed 105-mm rounds from Fire Support Base 20 on truck's location. A contact mission for 155-mm from LZ Swinger and 105-mm from Fire Support Base 20 on grids 810023 and 814025 was called by Company A. Also 105-mm from Fire Support Base 20 was fired at grid 816023.

4 March, 1969: 1st Battalion, 8th Infantry on 4 March, 1969 continued its reconnaissance in force mission. Company A moved from YB 822032 to 825042 to reestablish a new patrol base. Company A's 83B (ambush) location at 819019 observed 15 NVA approximately 45 meters from their position but took no action. They also sighted 10 flashlights moving toward their position. Artillery was employed with negative results. Company B continued Fire Support Base 20 security with local security patrols and 2 ambushes at coordinates 795060 and 835057. Company C moved from their previous night location to 773020. They encountered some antipersonnel mines general grid 7503. The mines were 2"X2" with a black plastic case. No injuries were suffered because of the mines. Company C also discovered another truck, vicinity 777025 with sleeping huts and a bunker complex nearby. Replacement parts, some personal equipment and maintenance gear was found with the vehicle. The truck was in good running order and it was driven from its location to a suitable LZ at 773024. The vehicle was destroyed upon order by Brigade. Company C also fixed a position on the enemy artillery at grid YB 777018 that had been firing on 3rd Battalion, 12th Infantry. Counter battery fire was employed and this succeeded in silencing the enemy battery. Company C moved to their night location at YB 773028. Company D moved to 761045 without incident. They set up security and ambushes along the trails. Reconnaissance platoon continued to work in liaison with Company A. Mortar platoon minus supported battalion operations from Fire Support Base 20. One 81 section supported Company A's activities for A's location.

Air Support: None

Artillery: Reconnaissance by fire by 105mm at Fire Support Base 20 for Company D. 105mm employed at grid 777018 fired on suspected enemy artillery position. Fifty rounds for this area added to night firing program. 105mm and 155mm fired at grid 777016 against suspected enemy artillery position.

5 March, 1969: 1st Battalion, 8th Infantry on 5 March, 1969 continued reconnaissance in force with Companies C and D. Company A's 83B at grid 819016 initiated the ambush resulting in 2 NVA killed. Two AK-47 rifles and one 9mm pistol CIA. The same element moving back to Company A's night location observed 2 NVA. The NVA were taken under fire. One NVA was wounded and captured. He was extracted and flown to Polei Kleng. Ambush 83 C at 813022 initiated an ambush at 2005 hours resulting in one NVA killed and 2 U.S. WIA. Fire from ambush's rear resulted in the 2 WIA (U.S.). Contact believed to be with the flank element of a large unit. Artillery was employed in same area with unknown results. Company also secured LZ for Company C's extraction. Companies C and A moved to co-location at 822032. They established a patrol base employing maximum platoon-sized ambush elements. Company B continued security of Fire Support Base 20 with local security, patrols and 2 platoon-sized ambushes at 805065 and at 834056. Company C located at 773026 moved to LZ at 800023. During the move they utilized reconnaissance by fire. At 1300 hours the point element spotted 1 NVA, vicinity 807025, and took him under fire. At 1543 they received heavy fire from three sides of their position. Fire came from trees and concealed position. The elements involved in contact could only move with extreme difficulty. Contact was so close that breaking contact was difficult. The recovery of US KIAs, and WIAs was done with extreme difficulty. The 7th of the 17th Cavalry assisted in extraction and suppressive fires for Company C. It is believed that element was in contact with an L-shaped ambush. During their extraction, enemy artillery was fired at Company C's LZ. No casualties or damage resulted. Gunships firing at suspected enemy location 777017 received intense ground fire. Incoming artillery ceased after gunships were employed. FAC requested but none available. Company C's extraction was completed at 1909 hours. The results of contact included, 7 NVA KIA (BC) 2 U.S. KIA, 12 U.S. WIA. One U.S. later died of wounds. Companies C and A moved to 822032 to establish patrol base and to conduct maximum platoon-sized ambush elements. Company D moved from 761045 to new night location at 773056 employing one platoon-sized ambush, vicinity 782056. Reconnaissance platoon continued to operate in liaison with Company A. Mortar platoon minus continued to support battalion operations from Fire Support Base 20. One 81 section operated in support of Companies C and A at YB 822032. Combat sky spot called for at 2400 hours on enemy artillery location 777016 from information received from Battalion Commanding Officer, liaison (Artillery) Officer Company C, and gunship observations.

Air Support: Troop A, 7th of the 17th Cavalry supported Company C's move with slicks and flew cover for them as they moved. They also assisted Company C in breaking contact by firing close in fire with their gunships. Gunships also fired suppressive fires on suspected artillery location grid 777016.

Artillery: From Fire Support Base 20, 105mm fired on grid 819016 for Company A at 0905 hours. At 1030 hours 105mm and 155mm fired 92 and 50 HE respectively on suspected enemy battery position. At 1300 hours, 155mm fired reconnaissance for Company D. Reconnaissance by fire at 1315 hours by 105mm for Company C at grid 790021. Reconnaissance by fire by Company D 777047, 155mm. Reconnaissance by fire at 1355 hours for Company C at grid 790022, 30 HE, 105mm. At 1450, 155mm and 105mm counter fire directed against 776016. At 1845 hours at grid 777016 105mm emplaced to silence enemy being placed on Company C.

6 March, 1969: 1st Battalion, 8th Infantry on 6 March, 1969 continued reconnaissance in force with Companies A, C and D. Company A's emplaced platoon-sized ambushes at grids 819027 and 818027 at 1814 hours. Company A experiences incoming 105mm howitzer. Counter battery from Fire Support Base 20 emplaced at grids 810020 and 811039. After artillery was employed incoming ceased. Company B continued to secure Fire Support Base 20 with local security, patrols and ambushes at 805065, 810085, 824086 and 819077. Company C continued reconnaissance in force from 828040. Two platoon-sized ambushes were employed at grids 820040 and 828035 with 4 NVA engaged with negative results from the later grid. Company D continued reconnaissance in force from 777052 and moved to Fire Support Base 20 at 2345 hours. They observed an enemy bunker complex at 793059 showing recent use. Reconnaissance platoon worked in liaison with Company A. Mortar platoon minus supported battalion operations from Fire Support Base 20. One 81 section supported Companies A and C operations.

Air Support: HH47 adjusted 105mm's from Fire Support Base onto grid 806032 (possible bunker complex) HH46 adjusted 3 rounds Firecracker, vicinity 806032, onto suspected enemy personnel positions.

Artillery: At 0750 reconnaissance by fire for platoon minus continued to support battalion operations from Fire Support Base 20 with 1 81 Company A at grid 807021, 105-mm. At 1055 hours, 4.2 inch and 105-mm for Company D at grid 797054, enemy in open. At 1820 hours Company A received incoming. Counter battery was directed on grid 810020. At 1825 hours counter mortar on grid 811039. (See air assets for 2 additional missions) NFP 805040, 100 rounds of 4.2 inch. YB 777016, 150 rounds 105mm.

7 March, 1969:1st Battalion, 8th Infantry on 7 March, 1969 continued reconnaissance in force with Companies A and C in the A.O. Company A continued security of night location, vicinity YB 825027, utilizing OP, LP, patrols. Their platoon-sized ambushes at 819024 and 818027 kept up their surveillance. Two NVA were sighted near Company A's CP location. They were taken under fire with negative results. Company B continued security of Fire Support Base 20 with local security, patrols and platoon-sized ambushes. Ambushes were employed at YB 819079 and 819077. Company C continued security of their night location with local LP's and OP's. They employed platoon-sized ambushes at YB 820040 and 828035. One NVA was sighted near Company C CP and was taken under fire with negative results. Company D continued to secure Fire Support Base 20 with local LP's and OP's. Platoon-sized ambush at YB826030. Reconnaissance platoon worked in liaison with Company A. Tracer 5 at YB 826030. Mortar section at Company A and C's location.

Air Support: Troop A, 7th of the 17th Cavalry operated in the A.O. At 1635 Comic Blue 31 reported sighting 2 artillery pieces at grid 779028. Gunships were employed and they reported destroying one piece and damaging the second.

Artillery: At 1300 hours 155mm fired firecracker on suspected enemy artillery position. At 1610 105mm fired in

313

support of Company A receiving small arms fire. Night fire program: 75 rounds 4.2-inch mortar on grid 793058.

8 March, 1969: 1st Battalion, 8th Infantry on 8 March, 1969 continued its reconnaissance in force mission with Company A. Companies B and D continued local security and patrols from Fire Support Base 20 employing one platoon-sized ambush each. Company B's ambush vicinity being YB 808078 and Company D's vicinity being YB 838075. Company C continued to secure their previous night location with local security patrols and two platoon-sized ambushes located at vicinity YB 827036 and YB 825027. Reconnaissance platoon continued to operate in liaison with Company A. Mortar platoon continued in support of battalion operations from Fire Support Base 20. Generally the Battalion's operations had negative results.

Air Support: Cider 10 (FAC) employed an air strike at grid vicinity YB 778018. The 7th of the 17th Cavalry's red birds reported destroying 1 NVA truck (2 ½ ton) and killing 1 NVA soldier in the vicinity of 105mm howitzer position. They also reported sighting another truck at the same general grid. Comic 31 also sighted another truck, vicinity YB 780022. Dust off was utilized at Fire Support Base 20 to remove one injured engineer.

Artillery: Vicinity 773026 the Battalion Liaison Officer employed 110 HE rounds of 105mm howitzer and 15 firecracker rounds of 155mm on enemy in open vicinity YB 847007. Results were three confirmed NVA KBA (Artillery). Vicinity 773026 the 7th of the 17th Cavalry employed 155mm on suspected enemy location. Vicinity 77017 Cavalry employed 105mm against an enemy artillery position with unknown results. Vicinity 834074 Company D employed mortars from Fire Support Base 20 in a reconnaissance by fire program. Night firing program: 110 rounds of 105-mm against suspected enemy artillery

314

positions and areas of enemy sightings that day.

9 March, 1969: 1st Battalion, 8th Infantry on 9 March, 1969 continued its mission to interdict the enemy's movement within the A.O. Company A conducted a BDA from their night location at YB 853025 and returned to the night location YB 826028 due to air strikes being employed in the vicinity of their BDA mission's A.O. Company A also employed 2 platoon-sized ambushes vicinity 817022 and at 824014. Company B continued local security of Fire Support Base 20 plus one platoon-sized ambush vicinity 818065 C Company located vicinity 828040 continued local patrols and security and its ambush missions to the southwest, west and northeast. A 2 platoon-sized ambush was employed vicinity 828036. Company D continued Fire Support Base 20 security mission employing local security, patrols and one platoon-sized ambush vicinity 817089. Reconnaissance platoon worked in liaison with Company A and moved to Company A's location. Tracer 6 was employed vicinity YB 828032 with the mission of ambushing the trail in that vicinity. The mortar platoon continued to support battalion operations from Fire Support Base 20.

Air Support: Comic Blue 6 reported enemy trucks vicinity 777018 and 780024. These trucks had been previously destroyed by an air strike but they had been covered with foliage during the night. Artillery emplaced with unknown results.

Artillery; Night firing program. 167 rounds of 105mm howitzer were employed on routes of regress to the southwest. An arc-light in the area where enemy were sighted in the open near a suspected mortar position was also fired upon.

10 March, 1969: 1st Battalion, 8th Infantry on 10 March, 1969 continued its reconnaissance in force mission with two companies operating from patrol bases utilizing maximum platoon-sized forces and local patrols. One company undertook mission to extract enemy artillery pieces at grid 779028, which was successfully accomplished. One company secured Fire Support Base 20 with local security patrols and two platoon-sized ambushes. Reconnaissance platoon's Tracer 6 was utilized as ambush vicinity YB828030 (negative results). Company A continued reconnaissance in force vicinity YB 825036. Local security patrols and two platoon-sized ambushes were employed in this area with negative results. One platoon was on standby to assist Company D's operation. Company B continued Fire Support Base 20 security mission; employing two platoon-sized ambushes, local security, and local patrols encountering negative results. Company C continued reconnaissance in force mission operating from patrol base vicinity YB 828040 employing two platoon-sized ambushes, local security and local patrols with negative results. Company D received mission to retrieve two enemy held 105mm howitzers vicinity YB 779028. Company D was lifted from Fire Support Base 20 to a LZ vicinity YB 770026. With combat assault complete 1159 hours, they regrouped and moved overland to objective area. Light contact was encountered vicinity YB 777018 from secured artillery pieces in bunker complex. A LAW was employed against bunker with fleeing NVA killed by Company D forward security element. Results of action: Two U.S. 105-mm howitzers recaptured and taken to Polei Kleng, one NVA KIA with personal effects and SKS carbine, two trucks previously burned by napalm were completely disabled with thermite grenade, explosive charges, and burning gasoline. These same two trucks contained about 4500-lbs. rice, 50 lbs. beans and a 55-gallon drum of gasoline. Another truck, well dug in and camouflaged, was uncovered and destroyed with thermite grenade, explosive charges and burning gasoline. Captured equipment, including communication equipment, wire, 1942 Honeywell quad (destroyed), plus various personal effects were captured; 30 rounds 105mm Chicom fixed ammunition was destroyed in place. The operation revealed a large enemy complex in this vicinity approximately one kilometer wide and one kilometer long. Company D received ground fire on pickup zone on airlift back to Fire Support Base 20. Artillery was employed on LZ vicinity in the form of a preparation with a total of 199 rounds being expended for operation. Artillery was also employed on PZ after final extraction of Company D with results unknown. Friendly casualties consisted of one U.S. WIA. Reconnaissance platoon continued working in liaison with Company A. Tracer 6 was located vicinity YB 828030 serving as an ambush. Mortar platoon continued to support battalion operations from Fire Support Base 20 with all mortars except those located at Mary Lou. One new 4.2 mortar was received at Fire Support Base 20 to DX one worn out of same dimensions.

11 March, 1969: 1st Battalion, 8th Infantry on 11 March, 1969 continued its reconnaissance in force mission with Company B. securing Fire Support Base 20 utilizing local patrols and security, and platoon-sized ambushes to the southwest, south and southeast of Fire Support Base 20. Companies A and C received mission to conduct BDA vicinity YB 870984. These two companies moved overland toward that location with negative results. Reconnaissance platoon continued to operate in liaison with Company A. Mortar platoon continued to support battalion operations at Fire Support Base 20 employing 7 81-mm mortars and 4 4.2 inch mortars. Four additional mortars are located at LZ Mary Lou. Artillery from A Battery 1st of the 29th Artillery was employed against enemy anti-aircraft gun position vicinity YB 827021 by Headhunter 46. Previously these guns had fired on Hummingbird 1 assisting in Company A and Company C BDA.

Air Support: Cider 10 (FAC) and 15 worked area vicinity YB 827011 and employed air strike. This was the area that enemy 105-mm artillery guns were extracted the previous day.

12 March, 1969: 1st Battalion, 8th Infantry on 12 March, 1969 continued operating in assigned A.O. with Companies A and C conducting BDA and Company B and D conducting local security on Fire Support Base 20. Heavy contact was encountered by Company A during BDA vicinity YB 852003 with possible enemy company dug in. Results of action were 22 NVA KIA, U.S. casualties 2 KIA, 15 WIA and 3 MIA. Company A withdrew to night location vicinity YB 852011 to regroup and reorganize. They conducted local security in vicinity of night location. Company C continued BDA mission in conjunction with Company A moving on a parallel axis with Company A. Company C encountered light contact vicinity YB 851999 with possible enemy squad dug in. After action Company C maneuvered to vicinity night location YB 847006, to regroup and reorganize. Results of action were 1 NVA KIA, 1 U.S. WIA. Company C conducted local security vicinity night location. Company D was on standby to combat assault into Company A's location and to reinforce or relieve in place and continue BDA mission, with Company C. Reconnaissance platoon continued to work in conjunction with Company A on BDA mission. Tracer 5 was being utilized as flank security for Company A. When contact was initiated Tracer 5 was cut off resulting in six MIA. Two men (one WIA) trying to escape and evade back to Company A's night location were detected by radio contact. Mortar platoon continued support of battalion operations on Fire Support Base 20 with 7 81-mm mortars and 4 4.2-inch mortars. Mortar platoon fired support fires with Companies in contact and continued to support both Companies A and C throughout the night.

Air Support: Hummingbird 5 evacuated one U.S. WIA from Company C contact. Medevac was employed vicinity Company A's location for 5 WIA and vicinity Fire Support Base 20 for 1 WIA. Comic Blue 47 with the 7th of the 17th Cavalry supported both Companies A and C and Tracer 5 along with Comic Blue 6 (7th of the 17th Cavalry) during the day's contact. Spooky 21 supported Companies A and C in contact throughout the night.

Artillery: Artillery support from A Battery 6th of the 29th Artillery was fired in support of Company A contact throughout the day. A total of 405 rounds were expended in night fire program in support of Companies A and C.

Combat Losses: Green memo book containing call signs and frequencies of Company A and Battalion net; SOI (compromised with appropriate action taken); total of 7 M16A1 rifles; one starlight scope; one An/PRC-25 radio; 58 rucksacks; ten D-handle shovels; 16 machetes.

Total NVA KIA for 12 March 1969 was 33. Total U.S. casualties were 13 WIA, 4 KIA and 2 MIA.

13 March, 1969: 1st Battalion, 8th Infantry on 13 March, 1969 continued operations in assigned A.O. with Company A regrouping and evacuating WIA and KIA and receiving light contact while moving from previous position to link up with Company C. Prior to the move Company A employed patrols to retrieve missing and killed personnel absent from company. All WIAs and KIAs that were found were evacuated from nearby LZ. Also resupply was accomplished during this action. During the move to the site to link with Company C, Company A experienced light contact resulting in 3 NVA KIA and 4 NVA possible wounded. Also Company A received incoming mortar attack during move with negative friendly casualties. Company employed artillery extensively to cover their advance on the flanks and front formation. Air strike was employed against possible enemy mortar position with unknown results. Company B remained on standby to reinforce and/or assist Company C in their operations. Company C located vicinity YB 847003 remained in position throughout the day awaiting arrival of Company A. Company C sent element to link with Company A and guide them to Company C position. Company C maintained local security and two platoon-sized ambushes near their vicinity throughout the day. Company D along with Company B continued security mission Fire Support Base 20 employing local security, local patrols and Company D supplying one platoon-sized ambush. Reconnaissance platoon continued to work in liaison with Company A with mission to retrieve KIA and WIA. They moved with Company A to new location and established patrol base. At that time reconnaissance platoon had one KIA, one died of wounds (DOW) and 3 MIA from previous day's action. One MIA walked into Company A's previous night location and informed element that the other MIA was dead. Mortar platoon supported battalion operations on Fire Support Base 20, firing no missions on that day.

Air Support: The 7th of the 17th Cavalry's Comic Blue 12 and 15 employed air strike on possible enemy mortar position firing on Company A and C position vicinity YB 850005. Headhunter 46 supplied surveillance and employment of artillery in support of battalion operations. The 7th of the 17th Cavalry supported Company A's operations, which consisted of extraction of WIA and KIA. Medevac also employed in vicinity Company A's previous night location.

Artillery: Artillery support for Company A was fired by Battery A, 6th of the 29th Artillery. This support helped to retrieve all of Company A's WIAs and KIAs. Artillery also covered Company A flanks and frontal portion of formation while moving to link with Company C. Artillery was employed on possible enemy bunker complex vicinity Company A's previous day's contact.

14 March, 1969: 1st Battalion, 8th Infantry on 14 March, 1969 continued operations in assigned A.O. with Company A and C operating from vicinity YB 847003 employing one platoon-sized reconnaissance patrol each. Fifteen rounds assorted 82mm and 60mm mortars were received in location of Companies A and C from enemy positions on three occasions throughout the day. Each time that artillery was employed from Fire Support Base 20 resulting in suppression of enemy fire. Throughout the night Companies A and C employed squad-sized ambushes for local security. Company C employed two platoon-sized patrols who encountered, vicinity YB 856992 to YB 852995 to YB 859994 what appeared to be a large U-shaped enemy bunker complex. They also observed approximately 20 individuals in vicinity of this area and heard voices and what appeared to be large artillery pieces firing vicinity YB 842000. Artillery was employed with negative results. Companies B and D continued Fire Support Base 20 security employing local security patrols and Company B employed one platoon size ambush, vicinity YB 820043 with negative results. Reconnaissance platoon continued working in conjunction with Company A at their night location. Mortar platoon continued supporting battalion operations at Fire Support Base 20.

Air Support: Spooky 22 supported Companies A and C vicinity YB 847003. Headhunter 46 and 6 reported heavy enemy activity at vicinity YB 8697 to YB 8797. It was checked extensively and revealed heavy trail network with extremely recent use.

Artillery: Artillery support from Battery A, 6th of the 29th Artillery was fired on grids YB 852005 CB, YB 854010 adjusted onto enemy bunker, YB 854002, support of Company C platoons, YB 849008, enemy in open for Company A, YB 862997 Company C reconnaissance by fire, YB 856996 Company C reconnaissance by fire, YB 835995 Company A CB, and YB 855000 CNF. Night Firing Program (CFP) Night fires at Fire Support Base Swinger, 500 rounds HE grids YB 853995, YB 859994, YB 857992, YB 850998, YB 838996, YB 838992, YB 838989 and YB 820006; 105-mm howitzer from Fire Support Base 20. Five roadrunners were employed at grids, YB 8300, YB 8599, YB 8699 and YB 8698 – 100 rounds HE.

15 March, 1969: 1st Battalion, 8th Infantry on 15 March, 1969 continued operations in assigned A.O. with Company A and C operating from patrol base employing ambushes and patrols. Company A and C were mortared two times in their patrol base location vicinity YB 847003. A total of 12 rounds were received resulting in 7 U.S. WIA. Companies C and D continued security mission of Fire Support Base 20 employing local patrols, local security, and three platoon-sized ambushes with negative results. Reconnaissance platoon continued to operate in liaison with Company A. Mortar platoon continued support of battalion operations on Fire Support Base 20.

Air Support: Cider 13 and 14 operated in A.O. employing an air strike at vicinity YB 862997 for support of the 7th of the 17th Cavalry sighting of possible U.S. MIA in that vicinity. The 7th of the 17th Cavalry operated in A.O. and sighted enemy in open. They employed ordinance with results unknown. Also in same vicinity sighted U.S. MIA in bomb crater. Extraction was attempted with negative results due to enemy ambush. U.S. individual was sighted vicinity 850998. Medevac was utilized at Company A and C location vicinity 847003 for 7 WIA. Headhunter 46 worked A.O. with negative results. Two MIA, lost in action of 12 March 1969, walked into Company A's position unharmed. This accounted for six MIAs of T-5 element. One was KIA, one individual still MIA at this time.

Artillery: Artillery from Battery A, 6th of the 29th Artillery fired on grid YB 855002 which was suspected enemy in open with fire coming close to friendly element at 2020 hours. Artillery also fired a night firing program of 150 rounds 105mm from Fire Support Base 20, and 100 rounds 155mm from Fire Support Base Swinger. The purpose of these fires was dual. First to supply support for Companies A and C at vicinity YB 847003 against close in concentrations and also H and I.

16 March, 1969: 1st Battalion, 8th Infantry on 16 March, 1969 continued operating in assigned A.O. with Companies A and C operating as a Task Force (Task Force Alpha) moving from previous night location to vicinity YB 817030. During move 2 NVA were sighted, taken under fire, with negative results, vicinity YB 838068. Also in same area another NVA was sighted and killed. In same location the 7th of the 17th Cavalry sighted two 2-½ ton trucks, a large object that was unidentifiable and a few bunkers. Cavalry destroyed both trucks with WP and turned one over on its side. They also destroyed a large caliber machine gun or anti aircraft gun and killed undisclosed number of NVA. Cider 13 dropped heavy bombs in same vicinity. Companies A and C employed local ambushes in vicinity of their night location. Companies B and D continued security mission of Fire Support Base 20 with local Ops, LPs and three platoon-sized ambushes on road to southwest. Reconnaissance platoon was extracted to Fire Support Base 20 to regroup and reorganize leaving Tracer 6 to operate in liaison with Task Force Alpha. Mortar platoon continued to support battalion operations at Fire Support Base 20.

Artillery: Artillery from Battery A 6th of the 29th Artillery fired 15 Roadrunners to support Task Force Alpha with 150 HE rounds from Fire Support Base 20 and 75 rounds 155-mm HE from Fire Support Base Swinger. Task Force Alpha movement was assisted with reconnaissance by fire by artillery throughout the day.

17 March, 1969: 1st Battalion, 8th Infantry on 17 March, 1969 continued operating in assigned A.O. with Task Force Alpha's mission to interdict and suppress enemy movement vicinity of roads near their location. Task Force Alpha moved from previous location to YB 804034 and established patrol base. Company A sent two platoons to vicinity YB 788023 mission to crater and abertee ford that vicinity. This mission was successfully accomplished. Company C conducted two platoon-sized patrols vicinity YB 794022 and YB 789011. Ambush actions for Task Force Alpha were concentrated on roads to the east, north and south. Company C ambush vicinity YB 815022 observed three NVA moving northeast. These individuals were taken under fire at approximately 50-75 meters with negative results. Companies B and D continued security mission of Fire Support Base 20 employing local security, patrols and 4 platoon-sized ambushes designed to monitor road to the east, south and southwest of Fire Support Base 20. Reconnaissance platoon moved to Fire Support Base 20 for regrouping and reorganization. Mortar platoon continued in support of battalion operations at Fire Support Base 20.

Air Support: Cider 10 drew ground fire vicinity YB 731055 while working in A.O. Red-legs employed Firecracker at grid YB 724055 with one large secondary explosion. They fired on grid YB 731055 intelligence from higher with negative surveillance. Cider 13 performed air strike, vicinity YB 739055. Headhunter 46 worked A.O. employing Artillery and adjusting it on suspected enemy location.

Artillery: Artillery fired Night Fire Program on vicinity YB 735046 on suspected enemy location expending 108 HE, 105-mm.

18 March, 1969: 1st Battalion, 8th Infantry on 18 March, 1969 continued operating in assigned A.O. with Task Force Alpha's mission to interdict and suppress enemy movement vicinity of roads near their location. The battalion furnished patrols and local security of areas occupied by companies. Company A continued security of Task Force Alpha's Fire Support Base with Company C employing 3 platoon-sized ambushes. Company C minus conducted road cratering and abertee from coordinates YB 768031 to YB 771029. Craters were blown at grids YB 790030, YB 789030 and YB 797031. One platoon ambushed vicinity YB 797034. A bunker complex was found by Company C vicinity YB 779035 to YB 781035 to YB 779032. Approximately 75 bunkers with commo wire running between them, 2-man size camouflaged well, showing no signs of recent use. Company B continued Fire Support Base 20 security mission with local security, patrols and 2 platoon-sized ambushes vicinity YB 868068 and YB 851079. Company D also had road interdiction mission vicinity YB 846085. One crater 20' wide X 10-15' deep was blown in the road. Reconnaissance platoon was moved to Task Force Alpha with preparation for new mission. Mortar platoon continued to support battalion operations from Fire Base 20 and one section was sent to support Task Force Alpha's operation.

Air Support: Cider 22 employed air strike vicinity YB 720053 to YB 730049 for purpose of cutting road that vicinity. One Medevac was employed with Company B for two WIA.

Artillery: Artillery shot 5 Roadrunners of 105mm, 150 rounds HE in support of Task Force Alpha. Also fired 5 rounds of 155mm, 75 rounds of HE in support of Task Force Alpha from Fire Base Swinger.

19 March, 1969: 1st Battalion, 8th Infantry on 19 March, 1969 continued road interdiction, ambushes and patrols in the A.O. Company A had 2 platoon-sized ambushes operating in vicinity of Task Force Alpha. An abertee was constructed grid YB 805053 by one of the ambushes. They came under intense ground fire. They received one U.S. KIA and one wounded. The other ambush linked with ambush in contact vicinity YB 801043 to go back into area and retrieve KIA. They were unable to move back due to intense enemy fire. They pulled back, employed mortar fire from Task Force Alpha's location. Company C cut road vicinity YB 784024 and employed two platoon-sized ambushes vicinity YB 797028 and YB 794029. Mortar accident occurred Task Force Alpha's location resulting in 12 WIA. Medevac was employed. Company B continued security of Fire Support Base 20 with local security, patrols and one platoon size ambush, vicinity YB 822035. Company D conducted cratering mission of roads south of Fire Support Base 20. They employed two platoon-sized ambushes vicinity YB 865068 and YB 854074 with remainder of company securing Fire Base 20. Reconnaissance platoon continued to secure patrol base headquarters. Task Force Alpha with Tracer team continued screening southern portion of A.O. vicinity YB 791015. An Arc-light was employed with code No. 7179 at

0915 hours.

Air Support: Troop A, 7th of the 17th Cavalry made BDA of AL 7179. They received small arms fire during BDA vicinity YB 863987 by approximate squad sized element. Also rocket fire and small arms fire were received by Cavalry White Birds vicinity YB 849991. Cider 14 employed air strike vicinity YB 876003. A total of 3 dust offs were called to Task Force Alpha's location. Eight Helocib AN/GSO-128 Censors were employed by elements from Fire Base 20 with support from the 7th of the 17th Cavalry in vicinity YB 779026, YB 784023, YB 782025, YB 776026, YB 813019, YB 810023, YB 805022 and YB 815021. These sensors were to be used by our battalion as a test to estimate their value in a combat situation. A crew from Division was assigned to the battalion to monitor the portascope after the drop. When the Censors were dropped they were supposedly correctly activated. However, no indications were observed on the portascope to confirm activation right after one was dropped. Late the next day Artillery fired on these grids confirming negative activation of the Censors. A preliminary conclusion was that the Battery assembly was not correctly set in the Censors before they were sent to Fire Base 20.

Artillery: Artillery fired Night Fire Program with normal H & I accomplished.

20 March, 1969: 1st Battalion, 8th Infantry on 20 March, 1969 continued ambush patrols and interdiction of roads in assigned A.O. Company A minus from Task Force Alpha moved to vicinity of previous day's contact and swept area and recovered 1 U.S. KIA. Company A minus had contact again at grid YB 801052 resulting in one U.S. KIA, 11 U.S. WIA and 4 NVA KIA. Company A employed ambush vicinity YB 792021. Company C continued security of Task Force A, plus local security, patrols. They sent one platoon size ambush, vicinity YB 779035. They also sent two platoons to assist Company A minus with their wounded. Company B continued security of Fire Support Base 20 with local Ops, LPs and one platoon size ambush, vicinity YB 814089. Company D moved overland on reconnaissance mission to east of Fire Support Base 20. Company D joined 2 platoons in that area and conducted a recon in force to vicinity of YB 876074 employing 4 squad-sized ambushes vicinity night location. Reconnaissance platoon continued to operate with Task Force Alpha employing Tracer 4 on south portion of A.O. vicinity YB 798006. Mortar platoon continued to support battalion operations from Fire Base 20 with one section at Task Force Alpha's location. Task Force Alpha's mortars fired support of Company A contact. This day's contact revealed a loss of 3 M16A1 rifles and one M60 machine gun belonging to Company A. Company C constructed one abertee of 2 large trees vicinity YB 793024. Results of Company A's previous day's mission; vicinity YB 797052 abertee of approximately 8 trees 24-30" in diameter blown across the road, also vicinity YB 801052 abertee was blown with undetermined amount and size of trees vicinity of contact.

Air Support: One Medevac was utilized vicinity of Company A's contact with one being utilized at Task Force Alpha's location. The rest of wounded in contact stayed with unit.

Artillery: Artillery fired on sensor location grids to test their operation. Fired HE rounds, 105-mm from Fire Base 20 in support of A Company in contact. Regular Night Fire Program was accomplished (both 105mm and 155mm were fired).

21 March, 1969: 1st Battalion, 8th Infantry on 21 March, 1969 continued ambush patrols and road interdiction in assigned A.O. Company A conducted airlift from Task

Force Alpha to Fire Support Base 20 assuming security mission and employing ambushes vicinity YB 814082 and YB 819082. Company B minus conducted airlift from Fire Support Base 20 to Task Force Alpha with one platoon closing Task Force Alpha by ground prior to airlift. Company B minus moved overland to area of Company A's previous day's contact with mission to interdict road in that vicinity. However, this mission could not be accomplished. Therefore a secondary mission of destroying 11 enemy bunkers vicinity YB 812048 was accomplished. Company B employed one platoon size ambush, vicinity YB 816048. Company C continued security of Task Force Alpha with local security, patrols and two platoon-sized ambushes. A platoon with mission of ambush moving toward night location encountered 5 NVA, vicinity YB 815020. Results: Two NVA KIA. Company D minus continued a reconnaissance mission to the east moving from previous night location vicinity YB 876071 to night location vicinity YB 870053. They employed 3 ambushes (general area of night location). Reconnaissance platoon continued security mission of Task Force Alpha with Tracer 4 closing in preparation for reconnaissance platoon's extraction to Fire Base 20. Mortar platoon continued to support battalion operations at Fire Support Base 20 with one section at Task Force Alpha. Mortars were employed from Task Force Alpha's location during Company C's platoon contact with results unknown.

Artillery: Artillery fired for a combat mission for 5321 element at grid 815024. Negative surveillance hindered in the support of Task Force Alpha. Night Fire Program: two Roadrunners expended, 50 HE 155mm, 100 rounds HE 105mm, 36 rounds HE 4.2 inch mortar, 20 rounds HE 81mm mortars all in support of Task Force Alpha.

22 March, 1969: 1st Battalion, 8th Infantry on 22 March, 1969 continued operations with patrols, ambushes and road interdiction missions in A.O. Company A continued security of Fire Base 20, with local security, patrols and two platoon-sized elements used as ambushes vicinity 818088 and 814082. Company B minus conducted patrols with two platoons covering objectives vicinity YB 805042, 809049, 800031, 808021 and 808045. Abertees were blown at 815042. Company B minus joined other platoon-sized element at night location vicinity 808045. Company C minus moved to vicinity 812022 from Task Force Alpha location. There they made contact with unknown sized enemy force. Results: 1 U.S. WIA, 1 NVA KIA. Company C minus moved back to Task Force Alpha's location employing ambush vicinity 796026. Company D minus continued reconnaissance sweep to east of last night location vicinity 855055 to present night location 863037 employing 3 ambushes vicinity 856055, 859033, and 868035. Reconnaissance platoon continued security of Task Force Alpha patrol base awaiting orders to move to Fire Support Base 20. Mortar platoon located at Fire Base 20 continued support of battalion operations with one section located with Task Force Alpha.

Air Support: Cider 24 and Cider 15 and 10 employed two air strikes vicinity 761042 and 755044. Alligator 834 the helicopter supplying Task Force Alpha received ground fire resulting in a disabled air craft. One R/S bird Alligator 270 was received Task Force Alpha's location, with no ground fire prior to this. This helicopter was utilized to Medevac Company C WIA. Gunships were employed vicinity of where helicopter was receiving enemy ground fire, with unknown results. The gunships also received a heavy volume of fire vicinity Task Force Alpha.

Artillery: Approximately 2250 hours Artillery was employed on truck movement, vicinity 796-19. Mortars from Task Force Alpha's location were also employed with negative surveillance. Artillery was employed for reconnaissance by fire for moving elements of the battalion throughout the day. Also employed 150 rounds HE 105mm in support of Task Force Alpha and 60 HE 81mm mortars in Night Fire Program.

23 March, 1969: 1st Battalion, 8th Infantry on 23 March, 1969 continued ambush patrols, and road interdiction missions in A.O. Company A continued security of Fire Support Base 20 with local security, patrols and ambushes vicinity 819066, 819078, 820084, and 825083. Company B minus conducted reconnaissance sweep to vicinity 821037, 825024. Company B's 24 element encountered enemy contact approximately 350 meters west of Task Force Alpha's location. Mortars from Task Force Alpha's location were employed, along with Spooky gunship in support of this action. Results: one U.S. KIA, 8 U.S. WIA and 4 NVA KIA. Company C continued security of Task Force Alpha. Employed local security and reconnaissance patrols. Company D continued reconnaissance to east from night location, to new night location vicinity 870053, encountering light contact. Results: One NVA KIA. Ambushes were employed vicinity 848040, 845038, and 837037. Reconnaissance platoon continued security of Task Force Alpha. Mortar platoon continued to support battalion operations on Fire Support Base 20 with one section located with Task Force Alpha. Fire Support Base 20 received 7 incoming White Phosphorus 105mm, 20 HE 105mm. Also received various enemy small mortars (possibly 57RR or 60mm) before enemy 105mm was employed.

Air Support: Troop C, 7th of the 17th Cavalry worked in A.O. with unknown results. R/S birds from 119th AHC conducted support of Task Force Alpha receiving sporadic ground fire. Cider 15 and Headhunter 40 and 48 assisted in location of enemy artillery positions and adjusted artillery on to these with unknown results. Spooky 21 was employed in support of Company B 24 element contact.

Artillery: Arc light 7183 was employed at 2115 hours 3000 meters southwest of Task Force Alpha. Artillery was in support all day for the battalion. When incoming started 175mm from Ben Het were employed on grid 750092 with negative results. Artillery was in support of Task Force Alpha and also fired on suspected enemy artillery positions. Mortars were also employed from Fire Support Base 20 in support of Task Force Alpha.

24 March, 1969: 1st Battalion, 8th Infantry on 24 March, 1969 continued ambush patrols and road interdictions in the A.O. Company A continued security of Fire Base 20, local security and patrols. They employed platoon-sized reconnaissance patrols YB 818054 to night location vicinity 819066. They employed short range patrols to vicinity YB 818078 to YB 820038. Fire Support Base 20 received incoming artillery and indirect fire weapons. Number of rounds received unknown. Company B minus located at Task Force Alpha sent two platoons and CP on mission to construct abertee and obstruct vicinity YB 788023. The mission was not accomplished. Company B minus set up night location vicinity YB 797023. The 23 and 23 platoons were located vicinity of Task Force A. The 23 element of Company B experienced light contact with NVA at approximately same area as previous night's contact. Results: One NVA KIA, one U.S. WIA from gunship who was later extracted from Task Force Alpha's location. Company C continued security of Task Force Alpha with local security and reconnaissance patrols and the clearing mission extensively around the perimeter. They employed short range patrols vicinity YB 806037, YB 807036, YB

808034 and YB 806033. Throughout the day Task Force Alpha received incoming indirect fire from mortars and B-40 rockets along with sniper fire from east and west sides of perimeter (small arms). Company D minus continued security vicinity of their previous night location with local security and reconnaissance patrols. They employed patrols in a cloverleaf around vicinity of night location. Company D minus had a water patrol make contact with one NVA. Results: 1 NVA KIA, 1 rucksack CIA and negative U.S. casualties. Reconnaissance platoon undertook mission of security of Fire Support Base 20 with one section located at Task Force Alpha's location. Mortars fired support for Company B contact and defensive concentrations of Task Force Alpha.

Air Support: Cider 10, 12, 13 and 14 employed air strikes in vicinity Task Force Alpha's location. Daisy Cutter employed in vicinity YB 877044. Medevac was called to Task Force Alpha's location. It received heavy ground fire and was unable to land. Artillery was employed to Task Force Alpha to extract two of the most seriously wounded. Resupply was conducted by Alligator 270 which received heavy ground fire but was able to remove the most seriously wounded. Troop C, 7th of the 17th Cavalry operated in A.O. sighting NVA in open vicinity 849982. Gunships were employed by Company B 23 element contact with results unknown. There was one U.S. WIA. A1E Sky Raiders were also utilized in this vicinity after contact had terminated with unknown results. The Cavalry also conducted BDA vicinity Arc light 7183. Air strikes were employed near Task Force Alpha, vicinity YB 807033 with two secondary explosions resulting from air strikes and strafing runs. Arc light 7186P was employed at 2120 hours southwest of Task Force Alpha.

Artillery: Artillery was fired with two roadrunners in support of Task Force A. 100 HE 105mm rounds were fired on suspected enemy artillery location, 50 HE 155mm rounds were fired in support of Task Force Alpha. Reconnaissance by fire was employed to support battalion operations throughout the day.

25 March 1969: 1st Battalion, 8th Infantry on 25 March 1969 continued ambush patrols and interdiction of roads in assigned A.O. Company A continued security of Fire Support Base 20 with local security and patrols. They employed platoon-sized ambush vicinity YB 855074. This platoon's additional mission was to form outpost for Fire Support Base 27. Short range patrols were employed to vicinity YB 824085, YB 775055, YB 772028, YB 819084, YB 817077, YB 825082 and YB 855074. Company B minus departed night location YB 797023 for cratering mission on road vicinity YB 794020. After completion of mission Company B minus had contact at 1215 hours vicinity YB 755020 with estimated 20 NVA. Contact was broken and initiated again at 1413 hours. Results: 2 U.S. KIA, 11 U.S. WIA and six U.S. MIA, 4 or 5 NVA KIA. Company B's 21 and 22 elements located at Task Force Alpha with mission to secure that area. Task Force Alpha came under attack at 0700 receiving B-40 rockets and small arms fire. Gunships, air strikes and mortar fire were employed against enemy in open with results unknown. Results of ground action: 13 U.S. WIA, 1 U.S. KIA, 2 NVA KIA, possible 3 additional NVA KIA and 1 AK-47 CIA. At approximately 0700 hours LP on west side of perimeter of Task Force Alpha observed 3 individuals to the west. The LP closed and 81-mm mortar was fired. A reconnaissance squad was sent out to check the area. Three to five NVA took the element under fire approximately 25 meters outside the perimeter. The point man was wounded. The patrol could not recover the U.S. WIA so they employed fire and maneuver and withdrew to perimeter. A reaction force was hastily organized and sent to recover wounded man. This element came under mortar fire and small arms fire. They returned with their wounded to perimeter. The area of contact was submitted to automatic weapons, M-79 and M-16 fire. One small maneuver element was sent along north side of saddle and recovered wounded man. The element received B-40 rocket and small arms fire from three locations of the saddle while getting the wounded man. When all elements had closed vicinity of Task Force Alpha, gunships were employed in area of contact and positions of enemy fire. The gunships drew ground fire from four positions, northwest, west, southwest and south of the perimeter. Two sets of gunships were employed. Two sets of A1E fighters and eight sets of fast pacers were employed to the west, south and east of the perimeter. Results: 2 enemy firing positions silenced and 2 NVA KIA. Company C continued security of Task Force Alpha with local security and Ops. They employed short range patrols vicinity YB 806037, YB 805033, YB 803033 and YB 802035. Company D moved overland from previous night location to Task Force Alpha's location. They employed short range patrols vicinity YB 825082, YB 802033 and YB 802034. Task Force Alpha received 60mm and 82mm mortar fire sporadically throughout the day. Reconnaissance platoon continued security of Fire Support Base 20. Mortar platoon continued to support battalion operations from Fire Support Base 20 with one section located at Task Force Alpha. Mortars at Task Force Alpha fired in support of Company B contact and Company B minus contact.

Air Support: Gunships, A1E Sky Raiders, fast pacers fighters were employed vicinity Task Force Alpha. Cider 13, and 12 were utilized to adjust air strikes. A CS drop was employed vicinity road west to east YB 775055 YB 772026. Medevac was employed to Company B minus vicinity to extract wounded taking ground fire and hits. Resupply was accomplished to Company B minus resulting in one helicopter being hit. Resupply bird vicinity Fire Base 20 drew small arms fire. Spooky gunship was on station to assist Company B minus throughout the night.

Artillery: Artillery fired three roadrunners, two times that night utilizing 105mm and 155mm. One roadrunner of 50 HE 155mm was utilized in support of Task Force A. Reconnaissance by fire was utilized throughout the operation during the day. All artillery support available was used.

26 March, 1969: 1st Battalion, 8th Infantry on 26 March, 1969 continued operations in assigned A.O. Company A conducting patrols, local security and road interdiction. Company A continued Fire Support Base 20 mission employing local security and patrols. One Company A platoon moved from their previous night location to Fire Base 27 to secure this area for Company D who was to move from Task Force Alpha's location to this new location. Fire Support Base 20 began receiving incoming artillery and mortar rounds from enemy positions approximately 1320 hours. A total of 13 rounds of 105mm, 7 impacted inside the perimeter, were received. At 1400 hours this barrage ended. At 1535 hours Fire Support Base 20 again receiving incoming artillery that ended at 1600 hours. A total of 19 rounds were received with 18 impacting inside the perimeter. Counter artillery and mortar fire was employed during both instances resulting in stopping the enemy fire. Results of the artillery and mortar attacks were: 1 U.S. KIA, 2 U.S. WIA, Battery A 6th of the 29th Artillery suffered 2 U.S. KIA and 7 U.S. WIA as a result of the enemy attack. One more round of incoming artillery was received at 1800 hours with negative injuries and damage. Company B minus located vicinity 805026 evacuated 7 WIA from their location prior to linking with Company D who had been sent to their location to assist

Company B minus back to Task Force Alpha's location. Company C undertook mission to secure southeast and southwest portion of perimeter to allow Company D free movement to Company B minus location. Company D and Company B minus met and started moving back toward Task Force Alpha's location. On this move back, 4 of the 6 MIA joined Company B minus. After Company D and Company B had reached Task Force Alpha's location Company C withdrew elements to Task Force Alpha's location. Companies C, D and B at this time resumed mission to secure patrol base vicinity Task Force Alpha. Task Force Alpha came under intense small arms, rocket, mortar, and artillery attacks starting at 1100 hours and lasting sporadically throughout the afternoon. Alligator 110 attempting a landing at Task Force Alpha's location was hit with small arms fire as he sat down on the pad. B-40 rockets were fired from the west into the vicinity of the pad. Dust off 52 coming into Task Force Alpha also received ground fire and 1 gunship escorting them also received rounds. During this time the enemy fired 5 B-40 rounds, 6 82-mm mortar rounds and small arms into Task Force Alpha's perimeter. Shortly after this attack Task Force Alpha began receiving incoming 105-mm from enemy positions near the border. This continued sporadically until 1845 hours. A total of 44 rounds were received during this time. Results of the attacks were: 1 U.S. KIA and 5 U.S. WIA. Company D's 23 element made contact about 200 meters to southeast of Task Force Alpha while trying to move to short range patrol location. An estimated enemy squad was encountered by this element vicinity 810034. Results were 1 U.S. WIA and 1 NVA KIA. Mortars were employed and 23 broke contact and moved to different night location. Throughout the night Task Force Alpha received reports of sightings of from 1 to 2 NVA probing the perimeter. These individuals were taken under fire with M-79, hand grenades and mortar fire with results unknown. Companies B, C and D continued security of Task Force Alpha with local security and short-range platoon size reconnaissance and surveillance patrols. Reconnaissance platoon continued security of Fire Support Base 20. Mortar platoon continued support of battalion operations from Fire Support Base 20 with one section located at Task Force Alpha. Mortar missions were fired from Fire Support Base 20 and Task Force Alpha in support of ground operations and counter mortar fire was utilized on suspected enemy mortar and rocket positions vicinity Task Force Alpha and Fire Base 20.

Air Support: Air support was prominent throughout the battalion A.O. Air strikes were employed vicinity YB 730030, 770029 and vicinity Task Force Alpha and enemy artillery positions 746095 by Cider 12. Armed helicopters were employed throughout the day to assist resupply of Task Force Alpha. Ships from the 119th A.H.C. were able to resupply Task Force Alpha on two occasions. Both times they received enemy fire with one being hit. Medevac was accomplished two times, once at Fire Base 20 and once vicinity Company B minus location. Medevac was attempted vicinity of Task Force Alpha unsuccessfully. Alligator aircraft 606 and 270 were able to evacuate wounded. Headhunter 44 worked area vicinity Task Force Alpha supporting Company D move to Company B minus location and assisting in locating enemy position in that area. One CS drop was accomplished by Gulf 25A vicinity 775055.

Artillery: Battery A, 6th of the 29th artillery (Direct Support) supported battalion operations from Fire Support Base 20 firing in support of ground movement, counter artillery and harassment and interdiction. Two roadrunners and one point target were engaged by 155mm expending 80 rounds HE in support of Task Force Alpha. Three roadrunners and 2 point targets were fired upon by

105mm from Fire Support Base 20 expending 200 rounds of HE. This was also in support of Task Force Alpha.

27 March, 1969: 1st Battalion, 8th Infantry on 27 March, 1969 continued operations in assigned A.O. employing reconnaissance patrols, short range patrols and local security. Company A (-) located vicinity of Fire Base 20 continued security of Fire Support Base 20 with local Ops and LPs. Their 21 and 24 platoons were located on Fire Support Base 27 where they established an outpost. Company A employed 3 short range patrols vicinity Fire Support Base 20 and 2 short range patrols vicinity Fire Support Base 27. Fire Support Base 20 received incoming 105-mm at approximately 1047 hours. A total of 19 rounds received with 12 impacting inside the perimeter. The enemy artillery barrage ended at 1127 hours. Results were 2 U.S. WIA. Company B continued security of Task Force Alpha with local security, reconnaissance patrols and short range reconnaissance patrols being employed in that vicinity. Throughout the day, especially during the airlift of Company D from Task Force Alpha to Fire Support Base 27, Task Force Alpha received 2 B-40 rockets inside the perimeter and an unknown amount of small arms fire. Company C undertook mission to sweep from Task Force Alpha to vicinity of Company B minus previous day's contact, in general vicinity 800033. Company C moving from vicinity Task Force Alpha came into contact with enemy snipers to their front and left flanks with a B-40 rocket firing at them from their right front along with snipers. Company C pulled back to employ artillery in the area of contact. As they were pulling back they started receiving 105mm incoming enemy fire. A total of 15 rounds were employed on their position forcing them back into Task Force Alpha location. Results of contact were: 4 NVA KIA and negative friendly casualties. Counter battery artillery was employed on enemy gun vicinity

725071 with one gun observed destroyed by Hummingbird 5. Company C again attempted to go to vicinity Company B minus contact about 1430. About 300 meters outside the perimeter they received a total of 3 82mm mortar rounds adjusted on their position. This again forced them back into Task Force Alpha's vicinity. Gun-ships were employed in vicinity to Company C's front with results unobserved. One of the gun-ships was hit by enemy fire vicinity 810030 or 807030. Gun-ships expended and withdrew. Artillery and mortars were employed in vicinity of Company C contact where enemy forward observer was suspected to be. Results were not observed. The planned operation for Company C was abandoned due to the short remainder of moving time available after these two actions. During Company C's action there was a propaganda round fired into the vicinity Task Force Alpha by the enemy. The round contained propaganda leaflets exhorting U.S. soldiers to come over to their side. These leaflets also contained statements from an U.S. POW on his excellent treatment as a POW at the hands of the NVA. Company C 22D platoon experienced heavy movement southeast of Task Force Alpha at 2020 hours. They employed claymores and pulled back to the perimeter. Mortars from Task Force Alpha were employed on suspected location of the 3 NVA with results unknown. 22D moved back to new location vicinity of their old one and began surveillance again. Company C employed a total of 4 short range patrols to the southwest, south, southeast and east of Task Force Alpha. Company D minus conducted airlift from vicinity Task Force Alpha to Fire Support Base 27. The 24 platoon continued security of Fire Support Base 20. Company D minus was Reaction Company for the 7th of the 17th Cavalry. Company D minus at Fire Support Base 27 employed a total of 6 short range patrols while their 24 element employed 2 short range patrols vicinity Fire Base 20 for local security.

Reconnaissance platoon continued security of Fire Support Base 20 and employed Tracer team vicinity 822074 with negative results. 1st Brigade LRRP 4C became OPCON to the 1st Battalion, 8th Infantry and started moving from its night location vicinity 880062 to vicinity Fire Support Base 27 for extraction. Mortar platoon continued support of battalion operations from Fire Support Base 20 with one section located with Task Force Alpha. 4.2 inch mortar was fired in support of Company C's planned move to southwest of Task Force Alpha. The 81mm mortars located in Task Force Alpha was fired as counter measure on possible enemy forward observer location in support of Company C operation.

Air Support: Air support in battalion A.O. was prominent with airlift of Company D accomplished from Task Force Alpha to Fire Base 27. A total of 14 slicks and 2 sets of gun-ships were employed from the 119th Assault Helicopter Co in this action. One set of gun-ships was utilized in second contact of Company C, with one helicopter receiving damage to the aircraft by enemy ground fire. Troop C, 7th of the 17th Cavalry worked the A.O. briefly and short missions due to operational difficulties. Cider 12 was beneficial in adjusting artillery from Fire Support Base 20 on enemy gun emplacements firing on Company C. One medevac was conducted successfully from Fire Support Base 20. Headhunter 40 was employed throughout A.O. on possible enemy infiltration routes and positions. CS gas drop by Gulf 25A was completed at YB 7603 east to west successfully at 1455 hours.

Artillery: Battery A, 6th of the 29th Artillery (Direct Support) fired reconnaissance by fire missions throughout the day for the battalion. Cider 12 sighted enemy artillery positions vicinity 725071 and employed counter artillery. K-14 and Cider 12 adjusted 105mm from Fire Base 20 and 175-mm from Ben Het on these positions. K-14 spotted enemy in open running from these artillery positions and employed Firecracker resulting in 3 confirmed NVA KIA. Night Fire Program consisted of 50 155mm HE employed against enemy artillery position, and in support of Task Force Alpha. A total of 200 HE 105mm was employed on enemy artillery position and in vicinity of Task Force Alpha for their support.

28 March, 1969: 1st Battalion, 8th Infantry on 28 March, 1969 continued to operate in assigned A.O. employing local security, reconnaissance patrols and short range patrols. Company A minus continued security of Fire Support Base 20 with local Ops and LPs. The 21 and 24 platoons departed Fire Support Base 27 but did not close Company A minus location. Platoons 21 and 24 linked up at night location vicinity 832089. Company A employed 4 short range patrols around Fire Support Base 20 for purposes of security. Fire Support Base 20 received one round of incoming 105-mm. Company B CP and the 22 and 23 platoons conducted a reconnaissance patrol to the east of Task Force Alpha. The CP was located with the 23 platoon at night location 822032 while the 22 platoon chose 828037 for its night location. Company B minus employed 3 short range patrols vicinity 821031, 829038 and 804036. The remainder of the company stayed at Task Force Alpha's location for security employing local security and short range reconnaissance patrols. A total of 120 rounds of incoming 105mm artillery was received at Task Force Alpha's location throughout the day. Results were 4 U.S. WIA and 1 KIA. Movement was encountered throughout the night vicinity Task Force Alpha. Each time M-79 and fragmentation grenades were employed resulting in movement ceasing. Company C continued security of Task Force Alpha with local Ops and LPs. Company C also employed 4 short range reconnaissance patrols vicinity Task Force Alpha as a screen. There were several enemy sightings during this day. Each sighting was taken under fire with results unknown. Company D continued security of Fire Support Base 27 with local Ops and LPs and short range reconnaissance patrols. A total of 4 short range patrols were employed in this area as a screen. Light contact was initiated by Company D on an NVA truck convoy by adjusting artillery fire onto them. Results were unobserved. Reconnaissance platoon continued security of Fire Support Base 20 with negative results. 1st Brigade LRRP 4C closed Company D location and was extracted. Mortar platoon continued to support battalion operations firing in support of Task Force Alpha and Fire Base 20. One section located with Task Force Alpha with the remainder located at Fire Support Base 20.

Air Support: Air support in battalion A.O. was prominent. Headhunter 40 and 44 assisted in observing area vicinity Task Force Alpha and area of enemy gun emplacement. Medevac was accomplished vicinity Task Force Alpha without incident. Resupply at Task Force Alpha was completed. Resupply for other elements were completed without incident. Troop C, 7th of the 17th Cavalry worked A.O. sighting enemy truck convoy vicinity 817088. Cavalry expended and Company D fired artillery on convoy. Results were one possible vehicle destroyed. Two Combat Sky Spot missions were employed in area of enemy artillery emplacements with unobserved results. Gulf 25 employed one CS drop, vicinity 7404. Cider 10 assisted in locating and employing artillery and air strikes on enemy gun positions.

Artillery: Battery A, 6th of the 29th Artillery (Direct Support) fired in support of Task Force Alpha receiving incoming. 175mm and 105mm was fired vicinity gun emplacements at YB 727072. Throughout the day artillery was employed against these positions with results unknown. Reconnaissance by fire was also employed in support of Task Force Alpha with 105mm.

29 March, 1969: 1st Battalion, 8th Infantry on 29 March, 1969 continued operations in assigned A.O. with local security and short range reconnaissance patrols. Company A continued security of Fire Support Base 20 employing local security and short range reconnaissance patrols. Two short-range patrols were employed vicinity 819087 and 814085. Fire Support Base 20 received a total of 16 rounds of 105mm enemy artillery fire throughout the afternoon with 12 falling inside the perimeter. Counter artillery was fired into suspected enemy locations vicinity YB 716062, YB 731074 and YB 729071 with results unknown. B Company 21 and 24 platoons continued security of Task Force Alpha's location while Company B minus element continued reconnaissance patrols vicinity east and southeast of Task Force Alpha and closing Task Force Alpha's location during the afternoon. Heavy movement was encountered throughout the early morning, afternoon and evening with Task Force Alpha receiving B-40 rockets, grenades 60mm mortars and small arms fire from the northeast, east, south, southwest and west. A total of 19 B-40 rockets, 12 60-mm mortar rounds and 1 chicom hand grenade were received at Task Force Alpha's location. Snipers on the east, south and west harassed friendly movement throughout the day. Results of this action were 3 U.S. WIA, 5 NVA KIA and the following items were captured: 3 B-40 rocket launchers, 1 AK-47, 1 AK-50, 1 Chinese assault rifle and approximately 12 B-40 rockets. The NVA KIA was found in vicinity of east Side of Task Force Alpha's perimeter. One NVA was observed in the vicinity of the KIA waving a white flag. Task Force Alpha personnel implored this individual to Chu Hoi for about 2 hours. A resupply helicopter came into Task Force Alpha's location and at this time the NVA fled. A psychological operations team in a LOH tried to talk this individual shortly after he was gone from the vicinity of Task Force Alpha. The LOH received fire from vicinity YB 811033 from 3 NVA resulting in minor damage to the aircraft. Company B employed 4 short-range reconnaissance patrols in immediate vicinity of Task Force A for security and early warning. Company C continued security of Task Force Alpha employing local security and a total of 4 short range reconnaissance patrols vicinity of Task Force Alpha. Sounds of something being dragged through the jungle were witnessed during the early morning at Task Force Alpha. It is believed that the NVA were dragging their wounded and dead away. During the night following this action sounds of digging and sightings of NVA were prominent. On each occasion mortars and small arms were employed against the enemy. Company D minus continued security of Fire Base 27 with local security and short range reconnaissance patrols. A total of 5 short range patrols were employed in vicinity of Fire Support Base 27. Company D minus their 24 element was airlifted from Fire Support Base 20 to Fire Support Base 27 rejoining the main element. Reconnaissance platoon continued security mission at Fire Support Base 20 assisting Company A. Mortar platoon continued to support battalion operations from Fire Support Base 20 with one section located with Task Force Alpha. Counter mortar fire was employed by Task Force Alpha throughout the day on suspected enemy mortar positions to the west and southeast. Defensive concentrations were fired throughout the early morning and late evening on suspected enemy movement with results unknown.

Air Support: Air support was prevalent throughout the battalion A.O. Spooky 22 was employed in vicinity of Task Force Alpha during the early morning against suspected enemy concentrations preparing for a ground attack. Cider 12 assisted in visual observation of Task Force Alpha and employing artillery fire on suspected enemy artillery emplacements. Nine Combat Sky Spots were employed vicinity enemy artillery emplacements vicinity YB 716062, 731074 and 729071. Cider 13 Headhunter 44 and 40 were utilized throughout A.O. to adjust artillery on suspected enemy locations. Resupply of Task Force Alpha was accomplished with 2 slicks and 3 WIA were evacuated on the first helicopter. A total of 6 slick sorties were employed from Fire Support Base 20 to Fire Support Base 27 to airlift Company D 24 element. Gulf 25 employed 2 CS drops on enemy infiltration routes vicinity 752038 to 758035 and 762041 to 756047. One light observation helicopter was employed vicinity Task Force Alpha with Psychological Operations team aboard, resulting in light damage to the aircraft.

Artillery: Artillery support throughout the battalion A.O. was performed by Battery A, 6th of the 29th Artillery (Direct Support) vicinity Fire Support Base 20, 155mm located LZ Swinger and 175mm located Ben Het. Heavy radar and Infrared readings indicated heavy enemy troop movement toward Task Force Alpha along southern road vicinity 774008, 774023, 776024, 788022 and 774006. Headhunter 40 adjusted artillery from Swinger and Fire Base 20 onto the locations. K-12 air observer sighted 3 enemy artillery tubes vicinity 716062, 731074 and 729071. 175mm from Ben Het was adjusted onto these positions. Task Force Alpha received support from 4.2 inch mortar vicinity Fire Support Base 20 with 150 HE and 50 White Phosphorus being employed on suspected enemy locations. 105mm from Fire Support Base 20 was also employed with 800 rounds of HE being expended vicinity Task Force Alpha on suspected enemy locations. 155mm from LZ Swinger employed 65 rounds HE in support of Task Force Alpha. Two secondary explosions resulted from these supporting fires. One to the southeast and one to the west were sighted at Task Force Alpha.

30 March, 1969: 1st Battalion, 8th Infantry on 30 March, 1969 was in the process of moving all elements to Fire Base McNerny for stand down and regrouping. Company A located on Fire Support Base 20 moved from that location to Polei Kleng and remained there during the night. Enemy artillery harassed the movement from Fire Support Base 20 with a total of 40 rounds being received starting at 0100 hours and lasting until final extraction of all elements at 1830 hours. One U.S. WIA was evacuated from Fire Support Base 20 by Medevac as a result of the enemy artillery. Tactical Operations Center minus remained with Company A throughout the night at Polei Kleng. Companies B and C located with Task Force A were extracted to Polei Kleng. Company C was the first company to be airlifted out. As Company B was being extracted enemy pressure was exerted upon elements left at Task Force A. Gun-ships were employed in immediate vicinity of Task Force A throughout the extraction, with results unobserved. Enemy ground fire with small arms and B-40 rockets were experienced by helicopters attempting extraction. Results of the extraction was 3 helicopters and one gunship disabled by enemy fire. Company C and Company B moved overland from Polei Kleng to Fire Base McNerny. These two companies closed approximately 1830 hours at Fire Base McNerny and assumed stand down status. A total of 30 slick sorties were utilized during this extraction. Company D was extracted from Fire Support Base 27 with the final extraction completed at 1535 hours. Company D moved overland to LZ Mary Lou and stayed there during the night in preparation for the move to Fire Base McNerny. The extraction of Company D was without incident. Reconnaissance platoon was extracted along with Company A. Reconnaissance platoon remained with Company A at Polei Kleng. Mortar platoon was extracted along with Company A at Fire Support Base 20 with one section being extracted with Task Force Alpha. The mortar platoon minus remained with Company A at Polei Kleng. One section was located at Mary Lou with Company D while Company D while one section was located at Fire Base McNerny with Companies C and D.

Air Support: Air support during the battalion operation was excellent. Chinooks were successful in extraction sorties from Fire Support Base 20. UH-1H helicopters and UH-1C gunships from the 119th Assault Helicopter Co. succeeded in extracting Companies C, D and B. An Air Force Spat was employed vicinity Fire Support Base 20 to cover the extraction. Cider 15 assisted the Spat operation and also assisted with air surveillance in the areas of extraction. Gulf 25A employed CS drops vicinity 730060, 730030, 760060, 760030 and 7401.

Artillery: Battery A, 6th of the 29th Artillery (Direct Support) was extracted from Fire Support Base 20 with last extraction complete at 1730 hours. 175mm from Ben Het and 155mm from LZ Swinger was employed on enemy positions throughout the day's activities in support of the operation.

31 March, 1969: On 31 March, 1969 1st Battalion, 8th Infantry assumed stand down status at Fire Base McNerny. Company D moved from LZ Mary Lou and closed Fire Base McNerny at 1100 hours. Company A, mortar platoon minus, reconnaissance platoon, and Tactical Operations Center minus closed Fire Base McNerny at 1500 hours.

II.   Special Equipment:

Eight HE/OCIB AN/GSQ-128 Censors were employed vicinity YB 779026, 784023, 782025, 776026,

813019, 810023, 805022 and 815021 on 19 March, 1969. These items proved to be defective or improperly employed resulting in their being ineffective.

ALLEN M. BUCKNER

LTC, INFANTRY, COMMANDING

Department of the Army
HQ, 1st Brigade, 4th Infantry Division
APO San Francisco 96265

AVDDA-BRC
30 April 1969

SUBJECT: <u>Combat Operations after Action Report for Operation Wayne Grey</u>

Commanding General
4th Infantry Division
ATTN: AVDDH-CC-MH
APO 96262

1. Name of Operation: Operation Wayne Grey
2. Date of Operation: 1 March 1969 - 14 April 1969
3. Location: Plei Trap, Kontum Province, RVN.
4. Command and Control HQ: Headquarters, 1st Brigade, 4th Infantry Division
5. Reporting Officer: COL Hale H. Knight
                    Commanding Officer
                    1st Brigade, 4th Infantry Division
6. Task Organization: Annex A.
7. Supporting Forces:
   a. 6-29TH Arty (DS)
   b. C/1-92 Arty (GS)
   c. 1 plat C/6-14 (175MM) (GS)
   d. 7th Air Force
   e. B/4th Eng (DS)
   f. 4th Avn Battalion
   g. 52nd Combat Aviation Battalion
   h. 7-17th Cavalry (_)
   i. D/1-10 Cavalry

8.   Intelligence:

a. Intelligence indicated the 66th NVA Regiment and the 24th NVA Regiment with supporting artillery elements from the 40th Artillery Regiment along with sapper units were staging for attacks against Kontum City, Polei Kleng Special Forces Camp, fire support bases west of Polei Kleng and probable interdiction of the LOC's from Pleiku north to Kontum, Dak To and west from Kontum to Polei Kleng.

b. The 66th NVA Regiment moved north in late January and February, skirting the contacts between the 24th NVA Regiment and FWMAF in the Chu Pa Mountain area (YA9568). In late February, captured "Red" Documents, POW Interrogation Reports, and aerial reconnaissance of the Polei Kleng area and firebases west of Polei Kleng, indicating plans for offensive operations in the area. The K25 Engineer Battalion was identified in documents directing coordination with the 40th Artillery Regiment for construction of a road from Plei Moi (YA8493). The enemy's efforts to construct roads deep into the mountain range east of the Plei Trap, continued improvement of trails and roads from the Cambodian Border into the Chu Mom Ray area and signs of vehicular traffic in the northern Plei Trap and to the east indicating heavy supply activity and probable use of artillery or even tanks in the planned attacks.

c. Suspected enemy strengths and probable locations were:

Unit Location	Strength
66th NVA REGT VIC YA 8182	1275
HQ & Support Units	550

7th BN	240	
8th BN	250	
9th BN	235	
40th NVA REGT	UNK	
Tri Border Area		
K25 Eng BN/B3 Front	250	YA 8493
H67 Dispensary	UNK	YA 8381

d. Enemy Forces Encountered. 1 March, the 119th AHC airlifted the first of the 3-12th Infantry as a combat assault into key terrain (YA8396) to secure LZ Swinger as a firebase to support the assaults of the 3-12th and 1-8th Infantry Battalions, the company was in immediate contact with NVA in bunkers. Fighting to secure the base, they killed 30 NVA and captured an NVA WIA, a 12.7 AAMG, LMG, other small arms, and anti-helicopter mines. The enemy element was apparently prepared to ambush a helicopter assault on the abandoned firebase. Documents taken from the KIA and statements from the POW identified the unit as the K25B Engineer/Sapper BN. The AA MG also indicated at least a small supporting artillery element.

1. 1-8th Infantry Area of Operations: On 2 March, A/7-17 Cavalry, screening the combat assault of 1-8th Infantry swept the area capturing the two Russian two ton trucks and 61 rounds of Chicom 105 Howitzer ammunition. One of the trucks and ammunition were evacuated. On 5 March, at YB819019, an ambush killed 4 NVA and captured one NVA who later died of wounds. The POW and documents captured identified the personnel as a recon element of the C-10 Co, K9 BN, 66th NVA Regt and that the element was performing a route and position reconnaissance from the northern Plei Trap to the east of Chu Mom Ray (Hill 1773) and south toward Polei Kleng Special Forces Camp. As action continued in

the area south of FB 20, LZ Swinger received incoming 105mm artillery fire with suspected enemy locations to the NW near the location of the captured vehicles. Subsequent search of the area by the Air Cavalry, Cider RAC, and ground elements resulting in destruction of six additional trucks and the capture of two 105-mm howitzers at YB779028 on 7 March. The howitzers were old US weapons used by the enemy. Significant ground contacts were made by A and C/1-8th Infantry on 12 March, vicinity YB8500. Small element contacts continued throughout the month of March, with no new unit identifications made. In the 1-8th Infantry area of operations, ground contacts, the 7-17 Air Cavalry, air strikes and artillery fires resulted in 125 confirmed NVA KIA and 2 POWs. In late March, prior to evacuation of FSB 20 and TF A loc (YB804034), the positions received heavy 105 mm fire for several days from locations near the Cambodian Border vicinity YB724061. Artillery and air strikes destroyed one of the weapons and possibly destroyed 2 or 3 additional weapons. On 27 March, at YB830992, C/7-17 Cavalry observed what appeared to be a camouflaged vehicle park. The ARP was inserted and checked the area finding 3 rounds and 60 expended shell casings of 85 mm assault gun ammunition. The 3 rounds were evacuated.

2. 3-8 Infantry Area of Operations: A, C, and D Companies of the 3-8 Infantry combat assaulted into LZs south of LZ Mary (YA784916) and moved towards the enemy's rear and the suspected location of the H67 Dispensary (YA830815). On 3 March, vicinity YA808879, 3-8 Infantry made contact with an estimated NVA BN in well-constructed bunkers. Fierce fighting followed with D Company moving from the southwest to secure Hill 947 (YA813864) and B and C Companies combat assaulting on the ridge north of Company A's contact and moving south along the ridge. In this battle, confirmed NVA KIA and

captured several weapons. Documents captured in the contacts identified the K8 BN, 66th NVA Regt, and the 25B Engineer BN B3 Front. The enemy's determination to hold the ridgeline, and other intelligence later developed, indicate a control headquarters was located south of the contact area. Although not confirmed, an NVA B3 Front Forward CP may have been in the area. Enemy activity in the 3-8th Infantry area of operations remained extremely light for the remainder of the operation except for the harassing fires against LZ Swinger.

3. 3-12th Infantry area of operations: Following A Company's assault on LZ Swinger, elements of the 3-12th Infantry combat assaulted into the Plei Trap. In reaction to the 3-8th action, TF Swift (B, D, and Rcn/3-12) moved to the southeast to assist in sweeping the area and to attack south into Cu Don (YA8081). In scattered contacts throughout the area 3-12th Infantry elements killed 114 NVA. Major contacts were made at YA818840, YA820855, and YA828811, on 20, 29, and 30 March respectively. In all contacts except the 29 March sapper attack at LZ D-HANDLE, the enemy was well dug in and protected by the dense jungle and heavy overhead cover. In the 29 March contact, the enemy employed an 82mm mortar preparation followed by a company sized attack of sappers using B40 rockets and satchel charges. The enemy attack was repelled resulting in 26 NVA KIA. Documents captured in the contacts identified elements of the NVA 66th Regt and K25B BN and B3 Front. A document captured by D/3-12 on 26 March at YA808852 indicated an infiltration route running from SW vicinity YA7683, toward Polei Kleng.

e. Significant Intelligence: Captured documents, POWs, captured weapons, vehicles, and munitions confirmed the accuracy of intelligence information available prior to and throughout the operations. POWs and documents identified the 66th NVA Regt with the K7, K8, and K9 Bns, the K25B Engineer Battalion and elements of the 40th NVA Artillery Regiment. Observation of improved roads by aerial surveillance and ground reconnaissance along with the capture and destruction of Russian trucks, 105 mm howitzers, 105 mm and 85 mm Chicom ammunition confirmed the enemy's capabilities to provide logistical and fire support for attacks deep into South Vietnam.

f. Terrain: Throughout the area of operation, the terrain consisted of steep slopes and deep valleys. The jungle canopy was tripled layered with 150' high trees in many areas.

1. Observation: The dense jungle greatly reduced observation from the air and ground and prevented long range observation of likely avenues of enemy movement.

2. Fields of fire. The dense jungle severely restricted employment of flat trajectory weapons except at very close ranges or with extensive clearing of firing lanes.

3. Cover. The steep hill masses, deep ravines and dense vegetation provided good cover throughout the area of operations, except along the Plei Trap Valley floor and in the relatively flat terrain leading from the northern Plei Trap to the east and the north of Chu Mom Ray, (Hill 1773). Even in these areas, the cover was fair.

4. Concealment. Throughout the area, dense jungle and broken terrain provided excellent concealment against ground the air observation, often completely hiding hardened positions and trail networks that were later found when artillery, air strikes or chemical defoliation destroyed the canopy.

5. Obstacles. The steep slopes and dense jungle were obstacles to any type vehicular movement and hinder foot movement in the steepest areas. Steep banks make

most streams obstacles unless extensive work was done to provide a fording site.

6. Avenues or movement. Routes of movement generally follow the valley areas and cross the hill masses in the saddles. Major avenues in the area extended from the Cambodian Border (northern Plei Trap to the south along the Plei Trap Valley and to the east along the valley floor south of FSB 20 (YB8208) and north of Chu Mom Ray).

g. Weather: Throughout the operation, the weather was clear and permitted effective use of air assets except for ground haze that occasionally limited visibility and two severe thunderstorms accompanied by rain and high winds that disrupted aerial support. The heavy rains that delayed the final extraction from FSB 20 would have been a critical factor had they continued throughout the late afternoon and prevented completion of the extraction.

9.   Mission: 1st Brigade conducts offensive operations in Plei Trap area to destroy enemy forces, prevent reinforcement and supply of the 66th and 24th NVA Regiments from Cambodia, and prevent their withdrawal into Cambodia.

10.   Concept of Operations:

a. Phase I; The 1st Brigade conducted offensive operations with its three associated battalions: 1-8th Infantry, 3-8th Infantry and 3-12th Infantry and its direct support artillery battalion. 6-29th Artillery. Initially, the battalions conducted combat assaults into previously used firebases on the eastern Plei Trap to establish adequate artillery fire support positions. With artillery support established, rifle companies combat assaulted into the western Plei Trap behind main enemy forces and on his infiltration routes. Upon landing, the companies moved eastward quickly in reconnaissance in force operations into base areas and ambushed known enemy lines of communication. Maximum use was made of artillery and air strikes to interdict enemy interdict enemy movement of logistics. Once maneuver elements fixed enemy forces, all available firepower was brought to bear upon him (Overlay 1)

b. Phase II. The 1st Brigade continued offensive operations by establishing company size blocking positions astride access routes to interdict enemy withdrawal. Ambushes and short range patrols were placed on enemy routes of withdrawal. Artillery fire programs and chemical drops covered routes of egress not under observation of ground troops. Enemy troop units, which concentrated, were struck by B-52 bombers. Air Cavalry screened the western AO to detect and interdict enemy movement in or out of the area. Artillery was used to a maximum on all suspected and confirmed enemy locations. Air strikes were used to destroy enemy bunker complexes, and saturation bombing was used on enemy troops concentrated in the Cu Don. Once enemy resistance was broken, US Infantry swept the area in clean up operations. (Overlay 2)

11.   Execution:

a. General: On 27 February, 1st Brigade received the mission to deploy to Polei Kleng for staging an assault into the northern Plei Trap area. Reliable intelligence indicated that two regiments were staging for an attack on Polei Kleng and Kontum. The Brigade mission to prevent the withdrawal of the 24th and 66th NVA Regiments into Cambodia and to cut their lines of communication. On 28 February, all battalions were marshaled for deployment to Plei Trap. 1-8th Infantry and 3-8th Infantry convoyed to Polei Kleng while 3-12th Infantry extracted to Plei Mrong.

b. Initial assaults. On 1 March, the move into the Plei Trap began with A/3-12th Infantry combat assaulting into FB Swinger from Plei Mrong. The firebase was occupied by enemy troops who had prepared positions and anti-helicopter mines on the LZ. The artillery prep destroyed a 12.7 mm AA position and the assault went as planned. After a three-hour battle, bunker to bunker, the FB was secured and C/1-92nd Arty (155) was moved in. Enemy losses were 30 KIA and 1 POW. US casualties were 2 KIA and 14 WIA. Combat assaults were then conducted by B/1-8th Infantry into FSB 20 and C/3-8th Infantry into Firebase Pause followed by A/6-29th Arty and C/6-29th Arty respectively. At the end of the day, the fire support bases were established for troop assaults the following day.

On 2 March, simultaneous combat assaults were conducted by the 1-8th Infantry and the 3-8th Inf. D/1/8th and C/1/8th assaulted into LZ Susan and began RIF operations along the enemy roads in the area. Company A/1-8th Infantry made a combat assault into LZ Turkey. They were to establish a blocking position and conduct ambush operations along routes of egress. Companies A, B, and D/3-8th Infantry combat assaulted into LZ Mary to establish a firebase. Companies C and B/3/12 combat assaulted to YA734953 and YA743974. From there they would RIF to the east. The initial positioning was completed on 3 March. At this time the combat assault of Company D/3-12 was completed at YA 747923.

c. Plei Trap Road 1-16 March: With intelligence pointing to increased road activity in the northern Plei

Trap, C/1/8th Infantry and D/1-8th Infantry were assigned missions of conduction RIF operations east along the roads east of LZ Susan (YA742032). A/1-8th Infantry and Rcn/1-8th Infantry were put in a blocking position at LZ Turkey (YB 805015). During the combat assault of C and D/1-8th on 2 March, ground fire was received by a gunship just north of LZ Susan. A/7-17th Cavalry was committed to the area to screen the eastward movement of the rifle companies. At YB 765032, a Scout observed two enemy trucks with ammunition. The LOH received fir from the area and an air strike was employed resulting in two trucks destroyed, 6 NVA KIA, and 8 secondary explosions. C/1-8th swept the area and found the Russian made 1 1/2 ton trucks, 61 rounds of 105 mm ammunition, and 1200 lbs. of rice. At 1850hrs an ambush patrol from A/1-8 Infantry made contact with 2 NVA with a LMG at YB820015. Small arms fire was exchanged and during the sweep by 4A/1-8 contact was made with a dug in force. Small arms fire and artillery were employed resulting in 2 NVA KIA and 1 US WIA.

On 3 March, C/1-8 Infantry continued the RIF along the southern road while 1 platoon assisted with the evacuation of the captured truck. Contact was made with an unknown size force at YB 756036. A/7-17 Cavalry was screening the area, located and engaged the enemy resulting in 4 NVA KIA and 1 US WIA. D/1-8 Infantry continued the RIF along the northern road with negative results.

On 4 March the RIF continued along the southern road to locate the enemy artillery battery known to be in the area. That afternoon the 3-12th Infantry CP at FB Swinger received incoming 105 mm. A/7-17 Cavalry was sent to recon the suspected firing positions. Counter battery fire was employed by the artillery with unknown results. C/1-8 Infantry captured another truck vicinity YB777025. It was driven to an LZ but was destroyed due to lack of air assets for evacuation. On 5 March at YB 819019 an ambush patrol from A/1-8 Infantry killed 2 NVA. While moving back to the company location, 2 more NVA were seen and engaged, resulting in 1 NVA WIA/CIA. An ambush from C/1-8 killed 1 NVA at YB813022. After the ambush was sprung, the US troops received fire from the rear resulting in 2 US WIA. Artillery was employed with unknown results. At 1500 hours as C/1-8 continued the RIF along the southern road, heavy contact was made vicinity YA 807025. The order was given to break contact due to the heavy engagement in the 3-8th AO. Contact was broken and C/1-8 withdrew to an LZ and was extracted to A/1-8 location (YB822032). Results of the contact were 7 NVA KIA, 3 US KIA, and 11 US WIA.

On 7 March, A/7-17 Cavalry, searching in area of suspected enemy 105 locations, found 2 105 mm howitzers at YB779028. Air strikes and gunships were employed resulting in 1 artillery piece destroyed and 1 possibly destroyed. On 8 March, A/7-17th found a truck at YB 778018. An air strike uncovered another truck, which was also destroyed by artillery and gunships. At YB 780002, A/7-17 found a third truck, which they destroyed with artillery and gunships. On 10 March, D/1-8 combat assaulted to YB 770026 with the mission to extract the 2 105mm howitzers. At YB 777018, contact was made by the point element with 1 NVA. The NVA was killed and an SKS captured. In the immediate area of the howitzers, 2 disabled trucks were destroyed w/thermite grenades. Another truck was uncovered and also destroyed by thermite grenades. Thirty (30) rounds of Chicom 105mm ammunition were destroyed in place. The howitzers were extracted to Polei Kleng.

On 9-10 March, 3 B-52 strikes were employed on the area

360

to the north of FB Swinger. A/1-8 and C/1-8 were given the mission to make a bomb contact with an estimated NVA company dug in bunkers. C/1-8 Infantry, working squad at YB 847006. A/7-17 Cavalry screened during the battle. Tracer 5, forced to escape and evade that night. Results of the battle were 33 NVA KIA, 2 US KIA, 13 WIA, and 6 US MIA. From 13-15 March, A and C/1-8 followed up in the contact area to recover MIAs. On 13 March at YB 852011 contact was made by A Co. resulting in 4 NVA KIA. That night, A and C companies were mortared at their night location with no casualties suffered. On 15 March A and C/1-8 again received 8 rounds of mortar fire in their base resulting in 2 WIA. Three of the 4 US MIA returned to the patrol base that afternoon.

A/7-17 Cavalry screened in support of 1-8th operations throughout this time. On 15 March they found 1 enemy platoon at YA 861986. Gunships expended resulting in 10 NVA KIA. From a BDA of an air strike at YA 855955, the Scout section found 1 12.7 AA weapon destroyed and 5 NVA KBA. Another air strike at YA 854977, destroyed 6 bunkers and killed 9 NVA.

The Plei Trap Road operation was significant in interdicting an enemy main supply route. The destruction of 6 trucks and 2 howitzers curtailed movement of enemy artillery toward Polei Kleng and stopped the flow of supplies to the 40th NVA Artillery Regiment. With a US battalion astride its line of communication, the enemy was forced to decide on a new course of action rather than support an attack on Polei Kleng.

d. LZ BRACE 3-7 March: At 1530 hours, 3 March 69, A/3-8th Infantry closed into what was believed to be their NL at YA 803879. A security patrol was sent out from the perimeter and found 2 NVA fleeing east from the perimeter toward the top of the hill. A platoon pursued and became engaged. The remainder of the company reinforced and made contact with an estimated battalion perimeter. After a 1 1/2 hour firefight, the company, after sustaining several casualties and mission, withdrew into a perimeter and contact was broken. Gunships, AC-47 Spooky, and artillery were employed throughout the night, around the perimeter. At 0950 4 Mar, A 3-8th sent a patrol to check the area of the previous contact and locate the missing personnel. Contact was made almost immediately and the patrol withdrew to the perimeter. The enemy then launched an attack w/grenades and B-40 rockets. A/3-8th Infantry was forced to fight a retrograde movement to an LZ at YA 790885 and was extracted to Firebase Pause at 1500 hours.

At 1125 hours, 4 March, B/3-8th Infantry attempted a combat assault to YA828899 with the mission of moving down the ridgeline to reinforce A/3-8th Inf. The assault was postponed because automatic weapons fire was encountered on the LZ. A second attempt was made at 1328 and again fire was received. After a preparation by air strike and screening by A/7-17th, B/3-8th was inserted at 1540 hours and moved south, joining Rcn/3-8th at YA 825890 for their night defensive location.

D/3-8th continued to move up the ridge from YA800856 to establish a block and prevent enemy withdrawal to the south. While moving to Hill 947 (YA14869), the company found a well used trail with telephone wire laid along side it and the military symbols carved in the trees. Hill 947 was reached without opposition. As the company moved further north, contact was made with an unknown size force, resulting in 4 NVA KIA and 1 US recaptured. The returned US soldier revealed the presence of a larger enemy force to the north. D Co was then ordered to reoccupy Hill 947 and prepare a defensive position to block enemy withdrawal from the area. At 1640, D Co received a probe from an estimated two enemy squads. Throughout the night of 4-5 March, D/3-8th had heavy movement and probes by sapper units. Enemy attempts to neutralize outposts were thwarted. At 0750, 5 March, an estimated two enemy companies reinforced with sappers launched an attack against D Company's east side. The attack was preceded by mortars, B-40 rockets, and CS; however, it was broken by artillery and gunships. At 0825, D Co successfully counterattacked to retake OP's. For the rest of the morning, D Co received probes and sniper fire. At 1340, the enemy attacked again with 1 company on the east and 1 company on the west. Again the attack was preceded by a mortar barrage. A FAC spotted the enemy mortars and destroyed them with an air strike. The ground attack was repelled in fifteen minutes of fierce fighting. Enemy probes continued for the remainder of the day including sapper attacks on the first platoon perimeter. Spooky and artillery were employed around the perimeter and in enemy assembly areas.

B/3-8 continued its attack south on 5 March with Rcn/3-8 attached. A/1-35 was OPCON to 3-8th Infantry after being lifted to LZ Pause. C/3-8 then combat assaulted to YA828899 at 1035hrs. The lead aircraft received fire and the assault was postponed. Also B/3-8 began receiving fire from the hill at YA8288880 (BRACE) and employed artillery. At 1320, C/3-8 again attempted a combat assault to YA828899 and was successful. The company then moved south to reinforce B/3-8 and Rcn/3-8. The two companies linked just prior to darkness.

As the major enemy force had been located in the Plei Trap, the 1st Brigade consolidated forces throughout the area of operations to prepare to meet any new threat. In

363

the 3-12 Infantry AO, B/3-12 and D/3-12 were moved to LZ Mary. C/3/12 was extracted to FSR Swinger. In the 1-8 Infantry AO, D/1-8 was ordered to contact, and was extracted to LZ Turkey. 1-35 Infantry (-) CHOP 1st Brigade and began moving to Polei Kleng.

On 6 March, B and C/3-8 began a coordinated assault on BRACE. B Co moved within 150 meters of the top when they received heavy AW fire. An attempt by B Co to maneuver east and C Co to maneuver west were unsuccessful. Artillery fire with delay fuses were employed without success. The companies withdrew part way down the hill and air strikes w/750 lb delay fused bombs were employed. At 1700 the attack commenced again. At 1720 C Co secured the top of the hill and B Co joined shortly thereafter to consolidate a defensive position.

D/3-8 on Hill 947 repelled a ground attack at 0700 on 6 March. The attack was preceded by a mortar preparation, to include CS rounds. Again Scouts and gunships from A/7-17 Cavalry were used to neutralize the enemy mortars. After 20 minutes the enemy was driven off. After a perimeter sweep, D Co then made preparations for resupply and evacuation of the wounded.

In order to block enemy withdrawal to the west from BRACE, the 3-12 Infantry formed Task Force Swift (B, D, Recon /3-12). TF Swift moved overland from LZ Mary on 6 March to the southeast to block or destroy enemy forces in the area.

On 6 March, the 1st Brigade continued the attack on 7 March by airlifting C/3-12 from FB Swinger to Hill 947 to reinforce D/3-8. TF Swift was extracted from YA788883 to BRACE. The task force attacked and secured the middle hill (YA815872) on 7 March without contact. 1-35 Infantry (-) was airlifted from Polei Kleng to LZ Mary to conduct search and destroy operations and block enemy withdrawal to the west of BRACE. On 8 March Task Force Swift attacked south and linked with D/3-8 and C/3-12. No further contact was made. Results of the entire action were 241 NVA KIA, 32 US KIA, 125 US WIA, and 1 US MIA. LZ BRACE was the most significant battle of Operation Wayne Grey. The 3-8 Infantry engaged reserve elements of the 66th NVA Regiment and rendered them ineffective. The losses sustained by the enemy by body count alone prohibited further employment of that unit. Also, the 3-8 Infantry had fought and defeated the enemy in a conventional battle through proper employment of fire support and maneuver. The steadfastness and determination of the fighting man on the ground was the key to success in this battle.

e. Task Force Swift 10-14March: After consolidation on Hill 947, TF Swift received the mission to make bomb damage assessment of 3 B52 strikes which would be made to the south of Hill 947. On 11 March, the task force received mortar fire and countered with air strikes and artillery. At 1145hrs at YA817861, a SRP from C/3-12 round 4 NVA bodies and fresh blood trails. A platoon was sent to sweep the area. At 1420 hours the platoon made contact with an unknown size force at YA 818858 and received mortar fire. C Co moved to reinforce, and B Co moved to secure a withdrawal route. Contact was made with an estimated enemy company. Due to the proximity of a B52 strike, the companies broke contact and withdrew to the task force perimeter. On 12 March TF Swift attacked again and secured the objective at YA818956. Once there, they received mortar and small arms fire resulting in 15 US WIA. Air strikes and artillery were employed with

365

unknown results. Results of the action were 5 NVA KIA, 10 US KIA, and 56 US WIA.

On March 15, the 1st Brigade began a new phase of operations, moving into company-sized blocking positions and using ambush operations, artillery, air strikes, B52 strikes, and chemical munitions to block and interdict enemy withdrawal. In the 3-12th Infantry, A/3-12 was moved to LZ Mary on 13 March prior to a combat assault to a new LZ (LZ CIDER) YA829799. The assault was made the following day unopposed and was followed by C/3-12, Hq/3-12, and B/6-29 Arty. B/3-12 and D/3-12 moved overland to vicinity YA808856 LZ D-HANDLE. After A/3-12 assaulted to LZ CIDER, C and D/3-8 constructed a firebase at BRACE. On 16 March, Hq/3-8 and A/3-8 and C/6-29 Arty moved to BRACE from LZ PAUSE. In the 1-8th Infantry AO, D/1-8 closed into FB 20. Companies A and C/1-8 moved to Hill 467 YB803034 and were constituted into Task Force Alpha.

f. Plei Trap Road Interdiction 16-30 March: As the 1st Brigade began its second phase of operations, the 1-8th Infantry was assigned the mission of interdicting the Plei Trap Road so as to prevent enemy vehicular movement in the area through the monsoon. The mission was to be accomplished by running road interdiction to the east from FB 20 and interdiction on the south from Hill 467 (YA803035). Companies A and C/1-8 on 16 March began moving from YB847003 to Hill 467. The A/7-17 Cavalry while screening their move, located an NVA truck in the vicinity YB838068 and destroyed it. On 19 March an ambush of A/1-8 made contact with a dug in force at YB805053 resulting in 1 US KIA and 1 US WIA. The ambush pulled back and employed artillery. On 20 March A Co swept the contact area again making contact with an unknown sized force resulting in 4 NVA KIA, 1 US KIA, and 11 US WIA. On 21 March, A/1-8 was airlifted to FB 20 and B/1-8 was moved to Hill 467.

From 21-23 March ambushes and road interdiction were continued around the area. Contacts were small resulting in 5 NVA KIA, 1 US KIA, and 9 US WIA.

On 23 March activity increased with enemy attacks by fire. FB 20 received seven 105 WP rounds, twenty 105 HE, and various mortars and RR rounds. On 24 March, FB 20 again received an undetermined number of 105 rounds. Hill 467 received indirect fires, sniper fire and B-40 rockets on its east and west perimeter. Security sweeps of the area resulted in 1 NVA KIA. On 25 March, B/1-8(-) returning from a road interdiction mission, made contact with an estimated platoon of NVA at YB795020. Contact was broken at 1230 and reinitiated at 1413 resulting in 5 NVA KIA, 2 US KIA, 11 US WIA, and 6 US MIA. Simultaneously, Task Force Alpha came under attack with B40 and small arms. The attack was repelled resulting in 5 NVA KIA, 1 US KIA, and 13 US WIA. The task force continued to receive sporadic 60mm and 82mm fire.

On 26 March FB 20 again received incoming 105mm during the afternoon. A total of 20 rounds impacted in and around the firebase resulting in 3 US KIA and 8 US WIA. Also B/1-8(-) linked with D/1-8 and moved back to Hill 467. Four MIA from B/1-8 rejoined the unit at that time. Shortly thereafter, Task Force Alpha began receiving incoming small arms and B40, 82mm mortar, and 105mm artillery. No casualties were suffered. On 27 March FB 20 received 19 rounds of 105mm resulting in 2 US WIA. Air strikes and artillery were employed in counter battery. Task Force Alpha received sporadic sniper and B-40 rounds, especially during the airlift of D/1-8 to FB 27. C/1-8 was sent to sweep the perimeter but was forced to return when they received incoming 105-mm artillery. A total of 15 105 rounds impacted including one propaganda round with leaflets exhorting the US soldiers to surrender. No US casualties were suffered. On 28 March Task Force Alpha had several sightings and movement. Mortars and artillery were employed with unknown results. Also they received 120 rounds of incoming 105 mm resulting in 1 US KIA and 4 US WIA. D/1-8 reported a convoy of NVA trucks north of FB 27. Artillery and mortars were employed with unobserved results. On 29 March, FB 20 received a total of 16 rounds of 105 with no casualties suffered. Artillery and air strikes were again employed on suspected firing positions. At Task Force Alpha sporadic sniper and B-40 fire were received. Small arms, mortar, and artillery were employed, resulting in 5 NVA KIA and 1 US WIA. On 30 March, 1-8th Infantry began a tactical withdrawal from their AO. Task Force Alpha was evacuated with aircraft and ground troops receiving small arms and B-40 fire. No casualties were suffered. In the evacuation of FB 20, the enemy fired a total of 40 rounds at the firebase. An Air Force smoke screen was used to cover the move with the extraction being completed at 1830 hours. D/1-8 was extracted to Polei Kleng from FB 27 without incident.

The 1-8th AO had twofold significance. First, the intensity of the attacks by fire indicated the enemy intention of inflicting casualties and damage on American firebases and preventing resupply. Second, the enemy ground activity around Task Force Alpha was designed to contain American forces while enemy equipment was withdrawn or hidden in the area. No major attacks was ever launched against the patrol base; however, the harassment to cover movement from the area as evidenced by repair work on the craters and abatis made by the 1-8th Infantry on the Plei Trap road.

g. On 15 March - 14 April: The Cu Don is a mountain on an extension of the ridge south of BRACE. It was a known enemy base area and suspected to be on the withdrawal route of the 66th NVA Regiment. As the first Brigade entered Phase II of Operation Wayne Grey, the 3-12 Infantry received the mission of establishing blocking positions and interdicting enemy movement through the area. On 14 March, The enemy action in A, Recon, and C/3-12 combat assaulted to LZ CIDER (YA829799) to establish a firebase. The following day, B/6-29 Arty moved to LZ CIDER. B/3-12 moved to a patrol base at YA818856, and D/3-12 established a firebase for the 4.2 mortars at LZ D-HANDLE (YA821853).

On 18 March, 3D/3-12 on a RIF became heavily engaged at YA817839. 2D/3-12 was sent to reinforce and made contact with an NVA force, which came between the two platoons. With support from air strikes, artillery, and gunships, the platoons were able to link and break contact. Results were 7 NVA KIA, 4 US KIA, 19 US WIA, and 3 US MIA. On 19 March, the bunker complex at YA8178839 was attacked by air strikes all day. That evening LZ CIDER was probed with small arms and M79 fire resulting in no friendly casualties and 1 NVA KIA.

On 20 March, D/3-12 attacked south to capture the bunker complex on Hill 800 (YA817839). The attack was supported by air strikes, artillery, and gunships. Enemy forces held the position, but 2 MIA were recovered. D Co withdrew to LZ D-HANDLE from 1845-2315hrs. LZ CIDER received a heavy weapons attack from 82mm mortars and 75 mm RR. There were no casualties and only slight equipment damage.

D/3-12 attacked Hill 800 again on 22 March after heavy air and artillery bombardment. The hill was seized without opposition and all US MIA were recovered. 4 NVA KBA were found in the bunker complex. From 23-26 March 3-12 Infantry units conducted patrols and ambushes throughout the area of operations.

On 27 March, 3A/3-12 on a local security patrol, made contact with 4 NVA at YA826811, killing 2. The platoon was then engaged by automatic weapons and B-40 rockets. They withdrew 200 meters and sent the WIA back to LZ CIDER. A/3-12 moved from LZ CIDER, linked with the platoon, and moved into the contact area after an artillery preparation. Again automatic weapons fire was received. The company withdrew to LZ CIDER leaving 8 MIA in the area of contact.

On 28 March A/3-12 again moved to vicinity YA826811 to recover the MIA. As the company entered the contact area, they received small arms fire from an estimated 2 platoons. Contact was broken and artillery and mortars were employed. As the company withdrew, they received 60 rounds of 82 mm and 60mm mortar fire. No casualties were suffered.

At 2245 on 28 March, SRP 43 at YA812845 near LZ D-HANDLE reported observing 9 NVA. Mortars were employed to force the NVA toward B/3-12 ambush. The NVA, however, moved toward SRP 43 and claymores were employed resulting in 4 NVA KIA. At 290600, the ambush platoon from B/3-12 observed 3-5 NVA at YA823858. As they waited for the enemy to enter the killing zone, they received 3 rounds of B-40 rockets resulting in 4 US WIA. The platoon then observed 15-20 NVA moving north carrying 3 NVA. The unit engaged with small arms and artillery resulting in 5 NVA KIA and possible 10 NVA killed by artillery. Also at 0600, at LZ D-HANDLE, the enemy launched a sapper attack under cover of a weapons attack. B and D/3-12 received 50 rounds of 82-mm mortar and sappers destroyed two bunkers with B-40 rockets. The attack was repelled by small arms and artillery. A patrol from B/3-12 later killed another 2 NVA during a sweep of the area. Results of the entire action were 27 NVA KIA, 2 US KIA, and 28 US WIA.

On 30 March, A/3-12 moved to recover the MIA from the contact of 27 March. The bodies were found vicinity YA826811, but the enemy again attacked with small arms and mortars. The company was ordered to withdraw and did so fighting its way back up the hill to YA834814. C/3-12(-) was dispatched to help secure the night location. Contact was broken at 1900hrs and C Co linked with A Co at 2000hrs. At 310035 March, A and C(-)/3-12 received small arms and 150 rounds of 82 mm, 60 mm, and 75 mm RR from vicinity YA830815. Artillery, mortars, and Spooky were employed. There were no US casualties.

In reaction to the locating of a large enemy force in the vicinity of the Cu Don and the enemy's willingness to remain in fight, five B52 strikes were struck in the area to prepare for the combat assault of 1-22 Infantry. On 2 April 1-22 Infantry CHOP 1st Brigade. A and C/1-22 AL to LZ CIDER and moved overland to YA821795. B, D, and Rcn/1-22 combat assaulted to YA806827.

On 3 April, the 1-22 Infantry attacked toward Objective Red (YA8280). 2C/1-22 made contact with an unknown size enemy force at YA816795. The platoon was reinforced by C/1-22(-) and ordered to withdraw. Results were 1 NVA KIA, 1 US KIA, and 14 US WIA. B/1-22 made contact with an unknown size force at YA805818 resulting in 1 KCS WIA. The company withdrew to its NL vicinity YA808822.

On 5 April C/3-8 AL from YA826906 to Hill 871 (YA806825 CHOP 1-22 Inf. 1-22 Infantry moved recon patrols to objective areas to establish blocking positions. 1D/1-22 on recon observed 4 NVA in bunkers vicinity YA813823. The platoon withdrew and air strikes and artillery were employed. The platoon sent recon patrols in the afternoon into the area and found an extensive bunker complex. As the unit reconnoitered the hill by fire, the enemy suddenly attacked from bunkers on top of the hill and from the flanks with small arms and B-40 rockets. 2D/1-22 was dispatched to assist in the evacuation of casualties and also made contact with a flanking enemy force. Contact was broken at 1620 resulting in 23 NVA KIA, 20 possible NVA WIA, 1 US KIA, 5 US KIA (MIA), and 17 US WIA.

From 6-9 April, the objective area was saturated with air strikes and artillery. LRRP teams were employed to recon the area for evidence of enemy forces in strength. On 10 April, D/1-22 moved to YA815824 and recovered 4 MIA. L1B found 9 MIA from A/3-12 Inf. On 11 April D/1-22 recovered 1 MIA and C/3-12 recovered 2 additional MIA. All were evacuated.

On 13 April 1-22nd Infantry was final extracted from the Cu Don to Polei Kleng and CHOP 2d Brigade. A, C, and Rcn/3-8 Infantry were also extracted and CHOP 2d Brigade. On 14 April 3-12 Infantry (-) and 3-8 Infantry (-) were extracted to Mary Lou. 3-12 Infantry prepared for deployment to Camp Radcliff. 3-8 Infantry (-) CHOP 2d Brigade.

The battles in the Cu Don are significant in the fact that an enemy base area was disrupted. The tenacity with which the enemy defended the area gave evidence that he had something to protect. His attacks by fire and harassing sniper fires were designed to hold US forces until he could evacuate or hide his equipment. When US forces came close to his base, his defenses were organized as ambushes. Despite these designs, the 3-12th Infantry and the 1-22nd Infantry were successful in inflicting heavy casualties on the enemy. An unknown number of the enemy were undoubtedly killed in the heavy air and artillery bombardment. As the operation concluded, indications were that the enemy had retreated toward Cambodia.

h. FB SWINGER: Throughout Operation Wayne Grey, FB Swinger was subjected to sporadic attacks by fire. This fire was primarily 82 mm mortar and 75mm recoilless rifle directed at aircraft and at the 155mm artillery battery. Artillery and mortars were always employed in counter battery fire. Air cavalry screened the area northwest and northeast of the firebase, but never detected the firing positions. Air strikes were employed on several suspected locations with no observed results. B52 strikes were employed on five occasions when intelligence indicated a troop concentration in the area. However, the enemy persisted in directing harassing fires at the firebases.

12.   RESULTS:

a. Enemy Losses:

KIA	575
POW	4

b. Enemy equipment captured or destroyed.

AK-47	57
SKS	13
CHICOM rifles	3

373

CHICOM assault rifle	1
SOVIET Carbine	1
RPD IMG	9
M60 MG	2
M16 rifle	3
RPG Rocket launcher	5
.50 cal MG (destroyed)	1
12.7 AA (destroyed)	1
12.7AA	1
60mm mortar	1
60mm Mortar (destroyed)	1
105-mm howitzer	2
105-mm howitzer (destroyed)	1
Soviet trucks (destroyed)	6
Soviet trucks	1
CHICOM AM/FM radio	1

6560 rounds 7.62mm
256 rounds 12.7mm
25 rounds 60mm
51 rounds 82mm
3 rounds 85mm
4 rounds 75mm
91 rounds 105-mm
22 rounds B40 rocket
110 CHICOM grenades
50 booby traps
35 lbs TNT

c. Friendly Losses:

US KIA	106
US WIA	437
US MIA	8

d. Friendly Equipment Losses and Damage:

M16	59
M16 (damaged)	1
M79	4
M60	5
PRC 25 radio	18
PRC 25 radio (damaged)	2
PRC 27 radio	2
KY 38 (X-Mode)	1
Starlight scopes	2
Starlight scopes (destroyed)	1

13. ADMINISTRATION MATTERS:

a. Supply: Battalion trains were based at Mary Lou. Resupply was accomplished by convoying items to Polei Kleng and airlifting them to forward firebases. The LOC at Polei Kleng was subjected to 12-mm rocket and 75mm RR attacks which disrupted resupply activities for 2 weeks. However, a sufficient amount of all classes of supply were delivered without extensive delay. Combat loads, ammunition, and weapons were adequate for performance of the mission.

b. Maintenance: Maintenance was performed by elements of 704th Maintenance Battalion at Mary Lou.

c. Treatment of Casualties: All casualties were evacuated by air in MEDEVAC helicopters or resupply helicopters directly to the medical clearing company at Mary Lou. This evacuation was normally timely and effective however, the tactical situation at times prevented a rapid response.

d. Transportation: helicopters were the primary mode of transportation during the operation. Support rendered by the 52nd Combat Aviation BN was outstanding, especially on mission requiring much courage and skill from the pilots. The major problem area was the inadequate refueling facility at Polei Kleng. An excessive loss of blade time was experienced especially for CH47 aircraft, which had to refuel at Kontum or Mary Lou.

e. Communications: The Brigade maintained four FM nets (Command, Intel, Aviation, and Secure Voice) for command and control of the operation. Also 8 VHF circuits were used for hot lines to Division and for common user circuits. Radio teletype worked on the Division Special Purpose Net.

14. SPECIAL EQUIPMENT AND TECHNIQUES: LRRP teams were employed in Operation Wayne Grey in a unique fashion. Rather than use them to develop intelligence by locating the enemy, they were inserted into an area where the enemy location was confirmed. Since combat troops experienced difficulty in scouting this type of situation, LRRP teams with their special training in jungle movement, camouflage and concealment, were employed to detect enemy strength in the area. In this mission in the Cu Don LRRP teams were successful in locating eleven US MIAs and clearing an area for employment of combat troops. Once their reconnaissance role was completed, they were withdrawn from the area.

15. COMMANDERS ANALYSIS:

a. Operation Wayne Grey was planned as a spoiling attack to disrupt the enemy post Tet offensive against Kontum by severing his line of communication into a sanctuary. This purpose was accomplished as evidenced by the lack of major enemy offensive action in the vicinity of Kontum City. The initial combat assaults into the Plei Trap surprised the enemy and caused him to deal with an unexpected threat to his rear. The battle of LZ Brace was an encounter with reserve elements of the 66th NVA Regiment. Losses sustained by the enemy in that action undoubtedly forced him to reverse his course of action. The reconnaissance in force along the Plei Trap Road, the capture and destruction of 2 enemy howitzers, and 7 enemy trucks prevented further commitment of the NVA 40th Artillery Regiment. With an American battalion astride its principal line of communication further offensive action endangered enemy maneuverability. In total the enemy timetable for a post Tet Offensive was disrupted, and he was forced back to sanctuary.

b. Operation Wayne Grey is an example of conventional warfare in an unconventional war. The enemy used artillery in support of his operation to include CS and white phosphorous rounds. Anti-aircraft weapons were employed to counter American air mobility. Enemy troops were well equipped. Almost every battle involved an infantry assault on an enemy fortified position. The assault was preceded by air strikes and artillery and was continued with these assets in close support. The enemy defended his position tenaciously making heavy use of mortars and rockets. Enemy attacks were mainly by fire to include attacks by fire on the Brigade Tactical Command Post and logistical helipads at Polei Kleng.

c. The Air Cavalry proved to be the most versatile force available to the Brigade Commander. Due to its capability to react in short time to any situation, it was most valuable in the shift of combat assets from one AO to another. In the execution of the normal reconnaissance role, the air cavalry was responsible for the aerial interdiction of enemy troop and logistical moves. It located and helped destroy 2 105-mm howitzers and seven enemy trucks. While working in support of ground engagements, the screening of flanks and engagement of enemy indirect fire weapons saved many lives and contributed to the success of infantry attacks. The courage, aggressiveness, and flexibility of the air cavalry made it a very valuable asset.

d. Air power played a key role in the fire support scheme of Operation Wayne Grey. Fighter sorties were used mainly in support of troop assaults and in the destruction of enemy bunker complexes. Fighters also interdicted enemy lines of communications with road cratering missions and by destroying enemy trucks and 3 artillery pieces. B-52 strikes interdicted large troop concentrations and routes of withdrawal. Smoke screens were employed by A1-E's in the evacuation of firebases subject to enemy indirect fire. Spooky aircraft provided close support to ground troops in contact. In the action at BRACE with D/3-8 Infantry, a Spooky aircraft helped account for 149 enemy dead around the perimeter. Shadow flights were used to screen for possible enemy movements in the western AO near the border. Integrated in the total scheme, Air Force personnel made an outstanding contribution to the accomplishment of the Brigade mission.

16.   RECOMMENDATIONS. None.

HALE H. KNIGHT
COL, INFANTRY - COMMANDING

Annex A - Task Organization

1.   Task Organization per 1st Brigade FRADO 8-69

        Headquarters; 1st Brigade
        1-8 Infantry
        3-8 Infantry
        3-12 Infantry
        6-29 Arty (-) (DS)
        A/6-29 Arty (DS)

C/6-29 Arty (DS)
B/6-29 Arty (DS)

B/4 Eng (-) (DS)
1B/4 Eng (DS)
3B/4 Eng (DS)
2B/4 Eng (DS)

2.   Changes in Task Organization

1 March	ADD	A/7-17 Cavalry
5 March	ADD	A/1-35 Infantry
6 March	ADD	1-35 Infantry (-)
15 March	DELETE	1-35 Infantry
20 March	DELETE	A/7-17 Cavalry
	ADD	C/7-17 Cavalry
25 March	DELETE	C/7-17 Cavalry
26 March	ADD	7-17 Cavalry (-)
3 April	DELETE	A/7-17 Cavalry
7 April	DELETE	C/7-17 Cavalry
	ADD	A/7-17 Cavalry
11 April	ADD	D/1-10 Cavalry

While I was doing my research and reliving the events that I had written in my journal, I realized what a terrible place the Plei-Trap Valley was. People were being killed as they were just trying to make it through the day. A soldier was killed as he walked away from an OH-6A helicopter. He stood up before clearing the outer edge of the main rotor blades. A cook was killed while making coffee in the mess hall. The first rocket hit just outside the door where he was standing. Another soldier was killed when a mortar tube exploded near the place he sat eating some C-rations.

The events of those days remain with all of us who served in that faraway place. What amazed me most was the fact many of the vets I talked to still remember things as if they happened yesterday. The following is an example of this.

As I was completing the final set-up of this book, I received this letter from my friend Bob Kilpatrick. He had spent his time in hell with me in the Plei-Trap Valley back in 1969. He was also a crew chief, and flew many long and dangerous hours in the Valley.

In the days before November 11, 2002 Bob was preparing to be one of the honored readers of the names at the Vietnam Wall in Washington DC. He had asked to read the name of John C. Schiffhauer (Shifty, as we called him) during his time of the reading. John was killed the first day we were in the Valley.

The following is the letter Bob sent to me. I can still remember some of the events that he speaks about as if it were yesterday. The days after March 1, 1969 became one long frightening dream. For that month-and-a-half we ate, slept, and breathed the events which we had no control over. The entire operation became one continuous period that could not be divided into days or weeks. His letter starts on the 2nd of March but it encompasses about a week of events that happened. I only know this because of four

380

years of research and thousands of pages of reports that have helped me define the actual time frame. I know how hard it is to share your feeling and memories of those times with others. For this, I thank Bob and hope that the words that he shared with me will help anyone who reads this understand what the Valley was really like.

The 2nd day of March 1969 was a tough one. My friend "Shifty" had been killed the day before. We had returned very late after a long day of combat assaults to learn that he had been shot in an LZ. I still had his blood on my clothes and boots from helping to clean up his helicopter in the dark. Again today I was up early, before dawn. After some breakfast, I picked up my rifle and machine-gun, then walked through the dawn to the revetment area where my helicopter was parked. I was a twenty-year-old US Army helicopter crew chief assigned to the 119th Assault Helicopter Company, stationed at Camp Holloway, near Pleiku in the Central Highlands of South Vietnam. In addition to ensuring that the helicopter received the proper maintenance, I flew each day behind a machine-gun in the open the left side door of the aircraft. Our gunner, my friend "Eggy," protected the other side of our ship, Gator 834.

The 4th Infantry Division had just started a major operation against the North Vietnamese Army in the Plei Trap Valley west of Kontum, and they were using us for helicopter support. The Ho Chi Minh Trail, the NVA's supply lifeline, entered the Central Highlands from Laos through the Plei Trap Valley, and the 4th Division's mission was to choke off the Trail at the Laotian border. The fighting had been very heavy all over the Valley.

As usual, our morning was a blur of tiny, "single-ship" Landing Zones at isolated, company-sized defensive outposts on hilltops and ridges all around the Plei Trap. We went wherever we were needed, hovering in with supplies of ammunition and water, then loading soldiers wounded in the overnight firefights onto our helicopter and trying to keep them alive during the dash back to medical care at Kontum. Later in the day we would return to drop off food and other less critical supplies, and to carry out the dead.

Our first mission of the afternoon was from a supply pad at Firebase Mary Lou in Kontum. They loaded us out on a resupply run to an LZ deep in the Plei Trap Valley, one where we had taken a lot of fire during the initial assault the day before. We called them "hot" LZs if there was shooting going on, "cold" if there was not. This one had been hot. Our cargo was the usual dangerous assortment of "ash and trash" -- cans of water, crates of ammo, grenades, C-4 plastic explosives, claymore mines, coils of concertina wire, and this time included a couple of cherry replacements with brand-new everything, looking pale and scared and very young.

The LZ was cold. The voice on the radio directing us in was cool and relaxed; under control, unlike the day before. Once we were down in the LZ, I saw that people were standing around, actually walking erect. The area had been cleaned up and fortified somewhat, and they had a pretty good pad cleared for us. Still, evidence of the previous day's combat was everywhere; shredded, limbless trees; a stale, burnt smell of the fight rising off blackened ground; an exhausted, vacant look in the grunts' eyes. Worst was the gut-wrenching, all-encompassing stench coming from a lineup of filthy, lumpy rubber ponchos with muddy boots hanging out of them at absurd angles, tied up haphazardly with rope.

We sat with our rotor idling, nervously still on the pad as a couple of the grunts pointed the replacements in the right direction and started to unload the rest of our cargo. The radio operator looked up and recognized me, so he came walking over. He told me that his Lieutenant, who had been directing the defense when we had fought our way in and out to extract some of their wounded the day before, was wrapped up in one of the ponchos next to us. They had been in trouble all night but had managed to hang on and the North Vietnamese had finally broken off the fight around dawn.

Other resupply ships had come in earlier in the day with more food, water, ammo, and replacements, and they were able to get the rest of their wounded pals out on them early. We were going to transport their dead, the shattered bodies that had been broiling all day in the sun.

I never saw a body bag in the field, not one. Some high-ranking commander had decreed that sending body bags out to the line outfits was bad for morale, defeatist. So 4th Division grunts in 1969, those who got blown to shreds or shot to pieces, usually made their last helicopter ride with most of their gory remains wrapped up in their own bloody rubber ponchos. It was a filthy twentieth-century equivalent of being carried home on your shield.

Our pilot saw the four soldiers pick up the first grimy poncho and take a step our way and simply said, "Aw, no," very quietly on the intercom. Today's co-pilot, a new guy, turned once and saw, then quickly looked away, back out the window on the opposite side. He said nothing. I liked him a little better.

Four or five dripping, reeking ponchos with various mangled body parts and contents hanging out were carefully lifted aboard by the guys working the pad. They were stacking the next one of their dead friends into our ship when most of an arm slid out and plopped into the dirt outside my door. The grunt standing the closest looked down, picked up his pal's arm, and casually handed it to me as he turned to go pick up another dead comrade. I took it by the elbow, picked up the bloody corner of his poncho, and tucked it inside as the other grunts loaded another carcass onto the pile.

A growing puddle of vital fluids was draining out of the nightmarish heap of ponchos and onto the deck of our helicopter. It was starting to pool around the soles of my boots, running over the edge of the cargo door. As soon as the last dead grunt was loaded I keyed my intercom switch and said to the pilot, "Let's get outta here." He pulled pitch and we got out of there.

The choking stench was horrifying enough, but the brown mist, the bloody cloud of body fluids that began to spray around the left side of our helicopter was incredibly, unspeakably worse, a living nightmare. As soon as we started to gain speed and altitude out of the LZ, the ponchos started flapping around, and the bile and blood started blowing and snapping out of the gory heap, all over and into everything, me included. Holding my breath, I yanked my helmet visor down and grabbed a greasy rag to cover my face below the visor while screaming over the intercom at the pilot to do something, to trim the ship so the stuff would stop covering me. But because of the wind direction and the way the airflow worked around the interior of the aircraft, there was nothing he could do; I could feel him try trimming left, then right, changing speed; nothing helped. It just kept getting worse, and worse, and worse. I sat and watched in horror as my hands, my arms, my legs, my guns, my ammunition, everything around me gradually turned brown with vile fluids.

By the time we got to the medical pad at Kontum about twenty minutes later, almost everything behind the pilots on the left side of the ship, all of me from my helmet to my boots, was encrusted, caked thick with layer after layer of brown, dried blood. I have no idea why I wasn't sick to my stomach, except that I had at some time during the trip arrived at a quiet, deadly furious mental state where I was looking only to even the score.

As soon as we landed a couple of sad-looking

grunts came over to unload the corpses, to add them to the horrifying lineup already in place at the side of the pad. The two of them had obviously seen most of a year and had their fill of it, and now they had more dead to deal with. Two other round-eyed guys, clean but sleazy somehow, in khaki safari suits with cameras and bags and meters hanging everywhere came jogging down towards our ship. They stopped short when they realized what we were carrying and one of them raised a camera to his face a few feet off to our side and began to focus on our cargo. It was the ultimate indignity; a final invasion of good men's privacy.

I watched as my hands flashed out and gripped the handles of my now blood-encrusted machine-gun to pull it back from its mount and swing and level the barrel directly at his damned chest, point blank, not ten feet away. He froze when his camera came to focus on the vicious-looking muzzle of my M-60. Looking up and behind the weapon he suddenly realized that the insane, faceless gunner aiming at his chest, about to chop him to pieces, was totally covered brown with blood from hands to head to toe.

He lowered the camera to his chest and his hands came up ever so slowly, palms out, as did his pal's. Their eyes had become huge and moist, and both ghouls just stood frozen in place, staring motionless up the bore of my weapon, preparing to exhale that one last breath. I sat there with my fists tightening on the gun grips, in a bitter fury, mentally machine-gunning the two bastards over and over again, and about to do it for real, my finger on the trigger. Nobody, including the grunt unloaders, was moving a muscle.

After what seems to have been hours, my friend Eggy appeared to my front, a little off to the side of the muzzle. He just stood there, hands at his sides, shaking his head, slow, waiting, just looking at me. I looked down

385

through my blood-smeared visor, from my bloody hands around the bloody machine-gun that had a bloody belt of ammunition leading into it, to my bloody jungle boots. Everything was crusted brown, thick with blood, so thick it was crumbling off in chunks, just like the rest of me.

I finally looked back up at the two photographers and was suddenly weak, drained, just sick of the whole surreal mess. I let go of the gun and slumped back against the bulkhead. Eggy turned and took a step towards the still motionless cameramen. His fist flicked out as soon as he got within range and one was down in a heap on the ground, cameras askew, and the other ghoul was running.

One of the unloaders solemnly low-fived Eggy on his way back around the ship, and they finished pulling the rest of the bodies out, kind of keeping an eye on me collapsed back in my seat, while the first parasite finally staggered to his sleazy feet and stumbled away. We all just sat there, surrounded by the leftover gore, our helicopter idling next to the pile of dead on the pad for a long time.

From that day on I kept a blood-encrusted foot-long strip of ammunition wired to the bulkhead next to me, a deadly, sacred talisman. The rest of the ammunition I cleaned meticulously of crusted gore, link by link, round by individual round, and I used it in the thick, hazy, murderous days that followed, trying my best to kill and kill again.

I threw my clothes away when we got back to Camp Holloway, but for some reason I kept the blood-soaked boots, put them away and didn't wear them again. When my tour was over, I carried them home and put them in the back of a closet. I laced them on just one time, several years ago, when I was asked to speak on Memorial Day in our town, East Hampton, Connecticut. Then I put them away again.

I will be wearing those bloodstained boots one more time. This year, at the 20th Anniversary of the

Vietnam Veterans Memorial, "The Wall," in Washington DC, all 58,229 names of the dead who are carved into that Wall will be read aloud over the four days before Veterans Day. It will be my honor to read the names of some of our dead from Panel 30 West. I know that one will be the name of my friend and fellow 119th Assault Helicopter Company crew chief, John C. Schiffhauer, who gave his life in the Plei Trap Valley that week and whose blood is on those boots that I will wear. I can only imagine that some of the names I read will be those of 4th Infantry Division soldiers unknown to me who died and whose blood mixed with mine on that day in March, 1969 and whose blood to this day is mixed with mine. A sacred trust will be honored and a circle will close on Veterans Day, 2002.

After thirty plus years, I share these same feelings with Bob. I will not attempt to determine what happened in Vietnam. Many people have tried to do this. Most have studied the events and all of the circumstances surrounding that period in our history. I can only say what happened to me. I would not attempt to write a story about the war on the ground. This is better left to people like Jack Leninger ("Time Heals No Wounds"), Tom Lacombe ("Light Ruck"), and Harry Dilkes ("Five Years to Deros"). Their war was a hell that I only visited.

This was a war in which only a small percentage of the troops fought the battles. But all of the troops who were there were on the front lines. The truck drivers who brought in the supplies faced the dangers of ambushes and mines every day. The cooks and clerks at the CP and Brigade Operations were under rocket and mortar attacks. Infantry and artillery faced the greatest dangers, but anyone who took part in this madness could have been killed or wounded at any time. The degree of danger cannot be determined by the loss of life. If one bullet is fired and one person might be killed, this is what war is.

To compare it any other way is stupid.

Joe Galloway, who co-authored the book "We Were Soldiers Once... and Young" called Vietnam air crew members "God's Own Lunatics". This is a title all of us wear with pride. "They came when called," he says. His other phrase, which I believe all Vietnam veterans wear, is even more precious. "They may have not been the greatest generation, but they were the greatest of their generation".

Glossary of Terms

A

AAA	Antiaircraft Artillery
AGS	Army Air-Ground System
ACAV	Armored Cavalry Assault Vehicle
AF	Air Force
AG	Adjutant General
AGL	Above Ground Level
Air Cav	Air Cavalry
AK-47	7.62mm Assault Rifle
ALO	Air Liaison Officer
ANGLICO	Air and Naval Gunfire Liaison Company
AO	Area of Operations
APC	Armored Personnel Carrier
ARC LIGHT	B-52 Bomb Strike
ARLO	Air Reconnaissance Liaison Officer
ARP	Aero Rifle Platoon
Arty	Artillery
ARVN	Army of the Republic of Vietnam
AASWCC	Artillery and Air Strike Warning Control Center

B

BDA	Bomb Damage Assessment
BLU	Bomb Live Unit

Bn	Battalion
BOQ	Bachelor Officers' Quarters

C

CAG	Combat Aviation Group
Cal	Caliber
CAR-15	Carbine version of the M-16 assault rifle
CAS	Close Air Support
CBU	Cluster Bomb Unit
C&C	Command and Control
CEP	Circular Error Probable
CFSCC	Combined Fire Support Coordination Center
CG	Commanding General
CHARLIE ECHO	Crew Chief (Crew Engineer))
CHICKEN PLATE	Ballistic armor chest plate worn by aerial crew members
CHICOM	Chinese Communist
CHINOOK	CH-47 Cargo Helicopter
CIC	Combat Information Center
CICV	Combined Intelligence Center, Vietnam
CID	Criminal Investigation Division
CLAYMORE	Antipersonnel directional mine
CO	Commanding Officer
COBRA	Bell AH-1G helicopter gunship with two crew members
COC	Combat Operations Center
COMNAVFORV	Commander, US Naval Forces,

	Vietnam
COMUSMACV	Commander, US Military Assistance Command, Vietnam
CP	Command Post
C RATS	Standard Army field rations
CRC	Control and Reporting Center
CRP	Control and Reporting Post
CS	Riot control agent similar to tear gas
CSC	Coastal Surveillance Center
CTF	Commander, Task Force
CTG	Commander, Task Group
CTOC	Corps Tactical Operations Center
CTU	Commander, Task Unit
CTZ	Corps Tactical Zone

D

DAS	Direct Air Support
DASC	Direct Air Support Center
DCO	Deputy Commanding Officer
DCS	Deputy Chief of Staff
Deadlined	Not operationally ready
Dep	Deputy
DEP	Deflection Error Probable
DEPCOMUSMACV	Deputy Commander, US Military Assistance Command, Vietnam
DEROS	Date estimated to return from overseas
Didi	Vietnamese slang for "get out of there"
DMAC	Delta Military Assistance Command

DMZ	Demilitarized Zone
DS	Direct Support
DUSTER	Nickname for the M-42 antiaircraft weapon, which consisted of twin 40mm cannon mounted on a tank chassis. It was used in Vietnam primarily for base defense and convoy escort.
DUSTOFF	Call sign of medical evacuation helicopters

E

F

FA	Field Artillery
FAC	Forward Air Controller
Fast Mover	Jet fighter or bomber
FDC	Fire Direction Center
FFAR	Folding Fin Aerial Rocket
FFORCEV	Field Force, Vietnam
Firefly	UH-1H mounted with spotlights, night observation devices, miniguns, and a .50-caliber machine gun
Flak Jacket	A sleeveless armored vest designed to protect the wearer from shell fragments
FM	Frequency Modulation
FO	Forward Observer
FOX MIKE	FM radio frequency

fps	Fragmentary (order)
FRAG ORDER	Fragmentary order, change in mission
FSB	Fire Support Base
FSC	Fire Support Coordination
FSCC	Fire Support Coordination Center
FSCOORD	Fire Support Coordinator
FWMAF	Free World Military Assistance Forces

G

G1GAM	Guided Air Missile
GDA	Gun Damage Assessment
GP	General Purpose
Grunt	Slang for Infantryman
GS	General Support
GSR	General Support Reinforcing
GUARD	Emergency frequency, 243.0 UHF and 121.5 VHF
GUN	Cobra ("Snake") AH-1G gunship
GURF	Guns Up Ready Fire (Report)
GVN	Government of the Republic of (South) Vietnam

H

HE	High Explosive
HEAP	High Explosive, Antipersonnel
HEAT	High Explosive, Antitank
HF	High Frequency

H& I	Harassment and Interdiction
HQ	Headquarters
Hootch	Vietnamese dwelling
Huey	Nickname for the UH-1 Series of Utility Helicopters
Hunter/Killer Team	One AH-1G and one OH-6A (also known as 'Pink Team')

I

ICM	Improved Conventional Munition
ICU	Intensive care Unit
ISUM	Daily Intelligence Summary
INTSUM	Intelligence summary
IPIR	Immediate Photo Interpretation Report

J

JAGOS	Joint Air-Ground Operations System
JCS	Joint Chiefs of Staff (US)
JGS	Joint General Staff (Vietnamese)

K

KBA	Killed by (Air) (Artillery)
KIA	Killed in Action
Kit Carson	Former VC or NVA who has defected to the ARVN and act as scout for US Troops
KLICK	Military slang for 'Kilometer'

KP	Kitchen Police
KTAS	Knots True Airspeed
KW	Kilowatt

L

lb(s) or #	Pound(s)
LOH	Hughes OH-6A light observation helicopter with one pilot and one or two gunner/observers
LOH	Light Observation Helicopter
LZ	Landing Zone

M

M	Model
M-14	7.62mm US Rifle, offspring of M1
M-16	Colt 5.56mm Assault Rifle, standard US issue
M-48	Battle tank with 90mm main gun
M-113	US armored personnel carrier
M-551	Sheridan armored airborne reconnaissance vehicle with 152mm main gun
m	Meter(s)
MACV	Military Assistance Command, Vietnam
MAF	Marine Amphibious Force
MAW	Marine Aircraft Wing
MI	Military Intelligence
MIA	Missing In Action

MIB(ARS)	Military Intelligence Battalion (Air Reconnaissance Support)
Minigun	General Electric 7.62-caliber electric Gatling gun firing 2000-4000 rounds per minute
MK	Mark
mm	Millimeter(s)
MP	Military Police
mph	Miles per hour
MSF	Mobile Strike Force

N

NDP	Night Defensive Position
Net Call	Radio call made to all stations operating on a single net
NGF	Naval Gunfire
NGFS	Naval Gunfire Support
NGLO	Naval Gunfire Liaison Officer
NVA	North Vietnamese Army

O

Old Man	Military slang for 'Commander'
OPLAN	Operation Plan
OV-10	North American Bronco FAC aircraft with one or two crew members

P

PIO	Public Information Office
PIPE SMOKE	UH-1's and CH-47's that recover downed aircraft
PPIF	Photo Processing and Interpretation Facility
PSP	Perforated Steel Planking
PUSH	Radio frequency
PSYOP	Psychological Operations
PX	Post Exchange

Q

R

Recon	Reconnaissance
RED TEAM	Two AH-1G Cobra gunships
REP	Range Error Probable
RESCAP	Rescue combat air patrol
Rocks	Rockets
ROME PLOW	Heavy bulldozer for clearing jungle
ROTC	Reserve Officers' Training Corps
RPD	Chinese copy of Russian PK crew-served machine gun
RPG	Rocket propelled grenade
R&R	Rest and Recuperation
RTO	Radio Telephone Operator
RVN	Republic of (South) Vietnam
RVNAF	Republic of Vietnam Armed Forces

S

SA	Senior Advisor
Satchel Charge	Explosive charge
SAC	Strategic Air Command
SEA	Southeast Asia
Shadow	USAF AC-119 fixed wing gunship
SITREP	Situation report
SLAR	Side-Looking Airborne Radar
Slick	Troop carrying UH-1 helicopter
Snake & Nape	Speed retarded bombs and Napalm
SOP	Standing Operating Procedure
SP	Self-Propelled
Spectre	USAF AC-130 fixed wing gunship
Spooky	USAF AC-47 fixed wing gunship
SSB	Single Side Band
SSZ	Specified Strike Zone
STZ	Special Tactical Zone
SUPIR	Supplemental Photo Interpretation Report

T

TACAIR	Tactical Air
Tac Ftr	Tactical Fighter
TACC	Tactical Air Control Center
TACP	Tactical Air Control Party
TACS	Tactical Air Control System
TAOI	Tactical Area of Interest
TAOR	Tactical Area of Responsibility
TASE	Tactical Air Support Element
TC	Track or Tank Commander
TOC	Tactical Operations Center

TOE	Table of Organization and Equipment
TOT	Time (on) (over) Target (also Turbine Outlet Temperature)
Track	Slang for armored vehicle
TRW	Tactical Reconnaissance Wing

U

UNREP	Underway Replenishment
Uniform	UHF radio frequency
US	United States
USA	United States (Army) (of America)
USAF	United States Air Force
USMC	United States Marine Corps
USN	United States Navy
UHF	Ultra High Frequency

V

VC	Viet Cong
VHF	Very High Frequency
Victor	VHF radio
Victor Charlie	Viet Cong
VN	Vietnam(ese)
VN	Vietnamese Navy
VNAF	Vietnamese Air Force
VR	Visual Reconnaissance

W

White Team	Two OH-6A Scout helicopters
WIA	Wounded In Action
Willie Pete	Military slang for white phosphorous
WP	White Phosphorus
X	
XO	Executive Officer
Y	
Z	
Zippo	Flamethrower (usually mounted on either a tank, APC or riverine craft)

About the Author

Ron Carey was born on April 29, 1949 in Chicago, Illinois. Raised in the small town of Plainfield, Illinois, he is the oldest of six children. In April of 1967 he decided to enlist in the Army under the "Delayed Entry Program" prior to graduation from high school. He reported for active duty six days after graduation on June 12, 1967.

He arrived in Southeast Asia in January of 1968. In March he was assigned to the 1st Flight platoon of the 119th Assault Helicopter Company in Pleiku. For the next ten months his missions included support for the 4th Infantry Division in the Dak To, Kontum areas near the Tri-borders of Vietnam, Cambodia, and Laos. During August and September his company was assigned to MACV-SOG missions out of FOB II near Kontum. At the end of his first year in Vietnam, he extended for another tour.

After his leave in January 1969, he returned to his company in February. He flew with the 1st Flight platoon until the end of April. During Operation Wayne Grey he logged almost 400 flight hours over the Plei-Tray Valley. In May he was assigned to the 3rd platoon. He continued to fly as a crew chief on a UH-1C ("Charlie" model gunship) until September. During his entire tour of duty he logged over 2200 flight hours.

He returned to the United States and was stationed at Ft. Eustis, Va. as an instructor, and was discharged in June 1970. In December of 1969 he married his high school girlfriend. They have been married for thirty-five years, and have three children and five grandchildren. He worked for the telephone company for thirty-two years before retiring in 2002. Ron and his family still live in Plainfield, Illinois.

The "Good Guys" always wear white hats. I arrived
in Vietnam the perfect soldier, eighteen years old
and invincible. Twenty months later, I was a
completely different person. This is a look at
Operation Wayne Grey through the eyes of that
young helicopter crew chief. It is impossible for me
to tell the complete story. The infantrymen of the 4th
Division fought and died in a place I only visited.
Using official Army records and the handwritten
memories from my personal journal, I have tried to
relate the day-by-day events from March 1, 1969 to
April 14, 1969.

ISBN 141203503-1

1638374

Made in the USA